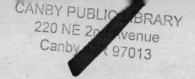
Praise for the novels of Morgan Howell

"Intriguing world building and wonderful characters made this an awesome book."
—Romance Book Wyrm, on
A Woman Worth Ten Coppers

"What makes *Coppers*—and, so far, Howell's writing as a whole—a standout is the complexity of her characters, and the sensitivity with which she portrays their struggles. . . . Howell brings the gritty, 'real world' flavor of urban fantasy to the more traditional landscape of high fantasy [and] manages to avoid the clichés of both."
—The Accidental Bard, on
A Woman Worth Ten Coppers

"What Anne McCaffrey and Naomi Novik have done for dragons, Morgan Howell has done for orcs. . . . Ms. Howell has written a spellbinding high fantasy novel that is refreshingly original and shows how talented a storyteller she is."
—SF Revu, on
The Queen of the Orcs: King's Property

"An unusual tale . . . Howell's depiction of orc culture is fascinating—these orcs are as big, strong, and dangerous as any in fantasy, but they also have moral and ethical issues of importance. This is not a book to read for fun on a rainy night—it's a book to think about."

—ELIZABETH MOON,
Nebula Award–winning author of
The Deed of Paksenarrion, on
The Queen of the Orcs: King's Property

"Dar never loses our admiration and compassion—qualities at the heart of any struggling hero. *King's Property* tests your own presumptions of 'the other' and brings to mind the cultural prejudices and wars born from betrayal that are so sadly evident throughout our own history."

—KARIN LOWACHEE,
author of *Warchild*, on
The Queen of the Orcs: King's Property

"In a crowded field, Howell has succeeded in creating an original and vivid fantasy. [The] characters display unexpected depths of humanity—even when they're not human. I was captivated by Dar. Highly recommended."

—NANCY KRESS,
Nebula Award–winning author of
Beggars in Spain, on
The Queen of the Orcs: King's Property

By Morgan Howell

THE SHADOWED PATH TRILOGY
A Woman Worth Ten Coppers
Candle in the Storm
The Iron Palace

THE QUEEN OF THE ORCS TRILOGY
King's Property
Clan Daughter
Royal Destiny

THE IRON PALACE

The Shadowed Path
Book 3

MORGAN HOWELL

BALLANTINE BOOKS • NEW YORK

A Del Rey Books Mass Market Original

Copyright © 2011 by William H. Hubbell

Interior map and illustration: © William H. Hubbell

All rights reserved.

Published in the United States by Del Rey, an imprint of The Random House Publishing Group, a division of Random House, Inc., New York.

DEL REY is a registered trademark and the Del Rey colophon is a trademark of Random House, Inc.

ISBN 978-0-345-50398-5

Printed in the United States of America

www.delreybooks.com

9 8 7 6 5 4 3 2 1

For my sons,
Nathaniel and Justin

These things crack a stone—
iron, frost, and love.

—Averen proverb

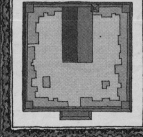

IRON PALACE

ONE

THE NIGHT roared with the sound of rain. Its damp chill flowed from the hut's unglazed windows and drove the old peasant and his wife to huddle by their hearth. There they shivered despite the fire. Then, mingled with the noise of falling water came the jangle of distant bells. They rang out in an uneven cadence. *Jang! . . . Jang! . . . Jang! Jang! . . . Jang!* The elderly pair glanced at each other uneasily.

"Karm preserve us!" said the woman. "A cursed one!"

"Mayhap 'twill pass us by," said her husband.

"Pray Karm it does," replied his wife. She arched her thumb in the Sign of the Balance. But as the couple listened, the bells sounded ever closer.

"Don't just sit there!" barked the man. "Get an offerin'. Mind ye, nothin' fine."

The man's wife rushed to a basket and hastily rummaged through it until she found three moldy roots. Then she hurried back to her husband and pressed them in his hand. "Ye do it, Toby. I'm afeared."

Grabbing the roots, the man opened the door and peered out into the rainy dark. Firelight spilled from the open door to tint the nearest raindrops red, but it illuminated little else. As the man stared into shadows and water, his ears told him more than his eyes. Cursed ones carried a belled staff to warn folk of their approach. Toby could hear the bells, but he couldn't see who jangled them; all he knew was that the wretch who bore them was coming closer. "I've food fer ye," he called out. "Show yerself, and I'll toss it yer way. Then pass us by."

There was no reply, only the sound of bells.

Mayhap its tongue's gone, thought the man. He'd heard tales of a cursed one whose entire face had rotted away. The peasant shuddered at the thought of it as he strained to see some movement. The bells sounded close before Toby finally viewed a dark figure staggering like a drunk across the rain-soaked field. It seemed more a phantom than a person, for Toby saw no face, only a pale orb with dark spots for eyes.

"I've roots fer ye," Toby cried. The figure kept advancing. When it was twenty paces away, Toby saw the face was wrapped in bandages with two eyeholes that likened to sockets in a skull. Toby tossed the roots at the advancing stranger. When they splashed on the wet ground, he slammed the door.

Jang! . . . Jang! . . . Jang! The bells sounded louder.

" 'Tis supposed to go away," said the woman. "Go away!" she shouted at the closed door. "We've fed ye, now leave us be."

The bells rang a few more times, then stopped. For a spell, the silence was a relief, but it quickly turned ominous. The pair listened for some sound that indicated the visitor was retreating. All they heard was falling rain. At last, the woman spoke. "Do ye think 'tis still here?"

"I don't know."

"Better look."

Toby walked hesitantly to the door, opened it a crack, and peered out. A sodden form lay motionless on the ground. A hand wrapped in filthy bandages still gripped a belled staff. The derelict was dressed in layers of rags and so wrapped with bandages that it was impossible to tell if a man or a woman had collapsed in the mud. " 'Tis here," Toby called back to his wife. "Mayhap 'tis dead."

"Oh nay!" exclaimed the women. "If 'tis dead, then the

curse will pass to us!" She grabbed a broom, opened the door wider, and prodded the still figure with the broom handle. " 'Tis alive yet!"

"Pah, woman. 'Twas yer proddin' that made it move."

Then the couple heard a soft moan. "Get the wheelbarrow," said the wife. "It hasn't died yet. Ye can take it to the hermit."

"But that means I'll have to touch it!"

"Do ye want yer fingers and toes to rot off?" asked the woman. " 'Cause 'twill happen if the curse passes to us."

The man said nothing, but he threw on his cloak and exited the hut, giving the prone figure a wide berth as he did so. Soon he returned with a rickety, wooden wheelbarrow. "Ye'll have to help me lift the wretch," he said.

The body had the stature of a man, but when the couple hefted it into the wheelbarrow there seemed little substance beneath the soaked rags. Nonetheless, the body's putrescent stench made lifting it a trial. They gagged from the odor that evoked disgusting images of what the filthy rags and bandages hid. Those images spurred the old man as he pushed his loathsome load across the field. Upon reaching the muddy road, he headed for the hermit's abode. *Don't die*, the peasant pleaded silently. *Don't die yet.*

Toby's destination was the ruin that housed a solitary man with a reputation for taking in the unwanted. The hermit, whose name no one knew, had lived there for many winters. A few folk said he was holy, while most claimed he was ill omened and kept their distance. Toby was one of the latter, and he had no qualms over leaving a cursed one at the man's door.

After passing through fields and woods, the road headed uphill toward the remnant of a castle. The stronghold of some forgotten lord, it had fallen long ago in an equally forgotten battle. Over the intervening generations, most of its stones had been carted away to build humbler structures, but the massive blocks of the keep remained. The hermit lived among them. By the time Toby reached the jagged-topped hulk, he was breathing hard. To his eyes, the ruin was an impressive sight, the largest building he'd ever seen. It was also an eerie place and haunted by all accounts. The rain and darkness enhanced that impression, and the peasant was anxious to finish his task and depart.

The keep's gateway was high upon its wall. The gate and the stone ramp leading up to it had disappeared long ago, so that the gateway seemed more like a huge window in the roofless wall than an entrance. A sizable crack in the wall's base served as the current means to enter. Toby pushed his wheelbarrow through it into the keep's lowest level. There, the thick walls of the basement storerooms remained, although all the floors above were gone. One of those storerooms had been roofed over to become the hermit's home.

Toby removed the cursed one's belled staff from the wheelbarrow before tipping its load in front of the closed door. Then he struck the staff against the flagstones hard and rapidly to jangle its bells. That done, he dropped the staff on the still figure by his feet, grabbed the handles of his wheelbarrow, and fled into the night.

TWO

DAVEN SLEPT lightly and had wakened when the wheelbarrow's wooden wheel rumbled over the ruined keep's stone floor. Nevertheless, he didn't greet his late-night visitor. The hermit's residence was the dumping place for sick and dying strangers, and he assumed that whoever was bringing someone to his doorway would prefer not to be seen. The jangle of bells confirmed his assumption. *Another cursed one*, he thought. Daven waited until his visitor had departed before opening the door.

The hermit didn't fear the wretch he found there, for he didn't believe the rotting curse passed to anyone upon death. He had cared for—and buried—nearly a dozen of those so afflicted with no ill effect. Nevertheless, he saw the benefit of the superstition, for it offered the cursed some protection. Likewise, the practice of giving them food to go away gave them a means to survive. It was a miserable existence, and Daven pitied the cursed. Despite their repellent and malodorous bodies, he made it his work to care for them as atonement for a deed that continued to haunt him.

The still form beyond the doorway smelled like a corpse, so Daven felt for a pulse. When he found a faint one, he gently dragged the cursed one into his home to tend him or her. First he lit a fire, then filled a pot with water and set it on the flames to warm. Afterward, he turned his attention to the cursed one's bandages. The soiled wrappings that the cursed wore served mostly to hide their sores. Seldom changed, they usually did more harm than good. Daven unwrapped a hand first, expecting to find festering stumps where fingers had been.

Instead, the hand was perfectly intact. Daven stared at it for a moment in surprise before exposing the other hand and finding it in the same condition. Then he pulled mud-caked cloth from around a foot. Not a toe was missing. The remaining foot proved equally undamaged. Nevertheless, something was rotting. Daven temporarily ignored the mystery of why someone would bandage healthy limbs and uncovered the face. When its wrapping fell away, he uttered a sharp cry and jerked back.

The face was that of a man. Though gaunt and covered with grizzled stubble, it was whole and without a single sore. Nonetheless, the face was marked, but not by affliction. It bore tattoos that made it appear frozen in a moment of rage.

Dark-blue lightning flashed down a furrowed brow and scowl lines were needled into the sunken cheeks. The closed eyes lay in pools of permanent shadow. In the dim light, the effect was menacing, but that wasn't why Daven was so startled. His last encounter with a Sarf—for the man's tattoos marked him as one—had nearly cost him his life. If his pursuer had been able to swim, Daven would have surely perished. He still had nightmares in which the Sarf found him to finish his assault. The man before him was a different Sarf, but for an unsettling moment, Daven thought the wrath needled on the face might be directed toward him.

That moment passed, and Daven calmed. The unconscious man had no sword, neither was he dressed in the customary dark blue. It seemed that the goddess had not sent him in retribution. Although Daven didn't recognize the face of the unconscious man, he recognized his tattoo. He hadn't seen it for more than twenty winters, but it was unforgettable. *He was Theodus's Sarf*, thought Daven. That was all he knew of him; he couldn't remember the man's name.

Daven turned his attention to caring for the unconscious Sarf. Thinking the source of the smell might be a festering wound, he began to undress him. When he removed a grime-covered overblouse, he found the decayed carcass of a hare dangling from the Sarf's neck like a pendant. It was the origin of the disgusting smell. Daven disposed of the carcass outside and burned the clothes tainted by its stench.

The Sarf lay unconscious throughout the process, and he remained so when Daven removed the rest of his clothes to bathe him. The man's body was almost skeletal. It was also filthy and crisscrossed with old scars. A jagged one that ran from the collarbone past the navel looked as if it should have been fatal. Yet the most remarkable thing about the Sarf's body was its chill. Usually the extremities of those suffering from exposure were colder than the torso, but the opposite was true with the unconscious man. That suggested an otherworldly cause. *A spell?* wondered Daven. He might learn the answer if the man revived.

When the water in the pot was warm, Daven gently washed the stranger's face, limbs, and chest before rolling him over to cleanse his back. He knew that he'd find runes tattooed there, but it didn't lessen his unease at the sight of them. The text they inscribed was both holy and secret. A Sarf couldn't read it, and uncovered the tattoos only for his Bearer, the holy one who was his master. Daven hadn't seen such inscriptions for more than eighteen winters. The runes tattooed on his Sarf—the same Sarf who had tried to kill him—were minimal compared to the extensive text needled on the stranger's back.

Better than anyone, Daven knew he shouldn't gaze at the marks. He was no longer a Bearer, and the unconscious man wasn't his Sarf. Moreover, Daven felt unworthy. He had turned his back on Karm. His Sarf had every right to slay him. Sometimes Daven wished that he had. Yet, worthy or not, the former Bearer felt drawn to the runes, and the impulse to read them quickly became irresistible. With trembling fingers, he reached out and brushed the archaic letters that transcribed an ancient language.

With so much time having passed since Daven had last read such a text, he struggled to decipher it. It didn't read like a narrative, for the Seers who made such marks wrote puzzles for which life provided the missing pieces. Their guidance wasn't meant for the Sarf but for his Bearer, and Daven felt like a sneak thief rummaging through another's most private possessions. He rummaged nevertheless, enthralled by what he discovered.

It was nearly dawn when Daven tore himself away from the runes. He dressed the stranger in a clean tunic and laid him on the mat that served as his bed. By then, he was convinced that Karm had sent the Sarf, not to slay him but to redeem him. His eyes teared at the notion of it. *Karm's truly the Goddess of Compassion*, he thought. However, the wonder of his redemption paled compared to a greater marvel. The runes had only hinted at it, yet those hints had stirred Daven to the core. He felt both energized and profoundly anxious. *Light and darkness will soon contend over the world's fate.* The outcome was far from certain, but the runes said that he had a role in the struggle. Daven resolved to do his utmost to fulfill it. He worried that he might fail, for there was much he didn't understand, despite numerous readings of the text.

Daven peered outside. The rain had stopped. The day promised to be a fair one, and he strolled out his door to witness its dawn. As Daven watched the eastern sky brighten and turn rosy, his thoughts returned to the enigmatic text on the Sarf's back. One name was woven throughout, and he didn't even know if it was that of a man or a woman. His only certainty was that much depended on someone named Yim.

THREE

WHILE DAVEN waited for the sun to rise, Roarc poled his reed boat along a narrow waterway that lay far to the north. The channel's tea-colored water was hemmed by reeds so tall they could have served as walls in a maze. Having lived his entire life in the Grey Fens, Roarc had spent nearly fifty winters navigating its tangled waters; yet even he got lost sometimes. He was in no danger of that at the moment, for his destination was his home. It was a limestone outcropping that fensfolk call a "hite." It jutted like a tiny mountaintop from the bog. Though in plain sight, reaching it by boat required threading a complicated course, which the fensman did with the assurance of long familiarity.

By Roarc's bare feet lay the night's takings from the traps, several dozen small fish. Additionally, there was a pair of traps that needed repair. Woven from reeds, they resembled spherical baskets with openings in the shape of inverted cones. Mending and making fish traps was a task for his wife, Rappali. She was skilled at reedwork, while Roarc—who was fifteen winters her senior—had stiffened fingers.

The waterway ended a fair distance from the hite. Roarc pulled his craft onto a sodden bank, took his catch and the fish traps, and followed a path to his home. The well-worn trail was easy to follow, but like the waterway, its route was irregular, for firm ground was rare in the fens. Much of the bog's lush plant life grew on floating mats of decayed vegetation that gave way when trod upon. A careless step could get one soaked or worse, so Roarc stuck to the path. When he reached the hite, the ground became stony and solid. Soon he was ascending the steep-sided outcropping to reach his home.

From the pathway he had a commanding view of the fens, and Roarc paused to observe the sunrise. To the north, about half a morning's journey by boat, lay the wide Turgen River. It invaded the fens by a maze of narrow waterways that petered out near Tararc Hite, the home of Roarc and his nearest kin. To the south were the fens proper. From where the fensman stood, it seemed a vast and lush prairie, not a treacherous, reedy bog. Scattered about the fens were thousands of limestone outcroppings. They came in all sizes. Some were no bigger than boulders, while a few looked like little mountains, complete with forests growing on their sides. Many, like Tararc Hite, were inhabited.

Roarc's home had been chiseled into the southern slope of the hite about halfway to its summit. Ten paces deep, it was sizable by fens standards, for many generations of Roarc's family had enlarged it. The front of the cavity was walled off with a stone facade that featured an ancient wooden door and a chimney flanked by two shuttered windows. The homes of Roarc's younger brothers, which lay elsewhere on the hite, were less grand and more cramped. When Roarc turned the bend, he saw Rappali already at work tilling the terraced field by the dwelling's entrance. He was pleased to see that. He was less pleased to see a goat tied near his doorway.

Rappali seemed to have anticipated Roarc's reaction, for she set down her mattock and greeted him with more good cheer than usual. "Good morn, husband. 'Tis a fine night's catch ya brought."

Roarc frowned. "I see tha goat girl came."

"Aye, last eve."

"That girl lacks sense. All tha way from Far Hite in tha eve. Tha fens will swallow her yet!"

"Yim's no girl," replied Rappali, "so why call her one? Her lad's almost as old as our Telk, 'bout seventeen winters by my reckoning."

"I name her girl 'cause she looks and acts like one. Raising a lad without a man! 'Tisn't fitting!"

"Just 'cause she refused yar brother—"

"And every other fensman who asked her. A lad needs a man ta guide him. Then he'd know how ta slaughter a goat."

"Ya know full well why he doesn't know," said Rappali, "and 'tisn't 'cause Yim lacks a husband."

"A lad *should* see blood. He's being raised unnatural. Why, I'm part minded ta send tha goat back."

"Fine. Then ya can send back tha cheese that she brought for our trouble. She promised us a hind quarter as well."

" 'Tis only an old milked-out doe."

" 'Tis dear ta her, poor thing."

"Why take her side?" asked Roarc. "She's an outsider. Mayhap a bogspit."

"Pah on that! Tha Mother guided her here."

"Tha healwife thinks different."

"That's 'cause Yim knows more 'bout birthing babes than she." Then Rappali put on her most conciliatory face. "Please, husband, enjoy Yim's cheese and kill tha goat for her. She's coming back this eve."

Roarc thought of Yim's cheese, which was renowned for its delicate flavor, and relented. Nevertheless, he made a show of deliberating and frowned when he spoke. "I'll slaughter and butcher tha goat after morn's rest," he said. He set down the basket of fish and the damaged traps. "Tend ta these afore I rise." Then he entered his home to sleep awhile.

Rappali grabbed the basket of fish and walked down to the bog to clean them. There she could also cut the reeds to mend the traps. She would have done both without being told and regarded her husband's insistence that she accomplish the chores before he rose as face-saving bluster. Roarc disliked slaughtering Yim's goats. The task didn't bother him; it was for whom he did it. Roarc wasn't fond of Yim, and his wife's friendship with her annoyed him.

Rappali assumed that her husband disliked Yim because she was an outsider. Fensfolk had little contact with the outside world and distrusted it. Sons who joined the ships that plied the Turgen almost never returned, and the few that did always seemed changed beyond recognition. Yim's sudden appearance had been the subject of gossip for many winters. There were folk who actually believed she was a bogspit, a being born from the muck in the bog. Such creatures were supposed to have bog water in their veins and were burned by real blood. That was said to be the reason why Yim wouldn't slaughter her animals.

Rappali knew Yim's blood was as red as anyone's, for she had found Yim just after she had given birth. Unconscious and covered in muck, Yim had looked dead. Yet she recovered, and Rappali admired how Yim had made a life for herself. Settling on isolated Far Hite with her newborn son and three goats loaned by Rappali's mother, she had raised a dairy herd and carved a life for herself and her child. Yim's cheese was the best in the Grey Fens, relished even by those who claimed witchcraft was used in its making.

Rappali believed Yim's story that war had driven her to the fens, where she could honor her oath to her dying husband that their child would never witness bloodshed. Rappali thought that Yim went too far in fulfilling that oath, but she never doubted her sincerity. Yim had experienced war, and her tales of its atrocities were chilling. *After what she's seen*, thought Rappali, *I don't blame her not wishing ta kill even a goat.*

Upon reaching the water's edge, Rappali began cleaning her husband's catch. Most of the fish were hand sized, so without their heads and tails they were little more than morsels to dry for later use. As the fenswoman scaled and gutted the fish, she thought of the other source of contention with her husband—Yim's son. Roarc was fond of the lad, but Froan unsettled Rappali.

Her reaction put Rappali in the minority, for most folk thought well of Froan. Telk, Rappali's only son, hung on Froan's every word, although Telk was older and larger than his friend. He wasn't alone in this; Froan had a knack for getting his way. Rappali found the ease with which he bent folk to his favor an unnatural trait. She believed it had something to do with his eyes. She had noticed them on the day he was born. The pale tan irises made the pupils seem all the more piercing. To her, they likened to twin holes into which one might fall and get trapped. She never spoke of this notion, for it seemed silly to fear a boy's gaze. Yet that fear had grown stronger over time. She sometimes thought that Yim felt it also.

FOUR

HONUS WOKE slowly, drifting into consciousness as one emerges from a fog. When he opened his eyes, he took in little of what he saw. He had become accustomed to waking in strange places, and even the fact that he was clean and freshly clothed made little impression on him. His belly was empty, but he was oblivious of that. The emptiness that gnawed at him was of a deeper nature and one that the living world couldn't ease. Honus slowly pulled himself into a sitting position, crossed his legs, and closed his eyes so he might trance and find some happy memory on the Dark Path.

That endeavor was foiled by a sudden sharp pain on his upper thigh. Honus tried to disregard it, but he felt a second pain and then a third. He opened his eyes and noticed for the first time that another man was in the room. He sat close by. The man had a full white beard and a matching tangle of hair. He wore a shabby robe and held a stick. Certain that the man had hit him with the stick, Honus tried to grab it. His hand grasped only air.

The stranger grinned. "Pretty slow for a Sarf."

Though it was obvious, it only then dawned on Honus that his disguise was gone. "I'm no Sarf."

"Your face says otherwise."

"My tattoos don't mark service to the goddess," replied Honus, his voice low and cold. "They display my hate for her."

"Your runes tell a different tale."

"A Sarf's runes may not be seen!"

The stranger smiled. "But, as you said, you're no Sarf. Besides, I needed diversion while I scrubbed your back."

Honus stared into the man's eyes, trying to discern the truth behind what he said. But as with his other skills, his powers of perception had diminished. He discerned only what was readily apparent; that the man was old, poor, and had a kindly face.

"I've heard of your affliction," said the man, "but so few can trance, I've never encountered it before. Yet I'm certain your chill comes not from this world."

"You speak nonsense."

"You know I don't," asserted the man. "You crave the dead's memories like a drunkard craves ale. It's made you squander your life on the Dark Path."

"So? It's *my* life."

"Your life's Karm's gift and therefore precious."

"It's a false gift that suits only the giver's ends," replied Honus. "Don't speak of my tormentor."

"Karm loves you."

"Ha! A lie to beguile the naive. You don't know my life."

"I do in part," replied the man. "It's inscribed in your runes."

"So my suffering was foreordained," said Honus, his voice heavy with bitterness. "I'm not surprised. But who are you to meddle? If you've the skill to read my runes, then you must know it's sacrilege."

Daven met the Sarf's aggressive stare with a mild look. The man on his sleeping mat was nearly dead; yet Daven was wary. He knew all too well how dangerous such men could be. Thus he replied honestly to the Sarf's remark. "It's not the first sacrilege I've committed and certainly not the gravest. Like you, I turned my back on Karm."

"Then you're wiser than I thought," replied the Sarf. "Now let me be."

Daven knew it would be the prudent thing to do, but he felt charged to take a different course. Judging from the Sarf's conversation, he seemed to have retained his wits even if he had turned away from the living world. *If I'm to guide him back to it*, he thought, *I must do so carefully.*

"Someone dumped you on my doorstep," said Daven. "If they hadn't, you'd no longer need to trance to roam the Dark Path."

The man's only reply was a grunt.

"When I unwrapped your face, I recalled your tattoos, though not you. Yet if memory serves, you were Theodus's Sarf. What became of him?"

"Slain."

"I'm sorry to hear that. He was a wise and virtuous man. It's said the Bearer is the measure of the Sarf." Daven bowed. "I'm honored by your presence."

"Don't be. I failed Theodus and . . ." The Sarf's face darkened, and he grew silent.

Daven took a gamble and divulged a little of what he had learned from reading the Sarf's runes. "You didn't fail Yim."

As soon as Daven spoke those words, he felt like a man who had pulled a stone from a wall and caused it to crumble. The Sarf's aloof facade fell, spilling anguish over his features. Daven saw the depths of the man's despair and knew that Yim was the key to understanding it. "Who was Yim?"

"She was my Bearer, and . . ." The Sarf paused as he struggled to control his voice. ". . . and she was more than that."

"She? Your Bearer was a woman?"

"Yes."

"Women Bearers are rare. I thought I knew all of them."

"Yim became my Bearer after the temple fell. Karm, herself, united us. Later, she strengthened that bond with love." The Sarf's eyes welled with tears. "Such love!" he said in a wistful tone. Then his voice hardened. "But it was only

Karm's ploy to use us, and when we fulfilled her need, she tore us apart forever!"

"And you still long for Yim?"

"For seventeen winters! Now the only joy I feel comes from the memories of the dead."

"Yet those memories aren't yours," said Daven, "and the heart isn't eased by shadows."

"They seem real enough for a moment, and during that moment I forget."

The Sarf's revelations gave meaning to some of the inscriptions on his back, causing Daven to consider which of his conclusions to reveal. *Clearly, I must tell him something.* The former Bearer chose his words carefully. "The goddess tore you asunder, but not forever." He watched the Sarf's face. A spark of animation briefly lit his forlorn eyes, but it quickly died. "I believe it's my fate to prepare you for what lies ahead. Yim needs you."

"My runes told you that?"

"They did."

The Sarf was silent for a long while, and Daven had the impression that he was struggling with his feelings. At last, the tattooed man sighed and spoke. "I'm no use to her. I don't know where she is, and I can't even fend off an old man's stick."

"Don't you want to help her?"

"Why ask pointless questions? What I want is unimportant."

"So you'll abandon her."

The Sarf flushed. "Yim abandoned me!"

"Not willingly. Not without regret."

"How could you know?"

"The runes."

The Sarf grew so agitated that Daven feared for his life. "Oh, the callousness of Karm! And of you for abetting her!"

"Karm wants to help you, and my role is to assist her."

The Sarf's only response was to stare at Daven with

disbelief. The pain and sorrow in the man's tear-rimmed eyes deeply moved Daven, and he waited awhile before he spoke again. When he did, his voice was quiet and humble. "It would help if I knew your name."

"Honus" was the whispered reply.

"I'm Daven. As you've probably guessed, I was once a Bearer."

"Daven?" The name seemed to have some meaning for Honus, for he appeared to mull over it awhile. When he spoke at last, he seemed puzzled. "Was your Sarf named Gatt?"

"Yes. Why do you ask?"

"I met him long ago. He said you had fallen."

"He spoke truly in a manner. When folk turned against the goddess, I fled their wrath and became a hermit. But where did you meet Gatt?"

"He tried to kill Yim." Then Honus cast Daven an unsettling smile. "Instead, he killed me." He seemed amused by Daven's puzzlement. "Didn't my runes tell you?"

Recalling an inscription that spoke of Honus as "twice-lived," Daven thought he finally understood its meaning. "They hint at a resurrection."

"That was Yim's doing. She was no common Bearer."

Daven did his best to conceal the excitement evoked by Honus's words. As a young man training in the temple, he had heard whispered rumors of a prophecy known fully only to a few Seers. It foretold the coming of a holy woman with extraordinary powers—someone called "the Chosen." *Could this Yim be her?* Daven was hesitant to ask. Instead, he thought of another enigmatic inscription and wondered what light Honus could shed on it. "The runes speak of three intertwined fates—yours, Yim's, and that of someone named Froan."

"This Froan's a stranger to me."

"Not for long, I think."

FIVE

FROAN MOVED cautiously toward the mired goat, testing the ground with his bare feet. The space between him and the doe seemed like a moist meadow, but he knew better. When the ground flexed ever so slightly, he assumed a prone position to spread his weight more evenly. Then Froan began to slither toward the panicked animal. Tall, lean, and strong, he was more man than boy. His features and walnut-colored hair made him favor his mother in looks, except for his piercing eyes. He was clad in only a goatskin breechclout, and the vegetation rasped his skin as he slid over the wet and reedy ground. Froan ignored the scrapes, intent solely on reaching the stranded doe.

"Silly Rosie," he said in a gentle voice, "the bog's no place for you. Now you're wet, and I know you hate that."

The frantic animal calmed a little after Froan spoke, but when she sank deeper into the boggy ground, she renewed her struggling. That only made her situation worse, for her churning legs further loosened the mat of floating vegetation. Froan sped up his advance, afraid that the struggling goat might break through the mat entirely and sink into the water beneath it.

"Easy, girl, I'm coming."

Froan reached the goat. He was keenly aware that he lay upon treacherous ground. It rippled beneath his prone form and water welled wherever he pressed. Froan dragged the end of a rope in his left hand. To pull the doe out, he would need to tie the rope about her chest just behind the forelegs. He plunged his left hand deep into the floating mat of muck and rotting vegetation to guide the rope under the goat's body. The deeper his hand went, the looser and wetter the mat became. When Froan's arm was submerged to the shoulder, his hand had passed under the goat's chest. He plunged his right arm into the muck on the other side of the doe in order to grasp the end of the rope and pull it around the animal.

Rosie's struggling hampered Froan's efforts, and he began to think that she would sink before he could secure her. The idea was infuriating. As always when rage gripped him, it was sudden, intense, and irrational. Within an instant, Froan went from attempting to save Rosie to wanting to kill her. Moreover, he acted on his impulse. He stopped groping for the rope and withdrew his right arm and hand from the wet, black rot so he could push the doe's muzzle into it and suffocate her.

Froan's hand was on the back of Rosie's head before he tried to stifle his fury. For a moment, he teetered between saving and destroying her. His entire arm trembled from the intensity of the inner conflict. Then his hand suddenly plunged into the stinking muck, grabbed the rope's end, and pulled it up. With blackened fingers, Froan quickly tied the rope to form a loop about the doe. Then he slithered to where the ground was firm. Rising to his feet, Froan tugged the rope.

The muck resisted Froan's efforts, then gave way to his wiry strength. Gradually, the doe moved forward and upward. All the while, Froan encouraged her. "Come to me, sweetheart. That's a girl, Rosie." There was nothing in his cajoling tone that betrayed his former rage. It had dissipated as quickly as it had arisen, but Froan still felt its aftereffects. In addition to guilt, he had the queasy feeling that something foul had possessed him. As a child, Froan had called his rage his "shadow," and he still thought of it as such—a dark thing that was apart from him yet constantly at his side.

At last, Rosie's forelegs were free. With the help of Froan's tugging, she managed to extract herself, leaving a hole filled with dark water. Even as the goat staggered to safety, the edges of the hole closed like a rapidly healing wound. By the time Rosie reached Froan, the hole was gone and the ground where it had been looked solid and firm.

Feeling guilty over his fit of temper, Froan sought to make amends. He stroked Rosie and rewarded her with a treat of faerie arrow. Rosie munched it contentedly, unaware of how close she had come to dying. Other goats had not fared as well when Froan's shadow had possessed him. Their bodies rotted in the bog, which was an ideal place for concealing misdeeds. While Froan regretted each instance, he also recalled them vividly. Compared to those moments of rage, the rest of his life seemed humdrum.

After Rosie had devoured her treat, Froan used the rope to lead her toward Far Hite. The way was complicated, for there was little stable ground about the outcropping. The hite got its name from its isolation, which was not due to its distance from the other hites but to the treacherousness of the surrounding bog. The fensfolk reckoned distance differently than people who lived on solid ground; the length of the safe route between two spots determined whether they were near or far. By that measure, Far Hite was aptly named. The only way to reach it was long and convoluted. A wrong turn could prove fatal, and after a wet spell, the way was mostly submerged.

When Froan's mother had moved to Far Hite, the place had been long abandoned. The bog had swallowed its former occupants, and most of the fensfolk expected the same to happen to the stranger and her child. After Froan was old enough to learn the complicated route, he was amazed that his mother had found it on her own. Others had tried and failed before her. Some had never returned.

Although no one visited Far Hite, many envied it as a residence, for it was large enough to support a goat herd. Moreover, trees grew on its gentle southern slope and its

northern side featured several natural caves. One was sufficiently large and deep to be ideal for storing milk and making cheese. Froan and his mother lived on the hite's southern
side in a cavity excavated by former residents. It was small
and rude, but it met their basic needs.

Partway home, Froan led Rosie away from the path and
tied her to the stump of a drowned tree. Then he reached
into his bag and scattered several faerie arrow roots on the
ground before her. As the doe began to eat, he patted her.
"Good girl," Froan said. "Now you can stay lost awhile
longer." With that, he headed toward Tararc Hite. Without
his help, milking would occupy his mother long enough for
him to visit Telk. Froan hated the tedium of the twice-daily
milking sessions and sought any opportunity to avoid them.

A short while later, Froan reached Tararc Hite and found
Telk working on his reed boat. "Telk!" he called. "Still fuss-
ing with that boat?"

"What are ya doing here?" asked Telk. " 'Tis milking
time."

"A doe strayed, and Mam asked me to fetch her," said
Froan. "She'll think I'm still looking."

The boat, which was constructed of bundled reeds, was
essentially an elongated raft with built-up sides. It tapered to
a point at its bow and stern, and the reeds curved up and inward at either end. Telk was working on the stern's curve.
Froan watched him briefly, then asked, "What are you doing
now?"

"Improving its lines."

"What for? You're only going to pole it through a bog.
Lay off that, and let's go to the island."

"I'm nearly done."

"I didn't come all the way here to watch you prettify your
boat," said Froan. "I came so we could prepare for our future. Now, come on."

Froan saw Telk's reluctance to leave off his work, but

that didn't faze him. He was accustomed to swaying others to get his way. The talent came to him so naturally that he noticed it only when it didn't work, as in the case of his mother. As Froan expected, his friend's sole resistance was to sigh as he set down his tools. Then he pushed the boat into the water. The craft's unfinished stern looked like a frayed brush, but it didn't affect its handling. After Froan waded out and climbed aboard, Telk began to pole the boat down the channel.

The pair had visited the island countless times, but Froan still didn't know the way to it. The narrow and tangled waterways flanked by tall reeds had a sameness that quickly confused him. However, Telk was like his father and always seemed to know where he was, despite the fact that the fens were changeable, varying with the season and the fluctuating water level. Froan quickly tired of gazing at reeds and turned to his friend. "One day, you'll guide a proper wooden boat up and down the Turgen."

Telk said nothing as he continued poling.

"Don't smile," said Froan. "And don't say you didn't. Mark my words. When I'm master of a ship, you'll be my helmsman. That's why we need to practice."

"Sword fighting?"

"Yes, sword fighting. You've heard Dobah's tales. The river's a rough place."

"Aye, if ya believe Dobah."

"I can tell if a man speaks true," said Froan. "Dobah's adventures were not as grand as he pretends, but the fighting was real enough. There are pirates on the river."

"Then we'd best avoid it."

"And avoid our chance for adventure and renown? Telk, we're not meant to milk goats and gut fish all our lives. We're destined for greater things."

"And must we seek that destiny on tha river?" asked Telk, as if the decision were all Froan's.

"Of course," replied Froan in a breezy tone. "And to prepare for that, we must learn to use a sword."

"But our swords aren't real."

"Someday, they will be," said Froan. "Meanwhile, we'll master our strokes and thrusts with wooden ones." He gazed up at his friend and easily read what he was thinking. *Telk believes he'll spend his life trapping fish, just like his father.* Without knowing why, Froan had always sensed his fate was to live elsewhere. Though the fens were all he knew, they never felt like home. That was partly because his mother was an outsider. Despite speaking like her, Froan had overcome that disadvantage. His compelling manner had caused the fensfolk to accept him. Nevertheless, he yearned to roam the wider world.

Froan was imagining his future adventures when the island came into view. The high reeds had hidden it until the last moment, so almost as soon as Froan spotted it, he and Telk were clambering up its limestone side. The place was a huge, low boulder about ten paces in diameter. Barely rising above the tops of the reeds, its most prominent feature was a small pine growing from a crack. Moss and short scruffy plants covered some of the boulder's surface, and the rest was bare rock. The wooden swords were hidden among the pine's branches. Froan retrieved them and gave one to Telk.

Neither young man had ever viewed a sword fight. The only sword they had ever seen was Dobah's, and they saw it only once. Their wooden weapons imitated his, but their swordplay was pure invention. By worldly standards, it was unskilled hacking. In the fens, blades were seldom used for fighting. Even daggers were rare. None of that dampened Froan's enthusiasm. He sparred ardently, and his aggressive tactics more than made up for Telk's greater reach.

The two practiced until dusk. By then, both were sweating and covered with red marks from each other's blows. "Can we go?" asked Telk. "My da will be looking for me."

Froan felt irritated, but he acted as if stopping were his idea. "That's enough for today," he said. "I should take the stray home before Mam gets fits. That doe's her favorite." He hid the swords while Telk untied the boat and brought it alongside the island's steep rock side. After Froan climbed aboard, Telk poled the boat into the narrow channel. He was silent awhile before he spoke. "Ya hit me pretty hard back there."

"But with wood, not steel."

"It still hurt."

"It was supposed to. You must learn to avoid the blows."

"Aye, but—"

"Be a man about it, Telk."

"I will," replied Telk in a subdued voice.

"I know I sound hard," said Froan, "but you never know when our chance will come. When it does, we must be ready."

When the boat reached Tararc Hite, Froan splashed ashore before it even touched the bank, for he was belatedly aware that he had overstayed on the island. He called back to Telk as he hurried off. "We'll practice again soon."

The failing light made traveling in the fens especially dangerous, but Froan sped through the bog confidently. He had inherited his mother's uncanny sense of where the safe ground lay, a sense some ascribed to sorcery. When he was younger, Froan had half believed the rumors and fervently hoped his mother could perform magic. But she had disappointed him. As he grew older, Froan had come to see her as ordinary. Though she was different from the fensfolk, she seemed equally as dull.

Turning a bend, Froan nearly collided with her. She was hurrying also and bearing a large empty sack. "Mam! What are you doing here?"

"Going to see Rappali. She has meat for us."

"I haven't yet found Rosie, but I—"

"Look by the old stump," said Yim. "She seems to have

found a rope and tied herself there." Without another word, she continued on her way.

Froan briefly glared at his departing mother, then continued onward to retrieve the doe.

SIX

RAPPALI EXPECTED Yim to arrive at dusk and was waiting outside her door when her friend came up the path. The goat's carcass hung from a nearby tree, minus a hind quarter, and Rappali held its rolled-up hide. Since her husband was home, she preferred to talk with Yim outside.

As Rappali watched Yim approach, she saw why Roarc called her a girl. For one thing, she dressed more like a maiden than a matron. Yim's sleeveless goatskin tunic ended above her knees, and she went about unshod except in winter. Her face was as youthful as her attire. Though Rappali knew her friend was well past thirty winters, Yim's face barely had a line on it. There was no gray among the dark walnut tresses that trailed down her back. Unmindful of her appearance, Yim kept her hair tied back with a strip of goatskin. Yet if Yim seemed oblivious of her beauty, others weren't. Men barely past Telk's age couldn't keep their eyes off her. One had even presented her with a marriage gift, which Yim refused, as she had all the other proposals.

As always, Yim greeted Rappali with a hug, "Thank you for your help," she said. "I'm sure Roarc grumbled over it."

"Oh, my husband likes ta grumble, and it does him good," replied Rappali with a smile. "Besides, he likes yar cheese, as do I."

"Well, Froan tires of it. He'll be glad for some meat."

"Did he visit my son today? Telk came home this eve covered with red marks and spouting some tale 'bout falling from a tree."

"Most like, our sons were together," said Yim, "for I met Froan on the way here. He seemed to be coming from your hite."

"What do ya think they were doing?"

Yim's face darkened. "Playing war, I fear."

"They're nearly men. They should be seeking wives, not playing."

"Men often never forsake that game, though their play becomes more deadly." Yim shook her head sadly. "I'd hoped it'd be different here."

" 'Tis different, Yim. True, some men go off, but not ta fight."

"So few return—who knows what they do?"

Rappali saw concern in her friend's eyes that bordered on fear, and she sought to reassure her. "Froan will grow up and leave off his foolishness."

Yim flashed an unconvincing smile. "I'm sure you're right."

" 'Tis getting dark," Rappali said. "Mayhap ya'd like ta bide with us till dawn."

"Thank you, but I can find my way by moonlight."

"Then we'll talk till moonrise. 'Twill be a treat for me, for Roarc's in a sulk." Rappali sat down on the low stone wall about the terraced garden, and Yim joined her. "I heard ya birthed Dori's child. Do ya think her husband was tha da?"

"I'd say the babe favored his mother," said Yim.

"But I heard his eyes . . ."

"The boy will be himself, no matter who the father," said Yim. "I don't see why folk prattle so."

"Because blood will always show," replied Rappali. "If Dori lay with that fisherman from Turgen Hite, then tha boy's going ta grow up mean."

"I'd think Dori would have some say in that."

"Pah!" said Rappali. "Look at my Telk and your Froan. They'll go their own ways no matter what we do."

"I hope not."

Rappali sighed. "'Tis the nature of men not ta mind their mothers."

Yim changed the subject and chatted with her friend until the moon rose high enough to light her way through the bog. Then she slipped her sack over the hanging carcass and cut it down to carry along with the goatskin. It was a heavy load, but she was used to hard work. After bidding Rappali farewell, Yim shouldered her burden and headed home.

As Yim walked alone, she brooded. Rappali was her closest friend—in truth her only one—but Yim didn't dare reveal her secret even to her. Thus she couldn't speak about what increasingly troubled her thoughts. It seemed ironic that Rappali had unknowingly spoken about it when she'd said "blood will always show." That was Yim's deepest fear, for Froan's father was a monster.

Tales of Lord Bahl's bloody rampages were known even in the Grey Fens, where folk assumed such terrors were distant. Yet their source wasn't distant at all. Bahl's cruelty and power arose from the Devourer, the malign entity that had possessed him. When Yim had bedded Bahl, that entity had passed through her to Froan. Yim was well aware of its malevolence, for having served briefly as a vessel for evil, a bit of it still lingered in her. Yim likened herself to a goblet that had held poison and was forever tainted.

That was the real reason Yim didn't slaughter her goats. The Devourer craved bloodshed because death fed its power. Since the sight of blood awoke that craving, Yim prevented Froan from seeing it. The only meat he ever ate was smoked until it was thoroughly dried. Whenever Yim prepared it, even she had to summon her willpower not to lick her bloody knife. *If I'm tempted, what hope has Froan?*

However, craving blood was merely an outward sign of the Devourer's need for carnage. Lord Bahl's name had been linked with war for generation after generation, as each son became like his father and took up the sword. As the Chosen, Yim had broken the cycle by seducing Bahl and fleeing with his unborn son. Afterward, peace had ensued. *But for how long?*

As of late, that question was constantly on Yim's mind. She feared that the Devourer would overwhelm her son and claim him as its own. She hadn't always felt that way. Froan had been an adorable child, and life with him on Far Hite—though hard—had been peaceful and often idyllic. As a toddler, Froan had been subject to rages, but Yim worked to help him tame them. For many winters, it seemed that she had succeeded. Yim loved Froan, set an example, taught him self-discipline, and hoped for the best. Nevertheless, she hid the knives.

With the onset of Froan's adolescence, Yim had become increasingly uneasy. It seemed that the dark thing inside him had been merely biding its time. Yim began to feel lonely as her son grew ever more distant. He started lying to her. Somehow he learned how to thwart her gaze so that she could no longer perceive what he was thinking. Yim soon found it necessary to veil her thoughts, for the power of Froan's eyes had strengthened. Like his father, he began to sway others to his will. His skill at this was rudimentary compared to Lord Bahl's, but Yim viewed Froan's growing abilities with distress.

What can I do? Yim asked herself. The question had long bedeviled her. *Love is my greatest strength, but can it overcome evil?* Lately, she had come to doubt it. *I gave up so much. Was it worth it?* Yim counted what she had gained. *I obeyed the goddess and fulfilled my destiny. I thwarted Lord Bahl and brought peace. Because of me, Honus lived.* As always, thoughts of Honus evoked longing. Memories of their moments of love—they seemed only moments—were both solace and torment in her exile. Yim still wondered where Honus was and what he was doing. With all her heart, she hoped that he had found happiness.

Yim was weary when she reached Far Hite, but she didn't head for home. Instead, she went to the hite's northern side to cut up the goat and smoke it while Froan slept. When Yim had first arrived at the hite, she made one of the smaller caves into a place for smoking and storing meat by constructing a door to seal its entrance. In anticipation of the night's work, she had already erected the smoking racks and gathered wood for the fire. Yim would do the butchering on a wide, flat stone outside the cave's entrance. Upon reaching her destination, she lay her burden down and went to light a reed torch so she could work in the dark.

As Yim approached the torch, something white caught her eye. She froze and her heart began pounding. There was a shape just beyond a nearby tree. Though it was vaporous and indistinct, it seemed to be taking the form of a woman robed in white. Yim called out in a voice quavering with emotion, "Karm?"

Then a breeze blew, and the shape dissipated. Yim realized that she had been peering at some mist caught in a beam of moonlight. She glanced about, saw more rising vapor, and knew that hope and a trick of the light had caused her to see what she most desired. "That wasn't the goddess," she said to the night, as if it needed convincing. "I haven't had a vision since I conceived Froan."

Yim was certain that she knew why: part of the enemy remained within her. *Karm can't speak to me without speaking to the Devourer.* Nevertheless, that understanding didn't lessen her sense of abandonment. The goddess's absence was yet another burden she had to bear. "Small wonder my eyes play tricks on me." Yim sighed heavily, then lit the torch.

Before Yim butchered the carcass, she took care of the hide. First she spread it out, hair side down, and liberally covered it with salt. Salt was a trade item in the Grey Fens, and precious, but there was no other way to cure a hide. Then she folded the skin, placing salted side to salted side, folded it again, put it in a loosely woven reed basket, and hung it in the cave. Afterward, she whetted her knife and began to cut the meat into thin strips. It took a long time to reduce an entire goat to ribbons of flesh and arrange them on the racks for smoking. Afterward, Yim lit a fire and disposed of the goat's bones while the fire burned to embers. Then she retrieved wood that she had soaked in the bog, covered the embers with the wet boughs, and set the racks of meat over them to smoke. By then, she was totally exhausted, and the sky was lightening with the promise of dawn.

There was one last thing Yim had to do before she could sleep: she needed to clean the blood from the butchering stone. With the day's first light, she could see it more clearly. Thick clots of dark maroon covered the smooth gray rock. Yim stared at the butchering stone wearily, feeling too tired to fetch the water to wash it. That was when the compulsion seized her to lick the stone clean instead. Before she knew it, she was running her tongue over its surface. While alarmed by what she was doing, Yim couldn't stop. She savored the salty, metallic taste that encompassed life and death at once, and it was a long while before she found the strength to break away.

Then Yim stood shuddering in the dawn, distraught over her weakness and the power of the evil thing inside her. She knew that it was nothing compared to the force of what lay within her son. Staring at the stone in the light of daybreak, she saw that it was mostly clean. As Yim went to get water to wash the remnant of blood away, she despaired for Froan.

SEVEN

A VAGRANT'S life had made Honus a light sleeper, and he woke as soon as dawn's light streamed through Daven's open door. The hermit lay close by, apparently asleep. Honus quietly rose into a cross-legged sitting position, closed his eyes, and commenced the meditations to trance, but instead of visiting the Dark Path, he felt Daven's stick across his back. "Thief!" shouted the old man. "I won't have it!"

Honus opened his eyes and saw that Daven had retreated out of reach. "Why name me that? I've stolen nothing."

"I, too, can trance," replied Daven. "So I know what you were taking—the memories of others."

"Memories the dead have discarded."

"Those who snatched offerings from the temple claimed the gifts were discarded, too. Your offense is no less great."

"Theodus never objected."

"Never?"

"Well, seldom."

"You mean he indulged your vice," said Daven. "That was a mistake. And see how it has ended. Yesterday you spoke of your feelings for Yim. If you're to help her, you must stop trancing."

"It's not so easy," replied Honus.

"It's oft easier to die than live. Is that what you choose? To forsake your love?"

"She forsook me."

Daven sighed dramatically. "We've been through this

before. She felt she had no choice. Will you hold it against her?"

Honus said nothing.

"Then abandon Yim for the memories of others, for happiness that isn't yours. But if you do, I'll tell you this: You'll soon visit the Dark Path and find you can't return. Already, it's entered your heart. Don't you feel an unnatural coldness? You must break free of it."

"How?"

"Eat. Rebuild your strength. Submit to my discipline."

"And who made you my master?"

"Didn't you say you've been apart from Yim for seventeen winters?"

"Yes. So?"

"Seventeen's a fateful number, for it clarifies what's tattooed upon your back. The Seer who made those marks foretold my role, and Karm inspired the Seer. You may have renounced the goddess, but she never renounced you. Won't you return her love?"

Honus sat silently as Daven waited for a reply. It was a long while before the old man shook his head and looked away.

The Most Holy Gorm's divining chamber was atop the highest tower in the Iron Palace, but sunlight never entered it. Only a single oil lamp broke the darkness of the windowless room. The smoky flame gave the air a pungent odor but didn't ease its otherworldly coldness. The lamp's pale light illuminated an iron door and walls of black basalt, a circle of blood painted on the stone floor, the corpse of the young boy sacrificed to provide it, and the Devourer's high priest. Gorm sat within the circle's protection and cast a set of ancient human bones upon the floor. They were yellow with age and inscribed with runes. As the bones clattered upon the cold stone, they appeared to move as if stirred by an unfelt wind, and it took some time for them to settle.

After the bones grew still, Gorm stared at them and noted their positions, where their shadows fell, and what runes were exposed. On three successive days, he had performed the ritual. Each time the revelation was the same. "Seventeen," he uttered to the chilly darkness. "Seventeen today."

The room slowly warmed as Gorm waited patiently within the circle of blood until it was safe to leave it. Even he wasn't immune to his master's malice, and the blood served as both offering and barrier. When the Most Holy One deemed it safe, he left the tower room and descended the long spiral stairway to the palace rooms below. Passing through them to the great hall, it was impossible to ignore their neglect. Gorm had been present when the foundation of the Iron Palace was laid, and had lived through the reigns of all its lords. The structure reflected the wax and wane of the lineage. Its iron exterior was oiled and black when Lord Bahl was in the fullness of his power, and rusty when that power passed to an infant heir. But never had the cycle reached such a low. Gorm walked past empty rooms shrouded in dust and gazed out dirty windows to view towers and crenellated walls encrusted with a thick reddish cancer.

Few servants remained, and even the garrison of the Iron Guard had many empty bunks. That was partly due to economy, for no plunder poured into the coffers, but it also reduced the number of potential wagging tongues. Gorm knew it was rumored that the heir was absent. He had done his utmost to suppress the talk, but it was hard to hide what was so plainly evident: The lord of the Iron Palace was but a husk with his seed missing. The most Gorm could hope for was an uneasy silence until the heir was found.

Gorm entered the great hall, his footsteps echoing in the empty, cobwebbed space. He passed the huge, cold fireplace and the unused banquet tables with their vacant chairs, all pale with long-gathered dust, to reach the raised platform at the room's end. There were two seats upon it, a large ornate one at the forefront, and Gorm's seat, slightly to the rear.

The latter was modest in appearance, and few realized it was where Bahland's true ruler sat. The ornate chair was occupied. Gorm bowed to the man sitting there out of habit, but there was no deference in his manner. "My lord, your son was born this day, seventeen winters past."

The man on the throne replied in a dull voice. "That long ago? How do you know?"

"The bones told me." Gorm gazed at Lord Bahl with thinly disguised contempt. *He was almost a god,* he thought. Gorm assumed that the Devourer had once so filled the man that little remained after it had departed. The pale, thin figure upon the throne resembled a squeezed rind, a withered and juiceless castoff. His eyes, which formerly had been so daunting, possessed the weary and haunted look of someone who hesitates to sleep for fear of dreams.

"Why tell me this?" asked Bahl. "It's useless information."

"Oh, it's far from useless. The time's auspicious."

"Auspicious for what?"

"To reach out to your son and persuade him to come home."

"How? Your precious magic bones have failed to divine his whereabouts. I can't speak to someone who can't be found."

"I've a means for you to do just that."

Bahl's expression grew uneasy. "Through sorcery?"

"Yes. It's the only way."

"Why now?"

"As I said, the time's auspicious."

"Then do it yourself. Magic's your province."

"Only a father may accomplish the feat. You sound fearful. Why?"

"Because I am. Your sorcery has cost me dearly."

"You failed our master, not I!" said Gorm, his voice echoing through the dark hall. "You would have been the world's sovereign—immortal and omnipotent—if you hadn't tupped that girl. Do you imagine the Devourer was pleased by your deed? Do you suppose that you're forgiven? Don't fear my sorcery. Fear our master's retribution." Then Gorm softened his tone. "This ritual is your chance for redemption. Your only chance, I might add."

Though it seemed impossible, Bahl's bloodless face grew even paler. "What must I do?"

"Join me atop the high tower at dusk."

After the Most Holy One had departed, Lord Bahl rang for a servant to bring him wine. An elderly man appeared from a side door to receive the request and departed the same way to fulfill it. Bahl seldom began drinking so early, but he needed to drown his apprehensions. Gorm terrified him, and he dreaded the idea of visiting the high tower. Nonetheless, he saw no alternative. After his downfall, he had learned who possessed the real power in the Iron Palace. It wasn't him. Bahl had come to believe that it had always been so. Even when he recalled the height of his power—when he commanded conquering armies and subdued men with a single glance—it seemed that true mastery lay elsewhere. *I was only power's vessel*, thought Bahl, *once full, now empty. But the power was never mine. I merely thought it was.* Such thinking made Lord Bahl bitter, but not rebellious. There was no rebelling against the Devourer.

The servant brought a goblet of wine. As Bahl drank, he gazed about the hall. A coat of dust lightened its black stone, and the bloodstains on the floor had long faded. The lord of Bahland tried to remember when the room was the seat of power and thronged with folk. Memories of those times had faded with the bloodstains. They seemed like scenes from another man's life and as vague as rumor. Much of what he recollected was nightmarish—ravaged towns awash in gore, men transformed into rabid beasts, brutal tortures, and a pervasive atmosphere of fear.

Bahl rang for another goblet of wine and wandered off with it. No one would notice his absence. The day promised to be like all the others—purposeless and idle. Gorm took care of the domain's administration. The Iron Guard reported to him. He levied taxes, made judgments, and issued decrees, all in Lord Bahl's name. No one objected. No one dared, Bahl least of all.

Bahl stepped onto a balcony that overlooked the bay and the sea beyond. Leaning against a rust-covered railing, he gazed out at the ocean as he drank. The day was heavily overcast and the restless sea had a dull, sullen sheen. There was no clear horizon, only gray water merging with gray mist. Lord Bahl finished his wine and retreated inside.

Dusk arrived. Acting on impulse, Lord Bahl had his servant dress him in black velvet and gold. He hadn't worn the outfit for ages, and it was moth-eaten. It also hung loosely from his diminished frame. Nevertheless, it somehow seemed appropriate for the ritual, for he had worn these clothes on the night he had lost his power. *Tonight I'll amend that error.*

When he was dressed, Lord Bahl ascended the tower stairs alone. He had climbed them only once before, for the tower was Gorm's domain. The windowless structure was pitch-black, and Bahl carried a torch to light his way. The darkness had the palpable quality of smoke that made the torchlight pale and watery. Bahl hurried his pace to pass through it more quickly.

The last time Bahl had stood atop the tower, he was only thirteen winters in age. He recalled that occasion vividly. It was sunset. Gorm was there with a woman whom Bahl had never seen before. She was dressed in a thin white robe and lay barefoot upon a large rectangular stone. Bahl remembered her as a blonde with the pale skin of someone shut away from sunlight. Bahl never knew if the woman was drugged or under a spell, but she must have been one or the other, for she was awake yet completely passive. She remained quiet and unresisting even when Gorm pierced her throat with a stone knife. He cut an artery, judging from the spurting blood. Then Gorm commanded Bahl to drink, and he obeyed.

The intervening winters never dimmed what happened next. No wine ever tasted as rich as that woman's blood or was as intoxicating. Moreover, it transformed Bahl as he drank it. Before that evening, he had felt incomplete, as if he were missing some vital part. The woman's sacrifice cured that. Bahl was convinced that he had ascended the stairs a boy but descended them a man. Although he had known the ritual was called the "suckling," only later did he learn the blond woman had been his mother.

The ritual was still on Lord Bahl's mind when he emerged onto the tower's windy summit. Gorm was waiting there, and he closed the iron trapdoor after Bahl stood upon the ironclad deck that capped the tower. The deck had not been allowed to rust, and its oiled surface was shiny and black. A slight slipperiness increased Bahl's feeling of vertigo, for the tower was the palace's loftiest, jutting like a spire high above its seaward wall. Moreover, the platform was only six paces wide, and it had no wall or railing at its edge. Bahl shuddered and moved to the center, which featured the waist-high rectangular stone.

Gorm smiled sardonically. "The last time you were here, the height didn't bother you. But no matter, this potion will cure your fear."

Bahl noticed that the priest held a goblet. "What's that?"

"A concoction to help you find your son."

"How?"

"It'll send your spirit forth. Blood will always find blood." Gorm cast another derisive smile. "Don't worry, it's not poison. Your spirit can return. Drink."

Bahl took the goblet and sipped from it. The liquid tasted both bitter and sweet. As the flavors warred in Bahl's mouth,

Gorm said. "Finish it quickly. Then you'd best lie upon the stone."

Bahl gulped down the rest of the potion, then climbed upon the block of basalt. Unbeckoned, a thought arose: *My mother lay here.* Bahl decided the potion tasted bitter. To easy his nerves, he spoke. "So, soon I'll meet my son."

"Yes, and in your old form with your powers restored. The Devourer has abandoned you in this world, but not in the other one."

The other one? thought Bahl. The phrase had disturbing connotations. *Don't worry. Gorm said this draught wouldn't kill me.* Bahl was beginning to feel a little dizzy, so he turned his gaze seaward to glimpse something substantial. But the sea was still a seething void of gray without a horizon; only it was darker than before.

The Most Holy Gorm waited for Lord Bahl to close his eyes and fall into an ensorcelled slumber. Then he turned Bahl's face upright and studied it in the dying light. He had performed the ritual many times and knew what subtle signs to look for. The eyelids quivered and the lips moved, then grew still. Soon Lord Bahl's breathing was as easy and regular as that of an innocent man. *His spirit's on its way,* Gorm thought. *Now my master can receive what's been long overdue.*

Gorm reached down and lifted a long, leaf-shaped blade fashioned from obsidian. One end of the black, glassy stone was wrapped in boiled leather to form a handle. Gorm gripped it with both hands and held it high. The knife was sharper than the finest steel, and when he plunged it downward, it easily parted Lord Bahl's chest. Gorm reached into the gaping cavity and tore out the heart. It was still beating when he threw it into the void.

EIGHT

AFTER SPENDING the night smoking goat meat, Yim had slept through much of the following day. Froan had performed the morning milking, and when Yim rose for the evening milking, she found that he had already led the herd to the milking shelter. It was located on the hite's eastern side where an irregularity in the steep, stone wall created a natural three-sided enclosure. Roofed over with branches and thatch, it allowed the goats to be milked out of the weather. Inside were two milking stands, goat-proof containers of dried faerie arrow, and crockery jugs for milk.

When Yim reached the shelter, Froan was already milking the first doe, which was contentedly munching a faerie arrow root. "Thanks for doing the morning milking," she said.

"You went to bed after sunrise," Froan replied. "I thought you needed the rest."

"I did." Yim led a doe to a milking stand, secured the animal, and gave her a root as a treat. Then she washed the doe's teats with water infused with cleansing herbs and began milking. After squeezing out a little milk to flush each teat, she set a jug in place and began to fill it. For a while, the only sound was liquid squirting into jugs as Yim and Froan expertly milked the herd. Yim broke the silence. "Telk's mother said you visited him yesterday."

"I wanted to see the boat he's making."

"His mother thought otherwise," said Yim. "She said Telk came home covered with marks. She believed you two were playing warrior."

"We were a bit. It was Telk's idea. He's fond of battles."

"That's because he hasn't seen one. Doesn't he know what happened to your father?"

"I've told him the tale."

"Honus was a good and gentle man. He deserved a better fate."

"You've oft spoke about his death but seldom about his life," said Froan. "Telk overheard his mam say you were Honus's slave. Is that true?"

"I was his slave, but only briefly. He set me free."

"How did you become a slave?"

"I was on a journey with my father, and we were attacked by bandits. They killed Father and sold me to a slave dealer. My fate was a common one in those times. Honus was a goatherd who needed a donkey. When he came to town to buy one, he discovered donkeys were dear and slaves were cheap. I was all he could afford. He paid ten coppers for me."

"Was that much money?"

"No. He spent six coppers on my cloak, and it was used and bloodstained." Yim smiled upon recalling it, then continued her tale. "On our first night together, I feared he would force himself on me. After all, I was his property. But he swore by the goddess that he'd never do so, and he kept his word. I think that was when I first knew he was no common man."

"Why did you free you?" asked Froan.

"Because he realized that no one can truly own another."

"But you stayed with him."

"Love binds tighter than chains. We married, and soon after, you were conceived. We were so happy."

"And then the soldiers came," said Froan. "I know the rest."

"War's not valor and glory," said Yim. "It's butchery and cruelty. Don't mistake it for a game."

"I just play with sticks, Mam, and only to please Telk."

Yim wanted to believe Froan, but she didn't. Nevertheless, she pretended that she did. While she was at it, she pretended Froan was Honus's son. It didn't stretch her imagination, for the boy had Honus's lean, strong body. *As did Lord Bahl.* His hair was almost as dark as Honus's. *But a walnut shade like mine.* However, the eyes were all wrong. *Honus's were blue.* Froan's eyes even differed from hers, for they were so pale that only the pupils were prominent. *Just like Lord Bahl's.* Similarities and differences aside, it was love that made Yim's pretense almost believable. Her devotion was the principal thing that Honus and Froan had in common. While one was a lover and the other a son, her love for each was equally intense. With the foresight that sometimes came to her, Yim knew that would never change.

Froan's fingers milked the doe with a rippling motion that imitated a suckling kid. Long practice allowed him to do it without thinking, permitting his thoughts to dwell upon his discontent. *Twice a day, every day*, he thought. *What a dreary life!* He despaired at the prospect, and once again felt a restless yearning for something different. He wasn't sure precisely what, other than an existence free of goats.

Froan glanced at his mother, who was gazing at him in an affectionate way that he found belittling, although he couldn't say why. It made him want to be elsewhere. But there was no hurrying milking, and Froan stuck with it to the last doe. Then he rose. "I'll take the milk to the cave," he said.

"While you're there, stop by the smoke cave," said Yim. "The meat there should be ready. If you bring me some, I'll add it to tonight's stew."

Froan forced himself to smile. "That'll be a treat."

Yim took a small jug of milk to serve at evemeal and departed. Froan consolidated the rest of the milk into two large crockery jugs that hung from a yoke. It was destined to be made into cheese, which was the staple food for him and his mother and also the item they bartered for their other needs. Although Froan knew that his mother's cheese was a favorite among their neighbors, he was sick of it. It reminded him of the wearying sameness of his life.

Froan hefted the yoke with its two dangling milk jugs and carried it easily to the northern side of the hite. The cave used for cheese making was there, close to the one for smoking meat. Since it was summer, the evening milking finished at sunset, and Froan arrived at his destination while some light still lingered in the sky. He entered the cave and untied the jugs to carry them farther back to a cool, dark chamber where milk kept well. Eager to be done, he didn't bother to light a torch, and soon he had to feel his way. He had just set the second jug down when he heard a whispered voice. "Son?"

Froan glanced about the dark chamber, but saw no one. "Mam?" he answered. It seemed impossible that his mother could be in the cave, but she was the only other person on the hite.

"Not her," answered the voice. "Someone else."

Froan peered in the direction from which the voice had come and detected a faint glimmer in the darkness. As he stared at it, the light elongated and grew brighter. "Who are you?" asked Froan.

"Who besides your mother would call you son?"

"My father?"

"Yes."

"But Honus is dead."

The glimmer continued to expand, assuming a vaguely human form composed of luminescent mist. It was the source of the voice. "Honus is neither dead nor your father. Your mother hasn't been honest."

"You mean I'm not a goatherd's son?"

The glowing mist resolved into the unclothed figure of a

man with features as crisply defined as if they had been cut
from crystal. Froan saw something of himself in the face, the
lean hard body, and the piercing eyes. There was a gaping
hole in the man's chest. Its torn edges quivered as he laughed
in response to Froan's question. "Is *that* what she told you?
Your father's a goatherd? How droll. And what did she say
she was? An assassin? A whore? She would have, if she
spoke true."

"And what do you speak?" asked Froan. "Truth or slan-
der?"

"The living need to lie. For gain. To evade justice. To
gather renown. Only the dead can embrace honesty, for
only they are beyond its consequences. Upon the Dark Path,
the sole coin is truth. So hear me out and be wiser for it."

"Who were you, then, other than my father?"

"A mighty lord of men. A conqueror." Bahl's spirit
pointed to his empty chest. "Your mother's victim."

Froan stood dumbfounded.

"Haven't you always sensed your differentness? Don't
you feel caged in this dismal bog?" asked the spirit. "That's
because you weren't destined for a common life. You possess
the patrimony of my line—a power over other men. Your
mother has worked to subdue that power, to render you ordinary. Yet greatness will out. Think how easily you sway
others to your will. With use, that power will grow. That's
what your mother seeks to prevent."

"Why?"

"Because the weak despise the strong. She would smother
your light rather than endure its brightness. And she would
justify her betrayal in the name of Karm, the goddess of
timidity."

"What you say stirs me," said Froan, "but your accusa-
tions dampen its appeal. Mam has cared for me all my life,
while you offer only words."

"I offer truth," replied the spirit. "Truth you can test
yourself. Not only does Honus live, he's a Sarf—the deadliest

of men. He's a killer, not a goatherd. Moreover, your mother forsook him so she might bed me. Spring this news on her and watch her face. It will confirm my honesty."

"And what good will that do?"

"It'll free you from a web of lies, so you might become your true self. That's no small thing. If you choose to seek your destiny, first visit a high and barren rock that lies near the river. It's shaped like two stone fingers pressed together."

"Twin Hite," said Froan, recognizing the place from its description.

"The power that oversees the world has worked its will to provide you an omen. Deep in a crevice near the rock's summit you'll find a token of your birthright, one that will help you achieve it."

"Who are you, and why do you speak in riddles?"

The spirit came closer, and for the first time, Froan felt the full power of its gaze. Then his doubt and wariness seemed foolish. He felt a deep kinship with the spirit and was ready—even eager—to believe all it said.

"My name you may not know until you gain the strength to bear it. Until then, it would only imperil you. Great lords have many enemies."

"Tell me how I might achieve that strength."

"It'll be easier than you think. Follow your instincts. Your first impulse will always be the right one. Remember that you were born to rule and laws are made for common men. Be ruthless, and you'll succeed where I failed. Always remember that there is strength in anger. Use its power to make your way." With those words, the spirit began to grow nebulous. "And heed this parting warning most of all: Never bed a virgin."

"Wait!" cried Froan. "Did my mother slay you? And when will I know . . ." His voice trailed off as the spirit faded altogether.

NINE

FROAN STARED into the darkness for a long while as a succession of emotions gripped him. He was perplexed, suspicious, and excited in turn without settling on one reaction. *What just happened?* he wondered. Froan had heard of visions, but the spirit didn't seem divine. The fensfolk spoke of boghaunts, the lost souls of persons swallowed by the muck; yet the apparition hadn't died by drowning. Thus it was possible that the ghost was what it claimed to be— the shade of his father.

Since much of what the spirit said affirmed Froan's deepest yearnings, he wanted to believe it. However, some of its claims were disturbing. *My mam a whore and a murderer?* That seemed as farfetched as it was unsettling, for Froan considered his mother naive and squeamish. Yet Froan felt that he couldn't pick and chose what to believe. The spirit had either revealed the truth or attempted to deceive him. There seemed only two possibilities: he was either the son of a lowly goatherd or the heir of a mighty lord. Furthermore, if he was destined for greatness, then his mother was a murderous whore. The alternatives were so extreme that Froan couldn't decide which was genuine. Fortunately, the spirit had provided a means to confirm its claims. All Froan needed to do was catch his mother in an unguarded moment and reveal what the spirit had said about Honus. Regardless of what happened next, Froan felt certain that he would learn the truth.

It was dusk when Froan left the cave and headed

homeward. Preoccupied with the bizarre visitation, he was halfway home before remembering that he was supposed to bring some meat. He rushed back to the smoke cave, opened its door, and grabbed some strips of goat from the rack inside. Then, after latching the door, Froan hurried to dinner.

When he arrived, his mother, who preferred to cook outdoors in warm weather, was stirring a pot nestled among orange-red embers. Lit by their dim glow, her face appeared serene but also mysterious. Froan had spent his entire life in her company, but he had given little thought to her existence before he was born. In that respect, she was as much a mystery to him as she was to the fensfolk. Thinking upon the matter, Froan couldn't decide if his ignorance was due to indifference on his part or evasion on hers. He had learned only recently that she had been a slave, and it wasn't his mother who had told him. *Perhaps her past is as sordid as the spirit said*, thought Froan. Although he was anxious to discover the truth, it didn't seem the right time to confront his mother, for the dim light would make it hard to read her expression.

Froan handed his mother the strips of smoked goat meat and retreated from the light, aware that his face might betray his turmoil. As she tore apart the meat and added it to the pot of simmering tubers and herbs, her expression became uneasy. She shivered and looked in his direction. "Did something happen to you?" she asked.

"No," replied Froan, taking pains to keep his voice even and casual. "I'm just hungry."

"Then you'll enjoy this stew. The meat will give it savor," his mother replied, still gazing at Froan's shadowed face.

Froan had been cold since birth, and he seldom noticed his perpetual chill, but at that moment he did. It had deepened. Moreover, his mother seemed to have noted the change, causing Froan to speculate that was why she shivered despite her nearness to the embers. *Is it my chill that makes her uneasy or something else?* It was another question that he must postpone asking.

Froan walked toward the entrance of the home that the two of them shared. "There's a chill in the air," he said, anxious to avoid his mother's gaze. "I'm going to get my cloak."

The door was open to admit the faint light from the evening sky, but Froan could have found his cloak with his eyes closed. The outer wall of moss-chinked stone enclosed a cramped cavity chipped into the rocky hite. It barely accommodated two narrow mattresses, some pots and baskets, and a space to cook. In the fashion of all fens abodes, the hearth was set into the outer wall, which also incorporated a chimney. Froan had to duck his head to pass through the doorway. Then it took only two steps before his outstretched hand touched his cloak, which hung from a peg on the far wall.

Froan slipped the goatskin garment over his bare shoulders, but he didn't immediately rejoin his mother. Instead, he imagined how his home would seem to his noble father. The cavity smelled strongly of smoke, although his mother has been cooking outside since spring. It also smelled of goats and the two people who tended them. Darkness obscured most of the meager possessions that hung from pegs or cluttered the tiny floor, but Froan saw them in his mind's eye. They seemed few and pitiful. He had heard tales of lords, how they wore colorful garments made of fine cloth, dined off golden plates on meat at every meal, and lived in stone-built houses the size of hites. *What would my father think of this tiny hole?* It was easy to guess: *It seems more a pen than a home.*

When Froan emerged into the night, his mother was still gazing in his direction. He found a shadowed spot and sat down. After a while, his mother broke the silence. "I'll do the milking next morn so you can go to Green Hite and deliver some cheeses."

"To whom?"

"Turtoc. He has smoked eels to trade. I know you're fond of them."

"Green Hite's a fair trek from here," said Froan. "How'd you learn about the eels?"

"Oh, I had cause to visit there." After a spell of silence, his mother added, "Most like, Turtoc will be tending his traps, but Treemi will be there."

"Who?"

"His eldest daughter. You've met her before. She's comely with golden hair."

"I scarce recall her."

"Well, she certainly remembers you. I sensed an attraction."

"She's but a girl."

"Not so! She's nigh on sixteen winters. And not only pretty but a hard worker and sweet tempered."

"Mam, what are you saying?"

"Fensfolk marry young, and—"

"Is that what you wish for me? To wed a fish trapper's daughter?" Froan recalled the spirit's warning that he should never bed a virgin. It suddenly seemed highly relevant.

"I wish you to be happy," replied his mother. "It'd be a good match."

"Forget it. I'm going to be like you and never marry anyone."

"But I did marry. I married Honus."

Froan had to fight the impulse to challenge that assertion, and he found the strength to do so from an unlikely source. It was the part of him that he called his shadow. Before, it had only spurred his anger, but on this occasion it tempered his urge to act. Then Froan saw the advantage of a more cold-blooded approach and changed his tone. "Of course," he said. "I forgot Honus. You were happy with him, weren't you?"

"To the day he died."

Froan was glad that the shadows hid his smile. "I'll see that girl tomorrow, and I'll keep an open mind."

"That's all I ask," replied his mother in a meek tone that Froan found annoying. *You're playing with me*, he thought. *Working to forestall my future.* For the time being, that future was still nebulous to Froan, a dream without specifics. Thinking upon it, he was eager for morning to come. *Daylight will reveal what the night hides. Then perhaps Mam's games will cease.*

Dawn found Froan wide-awake and still calculating how to best surprise his mother. He rose and ate a bit of cold stew, then waited for her to rise. When she did, she smiled at him. "No milking for you this morning."

"How many cheeses should I take to Green Hite?"

"Two. I've already spoken to Turtoc. We'll get six eels for them."

"You gave him generous terms," said Froan, guessing his mother's reasons.

"I wouldn't be surprised if Treemi gives you a few extra. Just use your charm."

Froan smiled. "I'll do my best." He didn't leave, but waited until his mother stepped outside to round up the goats for milking. Following her into the sunlight, he called to her in a gentle voice. "Mam."

She halted and turned.

Froan walked over to her until they were close enough to touch. "About last night," he said. "I know you wish the best for me." His mother's face took on a pleased look, mingled with a hint of relief. Froan gazed at her eyes, but was unable to peer behind them. With others, he could perceive far more—sense emotions and grasp unspoken thoughts. But when he gazed at his mother, Froan saw only what came to the surface. Nevertheless, he had grown skilled at reading her most subtle expressions. Nothing escaped his notice. He reached out and tenderly grasped her arms. "Mam, have you ever had a vision?" Watching his mother carefully, Froan noted his question both surprised and alarmed her.

"Never."

"I think I did last night."

"What did you see?" asked his mother in a voice that strained to seem casual but revealed growing apprehension.

Froan permitted himself to smile ever so slightly. "My father."

"Honus?" Apprehension turned to outright fear.

Froan, ever more certain where the truth lay, tightened his grip on his mother's arms as he spoke. "You mean the killer you abandoned? He's not my father." Froan watched the blood drain from his mother's face. When she struggled to break free, he held her fast. "Did you think I wouldn't find out? My sire's a lord, not a goatherd."

"No! No!"

"It's pointless to lie. Your face betrays you." Froan released his mother, who stood transfixed by shock. "I was born for greatness, and you'll not hold me back!" Then Froan smiled, turned on his heel, and strode away. He was ten paces down the path before his mother cried out to him. "Froan! Froan! Come back!" Her voice seemed on the verge of sobbing and sounded pathetic to his ears. Froan didn't even turn around.

As Yim watched her son stride away, she realized that trying to stop him would be both futile and foolish. Froan had managed to totally surprise her, and the shock of his revelation had left her stunned. Yim had no idea what to do, but she felt a wrong move would be disastrous. Since Froan had stormed off wearing only a breechclout, he was virtually guaranteed to return home. When he did, Yim would have a chance to sway his course. She suspected it would be her only one.

What chagrined Yim most was how all her sacrifices had been for naught. *Why did I presume I could hide Froan from the Devourer?* In retrospect, the idea seemed naive, even though she had vanished from the larger world. From the perspective of Averen or Bremven, the Grey Fens were as distant as the moon. The fensfolk had been so astonished by her arrival that some still didn't believe that she was human. Yet the bog had proved no sanctuary. *The Devourer is like the goddess*, thought Yim. *It overlooks all the world. It was merely biding its time until my son grew.*

Yim realized her mistake in relying on isolation and deception. Froan had learned the truth despite them. *But only part of the truth*, thought Yim. *He's learned his father was great and powerful, but I doubt he knows what that power cost him.* Yim saw that her only hope lay in revealing the whole truth about Lord Bahl to Froan, and in that effort, her previous deceptions would work against her. Froan had learned his true parentage, and having caught her in a lie, he would hold all she said suspect. Nevertheless, speaking truth was her only option short of violence, and Yim could never harm Froan. For seventeen winters, she had nurtured and loved him. Knowing that his flaws arose from his conception, she felt if Froan failed to overcome them, it would be her fault, not his. *Whatever it costs me*, Yim swore to herself, *I'll save him from his doom.*

TEN

FROAN DASHED through the bog in order to catch Telk before he left to check his fish traps. Certain that the apparition had been his father, Froan was anxious to visit Twin Hite and discover the token that the spirit said would be there. To do that, he would need Telk, for the hite was reachable only by boat.

Froan's haste paid off. When he reached Tararc Hite's far shore, Telk's reed boat was still in view. It was laden with fish traps, and Telk was poling it down the narrow channel. Froan called out. "Stop! Come back."

Telk immediately began to pole back toward the shore, obviously puzzled by his friend's unexpected arrival. Before he could say anything, Froan spoke. "I had a vision last eve."

"From tha Mother?"

"Of course, from her. She said we're to go to Twin Hite to receive a token of our fate."

"But Da wants these traps out by morn," replied Telk.

Froan gazed at Telk in the same manner that his father's spirit had regarded him and used his eyes to convey a sense of urgency. "The traps are unimportant," he said. "We've been charged by the Mother to do this. Besides, when your da checks the traps this eve, he won't know when they were set out."

"Nay, he won't," agreed Telk. He seemed infected by his friend's mood, for he picked up the pace of his poling. Soon his small craft touched the bank. Froan stepped aboard, confident that Telk would do his bidding.

*   *   *

Twin Hite was a prominent but rarely visited spot. Thrusting from the water to the height of half a dozen men, the spire of rock resembled an index and middle finger pressed together. It served as a landmark, but was good for nothing else, since its sides were nearly vertical. The only place a man could comfortably stand was on its lofty top. The hite lay close to where the bog merged with the Turgen in an area of tangled channels that was more river than fens.

It took a long while for Telk to thread his small craft through the maze of waterways, which often came to dead ends that forced him to find another route. The sun was high in the morning sky when he reached the hite and found no bank on which to beach his boat. "Now what?" asked Telk.

Froan had been silent throughout the journey, caught up in splendid daydreams. Roused from those reveries, he gazed up at the towering rock. "Pole around the hite until I spot a place to climb it."

Telk did as he was told, and on the far side of the hite, Froan found a place to attempt to scale it. A wide and jagged crack ran up the rock face, and its weathered interior provided a few holds. Telk maneuvered the reed boat until Froan was able to grip the rock, pull himself up, and begin climbing. The ascent was difficult and risky, but Froan approached it with a single-mindedness that vanquished fear. Soon Telk and the boat were left far below.

Froan had nearly reached the summit of the hite when he came upon an opening in the rear of the crack. It was a crevice that extended deeper into the stone. When Froan peered into its dark interior he saw a vague form. Curious, he entered the crevice, which widened to form a small cavity.

There, he discovered a man's body. When Froan's eyes adjusted to the dim light, he perceived that the corpse was ancient, little more than a skeleton wrapped in papery skin and moldering garments. The clothing wasn't that of a fensman and appeared exotic, furthering the body's air of mystery. Froan had no idea how the man had come to be in the crevice or the manner of his death. *Is this the token I'm supposed to find?* he wondered. *If so, what does it mean?*

Then Froan saw that the bony hands resting on the corpse's lap gripped an elongated object wrapped in cloth. The way the dead man held the bundle gave the impression that he was presenting a gift. Froan touched the wrapping and it disintegrated into dust, revealing a leather scabbard. When Froan gently pulled at it, the skeletal hands fell apart and tumbled to the crevice floor. Projecting from the newly freed scabbard was the hilt of a dagger with a brass pommel resembling the head of a snarling beast. Then the scabbard, like the cloth that had wrapped it, fell to pieces in Froan's hand to reveal a polished blade that had remained keen despite its long hiding. Reflecting the dim light, it shone like moonlit water.

The dagger's preservation seemed an omen, as well as the crumbling of its scabbard, which prevented the blade from being sheathed again. "I, too, have been hidden from the world," Froan said. He held the blade aloft. "But no more. My destiny has been revealed! I'm to take up this blade and claim my place!" The words rang within the narrow space, sounding grand and forceful to him—something a great lord would say. The weapon felt natural in his hand, less an extension of his arm than its completion. It seemed as if the blade always had been meant for him, and the thought gave him a heady sense of power. Already, the dagger was precious to him as both a token of his future and a means to achieve it.

Upon further examination of the corpse, Froan found a sword. Unlike the dagger, it had lain in a wet place and its scabbard had rotted away to expose a blade pitted with rust. Nevertheless, Froan decided to take it also. The upper portion of the dead man's cloak remained sound, and Froan cut two pieces from it to wrap the sword and dagger.

Then he cut long strips of cloth and used them to tie the pair of bundles to his back. Descending the crack with reckless haste, Froan reached the reed boat with his treasures. He held out the largest bundle to Telk. "The Mother has sent us signs," he said. "This one's for you."

Telk seldom questioned his friend's pronouncements, and he didn't on this occasion either. Instead, he seemed swept up by Froan's excitement as he pulled the aged cloth from the token of his fate. Froan caught the disappointment on Telk's face at the sight of the rusty blade, and he quickly spoke to ease it. "Yes, the sword's rusty. That's to test your resolve. Take a stone to the blade and make it gleam."

"I will, Froan. 'Twill sparkle like tha sun."

"Be quick with your work, for our time draws nigh. You must be ready."

"For what?"

"Adventure. Riches. Renown. Now pole us back so we might prepare. Gather your things in readiness for a quick departure."

Yim went through the motions of her morning routine with her mind elsewhere. Her thoughts dwelt solely on her son and what she would say to him when he returned. She could only guess about the nature of Froan's "vision" and what Lord Bahl had told him. She didn't even know if Bahl was alive or dead. Her only certainty was that her son hadn't been told the whole truth. *Would he choose to lose his soul for the sake of power and riches?* Froan's father had, but Yim wondered if he had had any choice in the matter. *Does Froan?* Yim worried that her son might have been doomed upon the moment of his conception. *But if that's true, then the world's doomed also.*

Hoping her sacrifices hadn't been pointless, Yim tried to devise an argument that would sway her son from following Lord Bahl's footsteps. After she came up with one, she rehearsed it out loud during the morning's tasks. "I hid the truth for your sake," she said for the dozenth time as she curdled milk to make cheese, "waiting until you gained the strength to hear it. Yes, your father was a lord with a great palace and a mighty army, but that power wasn't truly his. Its source was an evil being that possessed and consumed him. By the time I met your father, he was only a husk of a man. When you were conceived, that evil passed to you. It's the cause of your rages and unnatural urges. I know something of its power, for a trace lingers in me. It's a terrible legacy, and if you fail to master it, it will master you.

"Your father would have you become its slave, as he was. Heed him and you'll be doomed to a vile and bloody life. Do you wish to become a monster whose name evokes only fear? I brought you here so you might avoid that fate."

As Yim squeezed the water from the curds, she refined her argument. She also wondered if she should tell Froan that she was the Chosen, whose life's task was to bear Lord Bahl's child. *Should I recount my degradation while in Bahl's power? Reveal the nature of the Devourer? What tone should I take? Stern? Loving?* Yim wavered on those points before concluding that Froan's state of mind would determine the best approach. All she could do was wait for his return, then gauge his mood and decide how best to proceed.

It was midmorning when Yim was seized by the sudden fear that Froan might try to sneak away. Abruptly halting her cheese making, she ran back to their tiny home in a state of panic that eased only when she found Froan's things undisturbed. Yim realized that she had been lucky and that Froan could have easily slipped away forever. She resolved not to give him another opportunity and remained indoors.

The day passed slowly until it was time for the second milking. Froan had yet to come home. Still waiting for him, Yim heard the does grow distressed when no one emptied their swollen udders. Their bleating sounded ever more urgent until Yim knew that she must do something. Taking the goats to the milking shed was out of the question, so she led the head doe to a dense thicket near her home, knowing the herd would follow. Yim settled in a place where she could view her doorway and began to milk the does simply to relieve them. Their milk spurted on the ground and was wasted, but that seemed of no consequence. Yim was milking her fifth goat, when she saw Froan approach the doorway. His stealthy manner made her think that he had timed his arrival to avoid her. Froan appeared unaware of Yim's presence, so she waited until he entered their home. Then she followed him inside.

As Yim suspected, her son was hastily preparing to depart. Already, his winter boots and most of his clothing lay piled inside his spread-out cloak. Yim also spied household goods among them—a small cooking pot, a water skin, and some utensils along with a flint and iron. "Going on a journey?" she asked.

Froan started and whirled to regard her with a haughty gaze that reminded Yim of Lord Bahl. "That's not your concern," he said.

Yim struggled to keep her voice calm, and she even forced a smile. "Of course it is. I'm your mother."

"I had a father, too. What of him?"

"I hid the truth for your sake, waiting until . . ."

Froan appeared not to be listening. Instead, he reached into the pile upon his cloak and pulled out something wrapped in an ancient scrap of cloth. "My father gave me a sign," he said. "A token of my future." His right hand disappeared into the cloth and emerged holding a dagger.

At the sight of the blade, Yim's carefully reasoned arguments vanished from her mind. Her entire focus centered on the dagger. The weapon seemed to have transformed her son, as if it were some evil talisman. Seeing Froan brandish it stirred grim memories of soldiers' bloody deeds, and with those memories came rage. "How dare you?" shouted Yim. "How dare you bring that thing into our home?"

Without forethought, Yim grabbed Froan's wrist with both hands and twisted it. He gave a startled cry as his arm was wrenched into an awkward and painful position. His fingers flew open, and the dagger fell to the dirt floor. Both Yim and Froan lunged for it, but Froan grabbed the hilt first. Yim saw the blade move upward just as she was falling toward it. There was a burning sensation across her throat as she struck the floor. Then she quickly rose to a kneeling position and gazed up at her son.

Froan was backing away, dagger in hand, as he stared at her. His expression was unreadable, for it seemed that emotions were warring within him. Then one appeared to gain the upper hand—horror. Froan looked away, and Yim followed his gaze toward the blade. It was stained with blood. Then Yim understood why her throat burned. *It's been cut*, she thought. *That blood is mine.* She glanced downward. Crimson stained her tunic and the dirt floor before her knees. Yim looked at her son again, wondering if she was still capable of speech. Though her eyes met his, she could no longer see him clearly, for the light seemed to be fading. She tried to say "I forgive you," but growing darkness snuffed out her words. All Yim was able to do was gaze at her child as shadow enveloped him.

ELEVEN

FROAN WATCHED aghast as his mother fixed her eyes on him and attempted to speak. Her lips quivered, but instead of words, a single drop of blood passed her parted lips. The silence was terrible. The drop grew larger until it rolled down her chin, leaving a crimson trail. Then his mother's face turned deathly pale, and her eyes rolled upward. She collapsed with a slight twisting motion to lie still upon the floor. *I've killed her!* Froan thought, unsure if the deed was accidental or not. It had happened so quickly that his memory of the event was incoherent. His most vivid recollections were of how easily her flesh had parted and of his opposing reactions of horror and exultation. It seemed as if two persons had watched, each with feelings totally alien to the other's. Froan struggled to reconcile that he was both those persons, but it was impossible. He felt that he could be only one of them. He had either done something horrendous and abominable or he had avenged his father's murder and liberated himself in the process.

Torn between those two conceptions, Froan was unable to decide which was true. His emotions were too powerful and immediate for that. Then he felt an urge that was as appalling as his mother's death—a craving to taste her blood. The compulsion was so strong that Froan was bending toward his mother's gashed neck before revulsion made him shrink back. He quickly wiped the blood from the dagger with the scrap of cloth that had wrapped it, fighting the urge to lick the blade instead. The effort left him trembling. Fearing that if he didn't flee immediately he would succumb to his unnatural compulsion, he grabbed his cloak. In his haste, he was unmindful that many of the items he had gathered tumbled from his makeshift bundle. Taking it up, he turned to leave the only home he had ever known.

Froan took one last remorseful glance at the crumpled woman who had nurtured him all his life. Then he dashed outside. As he ran, his vision blurred with tears and his stomach churned. Soon he began retching and was forced to halt and vomit. Because he had eaten nothing since breakfast, only a thin stream of sour liquid issued forth. Nonetheless, his stomach convulsed for a long while. When it finally settled, he was thoroughly miserable. The future that had seemed so alluring felt tainted by his mother's death.

What's done's done. Froan's mind formed those words, though the thought seemed to have welled up from another source. Nevertheless, Froan saw the truth in it. *Mam's dead. Nothing will change that. I can only go forward.* Then the notion came to him that her death was yet another sign, one that he was forever severed from his former life. *The fens are no longer my home*, he thought.

Froan made his way to the caves on the northern side of the hite where he took a supply of cheese and smoked goat meat. He found a scrap of goatskin and fashioned it into a crude sheath. It was little more than a wrapping for the dagger's blade, but it allowed him to tuck the weapon into the waistband of his breechclout. Once that was done, Froan fled to Tararc Hite. He intended to spend the night by Telk's boat so he could catch his friend first thing in the morning.

As Froan threaded his way through the treacherous bog, his mind remained in turmoil. The part of him that he called his shadow spurred him onward. Its exultation over his freedom was undimmed by remorse. Froan recalled that his father had told him to follow his instincts, and he assumed that by obeying his shadow he was heeding that counsel. Nevertheless, regret slowed his steps. He knew that his mother wouldn't have wanted him to leave. *So?* said a voice within him. *She was a murderer and a whore. I don't know that! Do you doubt your father's word? Your mam lied to you. Her last words were "I hid the truth."* Perhaps she had a good reason. *Ridiculous! She loved me. She only used you like she used your father. Grief is weakness. You must be strong. There's no turning back. She's dead.* At least, there was no arguing the last point, regardless of how he felt about it.

Froan proceeded cautiously when he reached Tararc Hite, for Telk's father often returned from checking his traps at evening. Froan didn't want to encounter anyone. He was in no state for it. Moreover, he wanted to vanish without a trace. No one ever visited Far Hite, so his mother's body would go undiscovered. To the fensfolk, both his and her disappearance would be a common mystery.

Hiding among the reeds, Froan saw Roarc heading homeward with the day's catch. He waited until Roarc had passed before proceeding to where Telk kept his boat, which was on a different channel than the one his father used. When Froan reached the craft, he found the sword that he had given Telk hidden beneath some fish traps. He pulled off its wrapping and frowned. The blade bore some signs of sharpening, but it remained rusty. He found Telk's lack of diligence disappointing.

The neglected sword seemed an indication of the challenge Froan would face tomorrow morning. Telk was content with his lot in life, and without Froan's intervention, he would assuredly marry some fensman's daughter and settle down to breed children and trap fish. Whatever small yearning for adventure Telk possessed was the result of Froan's prodding. *And tomorrow morn, I must make him leave this place forever.* Froan realized that it wouldn't be a simple task, but one that he must accomplish. He needed Telk's boat and navigation skills in order to flee.

Despite Telk's attachment to his home, Froan felt confident that he could get him to forsake it. That confidence was based on the sense of power that the spirit's visit had awakened. Though Froan had fought his dark impulses throughout his life, he was beginning to see them as a source of strength, something that set him apart from his complacent friend and his meddlesome mother. It seemed to him that a mighty lord must see other folk as either pawns to be used or obstacles to be eliminated. Hadn't Froan's father told him that he was destined for greatness and possessed an innate power over others? Such power was a gift that shouldn't be forsaken through restraint.

As Froan contemplated the advantages that his shadowed side bestowed, he saw how violence had aided his transformation. His mother's death had stiffened his resolve. It was tragic but also fortunate in a way. He felt guilty over having that thought. Then he reconsidered what had happened and envisioned his mother's death as her fault. *She made me drop the dagger and then lunged as I was picking it up. What happened wasn't my doing. She killed herself.* The notion eased Froan's conscience. *I shouldn't feel guilty that some good arose by accident.*

Froan embraced that idea, for instinct warned that remorse would only impede him. It seemed a burden without benefit, one that should be discarded. Yet, sitting alone in the gathering dark, he found that hard to do. As a test of will, Froan attempted to force all memories of his mother from his thoughts. That proved impossible. Then he recalled his father's exhortation to be ruthless. He resolved that he would become exactly that. If he couldn't forget his mother, at least he could fight her weakening influence. He would harden himself. He would succeed where his father had failed. That resolution brought a small measure of calm, enough so that he was able to rest in preparation for the upcoming day.

Froan woke at first light, ate a bit of cheese, then took up a stone and began to work on the blade of Telk's sword. He had eliminated much of the rust by the time his friend arrived, though his efforts to give the sword a sharp edge were less successful. He smiled at Telk's surprise upon seeing him seated in the beached reed boat. Holding up the blade, Froan said, "You told me that you'd make it sparkle like the sun."

"I had chores. But I—"

"Did you gather your things, at least?"

"Mostly."

"Bring the bundle here. I want to see it."

"Why?"

"Because you promised you would," said Froan.

Telk responded as if the lie were true. "I'm sorry, Froan. I'll get it."

"Good," said Froan. "Be quick, but don't arouse suspicion." Then he turned his attention back to the sword.

It was a while before Telk returned. Like Froan, he had used his cloak to wrap his possessions. It was a small bundle, for everyone in the fens lived on the edge of want. Froan smiled when he saw it. "I knew I could count on you, Telk. And you can count on me. When the Mother came to me last night, she made me promise not to leave you behind."

Telk's eyes widened. "Ya had another vision?"

"Yes. After Mam went to sleep."

"But what's that part 'bout not leaving me behind?"

"The Mother said that we must go together. Go today."

"Today? Where?"

Froan could see uneasiness on Telk's face, and it annoyed him. Nevertheless, he smiled and replied in an easy tone, "To the river, of course, where awaits our good fortune."

"The river? Ya mean leave tha fens?"

"That was always our plan. You knew this day would come."

"I did?"

"We can't rot here forever," replied Froan, giving a harder edge to his voice.

"But I have chores, Froan. I just can't—"

Froan's annoyance flared into full-blown rage. "Telk!" he shouted, glaring at his friend and trapping his eyes. When he spoke, he held nothing back, so that fury made his words both hot and menacing. "You'll *not* desert me!"

Telk reacted as if he had been struck and the blow had shattered him. His face went slack, and his entire frame seemed to lose its vitality. The change was so abrupt and dramatic that even Froan was shocked by it. When Telk replied, his tone was meek and tinged with fear. "I'd never go against ya."

"Good. I knew you wouldn't." Froan smiled. Telk smiled back, but in a subservient and empty way. Froan rose and stepped from the boat to lighten it. "Now get your things aboard and launch the boat."

Telk obeyed without a word. When the reed craft was in the water, Froan stepped back into it. "Pole us to the Turgen."

Telk guided the boat through the channels in the direction of Twin Hite and the Turgen beyond it. He maintained a steady pace, halting only briefly to toss all his fish traps overboard. Froan took that as a good sign—proof that Telk was firmly under his power.

Telk faltered only once, and that was after they had passed Twin Hite. As they approached the river, the channels between the stands of reeds grew wider and their bottoms became deeper. Finally, the channel in which they were traveling seemed to disappear. The reeds no longer formed enclosing walls. Instead, there were only a few clumps of them set in open water that reached toward the horizon. Telk's pole could no longer touch bottom. With nothing to push against, Telk couldn't guide the craft, and it drifted aimlessly. Froan could see that his friend was unnerved. "Froan," Telk said in a frightened voice, "are ya sure 'bout this?"

"Give me the pole," said Froan.

As Telk handed him the pole, Froan felt some of his friend's uneasiness, for he had never gazed upon such emptiness. The Turgen was a broad river, and when Froan looked away from the fens, all he saw was dull water, a faint gray line that marked the distant shore, and the vast dome of an overcast sky. He felt smaller and more exposed than ever before in his life. Yet when the boat drifted toward one of the last clumps of reeds, Froan pressed the pole against that final bit of the fens and used all his strength to push the boat toward the river. When the pole became stuck in the muck, Froan released it rather than lose momentum.

The reed craft glided farther from the shore, and the current seized it. The boat spun slowly as the river claimed it, pulling it ever farther into its broad expanse. Like most fensfolk, neither Froan nor Telk could swim. They were entirely at the Turgen's mercy as it swept them toward strange places and an unknown future.

TWELVE

YIM WAS floating in a black void. *Where am I?* she wondered. The question seemed unanswerable. She didn't even know who she was. If she had a past, she couldn't recall it. Yim continued to float, and it would have been soothing except that her throat hurt. She tried to ignore the sensation, but it persisted. It was more than painful; it was puzzling and frightening. Furthermore, it was growing more intense.

The darkness dissipated, and Yim saw that she was lying on hard-packed dirt. It was stained with blood. The front of her neck felt on fire. She recognized her simple home and knew who she was. *I'm Yim. My son has cut my throat.*

With effort, Yim sat up. Then she tried to swallow, fearing that she might be incapable of the feat. When she managed, she gingerly touched her throat. Yim's fingers brushed a loose flap of flesh. The feel of it was ghastly, and she envisioned a gaping wound. Even the lightest pressure on it made her wince, and wincing caused further pain. Nevertheless, she traced the gash's blood-incrusted length. It went from one side of her neck to the other. In places, blood still dribbled from it.

Turning her body so as not to twist her neck, Yim looked around. It was late afternoon. Most of Froan's things were missing. What remained was spilled haphazardly on his bed. Yim saw a single boot, a wooden spoon, and a few other sundry items. They seemed evidence of a hasty departure. *He's gone*, she thought.

Yim was gripped by despair, but she fought it by clinging to life. Although she still lived, she also realized that her wound might prove fatal. She had lain on dirt through a night and part of a day, perhaps longer, which meant her injury was likely to fester. She had herbs that could be boiled to make a brew that prevented festering, but she couldn't stitch the wound closed. The healwife possessed the skill, but they weren't on good terms.

Cleanse the wound, thought Yim, *then worry about the stitching*. She rose unsteadily to pull the necessary herbs from where they hung from pegs. Crumbling their dried leaves into a small pot, she added water, and set the pot on the cold hearth. There was kindling and wood to make a fire, but when Yim couldn't find the flint and iron to light one, she assumed Froan had taken them.

There was a second flint and iron in the cave where she smoked meat. *I'll have to fetch them to make the brew.* Yet the little she had done already had left her dizzy and exhausted. Walking to the smoke cave and back seemed beyond her strength. *I'll rest a bit before I try.* Yim lay upon her bed and stared at the ceiling. A patch of darkness formed there. When it spread, she was too weak to flee. Yim watched helplessly as shadow consumed the world and her.

Meanwhile, Froan and Telk drifted on the wide Turgen. After nightfall, a mist settled on the water, making it seem that they were drifting in a chilly void. Froan silently huddled

beneath his goatskin cloak, unwilling to give voice to his uneasiness. Throughout the day, he had seen boats upon the
river, but none had approached them despite his waving.
Froan was beginning to wonder if they would drift unnoticed for days. That worried him, for the reed boat already
seemed to be riding lower in the water.

Telk was equally quiet. If he had misgivings, he betrayed
no signs of them. Froan was unsurprised by his companion's silence, but it made him consider the nature of Telk's
loyalty. It seemed more obedience than friendship. It occurred to Froan that a friend would have questioned his plan
to set out on the river in a boat lacking means for steering
and propulsion. It was apparent that by bending Telk to his
will Froan had changed him. In fact, Telk seemed broken,
even slightly mad. The body was intact, but the spirit within
had been diminished.

That's the price of leadership, Froan told himself. *To
lead is to be alone.* Gazing upon Telk's vacant face and the
wet void surrounding them both, the truth of that statement was painfully clear.

Elsewhere, Daven fought to keep from nodding off
while he watched Honus sleep. The elderly man was weary,
but concern that his charge would attempt to visit the Dark
Path made him loath to rest. *Nothing I've said has weakened his urge to trance.* The former Bearer shook his head
sadly, wondering at the depth of sorrow that could cause a
man to seek his happiness in the realm of the dead. *He's
been doing it for so many winters, the habit may be impossible to break.* Daven was convinced that it would prove fatal if continued. Already, he marveled that Honus was alive.
It seemed a testament to his former strength that he had
lasted so long.

Gazing at the neglected body on the mat, "strength"
was not a word that readily came to Daven's mind. Honus

had wasted to the point where he wavered on the edge of existence. His flesh hung loosely from his bones. He moved slowly and with effort. He seemed alive more by chance than any intention on his part. Daven knew that Honus would need more than nourishment and care to survive in his weakened state. He would require hope if he was to break free of the Dark Path's allure. To obtain it, Honus must become convinced that it was possible to find happiness in the living world. Daven had believed his revelations would achieve that. Yet the Sarf's despair had proved too formidable. *I've told him that Yim needs him. What else can I do?* Daven couldn't think of anything and hoped that Karm would provide the answer.

It still felt strange to Daven to look to the goddess for answers. When he had fled from his duties as a Bearer, he believed that he had forsaken Karm. It seemed only natural that the goddess had done the same to him. Yet reading Honus's runes had convinced him otherwise. Not only had Karm given him a chance to redeem himself, she had conferred a rare gift as well.

Long ago, when Daven had lived in the temple, he had heard tales of a Seer with an unusual power. She had no visions and was unable to prophesy, but she could sense impending turmoil as some folk could feel the approach of storms. It was as if she detected subtle strains in the world's fabric before events manifested them. She had warned of trouble from the west long before Lord Bahl's armies had poured forth. Daven had received the same ability upon Honus's arrival.

Sitting in the dark room, he sensed the world's pulse and felt the first tremors of looming conflict. Daven likened the impression to that of a frozen river at winter's end. Beneath seeming stillness was mounting pressure. Cracks were forming. Soon, what had been calm would slip into chaos. It had already begun. *Evil's abroad again*, he thought. *It seeks to restore its former power.* If it succeeded, Daven feared the end of all that was good and fair.

Daven also sensed his part in the scheme of things. He must strive to heal Honus as best he could, then send him forth into the fray. He could do nothing more, and he must do nothing less. Daven was far from certain that his efforts would avert the approaching doom. In fact, he had his doubts. The foe was long-lived and patient. Moreover, it learned from every past mistake. When Daven tried to sense what force opposed such a formidable enemy, he detected only frailty. Moreover, it seemed to be teetering on the brink of oblivion.

Within the Iron Palace's highest tower, the shadowy divining chamber duplicated the darkness of the night outside, a redundancy that made it ideal for sorcery. There, the Most Holy Gorm sat within the safety of a circle of blood and tossed his magic bones upon the stone floor. By the dim light of a single oil lamp, he watched as unseen forces arranged the rune-covered vertebrae and ribs in telling ways. After they stopped moving, he studied them and smiled. "Bahl's death has accomplished its purpose," he said to the empty room. "His spirit found his son. The game is now in motion."

Gorm scrutinized the runes that the bones exposed and spied a word spelled out in an ancient tongue. It meant "frost." He also found the symbols for "north" and "water." Other signs led him to conclude that all those things concerned the heir. Gorm was puzzled by the word "frost," though he was confident its significance would be revealed in time. "North" and "water" doubtlessly concerned the heir's whereabouts. As such, they were the first clues to the lad's location that Gorm had received. *The force that has been concealing him is weakening*, he concluded. It was a promising development.

Wanting to learn more about his opponent, Gorm looked for the vertebra that represented the enemy. At first, it seemed to be missing. Then the priest saw where it had bounced. It had landed far from the other bones, exactly on the edge of a shadow. Gorm blinked, uncertain that he was seeing correctly, for the vertebra was precariously balanced on the narrow, flat tip that projected from its rear. It was a highly improbable position, as unlikely as a flipped coin landing on its edge and remaining there. Obviously, the bone would tip over and fall either into light or shadow. Gorm waited to see which, convinced that the outcome would be a meaningful portent. However, the bone remained balanced until he grew impatient and blew in its direction. A single puff of air was all that was necessary to send it tumbling into darkness.

THIRTEEN

AT DAYBREAK, Yim didn't so much awake as drift into consciousness. She was feverish, and the pain in her throat had spread. Her entire neck felt on fire, as did her jaw and upper chest. Yim was also slightly delirious, but she had enough clarity of mind to know that the spreading pain was a bad sign.

I'll die if I stay here, Yim thought. The idea of seeking help was daunting, but fear spurred her to rise from her bed. It was a struggle to get to her feet and remain standing. Nevertheless, certain that her condition would only worsen, Yim realized that she should leave immediately. She paused only to grab her healer's kit, so that with her guidance,

Rappali might prepare curative brews and stitch up her wound.

As soon as Yim staggered outside, bleating does surrounded her. All were frantic to be milked. Pained by their swollen udders, they jostled and butted their mistress. Yim understood their distress, but she was in no condition to relieve it. She pushed onward, hampered by the herd until one doe butted her hard enough to send her sprawling. Yim's hard landing tore the crusts on her wound and fresh blood flowed from it. Pain and frustration drove Yim to weep. "I can't!" she cried between sobs. "I can't help you! I'm not sure I can help myself."

Yim rose shakily to her feet, keeping a wary eye on the doe that had butted her. Fortunately, the other does pressed around her, and their massed bodies prevented another assault. They also hampered Yim's progress. Only when she reached the bog did the herd hang back, wary of stepping on unfirm ground.

There was but a single way to and from Far Hite, and it was so convoluted and treacherous that only Yim and Froan used it. Since the route altered with shifts in the floating vegetation, Yim found the firmest footing largely by feel, her bare feet detecting subtle changes better than her eyes. This was especially true on a stretch where the winding route was submerged by black, stagnant water.

Yim's pain and fever dulled her senses just when they were needed most, and she was well aware of the risk she was taking by entering the bog. Convinced that she had no other choice, Yim moved onward, blinking her eyes to clear her vision. It was daylight, but everything seemed blurry and dark. Blinking didn't change that. Nonetheless, she continued to advance, hoping that memory and feel would get her through.

For a while, they did. But when Yim reached the submerged part of the route, she got into trouble. In her fevered state, she couldn't follow the ridge beneath the fetid water and quickly found herself waist-deep in the bog. Yim halted. Standing on one foot, she groped with the other to feel the incline. Her toes proved too numb for the task.

Yim planted both feet in the muck and stood still. If she slipped, stagnant water would contaminate her open wound. Such mishaps could make even a small cut fatal; as a healer, Yim had seen it happen. Yet standing didn't help matters. She was dizzy and disoriented. Furthermore, her feet were sinking ever deeper into the muck. Inaction wouldn't save her, so Yim stepped in the direction that she hoped would take her to shallower water. Weak from fever and impeded by the muck that gripped her feet, Yim pitched face-first into the murky water. Immersion in the foul liquid shocked her into frantic action. Clawing with both hands and feet, she found the submerged slope and scrambled up it to emerge gasping for air.

Yim felt doomed. Not only was she drenched with bog water and its thick decay, she had lost her healer's kit. Regardless, she struggled onward toward Tararc Hite. She had passed through the most treacherous stretch of the journey, and while the way ahead was long, it was also easier. When Yim reached the solid ground of the neighboring hite, she was totally spent. She staggered up the path, barely aware of her surroundings. When Yim encountered Rappali, she didn't recognize her.

Rappali dropped the basket of fish she was carrying when she saw the bloody and bedraggled figure on the path. For a terrified instant, she thought it was a boghaunt, for it looked and moved like a dead thing. Then Rappali's terror changed to horror and concern as she recognized her friend. "Yim! By tha Mother, what's happened ta ya?"

Yim answered with a single moan, then all her limbs went slack. Rappali was barely able to catch her as she fell. That's when she saw the ugly gash in Yim's neck. It was a gruesome sight, and Rappali's breakfast rose in her throat. That didn't keep her from holding on to her friend. Gripping Yim's torso with her left hand, Rappali slipped her right under Yim's knee to heft her up and cradle her. Then she staggered up the path with her unconscious burden.

When Rappali reached home, she placed Yim on the table. Roarc stirred from his morning rest and stared. "What did ya bring here, woman?"

"Yim. Someone's cut her throat."

"Is she dead?"

"Nay, not yet. Go fetch tha healwife."

Roarc yawned. "Have Telk do it. I need my rest."

"Telk hasn't been home since yestermorn."

Roarc grinned. "Probably seeing some lass. High time, too."

"So ya'll have ta go."

Roarc peered at Yim. "Pah! There's no point ta it. She's good as dead."

Rappali fixed her husband with a sharp look. "Mayhap so, but if ya want me ta share yar bed, ya'll go and go now! And don't tell tha healwife who ya're fetching her ta mend."

"I'll go," said Roarc, "but for yar sake, not hers."

After her husband left, Rappali used a damp rag to clean Yim as best she could. She wept while she did so, for her friend was a terrible sight. The entire front of her tunic was stained with blood that no amount of rubbing could remove, and her limbs were covered in muck, bog rot, and bloodstains. Cleaning around the gash distressed Rappali most, and it caused her to worry that whoever attacked Yim might have also attacked Telk. *Mayhap he's not with a lass at all but lying slain in tha bog!* The thought made Rappali frantic, and she began to gently shake Yim in hope that she could tell her something about the attack. Yim only moaned softly, as someone in a deep sleep. Seeing that shaking her friend was pointless, Rappali let her lie undisturbed.

* * *

Roarc didn't return with the healwife until late afternoon, and Yim had remained unconscious the entire time. The healwife was an elderly but vigorous woman with sharp features and dark, clever eyes. She glared at Roarc when she saw Yim lying on the table. "Ya said I was ta mend yar son, not this outsider!"

"Rappali told me ta say that."

The healer fixed her eyes on Rappali. "Did ya think I would not come if I knew tha truth?"

"It crossed my mind. But I only told my husband not ta say who ya'd be mending."

The healwife walked over to Yim and felt her brow. When she prodded the wound with her fingers, Rappali looked away, but she heard Yim moan. Then the healwife spoke. "I'll not mend anyone taday. She's beyond hope."

"At least sew up tha wound."

"Why? Ya'll only have a more comely corpse."

"Sew her up anyway."

"Is it worth a basket of dried fish? That's my fee."

"Ya'll have it," said Rappali. "Is there nothing more ta be done for her?"

"See tha flesh 'bout tha wound?" said the healwife. "'Tis fiery red, and like fire 'twill spread ta consume her spirit."

"Mayhap ya're letting her die from spite, though Yim was never yar rival."

"She tended births, births I should've tended."

"Only when begged ta do so, and then she never took a fee."

"Which was all tha worse for me!"

"So folk will be right when they say ya killed her," said Rappali.

"Nay, 'twasn't I who cut her throat."

"Aye, 'tis a grievous wound, and if ya cured it, folk would say 'twas truly a miracle. Pity tha deed's beyond ya."

The healwife thought a moment before she spoke. "I do

know of a draught that will either cure or kill her. 'Tis poison—poison that fights a wound's poison. If I give it ta her and she dies, will ya say I slew her?"

"Nay. I swear by tha Mother."

"Then set two pots of water ta boil," said the healwife, "and I'll do what I can."

Roarc, who had silently watched the exchange, approached the healwife. "My wife said we'll pay for tha sewing, and so we shall. But 'twouldn't it be fairer if Yim paid for tha draught?"

The healwife gave the fish trapper a cold look. "And what if she dies?"

"Then she'll have paid ya with her life," replied Roarc with a grin. "A steep fee by my reckoning."

The old woman didn't reply, but searched her healer's pouch for what she needed. She withdrew some herbs, three small dried mushrooms the color of dried blood, and a sewing kit containing a length of gut and a curved needle. Then she waited for the water to boil. When it did, she placed the herbs in one pot and the mushrooms in the other and then let them steep. Afterward, she cleansed Yim's wound with the herbal solution and neatly sewed it close. Yim lay perfectly silent and still throughout the entire process, an ill omen according to the healwife.

After Yim's wound was stitched, the healwife took the leg bone of a small animal from her pouch. It had been cut in half and the marrow removed to form a small, hollow tube that was closed at one end. Then she filled the bone with the mushroom brew. "Give her one bone full at sunrise and noon, and then two bones full at sunset," said the healwife. "I'll show ya how." She lifted Yim into a sitting position and eased her head back so that her mouth gaped open. Then she emptied the bone's contents directly down Yim's throat. "Ya can feed her clear broth tha same way."

"And how long should I give her tha draught?" asked Rappali.

"Till she wakes or dies," said the healwife. "Most like, 'twill take a while either way. She might last like this for days."

Rappali saw her husband roll his eyes at that news. "Yim's a strong one," she said. "She crossed tha fens by herself and gave birth alone. If anyone could live, 'twould be her. Thank ya for yar help. Only praise of ya will come from my lips, however this turns out."

Roarc gave the healwife her fee, then took her home. Rappali kept a vigil over her friend. The fiery red that marked much of Yim's throat remained, but it ceased spreading. Rappali was pleased by this until she noticed that Yim's color was fading also. Her lips turned almost white, and her skin took on a bluish pallor. Rappali would have thought that Yim had died except for the slight rise and fall of her chest. For a long while, Rappali simply watched Yim breathe. When she became convinced that her friend wasn't about to expire, she set about making fish broth for her.

It was dusk when Roarc returned home to find his wife still tending Yim, who lay in a corner upon a makeshift bed of cut reeds. "Too dark ta check tha traps," he grumbled. "A whole day gone ta waste." He walked over to look at Yim. "She looks dead."

"She's not."

"Well, not yet. Is Telk home?"

"Nay," said Rappali. "Roarc, do ya think—think that whoever did this ta Yim also hurt our boy?"

"Nay, he's with some lass," replied Roarc without conviction.

" 'Twould be tha first time."

"Then mayhap he's with Froan, larking about."

Though Rappali assumed that Roarc meant to comfort her, his words had the opposite effect. She had been wondering why Froan hadn't shown up, for she was certain that he would have missed his mother by then. *Yim never leaves him for long*, Rappali thought. *She's so devoted ta him. Too devoted, mayhap.* Rappali worried that Froan's absence was an ominous sign. She feared that her husband might be right; Telk could very well be with Froan. If he was, she doubted their activities would be described as "larking." She eyed the stitched-up gash across Yim's throat, increasingly convinced that it was connected with Telk's disappearance.

FOURTEEN

FROAN AND Telk's second day upon the river had been much like their first, and the third day followed the pattern of the previous two. The tiny craft remained a captive of the current, which pulled it ever farther from the shore. They were ignored by the other boats they spotted. The river was so broad that the boats often appeared as mere specks on the water. The only noticeable changes occurred in the surrounding landscape. The fens still covered the southern shore, but no hites could be seen in the seemingly endless expanse of reeds.

To the north, islands began to appear. They reminded Froan of hites in the way they jutted from the water. As the day progressed, they became more numerous. Most were small and rocky, but some were larger. Those were often wooded. Froan sometimes spotted dwellings on their shores. Occasionally, the boat drifted quite close to an island; but being unable to steer, they could only gaze at it as they glided by.

They still had an ample supply of cheese and smoked

goat, but Froan's concern over the boat riding low in the water had been valid. Continuous submersion in a fast-moving current was waterlogging the reeds, and the craft was becoming less buoyant. Froan feared that in a day or two they would be wallowing in the river. Telk seemed oblivious of the threat as he stared listlessly at the passing scenery and boats.

Toward the end of the third day, a low, sleek boat passed them. It had a mast, but its sail was furled and oars moved the craft against the current. Froan waved to it, as he had waved to all the other boats. At first, there was no response. Then the boat slowed and a man climbed over its side into a rowboat in tow. He untied it and rowed toward Froan and Telk.

As the stranger approached, Froan became wary. He slid the dagger tucked in his waistband toward his rear so his goatskin cloak hid it. Then he whispered to Telk, telling him to have his sword ready. Showing some animation at last, Telk grabbed his sword and laid it across his lap, hilt in hand. Then the pair anxiously waited as the man approached. He was short but burly, with a dark, tangled beard and a deeply tanned, sun-creased face. He rowed until his boat was three paces away, then pulled in his oars to drift close by. Gazing at Telk's sword he grinned. "Ye lads pirates?"

"Nay," replied Telk.

"Ah thought not. More like fensmen, by the look o' ye. Why are ye out here?"

"To make our way in the world," said Froan.

The man's grin broadened. "In a sinkin' boat with nary a paddle? Ye're none too smart, but mayhap yer clever enough to pull an oar."

"We can do that," said Froan.

"Then swim on over, and Ah'll take ye aboard."

"We can't swim," said Telk.

"Well, 'tis a pity," said the man. "But Ah'll pull alongside, so ye can board." He gazed at Telk as if sizing him up. "Ye go first, but afore ye do, hand me that sword. Those vittles, too."

Telk turned to Froan, silently asking his permission. As Froan nodded, the man maneuvered his craft until its side nestled against the reed boat. As Telk handed over his sword, Froan nimbly hopped into the other craft. The man appeared annoyed, but he attempted to hide it. "Whoa, young hare!" he said as his boat rocked from Froan's quick boarding. "Ye'll capsize us. Then yer way in the world will be straight to the river bottom. What's the big fella's name?"

"Telk."

"Now Telk, no hoppin'. Hand me the vittles, then step over easy."

Froan caught the man's eyes with his gaze. "After you take the food," he said, "don't leave him behind."

The stranger looked startled. Then he forced a smile as Froan continued to stare at him. "Why would ye say that?"

"Because you intended to leave me behind."

An uneasy silence followed. After Telk boarded the boat, Froan released the man from his gaze. The stranger looked away and said in a husky voice, "Ah don't know what ye're talkin' 'bout." Afterward, he picked up the oars and began to row.

As they neared the waiting boat, Froan steeled himself for what would happen next. One glimpse into his "rescuer's" eyes left him no doubt that his life was in danger and a single misstep would prove fatal. Yet instead of fear, he felt rage. His hatred for the man who had intended to take his food and abandon him was visceral. He was tempted to kill him on the spot, but he knew that would be foolish. Thus he put on a bland face to hide his feelings.

Froan studied the crew in the ship ahead. They varied in age, but all possessed a hardened look. He also noted that each man was armed. While Froan watched the crew, they

also gazed at him and Telk with the cold manner of preda-
tors. *They didn't pluck us from the river out of kindness*, he
thought. *Most like, we seem small but easy pickings.*

Sitting in the small boat, wearing only a breechclout and
a short goatskin cloak, Froan knew he appeared vulnerable.
Moreover, he imagined that the waiting crew saw him as a
boy, not a man. Yet while part of him had lived only seventeen winters, another part was far more ancient. A veteran
of a thousand battles, that part wasn't inhibited by fear or
the slightest shred of humanity. Its instincts were those that
Froan's father had counseled him to follow. As Froan drew
ever nearer to the waiting men, he understood that he
must heed those instincts to survive. Nothing from his life in
the fens and certainly none of his mother's lessons readied
him for the upcoming confrontation. Yet Froan was prepared, far more prepared than the waiting men could possibly imagine.

The rowboat reached its destination. Two lines were
thrown out, and the small craft was secured alongside the
larger one. Hands were extended, so Froan, Telk, and the
man who had brought them could be pulled onto the main
vessel. Froan gazed about it once he was aboard. Built for
speed, the slender boat was entirely open. There were six
pairs of benches, each bench long enough to accommodate
two oarsmen. A narrow aisle ran between the benches,
widening at the bow and stern. There was a single mast amidships, designed to carry a square sail. Five distressed-looking
sheep lay on their sides near the bow, their legs bound together. Beside them was a small pile of assorted goods that
appeared tossed there haphazardly. At the stern was a raised
platform, and two men stood upon it. One held the ship's
tiller. The other seemed to be the captain.

The latter man was tall, heavyset, and muscular. Like most
of his crew, he sported a full beard. It was red, and the man's
freckled skin had a sunburnt, pinkish cast. He was the only
man who wore a helmet, a simple steel hemisphere. Other-

wise, he was dressed much like the crew, except more richly. He wore heavy boots, baggy woolen breeches, a cloth shirt, and a leather vest with metal plates sewn on it. A sword, a hand ax, and a large dagger hung from a wide belt. The clothes looked both outlandish and lavish to Froan, who felt naked in comparison. Nevertheless, he met the man's gaze with almost arrogant confidence, then advanced toward him without his bidding.

As Froan walked toward the stern, he met each crewman's eyes to show he wasn't afraid. All of them were standing and watching expectantly, having pulled in their oars. The boat drifted silently with the current, guided by the man at the tiller. The quiet step of Froan's bare feet upon the planks was the only sound. He halted by the last set of rowing benches and stood close to the largest crewman, a massive man who was a full head taller than he.

The red-bearded man on the platform called to the crewman who had rowed out to the reed boat. "Catfish, wha'd ye haul in?"

"An oarsman, Bloodbeard. As ye ordered."

"*An* oarsman? By Karm's stinkin' feet, Ah'm seein' double." Bloodbeard peered down at Froan. "Or mayhap 'tis the big one's shadow."

"He hopped aboard," said Catfish, "afore Ah could stop him."

"Well, lad," said Bloodbeard, "Ah've no place fer ye. Since ye took it on yerself to hop where ye're not needed, ye can hop away as well. And if ye're shy o' river water, my crew will give ye a push."

"Before you say I'm not needed," said Froan, "best count your men." With those words, he whipped out his dagger and plunged it deep into the belly of the giant beside him. Then he tugged the blade across the man's abdomen, slicing it open. Just as quickly, Froan leapt toward the stern, narrowly avoiding the entrails that splattered onto the deck. The tall oarsman stood motionless for a moment, frozen by surprise and agony. Then he fell like a tree and lay moaning and writhing feebly upon the deck until Froan bent down and cut his throat.

As the man expired, Froan raised the bloody dagger to his face. Peering over its edge, he gazed at the crew as he ran his tongue along the blade's length. Froan had felt a surge of excitement when the man died, and that sensation was enhanced by the taste of his victim's blood. His eyes communicated that he was ready to kill again—indeed, eager to do so. The crew had been stunned by the suddenness and savagery of Froan's attack, and his aggressive stance further withered their courage. Together, they could have easily overwhelmed him, but Froan understood that fear would protect him. Thus he gazed at each man to make him feel singled out to die if the crew attacked. The tactic worked, and a standoff ensued.

It was Bloodbeard who broke the tension with a laugh. "Well, ye've proved a dark shadow indeed, and Ah've need o' black-hearted men on my crew. So Ah'll name ye Shadow, and invite ye to join us."

"And my friend, also?" said Froan. "We're a pair."

"Aye, Ah'll have him," said Bloodbeard. He regarded Telk. "I name ye Bog Rat. Take a place on a bench." As Telk meekly sat down in a vacant spot, Bloodbeard called out, "All right, men. After Shadow takes his plunder, dump Sturgeon overboard. Then put yer backs to the oars. There's enough light yet to find another prize."

Froan assumed that he had a right to the dead man's possessions and the captain expected him to exercise it. Yet as he walked over to the gruesome corpse, Froan was suddenly appalled by what he had done. His compassionate side—the one fostered by his mother—felt pity for the man he had slain. Then his emotions fought within him as he felt both triumphant and filled with remorse. The agony frozen on his victim's face nearly made him weep. Froan struggled to suppress the impulse and succeeded, for he was keenly aware that it would undo him. *Any show of weakness will send me to the river bottom*, he thought, feeling the crew's eyes upon him.

Froan forced himself to prod the dead man with his foot and roll him over. The pickings proved meager, since the man's clothes were far too large and also blood soaked. Froan searched Sturgeon's pockets, which were empty; pulled a silver ring from the man's hand; and removed his belt from which hug a scabbard and sword. Drawing the blade, he saw that it was neither well forged nor properly sharpened. Still, it was his first sword.

After Froan took his "plunder," the crew unceremoniously tossed his victim overboard and threw water on the deck to wash away the blood. When they slid out the oars to begin rowing, Froan took the dead man's spot. A stocky, brown-haired man of some twenty-odd winters was already sitting on the bench. They had pulled only a few strokes when the man said in a low voice, "That Sturgeon was an overbearin' bastard. 'Twas a pleasure to feed him to the river."

"I'm glad he won't be missed," replied Froan.

"Not that Sturgeon had no friends, so keep a wary eye. And Bloodbeard fancied him well enough, but he's the practical sort. Dead men don't row." Froan's rowing partner grinned. "Bloodbeard named me Toad on account of my wart," he said, pointing to his nose. "Ye're lucky he named ye Shadow."

"My true name's Froan."

"Don't that mean 'frost' in the old tongue? Seems fittin'. Way ye gutted Sturgeon was cold fer sure." Toad cast Froan a puzzled look. "And ye have a chill 'bout ye, like ye've been swimmin' in the river."

"I was born that way. It's how I got my name."

"Not that it matters anymore. Ye're Shadow, not Froan,

now." After a few more strokes, Toad spoke again. "That was some sharp work ye did. Real smooth. Where'd ye learn to use a blade like that?"

"It's a gift."

"One ye'll find handy, no doubt. Not that Bloodbeard goes in fer fightin' much, nevermind his talk. He favors easy pickin's."

Froan followed his instincts when he replied. "Some would say easy pickings are slim ones."

"And Ah might be one o' them," said Toad in a low voice. He glanced at Froan appraisingly. "Ye're dressed like a fensman, but ye don't talk or act like one. Most can't fight and are only good fer pullin' oars."

"I was raised in the fens, but my mam came from other parts."

"Where?"

"I don't know," said Froan. It was true, and he felt a twinge of regret when he realized that he'd never find out.

With Toad as his instructor, Froan quickly mastered rowing. It was simple work, but punishing to someone unaccustomed to it. Despite cutting strips of goatskin from his cloak to cushion his hands, they soon felt raw, and it wasn't long before Froan's back and arms ached as though he'd been pummeled. Bloodbeard set the oarsmen's pace by hitting a small wooden hoop with hide stretched over it, and his beat was a quick one. Propelled by rapid strokes, the boat darted swiftly about the river like a water strider searching a brook for prey.

Although they approached a few vessels, the captain chose not to pursue any of them. One appeared too large and had armed and armored men pacing its deck. Another was laden with lumber. The final boat was a tiny one manned by a fisherman who looked relieved when they passed him by. "If we'd happened on him earlier," said Toad, "he might be sittin' in yer spot now."

Froan was glad that the fisherman wasn't. Despite his sore muscles, he felt extremely fortunate. By a stroke of luck, he had fallen in with pirates, and anyone who aspires to lordship needs armed men. His situation seemed ripe with potential, although it was far too early to formulate any plans. For the time being, Froan intended to learn all he could and heed those dark instincts that had served him so well.

FIFTEEN

WHEN DUSK arrived, Bloodbeard gave up the hunt. He headed his vessel downstream and set a less strenuous pace for the oarsmen. The change came as a welcome relief to Froan, whose hands had blistered. Aided by the current, the boat moved swiftly down the darkening river. Nevertheless, it was midnight before the craft veered toward a small, wooded island. Froan strained to see it by starlight, but he could make out few features other than a pair of hills that rose from the isle's interior. Although the island was only a dark shape to Froan, it was apparent by the way the tillerman guided the boat that he was familiar with its shoreline.

Soon the boat swung into a cove. "Oars in!" shouted Bloodbeard. The boat glided toward a narrow beach. When its keel scraped gravel, the crew climbed over the sides without being told. Froan followed their example and jumped into waist-deep water. "Beach her!" bellowed the captain. Grabbing the boat's sides, the men pulled it onto dry ground. Then they unloaded the sheep and other loot from the bow. The beasts struggled in their grasp and made panicked cries. Although he was unfamiliar with sheep, Froan rushed over to help a pair of men who were trying to carry a ewe. The frantic animal was managing to kick despite its bound legs.

"If we cut its throat," said Froan, "we'll have an easier time carrying it."

"Aye, but Bloodbeard wants the mutton kept fresh," said the other, "so that's the end o' it."

Froan grabbed the sheep's flaying hooves. "Then I'll give you a hand."

The men headed away from the cove, and with Froan's help, they managed to carry their struggling burden. The path they followed wound uphill through a grove of trees, over a crest, and down into a depression between the two hills. There, hidden from any eyes on the river, several fires burned. A dozen people moved about them, and Froan was surprised to see that they were women and a few young children.

The firelight also revealed a haphazardly erected campsite. There were three shelters, and as Froan drew closer to them, he could see that they were constructed of sailcloth, scraps of lumber, branches, and small tree trunks. They seemed the work of men who were more adept at stealing than building. There were also crude pens made from branches that held an assortment of livestock. Judging from the trampled state of the clearing and the amount of garbage lying about, Froan surmised that the site had been occupied awhile.

Large kettles hung over two of the fires, and the women began ladling food from them as soon as men appeared on the crest of the ridge. By the time Froan had helped deposit the ewe in a pen and cut her loose, a meal of mutton stew accompanied by boiled roots was laid out on a pair of broad planks that served as a crude table. A wide assortment of vessels contained the food—wooden bowls, metal plates, and differing sorts of crockery—and the women who served the meal were equally varied. One woman wore a formerly elegant gown of pale blue cloth that had been reduced to dirty rags. Another was dressed in tattered peasant garb. The woman beside her wore man's clothes with the shirt torn open so her breasts were revealed. The only things the women seemed to have in common were their youth, signs of ill treatment, and a certain comeliness despite their disheveled and threadbare state.

Froan turned to one of the men who had carried the ewe. "Are those women captives?"

"Nay," replied the man. "Ye can ransom captives." He grinned salaciously. "Them wenches are plunder."

"The children, too?"

"Oh, they're just bastards. The ones we didn't drown."

As Froan walked over to the table, he noted that one of the serving women was pregnant and two of the toddlers running about had red hair. He grabbed a bowl of stew and a plate of roots. Then, since there were no benches or chairs about the table, he looked for a place in the clearing to sit. As Froan settled on a spot of ground out of the traffic, Telk came over to sit beside him.

"Froan," he whispered in an uneasy voice, "we're among pirates!"

"You must call me Shadow for now," Froan whispered back. "And we're not among pirates, we *are* pirates. I told you our sword practice would come in handy." Froan gazed into his friend's eyes and noted a trace of lingering madness. Probing deeper, he saw that while Telk had been rendered incapable of disobedience, abandoning home had gone against his nature. That conflict was the source of Telk's disturbance, and Froan felt that there was little he could do to relieve it. He didn't even try. Instead, he sought to bolster Telk's courage.

"I told Bloodbeard that you and I were a pair," whispered

Froan, "and I meant every word. They'll remember the day Shadow and Bog Rat arrived. Though I killed that man to save our hides, I'll tell you something." Froan fixed his eyes on Telk and let his power flow from them. It felt stronger than before. "It was a thrill to kill him. Spill a man's spirit, and it washes over you. It feels good, like warm sunshine or a hearty meal. Moreover, that bastard deserved to die."

"Mayhap so, but—"

"No buts about it. When it's you or him, it always must be him. And don't wait for your foe to make the first move. Strike hard and never hold back. Never! You're a pirate now. Be a bloody one and thrive!"

Froan watched with satisfaction as his words—and the power behind them—took hold. They enflamed Telk and drove out his fear. A gleam came to his lunatic eyes, and he grasped his sword hilt tightly. "Aye, I'm Bog Rat now. And Shadow, I'll do ya proud."

Froan grinned and slapped Telk's back. "I never doubted it."

Then the two turned to their food with appetites made ravenous by all their rowing. While they ate, the women began pouring ale and serving it. One of them approached Froan and Telk, bearing a pair of brimming wooden bowls. Barefoot and dressed in ragged peasant's clothes, she seemed a girl—perhaps only sixteen. A tangle of long, frizzy brown hair surrounded a pretty face that was marred by bruised, swollen lips. She gazed at Froan curiously before handing him a bowl. "They say ye're tha one what killed Sturgeon," she said in a low voice.

"I am," replied Froan.

The girl smiled, revealing that two of her front teeth had been knocked out. "Bless ye!"

Seeing promise in the girl's reaction, Froan returned the smile. "So my deed pleased you?"

"Aye."

"I know nothing of these men or their ways," said Froan in a low voice. "Perhaps we could talk."

The girl looked about anxiously. "Ah don't know."

Froan caught her eyes with his, then spoke in a low, compelling tone. "I'd be grateful if you did."

The girl fidgeted a moment before speaking. "Ah can't now. Later, when tha servin's over. Walk into tha woods, and Ah'll find ye."

Froan nodded, then sipped his ale as the girl hurried off. Though he had heard of the drink, it was new to him. At first, he thought it tasted like bog water, but he gradually grew used to it. When he drained his bowl, a different woman came by to refill it. Shortly afterward, Bloodbeard sauntered over to him. Both Froan and Telk rose as he approached.

"Shadow! Bog Rat!" called out the captain in a voice somewhat thickened by drink. "The newest o' my crew. We eat good, nay? And drink good, too. Prove handy, and ye'll feast every night and share in the booty."

"And the women?" asked Froan. "Do we get our share of them?"

Bloodbeard grinned. "Well, ye're a randy lad fer sure. Be 'ware that the wench in the blue frock and the one that's fat with child are mine. The rest are fer the takin'. Aye, 'tis a grand life fer the right sort o' fellow. And the wrong sort . . ." The captain cast a look of exaggerated menace. "Well, the river licks his bones."

"You'll find us the right sort," said Froan.

"Ah hope Ah will," replied Bloodbeard. "And 'bout those wenches: Some men are jealous, so pay heed o' who ye tup. Ah don't look kindly on fightin' over whores."

"I appreciate knowing where I stand," said Froan, "and thank you for it. Bog Rat does, too."

"Good," said Bloodbeard. "So that's settled." He sauntered off to have his bowl refilled.

"What an ass!" Froan whispered to Telk before getting more to eat.

As a woman ladled out more stew into Froan's bowl, Toad walked over to him. "Ah see Bloodbeard spoke with ye."

"Yes," replied Froan. "It seems we'll soon be fat and rich."

Toad grinned. "Aye, just like the rest o' us."

"Well, at least he spoke to me," said Froan. "That's more than most have done."

"Ye're fresh plucked from the river," said Toad, "and have yet to prove yer quality." He glanced about slyly, then lowered his voice to a whisper. "After what ye did, best sleep out o' sight tonight." Then he raised his voice again. "When we capture a ship, we'll take yer measure. Bloodbeard puts the new men on the boarding party to see how they fare. There's more to piratin' than pullin' oars."

"I'll remember that," replied Froan. Then he lowered his voice and added, "and the friend who said it."

Toad nodded and rejoined the men who were growing boisterous with the ale. Froan retreated to where Telk sat on the edge of the clearing. Telk soon lay down and dozed off, but Froan remained alert and observed the drinking men. Even before Toad's warning, he had no desire to join them. Rather, he would wait until they wished to join him. He knew that might take days or even moons, but he was patient. In the end, he felt certain that they would flock to him. It was his destiny.

The drinking went on far into the night, but eventually the men began to stumble off to the shelters. Froan looked for the girl who had spoken to him, but he couldn't spot her. Nevertheless, when the women stopped serving, he rose and wandered off into the woods, leaving his snoring friend behind. Once he passed beyond the edge of the trees, he halted and waited. Before long, he heard quiet footsteps and saw a dark figure moving toward him. Then he heard a whispered voice. "Shadow?"

"Here," Froan whispered back. The figure came closer, and he recognized the girl. "You've learned my name, but I don't know yours."

"Ah'm Moli."

"I'm glad you came. Almost no one's talked to me."

"Aye, they're afeared ta."

"Why?"

"Sturgeon had two friends, Pike and Chopper, and they're fixin' ta do ta ye what ye did ta him."

"I see," said Froan, feeling anger well within. "How will I know them?"

"Pike braids his beard. Chopper's missin' tha tip o' his nose. He carries an ax and is quick ta use it."

"You're brave to come to me. Why did you bother?"

"'Twas Sturgeon what broke my teeth, and"—Moli shyly looked down at her feet—"and there's somethin' 'bout ye. Ah can't say what exactly, but it sets ye apart. So Ah'm hopin' ye'll remember Ah did ye a good turn."

"I will, Moli. You won't regret tonight." Froan pulled Sturgeon's silver ring from his thumb—the only finger that it fit—and handed it to Moli. "Here. I want you to have this."

Moli gazed at the ring and then at Froan in surprise before she slipped it into a pocket in her skirt. "Ah must go. 'Twill go ill fer me if Ah'm seen with ye." Then Moli hurried to one of the shelters and disappeared into it.

Froan remained in the shadow of the trees and crouched down to watch the clearing. After a while, he observed two men emerge from a shelter. In the dim light they were little more than shadows, but Froan saw that one carried an ax. They entered another shelter, but after a short while exited it and entered the third one. *They're looking for me*, Froan thought. Soon they emerged from the shelter and began to search the clearing. They found Telk sleeping and stood over him as they whispered to each other. Eventually, they moved on, leaving Telk unharmed.

Froan moved on also, retreating farther into the woods. He trod quietly and cautiously until he was far from the campsite. When he found a dense stand of undergrowth, he crawled into it. Despite his fatigue, thoughts of his enemies prevented sleep. Froan lay awake, pondering how to deal with them. He didn't drift off to sleep until he had a plan.

SIXTEEN

THE PIRATES slept late, and it was well past dawn before Froan spied a man exit a shelter. A lifetime of early-morning milkings had accustomed Froan to rise at first light, and the habit served him well. He had returned to camp, found what he needed, and retreated into the woods well before anyone stirred.

Downhill from the campsite lay a dense copse of small pines. That was where the latrine had been dug. It was a simple trench, about three paces long. A horizontal pole that was lashed between two pines served for seating. It was the sole amenity, other than the privacy that the pines provided. The latrine was close enough to the shelters to be convenient, yet distant enough so that its stench didn't pervade the camp. It was near this malodorous spot that Froan found a place to hide.

From a clump of undergrowth, Froan could observe all who came and went. He did so gripping a device that he had fashioned that very morning, something he had never seen or used before. An image of it had come to him last night, and he had understood its function instinctively. It had been simple to make, for it had only three parts: Two of them were sections of a stout branch, cut to a length slightly longer than the width of his palm. These served as handles. The last part was a length of thin but strong rope he had pilfered that morning. It was tied to the middle of each handle. Stretched out, the rope was slightly shorter than his arm. Froan had no word to describe the thing he had made, but a more worldly person would have called it a garrote. All Froan knew was that it felt natural in his hands, and with luck, it would prove useful.

From his hiding place, Froan watched the first pirate enter the pines to relieve himself. Afterward, others came and went at irregular intervals. Nearly a dozen men and women had made the trip before he spotted a wiry man with a braided beard walking down the path in a manner of someone not fully awake. Assuming from Moli's description that the man was Pike, Froan silently crept toward the pines as soon as his enemy disappeared into them. Silently pushing his way through the branches, Froan discovered that fortune had favored him. Pike stood facing away as he emptied his bladder.

Froan moved quickly, advancing with the garrote in his hands. His arms were crossed when he threw the rope in front of Pike's throat. When Froan jerked his hands outward, a loop formed around his victim's neck. Then Froan pulled on the garrote's handles with savage strength, heedless of the blisters on his palms. Pike gave one rasping croak before the encircling rope crushed his windpipe. Urine sprayed wildly as the man's hands went to his throat to claw at what was choking him. It was already too late; the deadly cord had formed a deep furrow in his neck. Pike's trembling fingers could barely touch it, and they were rapidly growing weaker.

Excitement and hatred gave Froan added strength. Blood welled around the strangling rope as Pike kicked and jerked helplessly. Soon his movements lost their vigor, diminishing to feeble twitches and then to stillness. When Pike became deadweight, Froan felt a stimulating surge of power as his shadow exulted. Then his victim tumbled backward, and Froan was forced to catch him.

Aware that someone might enter the latrine at any moment, Froan hefted the dead man on his shoulder and pushed his way through the pines. He emerged on the downhill side of the copse and continued in that direction. The body upon his shoulder was heavy, but in his excited state, Froan scarcely noticed the weight. He rushed downhill until he reached the riverbank. There he walked into the current with his gruesome burden.

When Froan was chest-deep in the water, he slipped Pike's body from his shoulders. The garrote had remained embedded in his victim's neck, and Froan pulled it free. Blood flowed from the wound and briefly colored the water with a crimson cloud. The cloud elongated, grew pale pink, and dissipated as Froan watched. Then he turned Pike's body in the water, so it faced upward. Silver bubbles came from the dead man's mouth, and as the air left his lungs, his body grew less buoyant. When Froan released the corpse, it slowly sank and began to move as the current seized it.

Froan stood watching his foe drift away beneath the surface of the Turgen. It seemed to him that the man had become one of the river's denizens, moving in the fluid manner of aquatic creatures. When Pike finally vanished into the murky waters, Froan left, satisfied with his morning's work. He made his way back to camp by a leisurely route, pausing briefly to hide his garrote in the hollow of a tree. His skin was dry when he joined the pirates.

Some of them seemed surprised to see him, but Froan didn't acknowledge their reaction. He put on the bleary face of someone who had just awakened. Stretching and rubbing his eyes, he asked, "Is there anything to eat?"

"Cold stew," said a woman. "We don't light fires in daytime 'cause o' the smoke."

"Stew sounds good to me," replied Froan, grabbing one of the cleaner-looking bowls from an unwashed pile upon the table. The woman filled it.

One of the pirates who had borne a surprised expression spoke. "Shadow, where'd ye sleep?"

"In the woods," Froan replied, smiling. "I'm a fensman and fond of sleeping outside when the weather's fair."

While Froan was eating, Chopper emerged from a shelter. In daylight, the large round scar on the end of his nose was prominent. It not only gave the tip an unnatural shape, but its deep pink color rendered his face comical. However, there was nothing humorous in Chopper's expression as he glanced about. Froan briefly met his eyes and felt his enmity. He also noted the man's agitation, which grew as time passed. When everyone had risen, he finally voiced what was troubling him. "Has anyone seem Pike this morn?"

No one said he or she had.

Chopper stared at Froan. "How 'bout ye, Shadow."

"Who's Pike?" Froan asked innocently. It wasn't fear that governed his reply; he instinctively grasped the power of uncertainty. Fancy could be far more terrifying than fact. The plot against him was intended to be a secret, so Froan would let the plotter's fate be a secret as well. That way, the others could imagine what they might, and his reputation would grow from their speculations.

Froan watched with satisfaction as the news that Pike was missing became general knowledge. Each person's reaction was informative. Toad and Moli seemed pleased. Others became uneasy. The remainder were indifferent.

Eventually, the mystery stirred Bloodbeard into action, and he sent men to search the island. But Froan had taken care to leave no trail, and the river had carried away his victim. The men returned at noon, as puzzled as when they had left. When they informed the captain of their fruitless search, he was more than a little displeased. "By Karm's ass!" he swore. "How can a man just vanish?"

Froan had gathered with the others to hear the search party's findings, and he spoke up after the captain's outburst. "It reminds me of what you said last night."

Bloodbeard glared at him in annoyance. "And what was that, young pup?"

"Some fellows aren't the right sort," said Froan coolly.

Bloodbeard cast Froan a strange look, as if he were suddenly seeing him in a different light. The annoyance in his face had been replaced by one of uneasy respect. It didn't last long. Soon the captain frowned and shouted, "Enough o' Pike, the useless shit. Delayed our settin' out, he has. If he turns up, his booty's forfeit. And if he don't, good riddance. 'Tis past noon, so move yer arses. To the boat. We're shovin' off."

A short while later, the boat left the cove. In the daylight, Froan could see that the pirates' island was just one within a cluster. Varying in size, the rocky bits of land seemed like pebbles scattered by a giant. The boat headed downstream toward the nearest one. Aided by the current, the craft moved quickly and soon rounded the downstream side of the isle. When it did, the captain altered their course so they headed upstream toward another island. That proved to be but the first leg of an erratic course from one island to the next. Puzzled, Froan turned to Toad, who manned the oar beside him. "What are we doing?" he asked. "We seem to be going nowhere."

"We're confusin' anyone who spies us. 'Twon't do fer them to find our camp."

Toad's answer caused Froan to view Bloodbeard and his men differently. Their fear of discovery made them seem less bold, and to Froan's thinking, the elaborate departure route was evidence of timidity. *Only petty thieves with a boat*, he concluded.

A favorable wind blew from the west, and once the boat was sufficiently far from the island, Bloodbeard ordered the men to raise the sail. Froan had no idea what to do and was virtually useless as the men set to work. Nevertheless, he helped as best he could, watching carefully so he might be more adept the next time. Once the sail was unfurled, the boat surged forward. Afterward, an easy journey upstream consumed most of the afternoon. Froan knew they had reached the hunting grounds when Bloodbeard ordered the sail furled and the oars set out. Afterward, the pirates began roaming the river in search of prey.

Eventually, they sighted a pair of triangular sails, glowing gold in the slanting light of late day. They belonged to a boat that was tacking into the wind to sail downstream. The captain studied its zigzag course awhile before ordering his tillerman to head in an angle opposite to the one the other vessel was traveling. Toad explained to Froan what was happening. "That boat can't sail straight 'cause the wind's wrong. She must slant into the breeze to move forward and our captain knows it. It don't look like we're chasing her, but we are. When they slant their course the other way, we'll be right in their path."

"What if they don't change their course?" asked Froan.

"Then they'll run aground."

As he rowed, Froan watched the other ship. As Toad predicted, the vessel eventually made a sharp turn, slowed for a moment as its sails swung into a new position, and then picked up speed. Toad smiled. "Now she sees us, but what can she do? She lacks maneuverin' room."

Froan was fascinated by the game the two boats were playing. Bloodbeard's swift, oar-powered vessel could go anywhere, while the wind limited the other ship's options. Toad informed him that it was a cattle boat, built for capacity, not speed. In essence, its hull was a bloated version of their craft—single decked, half as wide is it was long, with high sides to fence in its animal cargo. Although it tried to evade pursuit with a last-moment course change, it was too slow to escape. Bloodbeard's boat pulled alongside the larger one, and his crew threw grappling hooks over the other vessel's side. The hooks were secured to chains, which the crew pulled to bind the two boats together. Close-up, the cattle boat seemed like a wooden wall that rose nearly a man's length higher than the rail of the pirates' craft.

When the two hulls touched, Bloodbeard shouted names. "Toad, Shadow, Chopper, Bog Rat, Serpent, Gouger, and Eel, ye board first." As he said this, the pirates set two hooked poles over the cattle boat's rail. A rope ladder, wide enough for three men to ascend at once, stretched between the poles. Froan lifted his eyes to the ladder's top and saw the opposing crewmen peering down at him. Each bore a weapon of some sort, and Froan decided that pirates were indeed bold men.

"Up! Up!' shouted Bloodbeard. "By Karm's milky tits, move yer arses! Gold awaits ye, or mayhap the Dark Path. Go and find out which."

SEVENTEEN

As FROAN hurried to the rope ladder with the others, his bloodthirsty half overpowered his fearful side. He surrendered to his violent urges because only they seemed capable of getting him through what lay ahead. By the time he gripped the ladder's top rung, his piercing eyes had taken on a malign gleam.

Someone swung a wooden club at his head. Froan fell backward, still gripping the rope with his left hand. The club sped past his nose, so close that he could feel a rush of air. Froan drew his sword with his free hand as he pulled himself back toward the ship. His assailant swung again. This time, the steel of Froan's blade met the club. The club splintered. Froan gazed at his opponent. He was a boy of perhaps fourteen winters. As he stared back at Froan, his face filled with terror. Then he dropped his ruined weapon, and while it clattered on the deck, he backed away with his hands held high.

Froan clambered over the ship's side and jumped onto its deck. As he did so, a bald, paunchy man bearing a sword advanced toward him and his fellow pirates. He held the weapon with his arm fully extended, as if the mere sight of a sword would ward off the attackers. Froan noted that the blade trembled violently. Almost as soon as he had made that observation, an ax slammed into the sword, wrenching it from the bald man's hand. Froan glanced to his right and saw Chopper, who raised his weapon and brought it down again. The ax head grazed the side of the bald man's head, severing an ear before biting deeply into his shoulder. The man dropped to the deck, screaming from pain and terror as his blood pooled on the boards. Then Chopper silenced him with another blow.

The killing stunned the opposing crew, and they stopped their resistance immediately. Dropping whatever weapons they had, they backed away to stand bunched against the far rail with their hands raised. A man who hadn't participated in the fray spoke up. "I'm captain of this vessel, and I surrender her to ye. Take what ye wish."

With the fighting over, Froan gazed about for the first time with an undistracted eye. The cattle boat's high sides had hidden the cargo until the pirates boarded. Upon the captain's surrender, that cargo had become theirs. It lay piled upon the wide deck, ready for the taking—bale upon bale of hay.

After Bloodbeard boarded his latest prize, he slowly paced its deck, glowering and striking his heels with every step. "By Karm's muddy feet!" he cursed. "Grass! A boat-load of grass!"

"I've coin, sir," said the captive captain timidly. He held out a worn leather purse. "A half-moon's worth of fares."

Bloodbeard grabbed the purse and spilled its contents onto his palm—perhaps two dozen coppers and a few silvers. There wasn't a single gold among them.

"I've food, too," said his prisoner. "A sack of grain, cheeses, a near-full keg of ale, and two casks of salt mutton, one unopened."

The news did nothing to lift Bloodbeard's mood. He returned the coins to the purse and tied it to his belt. "All right men," he bellowed, "take the vittles and ale aboard and anything else of use." He gazed at the captured ship's crew and passengers, who still cowered in a knot. Then he pointed to a husky young man of twenty-odd winters. "Ye there! Can ye pull an oar?"

The man swallowed nervously. "Nay."

"Can ye swim?"

"Nay."

"Well, better learn one or the other fast, fer ye're joinin' my crew. Ah name ye Shit Weed. Now come with me while yer new crewmates gather our booty." He turned to board his own vessel. "Hurry, men. Ah want to shove off quick."

As the other pirates began scooping what plunder could be had, Froan advanced toward the captives. When the bald man died, Froan had felt the same surge of power as when he had killed Pike earlier that morning. It seemed that it was unnecessary for him to do the killing to gain power from a death. Consequently, he felt confident and strong. The captives seemed to sense his power, for most paled under his scrutiny. After looking them up and down, Froan pointed to a man of his height who was dressed better than the rest. "You," he said. "Come here."

The man did so with a coolness that angered Froan. "Put a foot forward," Froan barked. When the man complied, Froan placed a bare foot beside the man's boot to take its measure. "Slip off your boots," he said. Then Froan smiled. "And your clothes, too."

The man's faced reddened, but he didn't move.

Froan poked the man's belly with his sword point. "I'd prefer your clothes without holes or bloodstains, but I'll have them either way."

After a glance at Froan's baleful eyes, the man removed his boots. Then he shed his clothes until he stood naked and then watched, fuming, as Froan donned his garments.

After Froan fastened on his sword belt, he glanced down at his new clothes and was pleased by what he saw. "These suit me," he said to his victim. Then he frowned. "But they stink of goats. Why?"

"Because I herd them," replied the man.

Froan smiled. "So you're a humble goatherd? I think not." He regarded the man and ensnared him with his gaze. He had never probed a stranger before, but the day's events had heightened his abilities. Although Froan couldn't discern the man's thoughts, he sensed deception and received hints of what that deception might involve. Froan pushed deeper and discovered all he could. Still, his perceptions were vague. He felt that he had uncovered clues to the truth, but not the truth itself.

"Where's your herd now?" asked Froan.

"At home," replied the man. "This hay's for them."

"That makes sense," said Froan.

The man looked relieved.

"But I don't believe you," said Froan. "You sold your herd." He studied the man's face and saw the color leave it. "A whole boatload of goats would fetch a tidy sum. And rather than returning home in an empty vessel, you've loaded it with hay."

"Nay, nay. I have no gold."

"Did I say you did?" Froan pointed to the boy who had attacked him. "Bog Rat, seize that lad."

Telk grabbed the boy, twisting his arm to secure him.

"The lad favors you," said Froan, "but I suppose he's not your son."

"He's not."

"Then you won't mind if my friend cuts his throat. What's a stranger's death to you? Bog Rat, open the boy's neck."

As Telk reached for his sword hilt, the man cried out. "Mercy! Spare him!"

Froan motioned for Telk to stay his hand. "Why?" he asked. "Is he your son or not?"

"Aye, he's mine."

"So you lied about your son, and I'm certain you lied about the gold. A third lie will cost your boy his life, so answer carefully. Where'd you hide the gold?"

"In the hay."

"Get it."

The man hurriedly climbed onto the stacked hay. He paused, seeming to count the rows of bales. Then he went to a bale and lifted it, along with two others beneath it, to retrieve a small cloth sack. Afterward, he climbed down and handed the sack to Froan, who smiled when he felt its weight. As the man retreated, Froan opened the sack and glimpsed gold. By then, the other pirates had gathered around him, "Well, lads," he said with a grin, "this beats salt mutton."

"Ye won't get away with this!" said the naked man. "The Merchants Guild will track ye down. Mark me, soon ye'll dangle from poles and crows will feed upon yer carcasses."

The man's threats enraged Froan, and fury heightened his a sense of power. Then words flowed easily from his tongue, almost without thought on his part. "Hear that, men?" he shouted in a voice filled with venom. Froan held up the sack of gold. "He deems this more precious than your lives."

Froan gazed at his fellow pirates and was thrilled by what he saw. The men appeared inflamed, and he was certain the effect went beyond the power of his words. Something far more primal and potent had emanated from him. Froan couldn't give it a name, but he could feel its force, and it exhilarated him. He pointed to the naked man. "This scum lied about the gold and denied his own son, but his threats are sincere. He'll stir men to hunt us down, and the others here will bear witness against us. When we're in chains, they'll slay us the coward's way—with tattling tongues."

Froan regarded each pirate in turn to fan his rage with his piercing eyes. "Will you abide that? If men must die, who should they be? Us or them?"

"Them!" shouted Chopper. Swinging his ax, he rushed at the unarmed captives and cut down the nearest one. His victim was just a boy. Telk, seized by a similar frenzy, was only a step behind him. He cleaved the head of the naked man. Then the other pirates joined in the mayhem and mercilessly slaughtered their screaming victims until the deck was littered with bodies lying in a crimson pool.

Froan watched, transfixed by the massacre. The sight of so much bloody death stirred and nurtured the shadow within him. He felt like a freezing man standing before a fire, or a starving one savoring his first meal in days. A hunger had awakened within him, one made keen by long denial. Unbidden, a thought arose: *From such nourishment comes strength.* Froan was still uncertain of the nature of that strength, but he had no doubt of its potency. Gazing upon the butchered captives, he sensed that his power had grown and foresaw where it could take him. It was an intoxicating vision of might and sovereignty—the lordship that his father had promised.

The bloodlust slowly faded from the pirates' faces as they wiped their weapons clean on the clothes of the slain. Yet Froan, knowing that he had stirred the men to murder, was confident he could do so again. He felt that he had just begun to exercise his powers and they would blossom with further use. Already, he was impressed by what he had accomplished.

"Finish looting the ship," Froan said and was pleased when no one questioned his order. As the men set to work, Froan reached into the sack and withdrew two gold coins. "Chopper," he said, "a word with you."

Chopper turned, regarding Froan with a mixture of madness and respect. Then Froan spoke to his former foe. "I don't know how Bloodbeard divides the loot," he said in a low voice, "but you deserve this." He clasped Chopper's hand and pressed the coins into it. Then he looked him in the eye and said, "You've lost two friends of late. It's time to find another."

Chopper gazed down at the gold in his palm and grinned. "Ah already have." He secreted the coins and resumed looting.

While the men carried off the food, ale, and sundry items, Froan grabbed some hay and rolled it into a cylinder. Then he went to an iron box at the rear of the boat. It stood on stone legs so that it didn't touch the wooden deck, and a kettle hung from an iron frame above it. Froan assumed that the box was used for cooking fires, and he hoped it held hot ashes. When he found that was so, he pushed the hay cylinder into the ashes and blew until it caught fire. Using his makeshift torch, Froan went about the ship, setting the bales ablaze. Then he climbed down the rope boarding ladder, the last man to leave.

"Well look at Shadow," said Bloodbeard in a slightly mocking tone, "all dressed proper now."

Froan said nothing. He merely strode over to the captain and handed him the sack. Bloodbeard opened it and grinned when he saw its contents.

"Captain," said Froan, "we'd best shove off. The other boat's afire."

Bloodbeard noticed the rising smoke and began to shout. "Loose those hooks and heave aback! Then oars out and away! Put yer backs to it."

As the pirates rowed away, the first flames rose from the cattle ship. Froan was rowing beside Toad when Bloodbeard strode up and roughly grabbed his shoulder. "Shadow," he said in a cold tone, "Ah gave no order to fire that ship."

Froan glanced up and readily saw the captain's menace. "That man whose gold you have swore to hunt you down."

"So? Ye should have reported it to me. 'Tis not your place to give orders. There's only one captain on this ship. Ferget that again, and gold or nay, Ah'll send ye to the river bottom."

"I won't forget, Captain."

"And to help ye remember, ye'll forfeit yer share," said Bloodbeard, already striding away.

EIGHTEEN

As FROAN watched the captain resume his post, the sense of power that he had felt aboard the captured ship began to wither. Bloodbeard's threat contributed to this change of mood, but it wasn't the primary cause. Memories of the slaughter on the burning boat no longer gratified Froan. Instead, they horrified him. He felt as if he had awakened from a nightmare to discover its terrors weren't imaginary. As their reality sank in, his face grew clammy and his hands would have trembled if he hadn't gripped the oar so tightly.

Froan's stomach churned with nausea as he relived the murders. It was as if he were still upon the blood-washed deck but no longer gripped by his shadow. Thus, in some ways, the memory of the event was more vivid to him than the actual experience. The sights, the sounds, and even the smells of slaughter returned to him with an undiminished rawness that he scarcely imagined possible. This time, he empathized with the victims' fear and suffering. They tore at him, filling him with remorse. Yet as terrible as those memories were, what horrified him most was that he had not only provoked the slaughter but had delighted in it. That knowledge both shamed and terrified him. *What kind of monster am I?*

As Froan struggled to answer that question, his shadowed side reasserted itself. *Would you rather end up dangling from a pole? Would that man have shown you mercy? The world's a harsh place where to be meek is to be a victim.* Froan glanced at Toad, who was rowing beside him. His companion was regarding him strangely, and with a chill, Froan saw that Toad sensed weakness. He could read it in his eyes.

See how your doubts have endangered you? said Froan's malign inner voice. *Do you suppose that Toad's your friend? He's only drawn to power. Show weakness, and he'll turn on you.* Froan knew that was the truth and realized he was in jeopardy. Panicked, he broke free from his conscience. Then his dark instincts came to his aid. He turned to Toad and muttered under his breath, "By Karm's stinking arse, I feel sick! It tears at my guts to abide the captain's threats and answer mildly."

Upon hearing that remark, Toad appeared reassured. It was a reaction enhanced by the return of Froan's baleful gaze. "Yer wise to bottle it up, Shadow," whispered Toad. "Don't fret, yer time will come."

Yim's bed of reeds seemed like a boat to her, and Rappali's home likened to a cavern where she floated on a sunless river. A part of her realized that wasn't so, but her impressions had an air of truth to them. Yim felt adrift in a shadow world between life and death. Her surroundings and the activity about her were insignificant compared to the central question: Would she live or die?

Sometimes, Yim felt that she had some say in the matter. At those times, she was uncertain which was the better choice. Curiously, the vestige of the Devourer that remained within her pulled toward life. That alone seemed a good reason to die. *But if I die, I'll never save Froan.* Yim reminded herself that she had tried to do that ever since his birth and had failed. She wondered what she could accomplish with additional time. *Probably nothing.* Moreover, if she contacted her son, she might actually aid her foe.

Yim recalled General Var speaking of a ritual called "the suckling," in which Lord Bahl sacrificed his mother by drinking her blood. Its purpose was to reunite that part of the Devourer lingering in the mother with the greater part that had passed to the son. Once unified in one person, the malevolent being was restored to it fullest power. Knowing this, Yim was puzzled. She was certain that Froan had cut her throat while under the Devourer's influence, thus she couldn't understand why he hadn't consumed her blood. It was obvious that he hadn't, for she was still alive.

At first, Yim supposed that Froan had been ignorant of what to do. She quickly rejected that idea. Though Froan knew nothing of the ritual, instinct should have guided him. Yim had drunk blood when seized by dark impulses, and she couldn't imagine Froan not doing the same. That led to a hopeful thought. *Perhaps something restrained him.* Yim thought it could have been Karm or perhaps Froan's better nature. Whatever it was, it seemed a cause for hope and a reason to live.

Yes, it's a reason, thought Yim, *but is it a good one?* Her death would return some of the Devourer to the Dark Path. Without her blood, Froan could still become the next Lord Bahl, but he would be a weakened version. *The Most Holy Gorm virtually said as much.* Yet what remained would grow in strength over time, though it might take generations to produce another Bahl who could threaten the entire world. *Generations of additional slaughter,* Yim reminded herself. A weak Lord Bahl would be a lesser evil, but he would still wreak misery and death.

As Froan's mother, I should stop him, thought Yim, reflecting on his potential victims. Yet if Froan achieved his father's power, the Devourer would eventually overwhelm him and rule a nightmare world forever. Yim was certain of that. She was far less certain that she could prevent it from happening. It might be possible, but it seemed a terrible gamble. As long as Yim lived, she held the key to the Devourer's everlasting domination. It pulsed through her veins and arteries.

Torn between her choices, Yim made none and continued to drift.

Froan's feelings wavered also as he rowed with the other pirates, but his choices were less complicated. While his shadow couldn't completely sway him, circumstances were on its side. Safety lay in ruthlessness, while a conscience brought misery as well as danger. *What good is there in mourning strangers?* On the cattle boat, Froan had felt exhilarated and powerful. That seemed far better than feeling miserable and sick. Nonetheless, he was unable to expunge his feelings of remorse and guilt. The best he could do was try to ignore them.

Prudence required Froan to put on a hard face, whatever his feelings, and he managed that feat. Having fooled Toad, he gave no other man cause to doubt his resolution or his menace. Thus, when the pirates arrived at their island camp, Froan was unsurprised that he was treated with new respect. The men in the boarding party, in particular, regarded him with awe. Chopper was the most transformed, and Froan observed that the maniacal air he had shown on the raid lingered in him. It was evident in Chopper's voice when they entered camp and he called out, "Wenches, bring out wine, so we might toast Shadow. 'Twas he who found gold and spurred us to manly deeds."

Bloodbeard's face darkened upon hearing that, although he said, "Aye, get wine."

"But let the first toast be for our captain," shouted Froan, "who chose the prize and ran it down." He glanced at Bloodbeard, who appeared only somewhat mollified by his gesture.

The woman with the tattered blue gown disappeared into one of the crude shelters and returned with a small oaken cask. Pulling its stopper, she began filling the various drinking vessels, which the other women brought to the men. When Moli presented Froan with a dented metal goblet, her swollen lips were twisted into a smile that managed to hide her missing teeth, "Ah'm happy fer ye, Shadow," she whispered.

Froan glanced into her eyes and saw that she spoke truthfully. He smiled and said "Thanks." Then he raised his goblet high. "To our captain!" he shouted.

"Our captain!" echoed the men.

"To Shadow and bloody deeds!" shouted Chopper.

"To Shadow!" said the men, some loudly and some in subdued tones.

Froan savored the wine as a token of his rise within the crew, but he sipped it sparingly, knowing that he needed to keep a clear head. He surveyed his situation, not with the awareness of a boy raised in a bog, but with the instincts of one far older and more cynical. Thus he knew his rise simultaneously endangered him. Bloodbeard was already wary and resentful, and he had adherents.

After the day's events, Froan was more aware of what surrendering to his instincts would mean, but he saw no other option. Bloodbeard would have tossed him overboard if he hadn't killed Sturgeon. Pike would have murdered him if he hadn't acted first. The slaughter on the cargo boat had turned Chopper from foe to follower. In each case, Froan saw how forbearance would have doomed him. He recalled his father's spirit saying that rules were for common men. *It seems mercy is also.* Nevertheless, Froan's conclusion saddened him. He glanced at Shit Weed, the crew's newest member, who stood apart and looked miserable. *But he only needs to row to live,* thought Froan. *That path is closed to me. I must climb higher or die.* Already, instinct told him that Bloodbeard wouldn't let him be and only the more ruthless would survive the coming confrontation.

Putting on a fell appearance while seeming festive, Froan participated in the night's celebration. All the while, he watched everyone. As the drinking continued, Chopper rambled on and on about gold and bloody deeds to anyone who would listen, and few dared not. Froan noted how Chopper drank heavily, and doubted he could offer much protection that night. Telk followed Chopper's example, and being unused to wine, soon staggered off to vomit and collapse in some bushes. Eventually, the night's carouse wound down. Froan thought it prudent to sleep alone in the woods, and when the moment was right, he slipped off into the trees.

Having kept a clear head, Froan had little difficulty making his way quietly through the dark woods. He hadn't strayed far from camp when he spied a dense expanse of ferns surrounded by dry leaves that would warn of anyone's approach. He stepped through the leaves as quietly as possible and settled among the bracken. His new clothes made sleeping on the ground more comfortable, but he wished that his victim had been wearing a cloak.

Froan was drifting off to sleep when he heard leaves rustle beneath someone's tread. He drew his dagger before he even looked around. All he could see was the black shape of someone moving in the dark. That someone was advancing toward him. Froan waited, ready to use his blade.

"Shadow?" came a whispered voice. "Shadow is it ye?"

Froan thought he recognized the whisper. "Moli?"

"Aye, 'tis me. Ken Ah be with ye?"

"Why?"

"Don't ye want me?" asked Moli.

Froan detected an injured tone in her voice. "You may have been followed."

"Nay. Ah made sure o' that."

Froan sat up so that Moli could see him. "Then come here."

Moli rushed over to him. "Ah brought a cloak fer us ta share," she said wrapping it around them both. The effect was to press them close together.

"Moli," said Froan with a note of surprise, "where's your blouse?"

"Wrapped 'bout my waist," she said, guiding Froan's hand to a breast. " 'Tis nicer this way. Don't ye think?"

Caught up in the novelty of touching a woman's breast, Froan was almost too preoccupied to answer. "Y-yes," he stammered. "Nice." His fingers continued their exploration. *She's so soft*, he thought. He toyed with a nipple and felt it stiffen.

"Aye, *nice*," echoed Moli in an earthy tone that sounded exaggerated to Froan, although he had no experience in such matters.

Moli rolled on her back, allowing Froan to touch her more freely. That was when he discovered the silver ring he had given her. Moli had suspended it as a pendant from a bit of cord about her neck. Froan touched his gift, pleased to think that it had spent the day between her breasts. Then he kissed Moli's nipples and sucked them. As he did, she made soft noises in her throat. After a while, she reached between his pants legs to stroke him. There was nothing fumbling or tentative about her touch. Finding Froan's swollen organ, she expertly fondled it through the cloth, heightening his desire. In doing so, she also freed him from his shadow, for the feelings she aroused had nothing to do with death. Thus Froan responded to her in innocence, and he gasped when she paused in her attentions to quickly remove her skirt so that she was completely naked.

Moli seemed to understand Froan's increasingly urgent feelings. She helped him lower his pants and then guided his manhood to her woman's cleft. Froan felt hair, then warm silky moistness. A sudden form of ecstasy followed so quickly that Moli had scarcely stirred before Froan was spent. He ceased moving and remained both atop Moli and inside her as the feeling faded into a tingling sense of well-being. Moli lay still also, except for languidly brushing his back with her fingertips. After a while, Froan found her bruised lips to bestow his first kiss ever. He pressed his mouth to Moli's only lightly, not wanting to cause her any pain. Then he withdrew from her to lie on his back.

Moli rolled onto her side so that she could rub a hand over Froan's chest, which was still covered by his shirt. " 'Twas wondrous fine," she said in a breathy voice.

Froan simply sighed, but he wholeheartedly agreed. He barely reflected that what seemed so marvelous to him must be commonplace to Moli. Most likely, she had been with another man the previous night. Froan didn't dwell upon it because Moli was distracting him by unbuttoning his shirt. Soon she was covering his bare chest with kisses. After a pleasant interval, her lips made a wandering trail down Froan's belly to his loins. Moli briefly dallied there until Froan's ardor was renewed, then she pulled off his pants and boots so that he was also nude.

The second time Froan tupped, it felt less urgent, but even more exciting. He was able to savor his lovemaking, and

Moli enhanced his experience by the way she met his thrusts with movements of her own. This time, she seemed more energetic, and it occurred to Froan that she might be enjoying the act as much as he. The idea was pleasing. Moli began to moan softly, and the sound further excited him. Then the world seemed to fall away, leaving only him and Moli. His senses were heightened, but they were focused solely on her smell, her voice, and the feel of her. When he exploded with pleasure, she kept moving, clasping him ever tighter until she seemed to undergo an explosion of her own, one that diminished more slowly than his. Moli grew still, but spasms occasionally shook her until she finally sighed and turned completely limp. Then Froan gazed at her in the starlight, filled with wonder. He withdrew, pulled the cloak over them both, and held her tight.

After a while, Moli sighed contentedly and said, "Ah could be yer woman, if ye want."

"My woman?"

"Aye, then no other man would have me, only ye."

"I'm not so sure they wouldn't try."

"Ah am. They'd be too afeared o' ye."

"You were Sturgeon's woman, weren't you?"

"Ah had no choice."

Froan's feeling of wonder dampened. "And now you're with me only because . . ."

"Because Ah want ta be yer woman," said Moli with a suddenness that betrayed her desperation. "Ah warned ye 'bout Chopper and Pike. Ye said ye'd remember. Please, Shadow, Ah've offered ye all Ah have. Will ye not take it?"

Froan pulled Moli's body against his, feeling her warmth against his perpetually chilled flesh. "I'll not abide another man to have you."

Moli pressed her swollen lips against his and kissed him. "Thank ye, Shadow. Thank ye." Then she became quiet, though she slowly brushed her hand over his chest. "Yer still cold," she whispered with a note of puzzlement, "but Ah'll warm ye." Moli pressed her bare body against his.

Froan appreciated her gesture, but he knew its futility. "I'm always cold," he whispered. "It's my nature. You'd better dress or you'll get chilled."

Moli put on her blouse and skirt, the only garments she possessed except her cloak. Froan dressed also, then lay beneath the cloak with "his woman." As she drifted off to sleep, Froan pondered their arrangement. He had enjoyed tupping Moli, but her motives perplexed him. They seemed more complex than trading sex for protection. Froan felt he was an unlikely protector. He wasn't the strongest among the crew, and he lacked experience with arms. Moreover, he had enemies—men who would become Moli's enemies as well.

Yet, while Moli seemed clever enough to realize that being with him brought risk, she had pursued him anyway. *Why?* His dark instincts told him nothing useful, for they lacked empathy and saw others as only pawns or obstacles. Moli might be either or both, but Froan felt that she was also more. As such, she bewildered him, evoking emotions that were not only new but also intense and confusing. *Mam might have helped me sort it out*, he thought. *But Mam's dead.*

NINETEEN

EVERY EVENING, Rappali ladled clear fish broth down Yim's throat, then gave her a double dose of the healwife's brew. Yim was vaguely aware of these ministrations and tried to express gratitude with her eyes. Since she was unable to direct her gaze or even focus, she doubted that her friend received the message. Afterward, the brew always caused everything to darken so that Yim felt she was swallowed by a void. The current evening had begun no differently, but sometime during the night the routine altered.

Then Yim felt that she was neither floating in a void nor lying in her friend's abode. Instead, she stood in a landscape that seemed to have more substance than a dream. As she looked up and saw a full moon in a starry sky, she also heard the rustle of leaves and felt the breeze that moved them. Gazing about, Yim had the impression that she was standing in the wild. The most prominent feature was an unusual pathway that appeared made out of silver. It wound through the low places much as a stream would. Yim was standing on the path's surface, which felt cool and spongy beneath her bare feet.

When Yim glanced down, she saw that she was wearing a simple white robe not unlike the one she wore on the night she became Honus's Bearer. Just thinking of that night awoke her longing for him. *That was long ago*, she thought. *Will these feelings never fade?* Reflecting on them, Yim hoped they wouldn't.

It seemed to Yim that she must find something. She had no idea what. Nevertheless, she began her search by walking down the silver path. It was slightly slippery and rippled with each step she took. As a result, Yim spent as much time gazing about her feet as at the way ahead. She walked this way for a long while before she rounded a bend and spied Honus squatting by the path's edge.

He had changed, but Yim recognized him immediately. He was older, of course, but he also looked worn. There were real lines on his face, not just tattooed ones. They spoke of grief and hardship, not the anger needled by the Seer. Yim nearly burst out sobbing at the sight of them. Instead, she halted and waited until she mastered her emotions. Then she spoke. "Honus."

Honus looked up, and his mournful eyes widened. "Goddess?"

Yim smiled at his mistake. "No. It's me, Yim."

"Yim," said Honus, speaking her name with such feeling that it conveyed a multitude of emotions—hope, wonder, sorrow, and most of all, love.

Yim was rendered speechless by its depth.

"Why are you here?" asked Honus.

Yim had to ponder his question before she knew what to say. "I don't know whether I should live or die."

"Live," replied Honus. It sounded more like a plea than an answer.

"But if I fail . . ."

"With life comes hope."

"You're a fine one to talk of hope," said Yim. "I see your despair."

"For many winters I've been estranged from hope," admitted Honus. "But I've just learned that my runes say I'm to help you." He shook his head, either in sadness or wonder—Yim couldn't tell which. "I didn't believe it until now."

"But this is just a dream," said Yim. "A delirium wrought by a potion."

"I think not," replied Honus. "All this is portent."

"So our long separation has made you a Seer?"

"No, but tonight is different."

"Then what do you foresee?"

"That we'll meet again."

"Oh, Honus, I've missed you so!"

"And I you," replied Honus.

Then Yim rushed toward Honus, arms outstretched. He rose to meet her embrace, but even as he moved, he began to fade. Yim's hand brushed Honus's tattooed face and felt its warmth. Then he was gone, and Yim hugged only empty air. All that remained was longing as keen as a knife in her heart. Yim squeezed her eyes shut to clear her tears, and when she opened them, she was inside Rappali's dark and quiet home.

Yim, who had lacked the strength to lift a hand or make the slightest sound, found herself standing on her makeshift bed. In the dim light, she could see Rappali and Roarc sleeping close by. She could hear the faint sound of their breathing and the crunch of reeds beneath her feet. The sensation of Honus's warmth still lingered on her fingertips, and Yim raised them to her neck to touch her wound as she imagined he would have done. She felt stitches and the raised line of a healing cut. *Who sewed me up?* Yim had no memory of it.

Yim's legs ached as though she had walked a long distance. Though fatigued, she was also alert and puzzled. *What just happened?* It had been over seventeen winters since Yim had her last vision, yet her memories of each contact with the goddess remained vivid. The encounter on the silver pathway seemed similar to a vision, but it also differed. There was no lingering chill, and Honus's guidance was unambiguous compared to Karm's. It evoked such hope and longing that Yim felt she had actually been with Honus. Though she didn't know how that could be possible, she was unable to dismiss it as a dream. Moreover, the strength of her feelings wasn't the only sign of a supernatural encounter. The vision—or whatever it was—had pulled her back into life.

There was no question about the latter. Yim felt fully returned to the living world. Her sensations had a richness to them. She savored everything about her: the herbal scent of her reed bed, the chirping of crickets, the familiar sights of her friend's home, the renewed vitality of her body. Yim saw all those things as signs that she was meant to live. *If so, then hope isn't an illusion. Perhaps I truly can rescue Froan and spend my days with Honus.* That would be the blissful consummation of all her desires and surely worth whatever risks she must undertake. The very thought of it invigorated Yim. She sat down upon her bed to wait for dawn and the beginning of the next phase of her life.

Far away, Honus was also awake. He sat upright in his bed and rubbed his cheek, certain that a hand other than his had just brushed it. Then he saw Daven rouse and reach for his stick. "You've no need for that," Honus said. "I'm not trancing."

"Good."

"Your stick's unnecessary now. Henceforth, I'll no longer seek the memories of others."

"I'm pleased but puzzled," said Daven. "What has brought on this change of mind?"

"I encountered my beloved," replied Honus.

Daven silently walked over to the hearth, where he threw dry grass upon the embers and blew until it ignited. Afterward, he fed kindling, then branches to the flame until it illuminated the small room. Only then did he turn again to Honus. There was curiosity on his face, and more than a hint of skepticism. "I'd like to hear this tale."

"I'm only a Sarf," said Honus. "Karm's purposes are beyond my understanding. But tonight . . ." He paused, briefly overwhelmed by wonder. "Tonight was different."

"You had a vision?"

"I'm not sure. Whatever it was, I sensed the goddess's hand. I felt I was somewhere else. Not in some dream, but a place within this world."

"A place you know?"

"It was too dark to say. But it seemed located in a waste. Luvein, or somewhere like it. I think there was a stream."

"And Yim was there?"

"She came to me, seeking advice."

Daven smiled. "A Bearer turning to her Sarf for wisdom?"

"It wasn't truly my wisdom; it was the wisdom of my

runes. Somehow I knew Yim couldn't read their ancient tongue, so I relayed what you had told me. I said I was meant to help her."

"You believe that now?"

"I do with all my being," said Honus. "I also told her that we'd meet again. I think that gave her hope."

Daven smiled. "And hope to yourself. I can see it in your face." He seemed to reflect a moment. "You called yourself a Sarf for the first time since we've met. Are you prepared to be one and submit to my discipline?"

"I'll do whatever's necessary."

"If your will has been restored, then there's hope for your body," said Daven. He gazed at Honus's skeletal frame and shook his head. "There'll be hard days ahead and scant time to accomplish what we must. Though it may not seem so yet, these are urgent times."

Froan woke with the first light of dawn. Moli still slept, her face just a hand's length from his. He gently brushed her hair aside so he might gaze at it. Though her cheek was smudged with dirt from sleeping on the ground, he had the impression that she had washed before their tryst. Her swollen lips were still dark purple and the surrounding flesh had the yellow-green cast of a slowly healing bruise. The sight of Moli's injury made Froan fiercely glad that he had gutted her assailant. It also evoked tender feelings.

When Froan gave those marred lips an impulsive kiss, Moli opened her eyes. For the first time, Froan noted that they were the shade of blue gray that clouds take on before a storm. They were beautiful to him. He smiled. "So you're my woman."

"Aye, Shadow, all yers."

Froan grinned and reached down to pull the hem of Moli's skirt above her waist. "So I can tup you right now?"

"If ye want ta."

The sight of the auburn mound between Moli's legs

aroused Froan, but the thought of tupping in the daylight was inhibiting. "Not now," he said somewhat reluctantly. "I should save my strength for rowing." As Moli pulled down her skirt, he noticed her dirty feet. "If we sack another ship today, perhaps I can find some shoes for you or a fine dress."

"Nothin' too nice, or tha captain will take it."

"He won't always be captain."

Moli paled slightly. "Be careful what ye say. He's a dangerous man."

"So am I."

TWENTY

YIM WATCHED Rappali awake and suddenly bolt upright in her bed. "Yim! Ya're alive!"

Yim smiled. "So it seems. I believe I have you to thank for that, though I don't remember coming here."

"Ya were half dead. Nay, more than half."

Roarc, roused by his wife's exclamations, blinked sleepily at Yim. "So ya're all better. Will ya be leaving now?"

Rappali hit her husband, but only lightly. "Hush! Tha healwife must see her first."

Roarc sighed. "Then I'll fetch her after dawnmeal."

"Yim, what happened ta ya?" asked Rappali.

"There was an accident."

"An accident? Yar throat was cut!"

"Froan didn't mean to do it."

"Froan?"

"See what comes from not having a husband," said

Roarc, looking vindicated. "A man would have taught Froan how ta handle a blade."

"You're right," said Yim, seizing on Roarc's comment. "We were cutting brush, and Froan was careless."

"So, his blade slipped and cut yar throat?" said Rappali, looking more than a little dubious.

"Yes," said Yim. "I know it sounds strange, but—"

"If Froan was with ya, why did ya come alone?" asked Rappali.

"I passed out. Froan must have thought he killed me. Most like, he fled."

"And ran off with our lad," said Rappali. She glared at her husband. "And ya thought so well of Froan!"

Roarc responded by frowning at Yim. "If ya had raised him proper, this wouldn't have happened."

In her heart, Yim agreed with Roarc. Moreover, she thought Rappali was right about Telk. If so, Yim was certain that Froan had lured him to a fate far worse than her friend could possibly imagine. It made her weep, which spurred Rappali to rush over and embrace her. "'Tisn't yar fault, Yim."

"I feel it is," replied Yim between sobs. "I'm so sorry."

Rappali began weeping also, leaving Roarc to gaze in consternation at the sobbing pair.

Eventually, Rappali calmed enough to set about making dawnmeal for the three of them. By then, Roarc had risen and dressed. He spoke to Yim. "What makes ya think yar lad's gone off?"

"When I came to, Froan's clothes were gone, along with things needed for a journey. So he's left Far Hite. And the fens also, I suppose."

"Telk's boat's gone," said Roarc in a dispirited voice. "So, 'tis most like our lad's with yars and we'll not see him for a while."

"We'll not see him *ever*!" said Rappali. She began to cry again.

*   *   *

Dawnmeal was silent and awkward. Yim was so over-wrought that she lacked an appetite and had to force her-self to eat. To her thinking, she had loosed evil on the world, and its first victim was her only friend. She was con-vinced that Rappali saw through her story about an acci-dent, even if her husband believed it. Rappali had always seemed aware of the dark thing that lurked within Froan, even though she didn't understand its nature. Thus Yim feared that her friend had more than an inkling of what re-ally had happened. That made her dread being alone with Rappali while Roarc went to fetch the healwife.

Fortunately, when the meal was over, Rappali urged Yim to rest and then went outside. Roarc departed on his errand, leaving Yim alone. She was both weak and tired, but rest was impossible. The hope that she had felt earlier was damp-ened by the prospect of the task before her. Nonetheless, Yim's resolve had been heightened. She felt responsible for what had happened and obligated to make amends. As such, Yim considered what to do.

It seems that Froan has fled with Telk by boat, Yim thought. *Most likely, he's on the Turgen and already far away.* Yim had neither access to a boat nor the skills to use one. She would have to pursue her son by land. *I may not know where he is, but I know where he's headed—the Iron Palace.* Yim could think of no more daunting destination. The horrors she had seen and experienced in the strong-hold near Tor's Gate paled compared to the tales of Lord Bahl's ancestral residence. It was a nightmare place by all accounts, the very seat of horror where atrocities had been perfected through generations of practice.

In the light of day, Honus's promise that he would help her and they would be together seemed more like a dream. Yim struggled to believe, but it was hard. *Even if what Honus said comes to pass, he didn't say how he'd help me or when.* Yim felt it was more likely that she would make her journey alone. At least, it seemed wise to proceed on that assumption.

I should leave as soon as I have the strength, Yim concluded. She began to think about what she should take. *A flint and iron . . . a water skin . . . my goatskin boots, though the soles won't last long on hard ground . . . my summer cloak.* The winter one made of hair-covered pelts was too heavy. *It's wiser to carry that weight in food.* Already, Yim's calculations made it apparent how chancy her journey would be. If winter caught her, she'd sorely miss the heavy cloak, but food was scarce in the Grey Fens and it was easy to get lost in its tangled ways. Whatever she didn't take, she'd give to Rappali along with her goats.

The morning passed. Rappali remained outside, and Yim eventually drifted off to sleep. She slumbered until she felt fingers groping her neck. Yim opened her eyes to gaze upon the healwife. The old woman ceased examining Yim's wound and smiled smugly. "Well, I've performed a wonder," she said. "Ya live, due ta my skill."

"Yes," said Yim. "And I thank you, Mother."

"So tha fee thief now calls me 'Mother.' Finally, some respect! I suppose ya'd like those stitches out."

"I'd be grateful," replied Yim.

"I'm not surprised, for gratitude is cheap. But I must be paid. Roarc paid for tha stitching, but not for tha brew that cured ya. And unstitching costs, too."

"I have cheeses, a hide, and some salt."

"Pah on those," said the healwife.

"We can pay you with dried fish, like afore," said Rappali.

"Keep out of this," said the healwife. "Tha matter's 'tween her and me."

"Then what do you want?" asked Yim.

"Yar oath that ya'll never tend another birth."

"Are you sure that's what you want?"

"Ever since ya came here."

"Then I swear by Karm, who fensfolk call the Mother, that I'll never tend another fenswoman again." Yim made the Sign of the Balance. "Does that satisfy you?"

"Aye." The healwife grinned. "'Twas easier than I thought 'twould be. Now lie down, and I'll pluck those stitches."

Yim reclined on her makeshift bed while the healwife reached into a pouch to produce a flake of glassy black stone, a pair of bone tweezers, and a handful of dried leaves. Giving the leaves to Rappali, the healwife said, "Put these in a clean pot with a little water, bring them ta boil, and let them steep." Then she set to work on Yim. First, she cut the stitches with the keen-edged flake, then used the tweezers to pull out the severed strands of gut. Yim felt each tug as a small, sharp pain. Soon she could feel, but not see, blood trickling down her neck. When the healwife cleaned the stitches with a scrap of cloth wetted in the hot herbal brew, the cloth came away deep pink. She turned to Rappali. "Wash her neck six times afore sunset and six times tomorrow. Then kill a frog—one with no spots—and wrap the cloth 'bout it and sink it in the bog."

Yim bowed her head to the healwife. "Thank you for your aid, Mother. May we talk awhile before you go?"

"'Bout what?"

"Since I'll no longer tend births, there are some skills I'd like to teach you."

"Ya've made that offer afore, and my answer's still tha same. Nay."

"But now women can turn only to you. Surely there's no reason to—"

"My mam learned me all I need ta know. Tha old ways are tha true ways."

"Please!" said Yim. "What harm can learning do?"

"Nay!" shouted the healwife. She turned to Roarc. "I'm done here. Take me home." As she followed Roarc out the door, she called back, "Mind ya, Rappali, no spots on tha frog or tha stitches may fester."

Rappali turned to Yim and sighed. "Where will I find a frog without spots?"

"You won't," said Yim. "So the healwife can blame you if her cure goes awry. But don't worry; it's the leaves that do the healing. The business with the frog is nonsense."

"Still, she healed ya."

"She had a hand in it, as did you. The healwife has skills, but not as many as she supposes. Without fresh learning, wisdom dwindles through the generations."

"Then why did ya swear not ta tend at births?"

"I'm leaving the fens, so the oath was an easy one."

"Leaving? Why? Ya'll not stop Froan, nor bring home my Telk. They're gone."

"I must stop Froan from becoming his father."

"I don't understand," said Rappali. "You said Froan's da was slain and that he was a goatherd."

"That tale's not true. Froan's father was a cruel and violent man. That's why I fled him."

"Then all that talk 'bout fleeing war was . . ."

"Truth. Froan's father was a soldier. I didn't want Froan to become one, too."

"But now that he's run off, he can do as he pleases."

"No! I can't allow it!"

"Come now, Yim. If tha da was fond of war, his son will have his nature. Blood will always show. Ya can't stop that."

"I must."

"How? What will ya do?"

Yim recalled her vision outside Bremven's gates. *Karm was covered in blood. She said it was mine!* Then Yim also recalled the goddess's instruction. "I'll do whatever's necessary."

TWENTY-ONE

FROAN PULLED on his oar alongside Toad, sweating in the afternoon sun. They had been on the river awhile, and the crew had fallen silent as they labored to propel their craft upriver. Froan had grown more accustomed to rowing, and his muscles strained less than on previous trips. In fact, he had come to appreciate the drudgery as a time to think. There was much to think about. Since he had left the fens, his life had grown complicated far more quickly than he possibly could have imagined.

For a while, his thoughts dwelt on Moli, for the tenderness and passion she evoked were new to him. He tried to ignore the more cynical explanations for why she had chosen him and concentrate on the simple fact that she had. Her seasoned lovemaking had made his first time with a woman marvelous. Froan found himself growing excited just thinking about it. Moreover, he felt inaugurated into the ranks of manhood by his deed. He couldn't brag to his fellow pirates that he had tupped a woman, for that would betray his inexperience. However, bragging proved unnecessary, for in subtle ways, Moli had let everyone know that she had become his woman.

The other women in the camp knew it first, since they were affected whenever one of their number slept with one man exclusively. When Moli trailed behind Froan as he walked from the woods, he was oblivious to the signal she was giving. The women were not. Bloodbeard's women noticed first, and they quickly whispered to the others. At dawnmeal, Moli waited on Froan with obvious attentiveness, and also made a point of taking special care of all his friends. Froan mostly noticed how Moli gazed at him adoringly, making him feel that he was the center of her world. His heightened powers of perception found no deception in her gaze. For whatever reason, she had staked her life on him.

Moli's commitment pleased but disquieted Froan. He wished that his feelings toward her could be totally separate from his dark impulses. He had fought his rages and violent urges all his life only to become dependent on them for survival. Necessary or not, Froan felt tainted by his deeds and wanted to shelter Moli from that side of him. Circumstances prevented that. He realized that to claim a woman might require him to defend that claim. Thus among the pirate band, even love could lead to violence. *Is that what I feel for Moli?* he wondered. *Love?* Froan was unsure what he felt, only that he could hardly wait to see her again.

The Way of the Sarf had seventy-seven trials, and Honus was struggling with the first one. He had last performed the Stone Circle Trial after his sixteenth winter, when he had earned his face tattoos. The Trials of the Way had lasted many days. For his first trial, Honus had caused two stones the size of large melons to travel in a circle through the air by tossing them from hand to hand. He had kept it up for half a summer afternoon. On the first afternoon of his rehabilitation, Honus juggled stones the size of apples. Quickly exhausted by the exertion, he became clumsy.

Daven watched, but said nothing when Honus dropped the stones again. Honus had lost track of how many times he had stooped to recover them, but it seemed he'd been doing so all afternoon. As Honus reached for the stones to begin yet another trial, he felt as he had as a child within the temple, striving for the masters. *Only now I'm old and tired, not young and eager.* When Daven's stick hit the back of his hand, Honus bowed his head. "Thank you, Master." Then he retrieved one of the fallen stones.

Honus reached for the second stone and felt a second blow. According to tradition, it was harder than the first. "Thank you, Master," said Honus in a calm voice. Calmness demonstrated the focused mind, and Honus knew that Daven was looking for flinching or any sign of emotion. Grasping the two stones in hands reddened by many blows, Honus began tossing them to make the stone circle. This time, the stones nearly made two dozen circuits before he fumbled. Steeling himself for a blow, Honus reached for one of the stones.

Daven's stick whistled through the air, missing Honus's hand altogether. "Were you thinking of the stick or the stone?" asked Daven.

"The stick, Master."

"And you call yourself a Sarf! Tell me: Is the true path wide?"

"No."

"Is it straight?"

"No."

"What lies on either side?"

"The abyss," replied Honus. His face reddened, but he bowed his head. "Master, I'm not an unmarked boy. I can recite the Scroll of Karm."

"So? Reciting is one thing. Understanding is another. Do you think the abyss is an unpleasant place? It's merely dark. A good place to hide. Or trance and stumble upon some happy memory. Then you could forget your clumsiness with stones."

"I told you, I renounced trancing."

"You weren't tired then. Your hands didn't hurt. The memory of your beloved was still fresh. Temptation bides its time and waits for weakness."

"I won't be weak."

"Temptation also favors pride. You *are* weak. Be humble and never forget it. You have no idea what you face."

Honus bowed his head low. "Do you, Master?"

"The guidance of runes is seldom clear, and yours are particularly difficult to understand. But know this: A hard path lies before you, narrow and crooked as the Scroll says. And I must prepare you for it. I hope you're up to the task, as I hope I am."

Honus bowed his head again. "I'm honored by your patience." He reached for the second stone, striving to be oblivious of the descending blow.

As dusk approached, the pirates had yet to board a single boat. They had spied a swift three-master and given chase, but the vessel had eluded them. Still, the captain didn't order the tillerman to steer for their island encampment, but commanded that the craft make a sweep closer to the northern shore. There, the pirates saw a long rowboat with a pair of men pulling the oars. As they headed in its direction, Toad told Froan that the boat was a fishing craft towing a net.

When the pirate vessel approached within fifty paces of the fishermen, Bloodbeard ordered his crew to pull in the oars. Then he called for Catfish and Froan to come astern.

When they stood before him, the captain grinned in a way Froan found unsettling. "Shadow, ye're a bloody sort, but yonder vessel's a different kind of prize. So Ah'll thank ye fer yer sword and dagger."

Froan hesitated, certain that whatever was afoot boded ill for him.

Bloodbeard's face hardened. " 'Twasn't a request, Shadow. 'Twas an order."

Froan looked around. With the exception of Toad, all his allies within the crew were boxed in on the rowing benches by men loyal to the captain. Froan, doubting it was happenstance, smiled at Bloodbeard. "That will keep them dry and

rust free, Captain, so I thank you for your thoughtfulness."
Seeing no other option, Froan surrendered his weapons.

When Bloodbeard took them, his grin broadened. "We
oft take a portion o' the fisherfolk's catch. Catfish knows
what ye need to do and will instruct ye as the pair o' ye row
out. Mind ye, no killin' tonight. The fisherfolk catch the fish,
and we take our share. That way, we can come back again
and again. Understand?"

"Sounds wise to me," said Froan. "If you fancy eggs, why
slay the hen?"

"Good lad," said the captain. "Now off."

Catfish grabbed two large empty baskets and tossed them
into the rowboat in tow before boarding the small craft and
taking up the oars. "In with ye, Shadow," he said. "Let's get
this done."

After Froan climbed aboard, Catfish began to row and
talk. "See how they've pulled in their oars? They know
what's comin'."

Froan glanced toward the other boat. The two men within
it were no longer rowing but sitting still and watching him.
As Catfish rowed him ever closer, Froan could sense tension in the men's work-hardened bodies and anger in their
gazes. He glanced at his companion to see if he was armed
and discovered that he wasn't.

Catfish looked amused. "So, young Shadow, now that
ye're a bold and cruel pirate, 'tis yer job to fill these baskets
with those men's fish."

Froan gazed again at the other boat. One of the fishermen
held a gaff in his huge and calloused hands. Its stout oak
shaft was tipped with a large iron hook. The way the man
gripped it announced that he had no intention of meekly surrendering his catch. Black rage boiled within Froan as he
saw Bloodbeard's ploy. *He's set me for a fall!* Humiliation
seemed the most hopeful outcome; it was more likely that
Catfish would row back alone.

Knowing this, Froan stood up to face the fishermen. He

had no weapon, only rage. He let it overwhelm him until the world seemed to fade and wrath dominated his very being. Having given free rein to the darkness within, it didn't fail him. Malice flowed from Froan and preceded him as heat does before a conflagration.

It withered the two men. Defiance fled their faces, which grew bloodless. They stared slack-mouthed in horror as if the incarnation of everything terrible was descending upon them. Then Froan sensed that that was what he had become—a wellspring of terror and madness. He didn't entirely understand what was happening as the power he unleashed focused on the two hapless men. He felt as if he were standing apart and observing his body as another used it.

When Froan was about ten paces from the fishing boat, the man who held the gaff dropped the makeshift weapon, and with a whimper, jumped into the river. He broke the surface only once, struggling in his heavy boots and waterlogged clothes. Then the Turgen claimed him, and he sank from view. Then the other fisherman plunged overboard and disappeared immediately. A few bubbles and an expanding ring of ripples briefly marked the spot. As they dissipated, Froan became aware that Catfish had stopped rowing. Froan remained standing as the rowboat continued gliding forward to gently bump the empty fishing boat.

Grabbing the two baskets, Froan hopped into the empty vessel. Setting the baskets down, he grabbed the gaff and swung it in a high arc so that its iron hook plunged into the bench where Catfish sat, barely missing his thigh. Though the pirate had been spared the full force of Froan's baleful gaze, he had been affected. Timidity had replaced the amusement in Catfish's face, and he yelped when the hook bit deep into the wood.

Then it was Froan's turn to grin. "It won't do to go floating off while I gather the fish," he said.

"Nay, Shadow," replied Catfish in a meek voice. "Never."

Froan turned to his task, but the hatred was slow to drain

from him. He had felt no surge of power from the deaths of the two fishermen. Apparently, drowning was too gentle a demise to nurture the dark thing within him. Thus he felt his shadow's hunger, and it lingered like a ravenous wolf about the hole down which its prey has escaped. Under its sway, Froan saw everything as though under bog water. The light seemed dull and the shadows deep. Sounds were muffled. The air bore a faint stench of decay that turned his stomach.

Only after Froan had half filled the baskets, did the darkness gradually retreat and the sensations of the living world grow immediate. Then Froan felt the boat bob underneath him, heard the soft lap of water, and smelled the tangy scent of fresh fish. He noticed that the boat he stood in was worn, but lovingly maintained. Its wood was smooth and oiled. There was no rot or disorder. Surveying the relic of two vanished lives evoked a pang of conscience that Froan quickly suppressed. *Nothing will sink me quicker*, he thought.

As he rowed Froan back to the pirate boat, Catfish was subdued. Most of his watching crewmates appeared likewise, though Chopper's manic eyes had waxed bright. Telk's had a fainter but similar gleam. Bloodbeard looked perplexed, but he forced a grin when Froan and Catfish hauled the brimming baskets aboard. "Why 'tis quite a haul. No tuppin' the ladies tonight; they'll be guttin' fish till dawn. And ye, Shadow, what a mug! To think that men would rather gaze at the river bottom than at yer face!" He shook his head in mock amazement. "What does Moli see in it?"

Bloodbeard's mention of Moli seemed to carry a vague threat, and for a moment, Froan considered turning his newfound power on the captain. Then he changed his mind, believing that would be rushing matters when he still had much to learn. Moreover, he was uncertain that he could summon the power at will. It had come to him without his beckoning, and it seemed his shadow had been in command.

Throughout the long row back to the island, Froan mused

over what he had done. As previously, he wavered between confidence and unease. Yet he saw no way to turn from his path, and often he didn't want to. More clearly than ever before, he could envision where his abilities might take him. A man who could project fear and enflame the hearts of followers could achieve great things. Such a man could give Moli far more than shoes and pretty frocks.

It was well past midnight when the pirates came ashore. The women had a meal waiting in the pots, and they groaned when Bloodbeard announced that they'd clean fish after the crew was served. Since even the captain's women were ordered to scale and gut the day's plunder, Froan resigned himself to sleeping alone. After a bite and a draught of ale, he retired to the bracken to sleep.

It was nearly morning when Moli found him. She looked exhausted. Fish scales sparkled in her hair, and her sticky hands smelt of fish entrails. Nevertheless, Froan undressed himself and her, then covered Moli with kisses. Then he made love with the desperation of one who has gazed upon horrors and craves to express some tenderness.

TWENTY·TWO

YIM'S FRAGILE state required her to spend the night with Rappali and her husband, but the next morning she was determined to return to Far Hite. Rappali urged her to stay, but Yim left even though she still felt weak. The trip through the bog was a drawn-out ordeal. Although Yim moved slowly, her surefootedness had returned, and by late morning she reached the hite. Only the goats met her, and they were indifferent. Having not been milked for days, the does no longer suffered from swollen udders. *They've all gone dry*, thought Yim, *and won't give milk until they kid again*. It didn't matter; Yim's cheese-making days were over. Nevertheless, she was disheartened.

After Yim reached Far Hite, many sights along the way home evoked memories. She spied a tree and recalled Froan as a laughing child dangling upside down from a low branch. She passed the rock where she used to sit and nurse him on sunny days. Nearby was the spot where she taught Froan his letters, scratching them in the dirt with a stick. Yim neared home, passing the kettle where she had cooked her last meal with her son, and then stepped through the open door. Inside, she smelled his scent mingled with all the others of her life. Then she spotted her bloodstains on the floor.

Exhausted by the trip home, Yim lay down and quickly fell asleep. Soon she was dreaming of Froan. He was running toward her, a laughing naked toddler with eyes alight. There was a soft collision as their arms entwined. She lifted him. His skin was cool despite running on a hot and sunny day. But that was Froan; he was never warm to the touch. Yim was so happy that she awoke, and for a hopeful instant, she still felt her child's weight in her arms. Then she saw her dream for what it was—not a vision or a portent, but only the figment of a mother's love and longing.

Unable to fall asleep again, Yim rose and went to the cave where she stored her cheeses. There she found that Froan had taken all but those that weren't yet fully aged. Yim was solely concerned with nourishment, not taste or texture, so she was glad that her son had been picky. She cut down a cheese to take home, then went over to the smoke cave. Froan had left its door open, and scavengers had cleaned out whatever meat he had left behind. Otherwise, everything was intact. Yim found the flint and iron, set up the smoking racks, and gathered wood and kindling for a fire. Then she collected oak branches to use for smoking and sunk them in the bog by weighing them down with stones. Finally, she retrieved her knife from its hiding place.

Though it had been many winters since Yim had slaughtered an animal, she remembered how to do it. After getting a length of rope, Yim searched the herd for an ailing goat and found a doe with udders so hard and inflamed that she could barely walk. Yim fed the doe a treat and stroked her until she was calm. Then Yim took a deep breath and made a quick cut across the doe's throat. Blood spurted onto the ground as Yim gently gripped the staggering animal. She needed to hold on only briefly before the goat collapsed. Then Yim tied one end of the rope around the doe's hind hooves, threw the other end over a tree limb, and hoisted the carcass up to drain the remaining blood.

Throughout all this, Yim felt the dark thing within her stir. She had expected its onslaught and resisted the vile urges it sent forth. Thus Yim didn't taste the flowing blood, though she was sorely tempted. Instead, she threw dirt upon the growing puddle beneath the carcass. While Yim expected the foul cravings, she was surprised that they seemed stronger than before. That troubled her. *Perhaps they only seem stronger because I'm frail.*

That was a comforting explanation, but not the only possible one. The Devourer's influence within the world had always waxed and waned with Lord Bahl's power. When the might of Froan's father was at its zenith, even the humblest of the Devourer's servants were empowered. Yim recalled the threadbare priest who had swayed a crowd with just his eyes and a rambling, inarticulate speech. It occurred to Yim that the strength of her unnatural urges might reflect the strength of the Devourer's grip on her son. If that was so, its grip was growing stronger. Yim had witnessed what it could do. She recalled her nightmare tryst with Lord Bahl—his cruel face and hardened body, his icy touch, his malign gaze, and his aura of terror and madness.

All those traits manifested the evil being that had nearly overwhelmed him. *The same being that seeks to overwhelm my son.*

Yim began to skin the carcass, realizing that she could add some meat to the evening's stew. With Froan gone, there was no need to smoke and dry it first. When blood covered her hands, she once more fought off the compulsion to lick them. She felt encouraged that her self-control stymied her adversary. It was a small victory, but still significant. *Every unseemly impulse and violent urge is a chance to overcome the enemy*, Yim thought, *and each contest builds my strength*.

Upon reflection, Yim could see that she had been fighting the Devourer even before Froan was conceived. She recalled Karvakken Pass, the night in Karm's ruined temple, and the thing that had possessed the black priest's corpse. Yim saw each instance as a battle in a prolonged struggle. It made her realize for the first time that being the Chosen meant far more than bearing a child. She had done that, and it hadn't ended her responsibilities. As Froan's mother, she must save him, and by doing so perhaps save the world. To accomplish either end she must defeat the Devourer. Some called it "god," but Yim knew better. It was only godlike in its power. Otherwise, it was the opposite of divine, a being bereft of compassion or wisdom that fomented hate and hungered for slaughter. Yim foresaw that if it thrived, it would consume the world.

This was her foe, and it dwelt within her as well as in her son. It had been brought to the living realm by the Most Holy Gorm, who was not holy in the least sense. Yim hoped that if a man could draw the Devourer from the Dark Path, perhaps a woman could drive it back. She had no idea how she could do that, nor any assurance it was possible. Her only certainty was that she must try and that she would.

The Iron Palace bustled with activity. Scores of women and girls were brought from the nearby town to remove the shroud of dust from its rooms and furnishings. As they labored, the palace grew more somber. Its walls and floors of black basalt lost their soft gray covering. The dark tone of the ancient wood was revealed. Even cleaning the windows didn't reduce the darkness. The light that filtered through the thick, greenish panes seemed swallowed by the cold rooms it shone upon. Outside, men and boys risked their lives to scrape the encrusted rust from walls, battlements, and towers, then oil the dark iron they exposed. Whenever one fell screaming to his death, it was said that the Most Holy Gorm smiled as one cheered by birdsong.

It was common knowledge that such activities signaled the ascension of the next Lord Bahl. However the ceremonies and public executions that celebrated the event had not taken place, nor had any been announced. None had seen Lord Bahl of late and no one had ever seen his heir, though only someone rash or foolish would say so. The Most Holy Gorm displayed an array of tongues—each imaginatively and gruesomely removed—on a row of hooks set into a wall at the town market. An overhang shielded them from the weather and a wire mesh kept the crows away, so that everyone might gaze upon them and be instructed on the prudence of silence.

The folk of Bahland learned the lesson well. They were taciturn and obedient. If a son was conscripted for the Iron Guard, they called it an honor. They paid their tithes without protest, even when it meant hungry winters and famished springs. There was no hue and cry when a small boy disappeared or when his bloodless body was found. One performed whatever task was required and kept mum about the nightmares that ensued. For this, the people were spared when the army marched out to slaughter other folk. And when the plunder poured in, some trickled their way, and the tithes were less burdensome.

If those in the town were closemouthed, they weren't unobservant. Their fates were bound to the iron edifice towering above the bay, and they watched it for portents. What they saw confused them. While the oiling of the palace was the sign of better times, there were no changes. The Most Holy One still ruled in Lord Bahl's name as he had done for many winters. The Iron Guard wasn't seeking conscripts. The armories weren't busy. Then, when the palace was restored to its former dark state, priests appeared as suddenly as crows driven by a storm. A few were well dressed and came on horseback. Most were clothed shabbily and arrived footsore. All hurried straight to the palace and bore the anxious look of driven men. Then the flow of black-clad priests stopped as abruptly as it had started. When the palace gates closed behind the last of them, all was still and silent again.

It was night. The moonlight seeping through the huge windows was so pale that the men standing in the great hall cast no shadows. Perfectly still and silent, the black priests seemed more like shades than living men. The sole sounds in the vast room were the slow footsteps of the Most Holy One and their echoes. He entered it, bearing the only light, an oil lamp with a smoky flame that trailed a pungent scent. All eyes followed him as he ascended the platform at the hall's rear and turned to address those assembled there.

"Dreams have driven you to me. You know of what I speak. The very fact that you're here numbers you among the select. You may be high or low within our order, but henceforth that makes no difference."

Gorm reached into his velvet robe and withdrew a circular iron pendant affixed to an elaborate silver chain. He held it aloft so that the polished silver caught the lamplight and sparkled in the inky hall. "The is the emblem of the More Holy One, and it bestows not only power but also youth upon he who wears it. For many winters, it has hung from no man's neck. Yet one of you may wear it—nay, one of you *will* wear it—and be graced as only our master can grace a man.

"You know that the Devourer is trapped within a man's body until the day of the Rising. We name that man Lord Bahl, yet our true lord is the god within him. And when Lord Bahl begets a son, the Devourer passes unto that son and its power wanes until the son reaches manhood. This cycle is the great secret of our order, and it will be broken only upon the Rising. May it come soon."

Then the assembled priests spoke as one. "May it come soon."

"Hear this, but never speak it," said Gorm. His voice was low, but its menace carried throughout the hall. "Lord Bahl is dead, and his son is missing. He has been missing since before his birth."

Despite themselves, the priests uttered a faint collective gasp.

"Now that the son has entered manhood, my sorceries have freed him to roam the world and achieve his destiny. And great shall that destiny be, for I foretell godhood and everlasting dominion. My auguries reveal that he's already testing his powers. Yet he's ignorant of his parentage and a novice in the arts of war. He has guidance from god, but he also needs the guidance of men.

"That has always been our role: to advance the Devourer in this world. Our god's too mighty to learn human ways, so we must serve as its hands, feet, and tongue. For this service we've always been rewarded, and the reward shall be great indeed to he who finds Lord Bahl's son. A thousand winters from now, that man will still be young and enjoy a privileged life because of his achievement."

Gorm held up the pendant again and jangled its silver chain. "Do this and prosper. Go forth and search the world. Listen for rumors of a young and bloodthirsty man. Seek him out. If he's our lord, you'll feel his power. Become his confidant and reveal his parentage. Speak of his palace and dominion. Aid him to enter Bahland in triumph. But speak not of the Rising. That lesson must come from my lips only."

Gorm surveyed the faces in the shadowy room. They looked ghostlike in the darkness, but the lamp's light gleamed in each eye like a tiny fire. He sensed eagerness in those eyes. They belonged to men drawn to power and inspired by a ruthless god. He understood their ambition, for it mirrored his. After centuries, it still gnawed at him.

On that night, Gorm had a sorcerer's certitude that all his labors were nearing fruition. The heir's mother would have a small but vital part to play in them, but she was a minor concern because her fate was sealed. The Devourer's growing power would soon drive her into his grasp, just as it had driven the priests. Gorm had already prepared her cell. He was more focused on the final bloodbath that would usher in the Rising. Though there was yet no Lord Bahl to lead it, the bones had revealed that the man who would find him was standing in the room.

TWENTY·THREE

STREGG DEPARTED the Iron Palace the same way he had arrived—on foot. As he walked, the dawn's light revealed what the dark in the great hall had hidden: the priest was an impoverished man. His black robe was patched and threadbare. His sandals were equally worn. Though Stregg had been at the secret meeting and heard the Most Holy One's words, he had little hope of ever wearing the coveted silver chain. As far as he could see, the sole benefit of his long and tiring journey was relief from the intrusive dreams that had driven him to take it. Ever suspicious, he was certain that Gorm knew more of the heir's whereabouts than he had revealed. *A favored few will get the fuller story*, he thought, *not me*.

Although accustomed to his low estate, Stregg was discontented with it. It embittered him, especially when he recalled tales of his great-grandfather's priesthood. That august man was long dead, but stories of his power and authority were handed down within Stregg's family as precious lore and tokens of better times to come. Stregg had grown up in a tiny hut, eating cabbages and roots while hearing accounts of long-ago banquets served in manor halls. Stregg's father and grandfather had been priests also, but by their day, wars had ravaged the countryside until there were no manors left.

A poor land makes for a starveling priest, and Stregg's homeland was poor indeed. For generations, armies from Bahland had preyed on it until the area south of the Turgen was known as the Empty Lands. It was a region dotted by burnt-out towns and moldering ruins, a place of forgotten names. It wasn't wholly unpopulated; there were scattered peasant dwellings, and a few villages remained. But nothing lingered that was worth a long march to pillage.

Stregg's appearance epitomized the want of the Empty Lands. He was mostly bone, with a tall frame that seemed to possess only enough flesh to animate it. His hatchet face was dominated by dark, sunken eyes. They appeared overlarge, and when their compelling gaze fixed on someone, that person found it difficult to look away. Though Stregg was well shy of thirty winters, his stringy and thinning hair made him look older. Its dark hue contrasted with his sallow complextion. Since Stregg's creed esteemed power as a sign of grace, he cultivated an imposing presence. Lacking physical strength, Stregg exuded a sorcerous air. The peasants in his homeland

were convinced that he was skilled in the dark arts, a belief
Stregg actively encouraged. Fear, however unfounded, was a
source of power.

Stregg had left at dawn, not because he was eager to return home, but because he wished to escape the condescen-
sion of the other priests. His poverty marked him as a failure
in their eyes, a man bereft of the Devourer's grace. Their
judgment galled Stregg. *It's easy to grow fat in Bremven,* he
thought. *Try getting a sack of roots from a hungry peasant.*

Taking a road that avoided the nearby town, Stregg
headed east. His long strides soon sped him away from the
Iron Palace. By late afternoon, he was traveling among less
worldly folk who were more easily intimidated by a priest.
Stregg's mood lightened somewhat, and he reflected that although he was lowly within his order, he possessed gifts
nonetheless. Even before he began dreaming of the Iron
Palace, he sensed his master stirring in the world. To Stregg,
it was a presence reminiscent of the faint tingling immediately preceding a lightning strike. Moreover, of late he had
begun to have violent dreams that were so vivid he felt he
was witnessing real events: A huge man was gutted on a boat.
Another was garroted while he pissed. Helpless captives were
slaughtered by maddened men. Such signs convinced Stregg
that the day approached when even the Devourer's lowest
servants would be raised high.

After Stregg had traveled for several days, the eastern
road dwindled to a trail on the grassy plain. Then he turned
northward. On the final leg of his journey, Stregg's pes-
simism over his prospects lessened, for he began to feel
closer to his master. It was a subtle thing, and Stregg wasn't
certain that he was heading toward the heir. Nevertheless,
it seemed logical that Bahl's missing son would be in the
north. If his mother had wished to hide, the Empty Lands
were an ideal place. Only the Grey Fens were more remote,
and they were deemed impassable. Stregg's steps quickened,

and at times, he fancied that he could feel the weight of silver around his neck.

As Stregg returned to his home, Yim prepared to leave hers. She slaughtered another ailing doe to smoke its meat for her journey and assembled other provisions. She tanned hides and replaced her bloodstained tunic. She fashioned a goatskin pack and made a water skin from a goat bladder. Yim gathered everything she thought she would need on the road, weighing each choice and changing her mind often.

There was one preparation that Yim couldn't rush; she had to rebuild her health and stamina. She ate well and rested often, but days passed before she felt recovered. When she did, she went to Tararc Hite. There she offered her herd to Rappali, who was reluctant to take the gift.

"I want yar company, not yar goats," Rappali said. "Stay, Yim. Ya've made a life here, and I doubt tha outside world's improved since ya fled it."

"You know why I can't stay," said Yim. "I must go for Froan's sake and for your son's."

"It grieves me sorely that Telk's gone, but gone he is. 'Tis fate, a thing beyond our changing."

"And it's my fate to leave, so I want you to have the herd."

Rappali's eyes welled with tears. "First Telk leaves, then you. 'Tis beyond abiding!"

"It's hard," said Yim, "but you'll survive."

"Aye, but will ya?" asked Rappali.

Yim didn't answer, for she wasn't sure. Instead, she changed the topic back to goats and made arrangements to bring the herd over.

Five days later, Yim returned to Tararc Hite at dawn to lead Roarc, his brothers, and their assorted kin to Far Hite. None had ever made the trip before, and after they experienced its treacherous convolutions firsthand, none wanted to make it again. Yim had corralled the herd to ease the transfer, but it was difficult nonetheless. The goats had to be carried over the wet portions of the route, which meant most of it. It took all day to fetch the entire herd. Afterward, Roarc roasted a goat to celebrate Yim's gift.

Courtesy required Yim to stay for the feast, so she did. She felt ill at ease throughout the meal, for it seemed to her that Roarc was also celebrating her departure. His brothers and their families appeared equally glad that the strange outsider was finally leaving. Adding to Yim's discomfort was her suspicion that the entire herd would be devoured before winter was over. It seemed emblematic of her life in the fens; all her work and sacrifice had come to naught.

Yim left the feast as early as politeness allowed, pausing to say good-bye to Rappali. The two friends moved away from the firelight and the others. Rappali forced a smile, but the moonlight revealed teary eyes. "Well, Yim, ya were always a stubborn one. Otherwise, ya'd have never made it here in tha first place."

"I doubt I would have survived if you hadn't found me."

" 'Twas fate, so 'twas tha Mother's doing, not mine."

"Still, I'm glad it was you."

Rappali seized Yim's hand. "Sometimes I have hopes of seeing Telk again. But as for ya . . . I know 'tis my last sight of ya."

Yim responded by embracing her only friend with a fierceness that bespoke her reluctance to leave and the certainty that she would. The two clung to each other for a long while. Yim didn't want to let go, but she did eventually. "Good-bye," she whispered in a voice thickened by emotion.

"Good-bye, Yim."

Making her way home by the light of a waning moon, Yim arrived at Far Hite well after midnight. It seemed particularly desolate without her animals. She walked down the empty pathway to her dark home, entered it, and sat upon her bed. *Now, nothing remains to hold me*, she thought. Nevertheless, something did—fear. With departure imminent, Yim feared her goal was beyond her capacity. She felt as she had upon the slaver's auction block—forgotten, insignificant, and utterly alone. From that bleak perspective, Yim saw her hopes of finding Honus and somehow saving Froan as only self-delusion and foolish bravado.

Pondering her future, Yim had only one certainty—she'd receive no help from Karm. She recalled the goddess's final visitation. *Karm said I had a choice. She claimed I knew what would be gained and lost through it.* Yim was convinced that all her visions had served to bring her to that moment. *That moment's past. I chose my path, and the rest is up to me.* Yim wasn't sure why that was so, though she suspected the goddess was constrained from further intervention. Whatever the reason, Yim believed it was futile to look to Karm for guidance.

"So what will you do?" Yim asked herself, speaking aloud to fill the silence. "Remain here?"

The idea had some appeal. Yim envisioned herself as a hermit, ignored by the world and ignorant of its tragedies. "And if someone chances to see me, they'll think I'm a boghaunt." Upon reflection, Yim concluded her imaginary observer would be mostly right. "For I'd be swallowed by the bog, only not yet a ghost." Such a life hardly seemed worth living. Having withdrawn from fens society, the only alternative to such an existence was to undertake her journey. To do that, she must accept that fear would dog her every step: fear that she would fail, fear that she would make things worse, fear that she would find Froan transformed into a monster, fear that the evil within her would gain the upper hand.

"Can I abide being so afraid?" Yim didn't know, but she

thought that she could endure it for a day. That day would begin when the sun rose. "When it does, I'll leave and not worry about the next day until tomorrow."

When the sun rose, Honus grabbed a sling and a handful of stones. Then he went out to hunt hares. Like everything he did, it was part of his training regimen. Hunting accomplished three objectives: It focused the mind; it enhanced skill; and if successful, it nourished the body. For Honus, it also provided a lesson in humility, for it proved the extent of his decline. He who had single-handedly slain thirty-six members of the Iron Guard had yet to bring down a hare after ten days of trying.

Exiting the ruined keep, Honus made his way to a grassy, eastward-facing slope where his quarry liked to breakfast. He squatted in the dewy turf, fitted a stone into the pocket of his sling, and became perfectly still. All Sarfs were trained to focus on the task at hand with minds emptied of all emotion except devotion for the goddess. "Achieve this," the masters had said, "and your every act will honor Karm, be it plucking a blossom or cleaving a man in two." Ever since Honus had submitted to Daven's discipline, he had struggled to regain that state of purity.

So far, he had failed, for bitterness tainted his feelings for the goddess. Honus strove to love Karm and believe that she loved him, but memories intruded to spoil his efforts. Try as he might, he couldn't forget his long stretch of desolation or its cause. Squatting in the wet grass, he doubted it was possible.

Forget Karm, he thought, *and think of Yim instead*. The idea was blasphemy, and Honus knew it. Regardless, he cleared his mind of everything except the hunt and his devotion to Yim. Then calm stole over him. He no longer felt wet or chilled or hungry. When hares hopped forth to nibble moist greenery, he watched them without bodily or mental distraction. His focus was perfect and so was his aim. Each stone he let fly was an act of devotion and had devotion's trueness. Three stones, three kills. It was over in an instant. Honus rose to gather his quarry with the confidence of a man who had finally found his way.

A breeze from the west eased the noon's heat as Froan rowed. His back and arms were easy with the work, as were his calloused hands. He knew by heart each turn of the irregular course from the pirate island. Froan had mastered other nautical skills as well, and whenever the captain ordered "up sail," he got to it as quickly as any man aboard. His pirate's life had settled into a routine of daily raids that brought slim pickings from easy targets. On those ventures, Froan served only as a crewman. Others were always chosen for the boarding parties. Ever since he had been sent out to collect the fishermen's catch, Froan hadn't left the boat except to come ashore at day's end. At nights, he ate with his crewmates, drank sparingly, and retired to the woods with Moli.

Faced with such a lulling routine, another man would have grown at ease, but not Froan. His powers of perception had sharpened, so he knew that the captain regarded him as a threat. Bloodbeard did everything to hide that fact. He was always affable to Froan, and he treated Moli no worse than he treated his own women. Whatever plotting he did was done out of sight with his closest men. Yet Froan could gaze into a man's eyes and see beneath appearances. In the captain, he saw animosity, cunning, and patience.

Froan was impressed that Bloodbeard recognized him as a rival, and he was curious what the captain would do. He decided to observe his adversary and learn from him, confident that when the clash finally came, he would prevail.

Bloodbeard's first move was to identify Froan's allies within the crew. Those were Telk, whom the captain called Bog Rat, Toad, and the men who had raided the cattle boat with Froan—Chopper, Serpent, Gouger, and Eel. In addition

to those six, Catfish had fallen from the captain's grace after
the incident with the fishermen. Froan noted how Bloodbeard closely watched all those men. Moreover, without being overly obvious, the captain isolated them from Froan
and one another. It wasn't hard to do, since the captain's
men outnumbered Froan's by more than two to one. Thus,
although Froan's life had been peaceful of late, the longer
circumstances remained calm, the more certain he was that
they were about to erupt.

When the pirate boat was clear of the islands, Bloodbeard
ordered the sail raised. Then the oars were pulled in, and the
pirates let the wind take them upriver to their hunting
grounds. The leisurely trip was nearly over when the captain
suddenly commanded that the sail be lowered. As Froan
rushed to tie the sail to its spar, he noted that the captain had
fixed his gaze on a distant ship the likes of which Froan had
never seen. It was a large craft, with two decks and a built-
up stern and bow. Yet, unlike a cattle boat, it was sleek and
fast looking. Oars bristled from ports in its lower deck,
while the upper one swarmed with armed and armored men.

"Oh, shit on us," said a crewman, "the guild's war boat."

" 'Tis turnin' toward us," said another.

"Oars out!" roared Bloodbeard, "and row to save yer
precious arses."

Froan dashed to his bench, grabbed his oar, and waited
for the captain's beat. It came quickly and was a rapid one.
"Long strokes, men!" shouted Bloodbeard. "If ye want to
rest, think o' danglin' from a pole. Fer dangle ye will, if they
catch us. And as they fit the noose 'bout yer neck, thank
Shadow fer firin' that cattle boat."

TWENTY·FOUR

FROAN EXPECTED to row with all his might in a race downriver, but the captain had the tillerman swing the boat toward the river's southern shore. The maneuver puzzled Froan, and he turned to the burly crewman rowing beside him, one of the captain's men named Snapper. "Where are we headed?" asked Froan.

"Fer the fens. Ye can't outrow a war boat."

Froan glanced toward the other vessel and noted it was already in pursuit and gaining. "You mean the captain intends to run aground?"

"There's precious little ground in that stinkin' bog, as ye should know. Our cap's lookin' fer a place to hide. Mayhap he'll find one. If not, 'tis the poles fer sure."

Froan glanced at the southern shore. As far as he could determine, it was a solid wall of reeds. As the pirates rowed closer to it, his impression didn't change.

"Bog Rat!" bellowed the captain, "climb the mast and guide me to a channel that'll take us out o' sight. One that goes far in, but don't get us stuck. Fail me, and Ah'll gut ye like a fish."

Telk left his oar and shimmied up the mast. When the boat neared the bog's outer edge, he called out. "Upstream, Captain."

The boat changed course, and began to travel parallel to the vast expanse of reeds. Closer up, it was apparent that the reeds didn't form a solid mass, but grew in clumps in the water. There were irregular channels between the clumps, but from Froan's perspective, he couldn't tell how deeply they penetrated the bog. He heard Telk call out again. "Up ahead, Captain." Bloodbeard had the men slow their strokes as Telk guided him from his perch. "Turn soon, Captain . . . we're near . . . almost here . . . now!"

The tillerman yanked his lever, and the boat turned sharply. Bloodbeard called out, "Oars in and use them to pole the boat."

Soon the boat was slipping among the reeds, poled by the men and guided by Telk. The pirates wove an irregular course among the channels, which became ever narrower until reeds brushed both sides of the boat. "Halt polin'," shouted Bloodbeard. "Bog Rat, off the mast. Snapper! Chopper! Cut it down. The rest o' ye men, grab yer bailers and hop over the side. Fill the boat till it's near sunk. And do it quiet."

That was the last order the captain spoke. After the mast toppled with a crash, all the frantic activity was eerily quiet. Bloodbeard commanded his crew with hand signals, and the loudest sound was water splashing into the hull. Eventually, the boat rode low enough for the men to climb aboard and reach over the side to fill it. When the railing was only a hand's length above the waterline, Bloodbeard signaled his crew to stop. Squatting low on the raised stern so his head didn't poke above the reeds, he was the only dry man on the vessel. His crew, including the tillerman, sat on the rowing benches, chest-deep in tea-brown bog water.

The war boat was screened from view, so the enemy might be near or far. It was impossible to tell which, and that uncertainty heightened the fear that gripped the crew. Froan needed no heightened powers to sense it; every man's face betrayed dread. He whispered to Snapper, "Surely they can't reach us here."

"They've no need. If they spot us, they'll drop anchor and wait. A few days soakin' in bog water bloats ye like a corpse. Then ye start to rot."

"Better to go out and face them," said Froan.

"And row through rainin' arrows to take on armored men?" Snapper spat a bubbly glob that floated near Froan's chest. "Ye thought ye were so brave and bloody, butcherin' merchants and boys. Takin' on a war boat's a different sort o' work."

Froan tried to imagine how his powers would help him in the current situation. *I could inflame the crew*, he thought, *but that would only spur them to suicide*. He readily saw how the bog would encumber their attack. The crew would be decimated before it even reached its superior foe, and Froan doubted he could terrorize enemies he couldn't see. *It's not worth the risk to find out*. Froan realized that he was stuck with the other men and would share their fate.

The sun sank low in the sky, and there was still no clue as to what that fate would be. Finally, Bloodbeard signaled a man named Mutton to come to him. After the captain whispered an order, Mutton shed his clothes, slipped over the side into the channel, and swam off toward the Turgen. Froan waited as anxiously as his fellow crewmen for Mutton's report, but the sun set without his return. Darkness fell, and since the moon was past its final quarter, it didn't rise until well after midnight. Sitting half-submerged in the dark and trying to slap mosquitoes quietly, Froan speculated on what had happened to Mutton. His shadow would have sensed a violent death, but not a drowning. *Perhaps he got lost—it's easy in the fens.*

At dawn, Bloodbeard sent out a second swimmer, and this one returned. His report was whispered down the length of the boat from man to man; the war boat was anchored within sight upriver. The captain's order was passed down the same way. They would sit tight all day and hope the war boat would leave.

That day was the most miserable in Froan's life. He was hungry, waterlogged, mosquito bitten, and exhausted. But worse than his physical miseries was his growing awareness that the crew blamed him for their plight. The war boat's appearance could have been happenstance, but Blood-beard's words—"As they fit the noose 'bout yer neck, thank Shadow fer firin' that cattle boat"—had provided them with a scapegoat. Froan could feel the men's anger grow the longer they suffered, and better than anyone, he knew the uses of hate. If they survived, the captain would be in a powerful position.

Toward dusk, Bloodbeard sent the swimmer out again. The man returned to report that the war boat remained anchored in the same spot. Then the order was passed down to start bailing. They would attempt to slip away in the night.

The boat was afloat again by dusk, but Bloodbeard didn't order the men to start poling until almost no light remained in the sky. The gloom hindered finding the way out. Even worse, without a guide on a mast to provide an overview, one channel looked like any other. The men poled their craft into one dead end after another. Froan could sense their growing frustration and anger. In one reed-hemmed channel they spotted Mutton's pale corpse floating like a ghost in the dark water. "That's all our fates, like enough," muttered Snapper.

Froan had no idea how long it took to find the river, but he was exhausted when the boat cleared the reeds at last. The moon had yet to rise, and the Turgen was a dark-gray expanse beneath a black sky. As the river's current seized the boat and the crew quietly drew in the oars as it had been instructed, each man was aware that the slightest sound might rouse the enemy. The tillerman guided the slowly drifting boat so it hugged the dark mass of reeds. Hopefully, that would prevent the craft's silhouette from showing against the river.

The war boat was invisible, but everyone knew it was close. That made the slow pace of the drifting boat especially agonizing. Froan craved to abandon stealth and find release in action, but he obeyed the captain's orders as dutifully as the rest of the crew. All the while, he kept his ears cocked for any sound that signaled they had been spotted. Once, he heard a distant voice drift over the dark river, but it wasn't followed by the splash of oars.

The boat continued to drift. When a faint glow in the sky announced the approach of moonrise, the whispered command was given to extend oars. Then, spurred by fear, Froan rowed with all the strength that remained in him. The idea of the unseen foe united the crew, and they rowed in unison without the captain beating the strokes.

Like the other men, Froan had peeled off his wet clothes and boots to let his wrinkled skin dry. In the moonlight, his flesh appeared as white as a fish's belly, and it felt as clammy until exertion warmed it. Despite their weariness, the oarsmen kept up a harried pace and arrived at their island hideout before dawn. Upon reaching it, the captain had them not only beach the boat but also drag it into the trees and out of view. Then they returned to camp and woke the women to have them reheat a cold dinner.

As Froan entered camp, Moli dashed up to him. Before he could say anything, she threw her arms around him to kiss his mouth long and hard. "Oh, Shadow, Shadow, Ah've been so worried 'bout ye!" Moli kissed him again. "Yer clothes are all wet! What happened?"

"A war boat chased us. We had to hide in the fens."

"But ye've come back ta me."

Froan saw tears flowing down Moli's smudged cheeks and tenderly wiped them away. "Yes," he said. "I'll always come back to you."

"Drink!" bellowed Bloodbeard. "Wenches, bring out ale. Ye too, Moli. Move yer slutty arse and serve the men Ah saved, no thanks to Shadow."

Moli cast Froan an anxious look before hurrying off. When she reached the ale cask, the captain gripped her arm. "Ah've been parched overlong, so see my mug don't run dry. Others can see to Shadow."

"Aye, Captain."

Bloodbeard squeezed Moli's arm so tight she winced. "And kiss the man who saved the crew." When Moli pecked his lips, Bloodbeard grabbed her face, digging his fingers and thumb into her cheeks. "A real kiss, ye whore. One that shows ye mean it!" Then he cupped the back of her head with one hand and pulled her toward him until their lips mashed together. As Moli squirmed in the captain's grip, she seemed to be choking on his tongue.

Watching this infuriated Froan, but he also saw through the captain's game. *He's goading me, hoping I'll do something rash.* Despite that awareness, Froan's thoughts turned murderous. He envisioned gutting Bloodbeard, as he had Sturgeon, or strangling him, as he had Pike. Then his cold inner voice reminded him that both those attacks had been surprises. Froan glanced around and saw that all Bloodbeard's men were watching him with weapons handy. *This is no time for a fight.* Froan forced on a nonchalant face, grabbed a bowl, and sauntered over to a stew pot. The fire beneath it had just been lit, and its contents were cold. Nevertheless, Froan dipped his bowl in the pot to fill it with stew. Then he retreated toward the woods, keeping a wary eye on his enemies.

As Froan reached the trees, he heard Bloodbeard's voice. It was especially loud, doubtlessly for his benefit. "Tonight, ye'll bed with me, Moli, and be tupped by a real man."

Upon hearing those words and imagining what lay in store for Moli, Froan almost charged back into camp, his sword swinging in reckless fury. *To be cut down before Moli's eyes,* he thought. Then Froan struggled to control his rage. He didn't seek to quell it, only channel it toward a more practical revenge. Born heir to that talent, he succeeded. Hot anger transformed into icy malice. As Froan slipped into the dark woods, his mind was awhirl.

TWENTY·FIVE

FEARING THAT the captain might send men to slay him while he slept, Froan bedded in a dense and distant thicket. Exhaustion caused him to sleep much later than usual, and it was midmorning when he returned to camp. Even so, Froan found no one up. He was helping himself to cold stew when Bloodbeard emerged from a shelter. The captain was fully dressed and armed, as were the two men who accompanied him, Snapper and Mud. Mud, another member of Bloodbeard's inner circle, was a huge man. His scarred face was surrounded by long blond locks and a voluminous beard. Both were tangled into thick, greasy ropes of hair. When he spied Froan, he cast him a derisive glance. "Look who's here, Cap."

"Well, well," said Bloodbeard, "our Shadow's crept out with the sun."

"Aye, there's no Shadow at night," said Mud, chuckling at his wit. "Just ask Moli."

"Where's that wench?" asked Bloodbeard. "Moli! Moli, drag yer whore's arse out here and serve me and my men."

Two more of the captain's men, also dressed and armed, emerged from the shelter. Behind them hobbled Moli. She seemed shattered, moving like an old woman who is pained by every step. She had been beaten so savagely that her eyes were only slits surrounded by swollen, discolored flesh. Her ragged blouse had been torn, forcing her to clutch it closed in order to cover her breasts.

Froan felt shamed by his failure to protect her. He was also outraged to the point of fury. Nonetheless, he fought to hide both emotions from Bloodbeard, who was watching him closely. The captain grinned. "Somethin' troublin' ye, Shadow?"

"Yes, Captain," replied Froan. "I never should've fired that ship. I stepped out of my place, and we all paid for it."

"Aye, we have," said Bloodbeard. He glanced pointedly at Moli. "All o' us. But mayhap ye can make amends."

While Bloodbeard was speaking, Moli went over to the pile of dirty dishes, picked up a bowl, and wiped it clean with the tail of her blouse. Then she filled it with cold stew and brought it over to the captain. Froan noted that her hands couldn't stop trembling and she seemed barely able to see. *What did he do to her?* he wondered as he struggled to appear calm.

Bloodbeard raised a hand, causing Moli to cringe. "Stupid sow! Where's a spoon?"

"Sorry, Captain, sorry," said Moli in a tiny voice as she hobbled to the pile of dishes as quickly as she could. There she found a spoon and rushed back to Bloodbeard, polishing it with her blouse as she went.

Bloodbeard took the spoon and smiled at Froan. "Now that she's broke in proper, Ah think Ah fancy her. Ye'll get more rest if ye sleep alone. A young lad needs his rest."

"Yes," said Froan. "And one grows bored of tupping the same wench every night."

"That's why Ah have three," said Bloodbeard. "Three, countin' Moli."

Froan kept his face neutral and shrugged. "Captain, you said I might make amends. I'd like to do that."

"Would ye? Well, good. Ah have an idea, and ye're just the one to make it work. But Ah'll need to get somethin' first." Bloodbeard began shoveling food into his mouth, and Froan didn't press him for details.

Bloodbeard didn't rouse his crew, but let them sleep in. He even allowed Moli to return to the shelter after she had ladled out cold stew to his men. It was midafternoon when he ordered the boat launched. The captain didn't head upriver, but set a course for the Turgen's northern bank. Froan assumed that the change was made to avoid the war boat.

The pirates prowled the north bank until they spotted a fishing boat. It was similar to the one that Froan had boarded—a long, two-man rowboat. Its two rowing benches were toward the bow, while the stern portion of the craft provided deck space to store and handle a net. A large, rectangular bin for holding the catch lay amidships. Four pirates were sent out to the fishing boat, double the usual number. To Froan's surprise, they slew the two fishermen and threw them overboard. Afterward, two of the pirates rowed the fishing boat to the pirate craft and secured it for towing. When that was done, Bloodbeard ordered a return to the hideaway. Froan was puzzled by the captain's actions, and he was further puzzled when the fishermen's catch was left in the bin.

At the evening meal, Bloodbeard was in a good mood, showing none of his former animosity toward Froan. When the drinking began, the captain spoke to him in a voice loud enough for all to hear. "Shadow, this morn ye spoke of makin' amends. Are ye still prepared to do that?"

"I am, Captain."

"Good man, fer it takes a man to own up to a mistake and an even better one to fix it. Ah've just the job fer one who's bold and darin'. Ye'll need men to help ye. Name six ye trust."

Froan sensed that Bloodbeard was setting a trap for him, but he saw no other option than to proceed. "Bog Rat, Chopper, Toad, Serpent, Gouger, and Eel."

Bloodbeard grinned. "Good choices, all true men."

"And what are we to do?" asked Froan.

"Why, ye're so fond of settin' fires, Ah thought ye'd torch the war boat."

"How?"

"Ah'll explain all in the morn. Tonight, let's drink."

Froan suspected that the captain had a reason for keeping him ignorant and it was futile to ask more about his mission. Instead, he strove to appear unfazed by its perils and grateful for the chance to redeem himself. In doing so, he hoped to prevent his men from becoming alarmed while convincing Bloodbeard that he was falling for his ploy, whatever it was. He was more successful in the latter than the former. Telk appeared worried, as did some of the others. Unconcerned by their apprehensions, Froan turned his attention to finding a way to speak with Moli.

Although she had helped the other women serve, she hung back in the shadows whenever possible. Her face was barely recognizable, and she seemed so forlorn and frightened that the sight of her tore at Froan. Aware that he was being watched, all he could do was wait until the captain and his men were in their cups. Then Froan skirted the light and approached Moli from the dark.

When she saw him coming, she tried to flee, and Froan was forced to grab her arm. When he did, she tensed and began shaking. "Moli, Moli," he whispered tenderly, "everything I told the captain was a lie. I said it only to protect you. No matter what he says, you'll always be my woman."

Moli said nothing, but tears flowed from the slits that were her eyes.

"Was it Bloodbeard who beat you?"

Moli nodded. Then she added in a barely audible whisper, "Others, too."

"Others?"

"Aye. When he was done, he gave me ta his men. 'Tweren't natural, what they done. 'Tweren't at all."

"They'll pay, Moli. All of them," said Froan in a cold, hard voice. "And they'll pay soon." Then he retreated into the dark.

*   *   *

It wasn't until the following morning that Bloodbeard revealed his plan. After dawnmeal, he took Froan aside and showed him two items that he had brought from storage. One was a large earthenware jug sealed with a stopper. "This is lamp oil," he said. He held up a rectangular metal box about two hand lengths high and one wide. There was a handle at the top, and both its top and bottom panels were perforated with tiny holes. "This is a dark lantern." He opened a door in its side to reveal its double-walled construction. The inner chamber had holes only in its side panels. "A flame in here sheds no light unless this door's open."

"So I spill the oil on the war boat and light it using the dark lantern."

"Aye, simple as that."

"And how do I get on the war boat?"

"That's what the fishin' boat's fer. Today, ye and yer men hide 'neath the catch in the fish bin while Mud and Snapper row up to the war boat. They'll have a friendly chat with them aboard to get a close look afore rowing upriver. The moon won't rise till near morn, so 'twill be a dark night. Past midnight, Mud and Snapper will guide the boat so it drifts up to the war boat. Then they'll wait while ye and yer men do the job. Leave yer boots behind and mayhap ye won't be heard. If ye are, yer men can hold back the watch while ye set the fire. Be quick, and ye'll be off afore the soldiers wake."

Froan was impressed with the captain's plan. While risky, it seemed to have a chance of success. "Can you tell me more about the war boat?" he asked.

"Why? Ye're not havin' second thoughts?"

It was impossible to miss the menace in Bloodbeard's tone. "Not at all," replied Froan. "I'd just like to know what I face."

"Ah've been on a war boat," said Bloodbeard. "Was forced to row a dozen moons fer stealin' a chicken. All the oarsmen are convicted men and chained three abreast to the benches. The soldiers are hirelings. They sleep in hammocks belowdecks."

"And their leaders?" asked Froan.

"The officers have fancy quarters on the stern."

"And there'll be a watch?"

"Should be one or two men, most like. The trick is to be quick. Fire the ship, then row off to watch it burn. And when ye return, all's forgiven."

Froan flashed a grateful smile. "Thank you, Captain."

Facing a long row against the current, the men left early. Snapper and Mud manned the oars, thus Froan and his men had it easy at first. There was no need to hide in the fish bin until they were farther upriver. Froan was glad for that, because hiding would be torture. The bin was little more than half the width of the deck and barely a man's length. For seven men to fit into the cramped space, they would have to form two layers. The day-old catch that would cover and hide them was already beginning to ripen. Fortunately, the bin had sides constructed of slats with spaces between them, allowing some fresh air to enter. With luck, they wouldn't suffocate.

Mud and Sapper rowed steadily, and by afternoon the fishing boat approached the stretch of river where the war boat had been anchored. Neither of the captain's men had spoken during the trip, but Froan had gazed into each man's eyes and saw betrayal in them. He was convinced that neither he nor his men were meant to survive the assault. *It seems Bloodbeard hopes to destroy two foes at once*, thought Froan. *The war boat and me.*

The rage that had simmered within Froan grew more intense, and he could feel his shadow stirring. Froan knew its power, which both assured and disturbed him. The two men rowing the boat had no idea what they would face if Froan unleashed his malevolent and savage side. But to do that, Froan would have to surrender to his darkest impulses, and he had seen the consequences. *How many will be slaughtered this time?* Froan had no idea, but already the shadowed part of him hungered for death and mayhem. It seemed to hint that bloodlust might consume him.

Once again, Froan felt that if he wished to survive, he had no choice other than to follow his malign side. Without his dark powers, he was helpless. Nevertheless, he shrank from embracing them, for he sensed that he was nearing a threshold beyond which there was no return. *Must I become a monster in order to live?*

His shadow answered, but not in a way Froan expected. No words or impulses welled up, just an image of Moli's battered face. Then love and hate combined, and Froan let go of all restraint. He felt a chill surge through his body as his being filled with malice. With it came a sense of power.

With a firm grip on his every feature, Froan gave himself the passive look of a beaten dog. He gazed at his feet when he spoke to Mud and Snapper in the fawning tone of an inferior. "So, how was Moli last night?"

Snapper answered first. "Like any slut, only bony."

"So-so," added Mud. "No better."

"Did she put up a fuss?" asked Froan.

"Not fer long," said Mud. "A few good blows and she did whatever Ah wanted."

Mud's words doomed him. He had spoken them with the easy confidence of a powerful man, but that was before Froan looked up at him. As soon as Mud met Froan's eyes he was overwhelmed by their withering intensity. The blood drained from his scarred face, and he stopped rowing to freeze like a hare seized by a wolf. Mud was helpless, though no jaws gripped him, only a pair of eyes. But those eyes weren't wholly human.

When Froan swung the fishing gaff, Mud was too terrorized even to flinch. With a meaty thump, the iron hook bit deep into the side of his neck. Then Froan yanked the handle, ripping out Mud's throat in a shower of blood. The huge man crashed onto the deck, and convulsed briefly before growing still.

Afterward, Froan advanced through a spreading crimson pool toward Snapper, who regarded him with abject horror. Mud's murder had invigorated the dark entity within Froan. When he spoke, he could hear new power in his voice, which sounded both cold and compelling. "What were the captain's plans? Were we really supposed to board the war boat?"

"Aye," said Snapper meekly, unable to look away.

"Then what?"

"Mud and me were to row off," replied Snapper. "Either ye'd burn with the ship or be cut to pieces."

Froan smiled coldly. "The captain must believe we're valiant men. Didn't he fear we'd surrender and talk?"

"Aye, he worried over it. So he planned to move to another hideaway, soon as ye were out o' sight."

"Where's this place?"

"Downriver a bit from the old hideaway. 'Tis a big island near seven others."

"And where will he set up the camp?"

"In a hollow on the south o' the only hill. 'Twill be by a pond."

Froan tossed the gaff down. "Thank you, Snapper."

"I can help ye, Shadow. Anythin' ye need, Ah'm yer man. And Ah only tupped Moli. Ah didn't hit her."

"I'm glad to hear that, Snapper. And there's one more thing you can do for me."

"Sure, anythin' ye want."

Froan spun and plunged his dagger into Snapper's chest with such force that it was buried to the hilt. "You can die," he said. Froan felt a second energizing surge as he withdrew his blade—a feat that required both hands. Then he kicked his dead victim, toppling him into the river.

As Snapper's corpse sank from view, Froan turned to face

his men. Toward them, he radiated a different sort of power, one that inspired a fearless form of madness, not terror. Froan saw their eyes light up with excitement, just as they had before the massacre on the cattle boat. The men's expressions lacked the frenzy of the earlier occasion because it wasn't required yet. Nevertheless, Froan saw how he dominated and inflamed their spirits. He had no doubt they would obey him even if it meant dying.

"There's much to like about the captain's plan," Froan said, "and we'll partly follow it. Prepare for your destiny. After tonight, nothing will ever be the same."

TWENTY·SIX

IT WAS late afternoon when Froan and Chopper rowed up to the war boat. The pool of blood had been washed from the deck of their boat, and what traces remained blended with the bloodstains of countless fish. Telk, Eel, Serpent, Toad, and Gouger lay in the fish bin covered by the slain fishermen's catch. Froan called up to the war boat in what he hoped was a convincing accent, "Halloo, good sirs. Do ye fancy a fish dinner?"

A soldier poked his head over the rail. "Do I see a sturgeon there?"

Froan whispered to Chopper, "Which one's that?"

"The big one," Chopper whispered back.

"Aye," said Froan. "Fer two coppers 'tis yours."

"Is it fresh?"

"Caught yesterday."

"A day old? Pah! Yer price is too dear."

"Afore ye say that, know there's pirates 'bout. 'Tis risky work ta haul a net."

"No more," said the soldier. "We've trapped them in the bog. They're as good as dangling from a pole."

"Then bless ye, sir, fer those fair tidings. And take the sturgeon with my compliments." Froan grabbed the fish from the bin and, balancing on his rowing bench, handed it up to the soldier.

Throughout the exchange, Froan took in every detail of the war boat he could observe, especially those that would affect his plans. The craft was essentially a floating wooden fortress. It had two stout masts, but neither supported spars and sails. Instead, they were capped by wooden-walled platforms for archers and the watch. Froan noted four men on each.

The war boat had low sides, despite having two decks, and Froan judged that boarding it would be fairly easy. Both the bow and stern were built-up, boxing in the main deck. The bow possessed one extra deck and the stern had two. The stern was of particular interest to Froan, for that's where the ship's officers would be quartered. The lower cabin had a door that opened onto the main deck. Froan assumed that the topmost cabin was the captain's and the small deck in front of its entrance was where he stood to issue commands.

Froan counted thirteen oar ports on the ship's side, which meant there could be as many as seventy-eight oarsmen aboard. Since they were chained to their benches, they'd be of no concern during his assault. It was more difficult to judge how many soldiers he would face. Though he could see little of the upper deck, and nothing of the lower one, he observed over a dozen fighting men, and he assumed that there were at least several times that number aboard.

After handing the soldier the sturgeon, Froan sat down

and took up his oars. "I'll fish easy knowing yer news. When ye catch the bastards, where will ye pole them?"

"Midgeport."

" 'Twould be worth a trip to see them dangling," said Froan. Then he began to row upriver. Froan and Chopper continued rowing until the war boat was out of view. Then they entered a channel in the bog. When they were hidden among the reeds, Froan said, "You can come out now."

Five men emerged from the fish bin. They were covered in slime and fish scales and looked worse for their ordeal, but none complained or even seemed glad that it was over. A part of Froan was disturbed by their behavior, for it seemed unnatural. He was particularly distressed to see Telk with a vacant expression on his filthy face. But Froan's shadowed part was unconcerned. It understood that the men had been reduced to tools. It was likely that some or all of them would die during the upcoming night, and a lack of emotions enhanced their utility.

If Froan's men were oblivious of their stench, he wasn't. He told them to rinse the fish slime from their clothes and bodies in the bog, and they obeyed. Afterward, he had them collect what dried, brown reeds they could find among the clumps growing in the water. These were placed in the boat's stern until there was a substantial pile. When that was done, there was nothing else to do except wait for nightfall.

The night was overcast, so there wasn't even starlight to illuminate the way. Froan and his men slowly drifted downstream in perfect silence. Telk used an oar as a rudder to ensure the boat hugged the river's edge. The fens were only a black expanse of shadow without definition, and the Turgen was scarcely brighter. The murk hid them, but it also hid the war boat. Froan stared into the dark to make sure that they didn't float past their target unaware.

Only Froan was anxious; his men had no qualms about

the work ahead. He was certain of that; for he had used his dark powers to replace whatever fears they had with blind obedience and rabid hatred. The only tension they felt came from waiting for a chance to kill. Froan almost envied their lack of inner conflict. While he was mostly eager to commence the night's bloody business, a part of him was appalled by the prospect. Though he tried, he couldn't wholly banish that feeling. So it remained, a nagging thorn he couldn't pull.

A dark shape loomed in the distance, clearing Froan's thoughts of everything except the task at hand. He signaled Telk to guide their boat toward the shadowy form on the water. Afterward, Froan made his way to the stern, where the jug of lamp oil lay beside the pile of reeds. He uncorked it and poured the oil on the dry stalks. Then he made his way toward the bow and briefly opened the door of the dark lantern a crack to ensure its flame was lit.

By that time, the dark shape had resolved into the silhouette of the war boat. It was anchored so that its bow pointed upriver, and since Froan wanted to board it near the stern, they would have to drift alongside the length of the boat. As the enemy vessel loomed ever larger, Froan was half expecting to hear the watch cry a warning from aloft. Telk guided their little craft past the war boat's pair of anchor ropes until he reached the bow. Then he steered so that they floated within touching distance of the hull. Just before they reached the stern, Froan gave the signal for Serpent and Eel to raise boarding poles with hooked ends designed to fit over a boat's rail. When the hooks grabbed hold, the fishing boat stopped drifting.

The rope boarding ladder stretching between the two poles resembled a large mesh. It was wide enough for two men to climb it at once. The pirates clambered up the ladder in pairs and dropped over the rail barefoot so as to make as little noise as possible. Froan was the last to grab onto the ladder, and still no alarm had been sounded. As soon as he stepped off the fishing boat, it began to drift away.

Froan watched it float downriver, unable to ascend the rope ladder because he held the dark lantern in one hand. He remained hanging from the ladder until the fishing boat was nearly past the war boat's stern. Then he opened the dark lantern to expose its flame and tossed it onto the oil-soaked reeds. That done, Froan climbed up to the deck of the enemy vessel.

As instructed, Froan's men stood pressed against the outer wall of the lower stern cabin. Froan joined them there, and as he did, a pillar of flame erupted from the fishing boat. Froan couldn't see it from where he stood, for the stern shielded him from its light. The flame did illuminate the masts, and Froan saw the two men on watch stare at it in puzzlement. The diversion allowed him and Chopper to ascend the wooden ladder to the captain's cabin unnoticed. Meanwhile, the other pirates burst into the quarters directly below.

Chopper entered the captain's cabin in a frenzied state, swinging his ax even before he spotted someone to kill. The only illumination came from three small windows in the cabin's rear. Ruddy light from the burning fishing boat shone on a man rising from a bunk. That effort was interrupted by Chopper's ax. It partly severed the man's neck with the first blow and finished the job with the second one. The head tumbled to the floor and rolled toward a wall. When Chopper bent down to retrieve it, he spied a cabin boy cowering in the corner and split the lad's skull without a moment's hesitation. Lifting the severed head by the hair, he handed it to Froan. "Here ye are, Shadow. Ah suppose 'twas the captain's."

"Good work," said Froan. "We're done here." As he moved toward the cabin door and the small deck outside, an aura of terror preceded him. The two violent deaths just moments before had fed the power he felt flowing from him. Froan projected its force more by instinct than conscious effort. In fact, he didn't have a clear idea what the force was, but its effects were readily apparent. As soon as he stepped onto the deck, the men on watch were paralyzed. One had been sounding an alarm by banging a cylindrical bell, which fell silent the instant Froan appeared. Beacons had been lit to illuminate the deck, and by their light, Froan could see that the men's faces were slack with terror.

A few soldiers had emerged from belowdecks, and they were similarly affected. Serpent rushed up to one who stood passively as he was cut down. Serpent would have slaughtered the other soldiers as well, but Froan stopped him with a single word. The soldiers were a resource that he didn't want to waste.

Eel, Telk, and Gouger emerged from the cabins below, each with a captive. Froan called to them. "Bring the officers to me." As his men obeyed, Froan turned his attention back to subduing the soldiers that continued to clamber up from belowdecks. Although it required no physical effort on his part, nonetheless he found it draining to terrorize so many at once. Froan was surprised to encounter limits to his powers. *Further slaughter will probably heighten them,* he thought, *but I need these men.*

A solution quickly came to him, for he was thinking as a seasoned veteran, not a lad who had spent his life milking goats. The tactics he had employed that night—the use of diversion and targeting the enemy's command—had come naturally to him, as if planning assaults were second nature. He recalled that his father's spirit had spoken of a patrimony, and he assumed his martial instincts were part of it. At the moment, he felt very much the leader. It was a good feeling. It made it easier for him to ignore his impression that he wasn't fully in charge of himself, regardless of how he dominated others.

Telk, Gouger, and Toad forced the captive officers up the ladder, then held them fast. Froan regarded each of his prisoners but didn't use his powers to terrorize them. Upon finishing his inspection, he spoke to all three. Holding up the severed head, he said, "This captain's no use to me. I need a new one. Who wants the job?"

When none of the officers replied, Froan walked over to the oldest one. "Will you serve me?"

"I won't serve a brigand," replied the man.

Froan calmly slit the man's throat and watched him die before regarding the two remaining officers. "Do both of you feel the same way?"

"I'll fight for pay," replied one officer, "but not out of fear." He was a wiry man with a hard and battered face that was missing an eye. A black stone was fitted into its socket.

"I like that answer. What's your name?"

"Wuulf."

"Well, Wuulf, we should talk," said Froan. He gestured to the late captain's quarters. "We'll do it in my cabin."

As the two headed for the cabin, Froan inquired if there was a means to light it.

"Aye," replied Wuulf, "the captain had an oil lamp. Would ye like it lit?"

"Yes."

Wuulf called down to the deck for a flame, and soon a soldier climbed the ladder with a rush candle clamped in his teeth. "Light the oil lamp," said Wuulf.

"Then stay a moment," added Froan.

The solder entered the cabin and lit the wick of a brass lamp that was suspended by a chain affixed to the ceiling. Its light revealed a well-ordered chamber marred by two grisly corpses. Froan glanced about the chamber in amazement, for he had never seen anything so elegant or finely crafted. Telk's home, considered one of the grandest in the fens, paled in comparison. Froan forced himself to tear his gaze from all the built-in furnishings and fix it on the soldier who had brought the candle. After giving the man a penetrating look, he spoke to him in a cold, compelling voice. "Hold your hand in the flame."

The soldier obeyed without hesitation, and as the flesh

of his palm began to blister, Froan turned to Wuulf. "Look in that man's eyes. Do you see any pain?"

"Nay."

"What *do* you see?"

"Nothing. I think ye've driven him mad."

Froan dismissed the soldier, then turned to Wuulf who was regarding him with a look of awe. "I can make you obey me just like that soldier obeyed me. But, as you saw, that obedience comes with a price. I'd rather have you serve me willingly."

"Aye, a fearless idiot makes a poor captain."

"I thought you'd see my problem."

"But why would I tie my fate to yers?"

"Because I'm destined to be a great lord. I've seen but seventeen winters and have only six men, but I've managed to take your ship."

Wuulf smiled ruefully. "Aye, ye did at that."

"I'll turn the oarsmen into my fearless and obedient horde, but I want willing soldiers to form the core of my army."

"Yer army? Ye aim high."

"I do. And high I'll rise. So will those who serve me."

Wuulf bowed his head. "Sire, I'm yer man."

"You may call me Shadow."

"From what I've seen tonight, I think 'twill be 'Lord Shadow' afore long."

TWENTY·SEVEN

WHEN FROAN stepped outside his new cabin, the deck below was filled with soldiers. They appeared subdued, but when he gazed at them in the flickering light of the watch beacons, he sensed they were growing restive. Although Froan had felt his power increase when he cut the officer's throat, he was glad that he had no need to use it on the men before him. Instead, he turned to his new captain.

Wuulf knew exactly what to do. "Comrades!" he called out. "Captain Grute is slain, and so's Lieutenant Smite. I'm captain now. And I've good news! We're no longer the Merchants Guild's men!

"From now on, we'll soldier for a new master, not stingy merchants. No more will we shed our blood for coppers. Instead, we'll serve an openhanded master. A master destined to rise high, and who'll raise us with him. Already, ye've sensed his power. Those who opposed him lie dead, and this vessel's his. Only fools fight such a man. Wisdom lies in fighting for him. Are ye wise, comrades?"

"Aye!" shouted the soldiers.

"Shout it so the guild can hear ye."

"Aye!" shouted the soldiers louder than before.

"Then meet yer captain's master . . . and yers—Shadow."

Froan stepped forward. Unlike his men, he still had his boots, and he had donned the late captain's cloak. It was black, and in the ruddy firelight, it blended with Froan's dark hair to give him the appearance of a shadow. But it was

Froan's aura of menace that created the greatest impression. It bypassed the eyes and went straight to the gut. Froan sensed it in the men's faces—the mixture of fear and awe that marked respect for a dangerous man.

Then Froan addressed them. "The pirates you sought have slipped your grasp. But not mine. This coming morn, you'll plunder the plunderers. All they possess will be shared among you, for I desire naught except to save a woman." He turned to Captain Wuulf. "This will seem a child's game. Bring who you need to my cabin, and we'll make plans for it."

Captain Wuulf immediately demonstrated the advantages of military discipline. Used to Bloodbeard's capricious style of leadership, Froan was impressed by Wuulf's efficiency. The new captain began by having the sergeants report to the captain's deck. There he ordered one to form a detail to remove the bodies from the captain's cabin and clean it. He told another to outfit Froan's men and find accommodations for them. Finally, he ordered all the sergeants to report for battle orders after the council concluded.

The council met as soon as the cabin was prepared. Captain Wuulf brought three additional men to meet with Froan. One was the other surviving officer, an ensign named Tarbon. He was a rough-looking and boxy man of thirty-odd winters who was completely bald. The boat's pilot and the oar master completed the council. When Froan described the pirates' new hideout, the pilot said he knew the island. After Froan said that he wanted a quick attack, the pilot and the oar master estimated a dawn arrival if they weighed anchor immediately and rowed at quickstroke speed. Then Froan told Wuulf and Tarbon what he wanted to do once the hideaway was reached. The officers soon departed to implement his orders, leaving Froan to settle into his new accommodations.

Froan slipped off his boots and experienced lying on bed linens and a feather mattress for the first time in his life. At home, he had slept on a bed made of bundled reeds, never imagining such softness existed. He savored the sensation of a comfortable bed almost as much as having others perform his bidding. Froan drifted off to sleep to the sounds of rapid oar strokes, shouted orders, and hurried footsteps on deck. Somehow, he found them calming.

A knock on the cabin door awoke Froan. Then he heard Captain Wuulf's voice. "Sire, we're at the island. The pirates' beached boat lies in view."

Froan was smiling as he pulled on his boots. The sun had just risen, but when he opened his door, Froan found the main deck teaming with men. Most were engaged in launching the two assault boats, which had been stored on deck. Froan paused to watch the men work, impressed by their precision.

The long rowboats were designed to ferry troops from ship to shore. Four rowers could transport a dozen armored soldiers at a time. Five trips would provide him with more than sufficient men to accomplish his ends. Froan thought of the humiliations he had endured, and it sweetened the prospect of revenge. He intended to savor every moment.

Returning to his cabin, Froan donned the late captain's chain mail tunic. It had sleeves that ended at the elbow and the mail extended slightly below his knee. It fit him well, but the helm was too small for his head. Froan also strapped on the captain's sword, which had a utilitarian hilt but a keen, well-forged blade. The sword belt also had a dagger in a fine leather scabbard. Froan used only the latter, preferring his own dagger. To him, it was more than a weapon: it was a token of his future.

Froan tied the black cloak over the chain mail, and thus outfitted for the morning's enterprise, he stepped back onto the raised deck. By then, the assault boats were returning for more men. The first wave of soldiers was already on the island, where they had secured the pirate vessel. *Now Blood-beard can't escape*, thought Froan. Knowing the pirates' habits, Froan doubted Bloodbeard or his crew would get a chance to try.

Froan arrived on the fifth boat trip along with Telk, Chopper, and the others. All the former pirates had been outfitted with leather chest armor and a leather helmet, both reinforced with iron plates. When Froan came ashore, Captain Wuulf greeted him. "No sign of the enemy, sire, other than his boat. It still has supplies aboard."

"I expect the camp will be equally disorganized," said Froan. "When we reach it, most likely all will be asleep."

"So I should stick to last night's plan?"

"Yes," said Froan. "Move quietly, and wait for my signal."

The hideout had been used several winters before, and Eel remembered the route to it. He led Froan and his companions down the path, but the soldiers held back awhile before following. The woods were so dense that Froan couldn't see much of what lay ahead. Nonetheless, the trail was easy to follow, for the pirates had made no effort to hide it. When the ground began to rise, the men encountered the carcasses of goats and sheep hanging from tree limbs. The fact that Bloodbeard had slaughtered all the livestock seemed a sign of a hasty relocation.

Froan and his men moved farther up the trail until the trees suddenly gave way to a clearing that contained a small pond. The pirates' new hideaway lay within that open space. No shelters had been erected; goods and sleepers were scattered haphazardly about the trampled ground. The only person awake was the woman who was bearing Bloodbeard's child. She was helping herself to something from a pot when she spied Froan and his men. Dropping her bowl, she hurried over to Bloodbeard and frantically shook him awake.

Bloodbeard sat up and dumbly stared at Froan, who

watched his enemy's face grow pale. "Captain, you look like you're gazing at a spirit."

"Mayhap Ah am, fer ye look different, Shadow."

Froan smiled. "I *am* different."

Bloodbeard flashed an uneasy smile. "Wake up, everyone!" he said in a boisterous voice. "Wake up! Our Shadow's returned." Then he leaned over and gently shook what seemed a bundle of rags beside him. He spoke to the bundle in an equally gentle tone. "Moli, dear. 'Tis morn and yer man's come back."

The bundle moved, transforming into a woman who gazed at Froan with slit eyes masked in purple. Moli's face was too swollen for him to read her expression, but when she spoke, he heard hope in her voice. "Shadow, is it truly ye? Ah can't see so good."

"It's me, Moli. I'm here to keep my promise."

"Take her, Shadow," said Bloodbeard as he groped for his sword. "She's yers. As Ah promised, all's forgiven."

"She's not yours to give," replied Froan. "Neither is forgiveness. You must speak to Mud and Snapper first."

"Should Ah?" said Bloodbeard, clearly puzzled by the last statement. Then he found his sword and grasped its hilt, "Well, mayhap Ah will."

"I'll call them," replied Froan. Then he shouted, "Mud! Snapper!" As the echo of his cry died away, the woods filled with the sound of many feet running through the undergrowth. Bloodbeard sprang up, unsheathed sword in hand, and most of his men followed his example. Froan drew his sword in self-defense, as did his companions. It proved unnecessary, for just then, the soldiers poured out of the woods. They quickly assembled into a wall of armed and armored men.

"You'd be wise to drop your sword, Captain," said Froan. "Tell your men to do the same."

"Ah think Ah'd rather go down fightin'," answered Bloodbeard.

"Why, Captain, I didn't come to fight. I've only come for Moli. This needn't get ugly. Just toss your weapon down."

Bloodbeard gazed at the force arrayed against him, and still he hesitated before throwing down his sword.

"Have the others do it, too," said Froan.

"Weapons down," said Bloodbeard with a sigh.

When all the pirates were disarmed, Froan said, "Come, Moli. You're free of him forever." She had started to hobble toward Froan, when he suddenly said, "Wait! The captain struck you, didn't he?"

Moli nodded.

"Well, I think it's only fair that you hit him back." Upon those words, two burly soldiers rushed forward, grabbed Bloodbeard, and pinioned his arms behind him. Froan permitted himself the slightest of smiles as the captain struggled in their grasp. "Why, Captain, surely you don't fear a woman's blow." He strode over to grasp Moli's hand. Raising it to his lips, he softly kissed her fingertips. "Such a dainty hand." He kissed it again and then frowned. "Too dainty, mayhap. It lacks the weight of a man's fist."

Froan nodded to the men who held the pirate captain, and they forced him to his knees. Then they bent him backward until he lay flat and facing upward. While that was being done, the line of soldiers parted to permit the passage of two of their fellows who struggled to carry a huge rock. It was approximately the size and shape of a man's torso. Lugging the rock to where the captain lay, they held it above his head.

Froan's smile broadened. "Yes, this makes things fairer. Moli, touch the stone to deliver the captain's blow."

Moli hobbled to where the two soldiers strained to keep the rock raised to shoulder height. Bloodbeard lay perfectly still beneath it, resigned to what would happen next. Moli, extended a hand. As soon as her fingertips brushed the rough stone, it was released. Mingled with a dull thump was a sound reminiscent of a cracking nutshell. The pregnant woman shrieked and began to sob. Froan tenderly grasped Moli's arm to lead her away. As he did, he nodded to Captain Wuulf.

Moli could move only slowly. Even so, Froan was halfway to a waiting boat before the massacre began. It was remarkably quiet. A few women screamed and a child bawled, but only briefly. The men died silently. Froan barely heard the killings, but he felt them. Each death brought a surge of energy. The sensation was so unique that he would have had difficulty describing it. It certainly wasn't warm, though it lacked the discomfort of a chill. It felt a little like the effect of drink without its befuddlement or like eating when he was starving, except he never became sated. Whether he could describe the sensation or not, Froan knew that he grew stronger each time he felt it.

"Shadow," said Moli, "what are those soldiers doin'?"

"Making those who hurt you pay, just as I promised."

"But Ah heard a woman screamin' and a babe cry. They never hurt me. Neither did most o' tha men."

"And they won't be harmed," said Froan, speaking his first lie to her. "The soldiers are killing only those who deserve it."

When the pair reached the riverbank, men helped Moli into one of the assault boats and then rowed her and Froan to the war boat. Moli squinted at the looming vessel, then asked, "Where are they taking us?"

Hearing fear in Moli's voice, Froan gently grasped her hand. "To my boat."

"*Yer* boat? Are ye a captain now?"

"I'm greater than a captain."

Moli's swollen face was barely capable of expression, yet her mouth dropped in amazement. "And Ah thought ye were goin' ta yer death."

Froan smiled. "So did Bloodbeard."

When they reached the war boat, men helped Moli

board. She was ragged and bedraggled, with a marred face that no one would describe as beautiful. Yet not a man dared show puzzlement over their master's choice of woman. His grip over them was already too strong for that. When Froan stepped onto the deck, he told a soldier, "Bring water to my cabin. It must be fit for bathing." The man hurried off as Froan led Moli to his new quarters. Upon entering them, she was as amazed as Froan had been. "This is *yers*?"

Froan smiled. "Yes."

" 'Tis like a fine house," said Moli, running a hand over a chair of polished wood, "only smaller. My folks had nothin' like this. We didn't even own a chair, just benches."

"I've begun my rise. This is only the beginning."

They heard a knock on the door and a voice. "Sire, I have yer water."

Froan opened the door. A soldier stood on the deck bearing a pot of water. It steamed slightly and dried herbs floated on its surface. "Set it in the cabin," said Froan.

The soldier did as ordered. "I brought a bathing rag, sire." He gave it to Froan, then departed.

Froan gestured toward the bunk. "I've clothes for you." The captain's linen nightshirt lay upon the sheets, a long-sleeved garment that would extend halfway past Moli's knees. "Soon you'll have something finer, but at least this is clean and untorn." He began to remove the tattered remnant of Moli's blouse. "I'll bathe you first."

"Oh, Shadow, ye're so good ta me."

Froan kissed her softly. "No more than you deserve."

Disrobing Moli revealed the full extent of her injuries. Her bruises weren't limited to her face. They covered much of her body, along with welts. Froan was even more upset by the dark purple crescents left by bites. They were all over her shoulders, upper arms, and breasts. Froan took up the rag and bathed Moli with a gentle touch, as if warm, scented water could cleanse away not only dirt but also pain. Every place that Froan washed he also kissed. He did so without passion but with the same tenderness his mother had shown him when he was a child and kisses were cures for hurts.

Froan didn't speak as he bathed Moli, and neither did she. Words were unnecessary. The only sounds within the cabin were the quiet ones of falling water and Froan's muffled weeping.

TWENTY·EIGHT

EARLY AFTERNOON found Froan on the small deck outside his cabin. Moli was dozing, and he had become restless. It felt strange to be idle while everyone else in sight was at work. *Busy doing my bidding*, he thought. On the island's shore, several large fire pits had been set up to cook the pirates' slaughtered livestock for a feast to celebrate his first triumph. When the breeze was right, Froan could smell the tantalizing aroma of roasting meat. Other soldiers were loading plunder onto the assault boats. One shipment had already been delivered. From what Froan could see, it was mostly foodstuffs and weapons.

A short while later, Captain Wuulf returned and reported to Froan. "Sire, we're done on the island, except for the cooking."

"Good," replied Froan. "Did you find the ring?"

"Aye," said Wuulf, handing Froan a silver ring threaded through a bit of cord. " 'Twas in the captain's pocket."

Froan's face softened, and he gazed at the trinket as if it were a great treasure before he tucked it away. "And the gold? Did you find it, too?"

"Aye, sire. 'Twas a bag of coin with some gold in it."

"I want it distributed among the men."

"Sire, it would be wise to hold some back for provisions."

"Why? We have a war boat. We can take whatever we need."

"Those pirates could live off river traffic because they were but a small band. A war boat is a ponderous beast with more than eight score stomachs to fill."

"Don't you have stores on board?"

"Aye, the guild outfitted us, but with less than a moon's worth of provisions. The soldiers get hardbread twice a day, and some salt mutton at evemeal. The officers eat a little better, and the oarsmen eat worse."

"I see," said Froan.

"Sire, I'm a rough sort, with a tongue unfit for flattery. I've made my way by selling my sword to whoever pays best, and plain talk is the only talk I know."

Froan smiled slightly. "And I assume I'm about to hear some."

"Aye. Ye have talent. The way ye handled that red-bearded fellow was a cold bit of work. I quite admired it. But an army wears down quick if ye don't treat it proper."

"The men will obey me. I've no doubt of that."

"Nor do I. But starving men make poor soldiers, so pay heed to their bellies. That is, unless yer sorcery can fill them."

"I'm ignorant of magic."

"Truly? How 'bout that man who held his hand in the flame? The men fear ye. I do myself a bit."

Froan shrugged. "It's just a trait of mine. I'm told it runs in my family."

"Some trait. Ye liken to Lord Bahl."

"Lord Bahl!" Froan exclaimed in an amused tone. "That old fable?"

"Fable?"

"Yes, like Jak Springshanks, who plucks birds from the clouds."

"Who said he was a fable?"

"My mam. She told me he was a fensfolk tale, a made-up monster to frighten children."

"Lord Bahl's real enough, as many folk have learned the hard way. When he was younger, 'twas thought he'd conquer all the empire. 'Tis said he had a way with men that made them reckless with their lives."

"So Mam lied to me."

"I meant no offense," said Wuulf quickly. "Mayhap she believed her tale. Fensfolk know little of the wider world."

"It seems the same can be said of me. So tell me, Captain, how can I best use these men?"

"Abandon the war boat. There's far more plunder on land than water. Better still, it stays put. Row to Midgeport and take the town. Since ye can make the oarsmen fight for ye, send them out to spill first blood. Yer soldiers can finish what remains."

"Then what?"

"Head east and seize a northern realm. Ye'll have to pass through the Empty Lands first. They're aptly named, but there are just enough villages to sustain a march. More settlements lie in the Western Reach, but nothing worth keeping. Beyond it lies the ruins of Lurwic, Bahl's handiwork. But after that are Falsten, Basthem, and Walstur, all worth the plucking. Grab any one, and ye'll be a lord. And south of them lies Argenor and even greater riches."

"Such a plan matches my ambition," said Froan. "You please me, Captain."

"The fighting will be harder farther east, for all the nobles keep troops. But by then ye'll be more seasoned."

And stronger, thought Froan. The morning's attack had resulted in scarcely more than two dozen deaths, but he could sense his enhanced potency. He had no doubt that when he inflamed the oarsmen and loosed them on Midgeport, the slaughter would be far greater. *If I feel strong now, how will I feel after a whole town dies?* It seemed likely that he would find out soon.

After five days of wandering, Yim had begun to worry that she would never see the end of reeds. They rose higher than her head and hemmed her in on all sides. Usually she could see little farther than she could reach. When she encountered a rare stretch of open water, she gazed over it to see reeds extending to the horizon.

Yim had arrived at the Grey Fens on horseback; leaving it on foot was far more arduous. Not only had her mount possessed the advantages of height and speed, Yim had come to believe that her steed had been faerie charmed. Although the bog had claimed him in the end, Yim had always believed that the horse had purposefully sacrificed his life for her sake. *Neeg only took that shortcut because I was giving birth.* Otherwise, the horse had threaded a way through the fens without mishap.

Over the past days, Yim's appreciation of that accomplishment had grown. Like Neeg, Yim had a talent for locating the driest ground. It involved feeling her way with bare feet and keenly observing her surroundings. But she quickly discovered that finding dry ground was not the same as finding one's way. There were no direct routes within the Grey Fens, and firm ground often turned in the wrong direction or came to an abrupt end.

Observing the sky kept Yim from becoming totally disoriented, but the heavens gave no clue as to how to reach her destination. Yim had wandered far enough southward that she could no longer see any hites, but she had no idea how much farther she needed to go. *If I were a bird, maybe not far at all.* Nevertheless, Yim feared that she might continue wandering for days. That would prove a problem. Her water skin had gone dry days ago, forcing her to drink bog water, and the pack that had been heavy with food was beginning to feel light.

Moreover, Yim had a new concern; she had begun to feel cool. The late summer sun made the vast wet expanse of reeds a muggy place, but the hot damp air had stopped affecting her. The change had been sudden, and it had occurred earlier in the morning. If the reeds had stirred, Yim would have thought the onset of her chill marked the coming of a storm. But every breath convinced her that there was no change in the air; it was in her.

The Devourer's growing stronger, thought Yim. *Somewhere, folk are being slaughtered.* The evil entity that had been quiescent within her for so long had been strengthened by violent death. While Yim had feared it would happen, she was still surprised when it did, for its suddenness was startling. First, there was a tiny shiver that she easily ignored. A short while passed, then there was a wave of cold. Moreover, the cold lingered. Yim imagined that the shiver was a single death and the cold was a massacre. *Is Froan already following in his father's footsteps?* Yim was almost certain that he was. Lost in a bog, she felt more impotent than ever. All she could do was slog on and hope.

For days, the fens had seemed changeless; a lush expanse of reeds and smaller bog plants growing from wet ground that often wasn't ground at all but a mat of decay floating over murky water. Yet whether the ground was sound or not, it all looked the same. The sounds changed little also. The rustle of stalks shaken by the wind and the squish following each step seldom ceased. Only the occasional birdcall provided variety. The monotony of her surroundings and the constant walking turned Yim's thoughts inward. After a while, it seemed the past was more vivid than the present.

In Yim's imagination, reeds gave way to mountain peaks, flinty ground, and alpine grass. She was a little girl, idly hopping from stone to stone. They formed a perfect

circle and in the center was a hut. *The Wise Woman's hut.*
Then Yim saw her new guardian coming out the door. Her
hair was brown then, not white. Only the night before,
Yim had told her about her vision, saying, "She who holds
the Balance said I'm the Chosen." When the Wise Woman
approached, Yim stopped hopping from stone to stone.
"Da says I'm to live with you. For how long?"

"A while," replied the Wise Woman.

"Will you be my mother?"

"Nay. You need no mother."

*That was a strange reply and strange that I should recall
it after so many winters*, thought Yim. She had always
deemed the Wise Woman cold, but lately she had been re-
thinking that judgment. *How much did she know?* Yim
didn't believe in fate, for fate implied a lack of choice. Nevertheless, she believed that the goddess prepared paths that
one might follow by choosing wisely. Yim wondered if she
had done so, and concluded that if she had, she owed a
debt to the one who had prepared her. Having nurtured a
child, Yim realized the Wise Woman's job couldn't have
been an easy one. *Readying a girl to bed Lord Bahl. It must
have been a heartbreaking task.* For the first time, Yim felt
sympathy for her guardian.

Then Yim wondered if she still retained any of the skills
she had acquired under the Wise Woman's tutelage. She
had lost her ability to learn the sex of an unborn child. She
hadn't tried to raise a spirit since she had called forth
Count Yaun's victims, and she doubted that she still could.
Such skills are gifts from Karm, Yim thought, *and I've been
fouled by the Devourer.* Her new chill served as a reminder
of that fact.

Yim ended the day's trek uncertain if she was any closer
to leaving the fens. She tried not to think of her ultimate
goal for fear that she would lose heart. One step at a time
was her plan, and she was sticking to it. As darkness fell,
Yim searched for a dry place to spend the night. In the fens,

"dry" was a relative term, and she settled for a place that was merely damp as opposed to one where water welled up wherever she stepped. Having selected a spot, she cut down armfuls of reeds. Those she used to make a sleeping pad by piling the stalks in layers, with each layer running at a right angle to the one below. It was an old fensfolk trick for staying dry, and it often worked.

After the pad was assembled, she ate her evemeal; two strips of smoked goat, a crumbling piece of young cheese, and a raw faerie arrow root, all washed down with bog water. It was too dark for Yim to see the mold that was spreading over her rations, but she could taste it. After Yim ate, she lay back to watch the sky.

The stars reminded her of the night when she walked upon the silver trail to find Honus. The memory of it had grown so vivid that Yim was convinced that she was recalling a real—if inexplicable—event. When she relived brushing her hand against Honus's face, she not only felt warmth but also the scratch of stubble. Each time she recalled the gesture, she relished the moment. It helped sustain her.

Thoughts of Froan sustained her also. She saw the evil within him as a separate entity. She loathed and feared it, but not her son. *His hard words and the blade on my throat weren't his doing. Not truly.* Yim turned her thoughts from their last encounter to happier times. They had been abundant enough, and remembering them was pacifying. When Yim grew drowsy, her remembrances turned fanciful and Honus entered them. As she drifted off to sleep, she watched Froan and Honus work side by side. They were planting grapevines on a hillside. In her near-dream state, the pair seemed like father and son.

The morning of Yim's sixth day of wandering in the fens began like the previous ones. The sky lightened. She rose, damp and chilled, to eat a meager dawnmeal. The mold spreading over her rations was evident in daylight, but there was nothing she could do about it except eat larger portions and consume all her food before it spoiled. With that in mind, she rubbed the gray-green fuzz off another strip of meat and ate it. Afterward, she shouldered the pack and rose to continue her trek.

Froan ate his dawnmeal later and in far more comfortable surroundings. The fare was both tastier and more substantial than Yim's, for there were ample leftovers from the feast. He dined in his cabin with Moli. Rest and a change of fortunes had improved her spirits, but her injuries obviously troubled her. It upset Froan to see her in pain. "We'll weigh anchor this morning," he said. "I hope to find you a healwife soon."

"Is there no healer among yer men?"

"Yes, but he knows only rough soldier cures, nothing fine enough for a lady."

Moli giggled. "A lady? Me?"

"Yes," said Froan. "For that's what you'll be."

"Ah'm but a peasant lass, caught by pirates and made their whore. Ah know nothin' 'bout bein' a lady."

"And I know nothing about being a lord, so we'll learn together." Then he leaned across the tiny table to kiss Moli. Afterward, he rose. "I've business ashore."

A short while later, Froan returned to the pirates' former hideout with a squad of soldiers. Captain Wuulf advised arriving with the bodies of pirates dangling from the war boat's masts to enhance the surprise attack on Midgeport. It would make them seem to be returning from their mission while drawing out the citizenry to gawk. Froan liked the idea, but mindful of Moli's sensibilities, he planned to display only the corpses of her molesters. To select them, Froan had to view the aftermath of the slaughter he had ordered.

Froan thought that he was steeled for the sight, but the first body he encountered was that of the crewman kidnapped from the cattle boat. His eyes were still open, and they seemed staring in horror at a woman dressed in peasant clothes. She appeared to have died seeking the comfort of his arms. Froan looked away, only to spy a toddler lying facedown in bloody water. *Such is the source of my power,* he thought. For a moment, he longed to turn from the path he was following. He wondered if it might still be possible. Then his thoughts turned cold. ***Better to prey than be preyed upon.*** Froan realized that he didn't wish to abandon safety and comfort any more than to reveal to Moli all he'd done to obtain them.

TWENTY·NINE

YIM WANDERED two more days before she began to encounter sporadic clumps of trees that sprouted from small patches of dry ground within the bog. That evening, she spent the night on one such patch. Able to light a fire, she singed the mold off her remaining strips of meat. The cheese had become inedible, and the roots were gone, so Yim augmented her rations with legs from frogs that she caught and roasted.

The following day, Yim came across further signs that she was nearing the edge of the fens. The ground was firmer, and the firm stretches extended for ever greater distances. The reeds didn't grow as high, allowing her to see into the distance. Nonetheless, treacherous ground still prevented her from traveling a direct route. It wasn't until late in the afternoon that reeds gave way to grass and the ground became solid. Then, tired as she was, Yim ran for joy awhile before falling to the earth, gasping for breath and laughing at the same time. The Grey Fens were behind her.

Yim eventually rose and resumed walking. It felt strange to travel in a straight line, and she found herself testing her footing with each step. It had become second nature to suspect the ground beneath her feet, and even knowledge that it was solid couldn't overcome the long habit.

If the footing was secure beyond the fens, it was the sole security Yim had. The bog's treacherous ground had made it safe in other ways. While Yim no longer had to worry that her next step might plunge through seemingly dry turf, neither did soldiers, bandits, or slavers. It had been a long time since Yim had felt vulnerable and endangered when traveling alone, but those feelings returned to her. *The world hasn't changed in my absence.* She lacked protection in a place where lone women often faced enslavement or worse.

Yim tried to recall her journey north to the Grey Fens, but it was hazy to her, for she had been feverish most of the time. She remembered that Honus had called the territory south of the Grey Fens the Empty Lands, although he said that some folk still dwelt there. Yim suspected that she had encountered no one on her trip north because Neeg had avoided settlements. On her current journey to Bahland, that wouldn't be an option. Yim was nearly out of food. Moreover, she would need news and directions. The risks seemed both substantial and unavoidable.

Before I worry over approaching strangers, I'll have to find some first, thought Yim. It didn't seem that would happen soon. The land beyond the fens appeared fittingly named. It was a flat and desolate expanse of grass that extended to the horizon without any sign of human habitation. The monotony of the view was broken only by occasional clumps of trees. Using the sun to determine the southward route, Yim headed in that direction.

The sun was low in the sky when Yim felt the first chill. Unlike before, there was but a moment before she felt the second one. More followed in such rapid succession that they blended together into a wave of cold that was spiritual as well as physical. Yim knew that people were dying somewhere in a manner the fed the darkness within her. The air seemed alive with screams that Yim felt but didn't hear. Something foul was relishing each one. Yim was certain that her son was orchestrating another slaughter and each death strengthened the thing that was poisoning him.

It was poisoning her also. Yim felt polluted and sick at heart. It was especially disturbing to be defenseless against the invisible assault. The massacre that fueled it was likely far away, though she had no means of telling. All she could do was endure its effects, knowing they would linger. Discouraged by the prospect, Yim headed for a tiny grove of trees where she could rest and find wood for a fire.

By dusk it was over. Midgeport had been overwhelmed. Captain Wuulf strode its blood-spattered streets to ensure the looting was done efficiently. After the preceding chaos, he took comfort from the rationality of theft. The attack had been anything but rational. In his entire career as a mercenary, Wuulf had never seen its like.

Thinking back, Wuulf realized that it had begun belowdecks after Shadow ordered the oarsmen unchained. They were a rough bunch sentenced to hard labor more to save the cost of wages than to serve justice. Most were petty criminals and troublemakers. Some were just unlucky. All bore a grudge. Wuulf had been concerned that they would turn on Shadow at the first opportunity, but he needn't have worried. The men had been in Shadow's palm from the instant he spoke to them.

Wuulf recalled only vaguely what Shadow had said. It hadn't been a memorable speech. Wuulf had heard other commanders say similar things in equally bloodthirsty tones.

The folk of Midgeport had been portrayed as an enemy unworthy of mercy. "Seek your revenge!" Shadow had shouted. "Don't hold back!" The words had been trite, but their effects had been extraordinary.

Never had the officer witnessed such a transformation. It had been so extreme that he was certain that its cause was otherworldly. Shadow had paced belowdecks, gazing at the newly freed oarsmen while the atmosphere became heavy with rage. It had been palpable, with an oily feel and a faint but acrid scent. Whatever force Shadow had employed hadn't been directed at Wuulf, and yet he had become angry and eager to fight. The effect had been far more pronounced on the oarsmen. Wuulf had watched them shed their humanity as if it were merely a mask. Faces contorted with rage. Eyes glared, bereft of sanity. Although the captain was a seasoned veteran, he had felt chilled whenever an oarsman looked his way.

Nevertheless, the impending violence had been firmly under Shadow's control. The oarsmen had likened to an arrow in a bow that was fully drawn—ready at any moment to speed forth in deadly flight. Shadow had been the finger on the bowstring, rendering the men powerless until he loosed them.

The war boat had sailed into port, its grisly trophies dangling from the masts. Lines had been thrown to secure the vessel as twin gangplanks were extended. A crowd had gathered to gawk at the dead, while belowdecks the pirates' looted arms were given to the oarsmen. Those men who didn't receive a weapon fashioned oars into clubs. Afterward, Shadow had climbed on deck as the oarsmen boiled from the hold and poured down the gangplanks. When the crowd drew back a little, Shadow had shouted "Now!" The arrow had been loosed.

What followed had shocked Captain Wuulf, hardened as he was. Soldiers were trained to kill, but they also strove to live. The oarsmen had seemed solely interested in death.

In their single-mindedness, they had slain without bothering to defend themselves and often died needlessly. Moreover, everyone had been a target—children and women, as well as men. From beginning to end, it had been mindless butchery. Once the docks had been expunged of life, the oarsmen poured into the town, slaughtering indiscriminately. Wuulf had ordered his soldiers to follow and gather up the survivors as prisoners. After what the townsfolk had experienced, those still living had regarded the soldiers as saviors.

When the oarsmen had doubled back, the prisoners were huddled in a courtyard near the docks. By then, Shadow had left the war boat and subdued the returning men as easily as he had inflamed them. Wuulf had been certain that they would have killed the prisoners otherwise. The oarsmen had fought savagely, but they were careless and unskilled, and only a third of their number had survived. Even after Shadow had calmed them, they possessed the vacant gaze of madmen. Covered with gore and heedless of their wounds, they muddled about aimlessly. Wuulf wanted no part of them.

Captain Wuulf knew Midgeport well, so he had sent a squad to commandeer its finest residence for Shadow. It was the home of a sheep broker. When his commander and his lady were ready to enter the town, Wuulf had ordered soldiers to escort them to their new quarters. Afterward, the captain had taken charge of the looting. As the plunder was gathered, Wuulf had made sure that the choicest items were sent to Shadow.

With darkness falling, Captain Wuulf called a halt to the looting for the night. The pickings had been good for the Empty Lands, but that wasn't saying much. Once the town had boasted a canal that linked the Turgen with the Midge River. Merchants had gladly paid a stiff toll to bypass the Turgen's treacherous delta, but that was long ago. Within living memory, the canal was a useless ditch filled with muck and cattails. The recurring invasions that had ruined the canal had also reduced Midgeport to little more than a village. The town's breached walls stood unrepaired, three-quarters of its dwellings were roofless and empty, and its wealthiest citizen traded in sheep.

As most of his soldiers headed for empty taverns to celebrate, Captain Wuulf strode to the sheep broker's former home to report to his commander. A pair of soldiers flanked the entrance to a dwelling that once had been grand, but currently stood half collapsed. The livable section had been crudely walled off from the crumbling portion. The work reminded Wuulf of an ineptly cauterized wound. He was glad that he had posted a guard; though unnecessary, it provided a touch of status to the decrepit pile.

Wuulf passed the guards and entered the house. Its former entrance foyer had been remade into a "great hall," though there was little greatness to it. Wuulf's late captain had negotiated the company's contract in that very room less than a moon ago. Wuulf, having been present, noted a few changes. Foremost was a large bloodstain on the wooden floor, though no bodies were evident. A table was piled with food and drink, a collection of purses, some gaudy crockery, assorted clothing, and a stack of women's footwear. Shadow's lady was seated near the ornate but crumbling fireplace. Dressed in a rose-colored gown, she was trying on shoes.

Shadow had also donned looted clothes. He was outfitted entirely in black, from vest to boots. The way he was grinning informed Wuulf that his commander was far more impressed by Midgeport than he was. That insight altered Wuulf's greeting. He smiled and bowed low. "Greetings, sire. Mayhap 'tis time to name ye Lord Shadow."

"Well, this town's a lordly prize. That's for certain."

" 'Tis a fair start, sire, but one that'll pale later on. I'll say this, though: Ye won't see its like again until we're past the Western Reach. So 'tis a fitting start for yer campaign."

"Advise me, Captain. What should I do next?"

"Let the men celebrate yer victory for a day, then order them to prepare to move out. They'll need to assemble wagons and teams and also gather a flock to feed us on the march. Sire, can ye ride a horse?"

"I've never even seen a horse."

"I'll fix that tomorrow and tutor ye in horsemanship." Wuulf hesitated a moment, loath to make his next recommendation, though he saw no way around it. "Sire, we lost most of the oarsmen. So 'twould be helpful if ye worked yer will on some of the townsmen."

Shadow smiled. "Nothing would be easier. My power's grown."

Wuulf sensed it was no idle boast. He could feel Shadow's power by the way he cooled the room despite a fire blazing in the hearth. The chill seemed further proof of his otherworldly might. That power made Wuulf uneasy, though he appreciated its usefulness. None of his soldiers had died while capturing the town, and only two had received minor wounds. The oarsmen didn't count, and neither would the townsmen who were destined to replace them.

In many ways, Wuulf felt lucky to serve a commander who made victory so easy. He envisioned the eastward march as an avalanche that would gather force as it advanced. Shadow would create a marauding horde, while he would provide the disciplined troops. It would be a perfect combination. Yet, while Wuulf was pleased to serve Shadow, he preferred the companionship of men whose blood ran warm and whose eyes were only used for seeing. As soon as Shadow dismissed him, he sought their company.

After Captain Wuulf departed, Froan resumed gazing about the room in wonder. Knowing that his officer was worldlier, Froan had restrained his exuberance to seem sophisticated. Once he was alone again with Moli, it returned.

To his fensman's eyes everything was grand and magnificent. The paneled walls, the large fireplace built of carved stone, the parquet floor, and—most of all—the novelty of windows with glass panes were marvels to him. Froan saw none of the room's shabbiness or neglect. He had unwittingly lived a life of want; thus the sheep broker's house seemed a palace.

Froan had expected Moli to share his excitement, but she didn't. As she tried on yet another pair of shoes, her bruised face bore a subdued and troubled expression. He watched her as she rose and walked about the room, carefully avoiding the dark stain on the floor. "That pair seems to fit you well," he said.

"Aye, they do. But Ah ken feel another's footprints in them."

"Pah!"

"Ah ken, Shadow! These are a dead woman's shoes!"

"You don't know that."

"Mayhap, but 'tis likely! We passed so many slain! Oh Shadow, did they all have ta die?"

Froan saw tears welling in Moli's eyes. "Moli, I'm born to rule in a world that heeds only power. Sometimes I must be ruthless." He walked over to gently kiss her. "But never to you."

Moli began to tremble. "Oh, Shadow, the things Ah saw! Mams and their babes . . ."

"Hush, sweet gentle one," cooed Froan. "From now on, I'll make sure you're spared those sights."

THIRTY

YIM HAD spent an uneasy night, feeling chilled despite the mild air and a campfire, and the morning's sunshine brought little relief. Her discomfort was exacerbated by memories of the period immediately before the Devourer had settled in her womb. She recalled feeling cold all over. Even worse, she had been subject to violent urges that were difficult to stifle. Yim feared that she was approaching that state again. *Could I become as icy as Lord Bahl? As evil?* It was a terrifying idea.

Yim pondered her situation. She knew that the Devourer had entered her when she seduced Lord Bahl. It had passed to Froan upon his conception, but not entirely. A vestige lingered in her even after her son's birth. Furthermore, recent events indicated that the part of the Devourer remaining in her was linked somehow to the part within Froan. In essence, they were a single entity. *As it grows stronger in Froan, it also grows stronger in me.* Envisioning the connection between her and Froan led Yim to conceive of it as something separate from them both.

That concept gave rise to an intriguing question: *If the Devourer is separate from me, can I drive it out?* Yim stopped seeing the dark thing within her as a taint or an evil trait. Instead, she envisioned it as a kind of parasite. She knew herbs could drive out some parasites. Others could be cut away. Yim didn't believe that such techniques would work against a spirit. Nevertheless, she wasn't discouraged, for she had experience with spirits. In the past, she had called them forth by the force of her will; perhaps she could drive one back by the same means.

Yim sat on her heels, shut her eyes, and tried to recall the meditations for contacting a spirit that she had learned as a girl. They came to her with surprising ease. However, she wasn't trying to raise a ghost, so she didn't send her thoughts to the Dark Path. Instead, she turned them inward. For a while, nothing seemed to happen. Yim concentrated harder. Then the sensations of the world slowly faded until only the self remained. Yim felt blood course through her body, the tingle of thousands of nerves, the weight of her bones, and air flowing into and out of her lungs. Then those sensations faded like those of the world as Yim delved deeper into her being.

Yim saw herself as a vessel of light that was partially dimmed by something murky and alien. Using only her will, she pushed, and the alien entity retreated. As it fled, it condensed and grew slightly darker. She pushed again, and the darkness became more discrete. Yim found that pushing wasn't effortless, so she rested a moment before pushing harder. This time, the entity resisted and managed to slip away. Then it began to diffuse.

Opening her eyes, Yim found herself in the grove. Her feet felt warmer than the rest of her body, but they soon chilled. Regardless, she was excited to have physical confirmation that she hadn't merely imagined the struggle. After a brief rest, she made another attempt, passing through the preliminaries a bit faster the second time. As soon as she perceived the darkness, she attacked and drove it back until it reached some sort of barrier. Though the barrier trapped and contained the dark, it also prevented Yim from expelling it.

The effort exhausted Yim. She ceased her struggle and opened her eyes. Her entire body, except for her left hand, felt warm. The hand was especially cold, as if she had plunged it into an icy pond. As a chill spread throughout

Yim's body, her left hand warmed until it was no warmer or cooler than any other part of her.

Yim pondered her latest experience. It seemed that the barrier she encountered had been her physical self. In the meditative state it was difficult to perceive the boundaries of her body, yet they were obviously there. Yim assumed that she had cornered the Devourer in her left hand. That was the barrier it couldn't breach. That seemed logical, for the spirit of a living person was confined to his or her body. Apparently, the Devourer within her was similarly constrained.

Then it occurred to Yim that there were exceptions to that rule. She knew one's spirit left the body during trancing. Furthermore, she had called forth spirits from the Dark Path. The exceptions perplexed her until she realized that the Dark Path figured in both. The realm of the dead paralleled the living world and permeated it. The spirit of a trancing person left his or her body to enter it. The spirits of the dead had no bodies, so they could briefly enter the living world. That provided a clue for how the Devourer could link her and Froan without leaving either body.

She knew that the Devourer remained a denizen of the Dark Path, although Gorm had used sorcery to bring a portion of it into the living world. In her mind's eye, Yim envisioned a hand extended over a muddy puddle with two fingertips dipped beneath the water. Creatures in the murky puddle couldn't see the hand, so the fingers seemed unconnected. The boundary between the Sunless Realm and the living world acted in a similar way, although it was not so easily breached as the surface of a puddle. As of yet, the Devourer had been unable to plunge entirely through it.

Gorm had told Yim of his centuries-long effort to release the Devourer from the Dark Path. If he succeeded, a being formed from memories of slaughter would be loosed upon the living world. There, it would strive to create more such memories. Inevitably, it would consume everyone in a reign of horror too terrible to imagine. *Why can't Gorm see the consequences of his actions? How can he believe that he'll be spared?* Gorm's delusion gave Yim all the proof she needed of his utter madness.

Spurred by a heightened sense of urgency, Yim began another bout with her inner darkness. This time, she didn't bother to sit on her heels but remained standing to go through the meditations. The vigor of her assault allowed her to trap the darkness quickly. Then she opened her eyes. One hand felt icy. Yim peered at her sunlit palm and spied a dark spot there. It was small, nebulous, and blacker than the darkest shadow. Instinctively, she tried to fling it away as if it were a glob of excrement or something equally foul. The effort was futile. As the spot quickly faded into her hand, Yim conceded that it was bound to her.

Although Yim felt discouraged, her experiments led to some positive conclusions. First of all, she and the Devourer were separate, despite the intimacy of their association. Furthermore, she possessed some control over it. She believed that the same would be true for Froan. It gave her hope that he could fight the thing that afflicted him and avoid succumbing to it. *This is the message I must take to Froan*, she thought. *The goodness in him can triumph!*

Desperate for any scrap of hope, Yim didn't try to figure how that triumph might be achieved. For the moment, its mere possibility was enough to sustain her. She had a long journey ahead and ample time to delve into that problem. Moreover, Yim felt it was likely that her instincts would guide her in the end. Meanwhile, she could prepare for that future confrontation by occasionally sparring with her shadowy inner foe.

Yim's struggles left her hungry, and she searched the grove for anything edible. All she found were a few woody mushrooms growing on a tree trunk and several large grasshoppers. After she plucked the wings and barbed legs from the latter, she gobbled them down with the mushrooms. The insects' chitinous shells stuck between her teeth, but they were quite satisfactory otherwise. Yim smiled to herself as she imagined how Honus would have reacted to her meal. *He was always squeamish when it came to food.*

Having eaten, Yim began to walk south, keeping an eye out for grasshoppers as she did. She hiked all day, except for brief pauses to rest. Along the way, she found streams to drink from and refill her water skin. She also encountered the tumbled stones of former dwellings. Usually they were fire blackened. In the late afternoon, she stumbled across the ruins of an entire village. It, also, seemed to have been razed by fire.

When the sun neared the horizon, she found the shell of a hut. Since it would provide shelter from the wind, she decided to spend the night there. The partial stone walls were the only evidence that people had ever occupied the spot. The roofless interior of the hut looked no different from the surrounding grassland, and it didn't contain a single scrap of metal, shard of pottery, or anything else made by human hands. Yim couldn't tell if time or looters had scoured the structure. Either way, its air of desolation was the same. There was no wood for a fire, so Yim simply leaned against a wall, opened her small bundle of wingless and legless insects, and ate her crunchy evemeal.

The next several days were much the same. Yim continued walking south through a landscape empty of people. She continued her bouts with her inner foe. Sometimes, it seemed to her that her chill had lessened. Other times, she thought that she merely had grown accustomed to it. Having finished the last of the smoked goat, Yim subsisted on whatever she could forage, which was insects and a few wild plants.

The weather turned sharply colder on the fourth day of travel, giving Yim a foretaste of autumn. She donned her cloak, but kept her thin-soled goatskin boots in her pack.

The sudden cold made insects scarce, and that scarcity persisted even after the weather turned mild again. By then, Yim's empty belly ached from hunger.

The land had become hilly, and Yim saw the territory ahead only when she crested a hilltop. She was heading up a slope when she heard a sound that stopped her short—the bleating of a goat. Following her ears, Yim discovered a solitary doe in a nearby hollow. The doe's udder was swollen with milk, indicating she was probably someone's dairy goat. Yim glanced about but saw no sign of a herder or human presence of any kind. *Perhaps she's a stray*, thought Yim.

Mindful that goats were often wary of strangers, Yim approached the animal calmly and gradually, all the while speaking in a gentle, cooing voice. With every step, Yim's stomach pangs grew more intense as she thought of the doe's rich milk. When Yim reached the doe, she gently stroked the animal's back. While approaching a strange doe was difficult, Yim knew that milking one was virtually impossible. Goats liked a fixed routine with the same person milking them. Moreover, a milking stand and treats were considered essential. With the odds so stacked against success, only desperation caused Yim to bother trying.

While continuing to stroke the doe and talk to her, Yim knelt down by the doe's rear flank and pressed her head against it. Then Yim gently grasped a teat. The doe started, then calmed. Yim always had a way with animals, and she was especially experienced with goats. Nonetheless, she was astonished when the doe submitted to being milked. Yim kneaded a teat with her right hand to spurt warm milk into the cupped palm of her left, which she then pressed to her lips to slurp down its contents. Each small taste was exquisite, providing not only the nourishment Yim craved but also evoking memories of her life at Far Hite.

It was an extremely slow way to milk a goat, and one that required Yim's total concentration. Her focus was further increased by her near-starving state. Thus the first time Yim was aware of the man's approach was when he shouted, "Thief!" She turned in the direction of the shout as the goat scampered off. A man in peasant garb was striding toward her. Already, he was only a few paces away. Before Yim could rise, he closed the distance to within striking range of his staff. It was a stout piece of wood, and he held it ready to deliver a blow.

THIRTY·ONE

DESPITE HER fear, Yim was too exhausted to run. Furthermore, she thought it would be futile. The man was ready to strike, and any attempt at flight was likely to provoke him. Hoping to avoid serious injury, Yim sought to protect her head by covering it with her arms and hands. Then she bent down, curled into a ball, and tensed for a beating. No blows fell. "Ah called ye thief," said the man. "What do ye say ta that?"

Yim peeked up. The man was watching her intently, his large, gnarled hands still holding his staff high. "I was starving, so I took the milk out of need," she said. "I'll repay you for it."

"How? Have ye any coin?"

"No, but I'll work off my debt."

"Pah! Ye're like ta eat more than yer labor's worth."

Yim continued to observe the man, who looked old but hardy. His grizzled face was sun-darkened and lined, a match for the gray hair that fell in tangles from the edge of his bald pate. Gazing into his dark eyes, she perceived that the raised staff was only a bluff. "I've experience with goats," Yim said. "I kept a herd."

"Where?"

"The Grey Fens."

"Ye've journeyed far," said the man. "Why?"

"To find my son. He ran off."

"He wouldn't have come this way. No one does." The man lowered his staff as he squinted at Yim. "Someone's cut yer throat," he said. "Not long ago, by tha looks o' it."

"It was an accident."

"Pah!" The man continued to scrutinize Yim. "Ah think yer son did it."

"No."

"Yer face tells a different tale." The man shook his head in sympathy, as if he understood far more than he said. "Ye're too tired ta hide tha truth, so tell me if Ah was seein' right: Were ye really milkin' that doe?"

"Yes." Yim held out her left hand, which was sticky with goat milk. "Take a sniff, and you'll know I speak true."

The man grasped Yim's extended hand and smelled her palm. "Aye, it smells o' milk, but Ah still don't know how. Only mah wife ken milk that doe."

"I understand goats," Yim said. "I herded them for seventeen winters."

The man gazed hard at Yim as if he was trying to come to a decision. "What have ye et o' late?" he asked at last. "Other than my goat's milk."

"Roots and seeds. A few grasshoppers."

"We eat plain fare, but 'tis better than that. Ye said ye're willin' ta work. Did ye mean it?"

"Yes."

The man pulled a short length of rope from a pocket and handed it to Yim. "Then ye ken fetch tha doe ye milked."

Yim took the rope, then looked about. The doe was still in sight, grazing at the far side of the hollow. "Does she have a name?" Yim asked.

"Aye. Muka, and she's a contrary beast."

"Muka," called Yim in the same calming tone she had used before. "Muka, come with me." She walked slowly toward the goat, talking all the while. Muka continued grazing, and when Yim reached her, she didn't resist the rope being tied about her neck. "Good girl, Muka! Now come. You're going home."

Yim led Muka back to the waiting man, who stood watching in amazement. "Ye saved me half o' day o' trampin', and earned yerself a meal," he said. "Ah'm Hewt and mah wife is Witha."

Still somewhat wary, Yim thought a moment before she replied. "I'm Mirien," she said.

"Well, Mirien, ye look wore out. Ye sure yer boy's worth such trouble?"

Hewt took the rope from Yim and then guided her and his goat to his hut. It proved to be a long hike. He crested the hill, descended into the narrow valley beyond, which he crossed to climb the ridge on its far side. The ridge overlooked another valley that was wider than the previous one. Directly below lay Hewt's hut, nestled in a fold at the ridge's base. Yim's guide was silent during their walk, allowing Yim to ponder the unexpected turn of events. She felt apprehensive, and as she followed Hewt, she wondered if she would regret her offer to work for him.

Hewt's hut was a low building made of sod with brambles planted upon its roof, probably to discourage goats from grazing on it. Yim was surprised to see that a ring of half-buried cobblestones surrounded the hut, marking it as a Wise Woman's dwelling. Its facade featured a single door and several small square holes that served as windows. The door was open and a voice emerged from it. "Hewt, do Ah hear someone with ye?"

"Aye, 'tis a lass. She found Muka. Her name's Mirien."

Hewt's reply drew Witha outside. Her tangled white hair,

deeply lined face, and bent posture made her look older than her spouse and more infirm. Witha's blue eyes were filmed over, and she moved as one who was nearly blind.

"She's offered ta work fer a while," said Hewt.

"Why?"

" 'Cause she's wore out and hungry after lookin' fer her son. She has a way with goats and could help with tha milkin' and other chores."

" 'Twould be as when Rowena—"

"Nay, love," said Hewt quickly. "Mirien don't plan ta stay."

"Mayhap, but that ken change," answered Witha. "Come inside, Mirien."

As Hewt led the goat away, Witha went back into the hut. Yim followed her. The room was dark, for the thick turf walls prevented the windows from scattering much light. The dim interior smelled of herbs and woodsmoke, reminding Yim of her guardian's hut. The floor was hard-packed earth, but the walls were paneled with boards that bristled with wooden pegs. Dried herbs dangled from most of them.

"You're a Wise Woman," Yim said.

"Aye, but a blind one, so few have faith in mah skills." Witha gestured to a small table with benches on either side. "Please sit."

As Yim sat on a bench, Witha went into a side room and returned with a hunk of bread, a small earthenware bowl of yogurt, and a wooden spoon. Next she brought out a cup of goat milk. After placing these before Yim, Witha sat down on the opposite bench and let her guest eat undisturbed. She spoke only after the bread, milk, and yogurt were gone. "Ken Ah touch yer face? Mah fingers are like eyes ta me."

"Of course," said Yim, guiding the old woman's hand to her cheek.

Witha's fingers softly brushed over Yim's features. "Yer young."

"Not so young. I've thirty-six winters."

"Ye feel younger." Witha's fingertips rounded Yim's chin and traveled down her neck until they touched her scar. Then the old woman's expression became agitated, and after she traced the raised mark left by Yim's wound, she burst out sobbing.

"What's the matter?" asked Yim.

"They cut her throat, too. Our daughter . . . our Rowena."

"I'm sorry to remind you of your grief. Perhaps I should g—"

Witha gripped Yim's wrist. "Nay, nay. Don't leave. Stay as long as ye wish." Yim's host lowered her voice to a whisper. "Ah knew ye'd come."

"How could you know that?"

"After Karm took mah sight, she spoke ta me." Witha fixed her milky eyes on Yim as though they could still see clearly. "Don't feed tha dark. 'Tis stronger than ye think."

"I . . . I don't know what you're talking about."

"Neither do Ah, Mirien. But that's what tha goddess said."

"Then I guess I should be mindful at night," said Yim, trying hard to keep her voice calm. "Did Karm have any other advice?"

"Nay, dear, but Ah have some o' mah own. Ye need ta rest and build yer strength. Ah don't know fer what, but Ah ken feel weariness in yer face and hear it in yer voice."

Yim ended up taking Witha's advice. She did so warily at first, not because she distrusted the couple, but because she had ceased to believe in the possibility of good fortune. Nevertheless, after a lonely and arduous journey, she had a roof over her head, sufficient food, a dry and warm place to sleep, and the company of two kindly people. Having assumed a slain girl's name, Yim found herself assuming a slain daughter's role. She performed Rowena's chores, slept in her bed, and at Witha's insistence, inherited Rowena's clothes.

Yim's new clothing was less outlandish than her goatskin outfit, which was why she accepted the gift. It was peasant garb, plain and durable, consisting of a sleeveless linen shift that was worn under a woolen skirt and blouse. The rust-colored skirt reached midcalf and had a pouchlike pocket in the front. The blouse was collarless, with baggy sleeves that ended high above Yim's wrists. It was gray and laced up in the front. She also received a hooded cloak and a pair of sturdy boots that were only slightly larger than her feet.

Yim repaid Hewt and Witha's generosity by working hard. She milked goats, made cheese, watched the herd, gathered herbs, and generally made herself useful. Yim found the routine comforting. Although she felt that she should resume her journey, each day she found a reason to postpone leaving. In truth, the longer she stayed, the more she wanted to linger. When Yim considered why, she realized that she was experiencing the family life she had always yearned for as a child. It was a pleasant fiction for all of them: Witha and Hewt were the parents Yim never had, while she was the daughter they had lost.

The hut's isolation enhanced the illusion, for no visitors came to question it. Though others dwelt in the valley, raising goats required folk to live scattered apart. Yim never met her neighbors and the tiny village at the valley's western end seemed remote. She never thought of visiting it, for there was too much to do. Fall was coming. Fodder needed to be gathered and stored. Excess animals had to be slaughtered and their meat preserved. Yim saw how those tasks would go easier with her to help. Being needed felt good, and she stopped thinking about leaving "tomorrow" and began to think about leaving "soon."

As Yim settled into her new routine, the sudden chills that marked violent deaths began to afflict her again. It wasn't like the last time: the icy pangs were fewer in number, and although they tended to occur in clusters, they were spread out. As before, Yim had no sense of where the deaths were occurring. Nonetheless, each chill reminded her that whatever hardship and dangers she encountered on the road would pale next to the horrors of the Iron Palace. Each icy stab evoked them and made Yim's peaceful interlude seem precious.

THIRTY-TWO

YIM HAD been with Hewt and Witha for over half a moon when autumn weather arrived. The nights turned crisp and their chill lingered late into the mornings. Aware that there might be a frost any day, Yim decided to renew Witha's supply of healing plants while she could. After the morning milking was over, she took a collecting basket along with her herder's staff as she led the goats up the ridge to forage. The trail was rocky, so she wore her "new" boots, which fit well enough after she stuffed some dry grass into the toes.

Around noon, Yim and the herd reached a southern-facing hollow near the ridgeline. As the goats happily grazed on wild carrots, asters, and thistles, Yim found a stand of va-lerian. The plant's roots were good for treating headaches, cramps, and insomnia. She had dug up several plants when she felt the first chill that marked the moment of someone's violent death. It seemed stronger than those she had experi-enced before, but like them, it felt like a sliver of ice stabbing deep into her chest. There was cold and a hint of pain, then the "ice" seemed to melt away to leave a more general chill. After a moment passed, Yim felt a second chill. Then life re-turned to normal.

In the days since the icy pangs returned, Yim had perceived patterns in them and devised scenarios to explain
their causes. She envisioned a group of men, or perhaps a
small army, marching through a thinly populated land. It
slew whomever it encountered. A single pang represented a
solitary traveler or someone living alone. Two pangs in
quick succession meant a man and wife surprised in their
home. If more pangs followed soon afterward, the couple
had children. A slaughtered village felt like a hailstorm.
Fortunately, she had endured only three of those.

It was a dismal fact that, while Yim's chills were sporadic,
they happened frequently enough to become routine. Usually she paid little attention to them. When Yim experienced
her latest bout, she paused in her digging for only a moment. Then she sighed and resumed her work; there was
nothing else to do. Throughout the afternoon, Yim continued to search for herbs and feel momentary chills. For a
short while, they came in such rapid succession that she
was forced to pause her work until the pangs spaced out
again. By late afternoon, her basket was filled with herbs,
and she began to drive the goats toward the hut. Only after
Yim exited the hollow did she notice the smoke. Peering
from her high vantage point, she saw that the western end
of the valley was hazy with it, and there were separate
plumes rising from within the valley as well.

Yim paused, puzzled by what she saw. Then she felt more
chills as another plume of smoke appeared. It rose from a
spot on the other side of the valley not too distant from
Hewt and Witha's hut. Starting as a thin gray line, it quickly
thickened into black billows that stained the sky. Yim was
close enough to see the flames that created the smudge. Then
with sudden and horrible clarity, she understood both the
cause of her chills and the smoke. *Men are moving up the
valley, slaying folks and burning their homes!*

Yim forgot the goats. She tossed aside the basket of
herbs, and taking only her staff, dashed down the steep

trail. Her sole thought was of Hewt and Witha and the destruction advancing their way. As Yim ran, hope and terror alternately spurred her onward. Whether gripped by one or the other, she put every bit of her will and energy into reaching the hut. Whenever she fell, she immediately rose and sprinted off, mindless of her hurts. By the time Yim reached the hut, she was breathing in ragged gasps.

She had arrived too late. Hewt lay in the yard. He was so mangled that Yim recognized him only by his blood-soaked clothes. She cried out and halted, paralyzed by grief and nausea. Then a gore-spattered man appeared in the doorway. When Yim spied the bloody sword in his hand, a new emotion purged her of all others. It was hatred. Sorrow, fear, and prudence vanished as the urge for vengeance became all-consuming. Yim surrendered to it. Without an instant of hesitation, she raised her staff and charged the man.

The man in the doorway wore tattered clothes that bore evidence of his deeds. Some of the bloodstains were old and dry, while others were still wet. His brutish face was a mask of rage from which soulless eyes gazed out. But when he beheld Yim, his expression underwent a transformation. To Yim, it seemed that her fury preceded her and withered the man. His face slackened even before her staff smashed into it. Yim felt a surge of jubilation as she heard the man's skull crack from the impact of her blow. As the man teetered, she struck him again. He crumpled, and Yim struck him as he fell. By then, his head likened to a battered leather bag sewn with hair and misshapen human features. Blood poured out of every opening—nostrils, mouth, eyes, and ears—and yet Yim continued to smash away. The man was dead, but in her fury, that wasn't sufficient. She wanted to reduce him to a pulp.

The only reason Yim stopped striking the corpse was that she spied movement within the hut. Grabbing the dead man's sword, she rushed into the dim room. Witha's body lay on the dirt floor, which was darkened by her blood. A huge man holding an ax towered over her. His expression was hard to read in the half light, but it seemed blank. His posture was certainly passive. He stood absolutely still, the ax dangling limply in his grasp. Those were only fleeting impressions to Yim, for she was focused on mayhem. Killing the first man had served only to heighten her rage, not quench it.

Closing the distance with a few bounds, Yim drove the sword into the man's belly, pushing with all her might until the point broke through the other side. Then the blade slid easily through the man's torso until its hilt guard pressed against his belly and hot blood gushed over Yim's hands. Exhilarated, she tugged the blade sideways to enlarge the wound. The man groaned and toppled, his fall wrenching the sword from Yim's grasp. He was still alive when she pulled it out to wildly hack at him. Yim had partly severed the man's arm before one of her blows bit deep into his neck and ended his life. Yim felt another ecstatic surge; then she continued hacking.

The sound of voices interrupted Yim. She darted over to the doorway and peered out. There were three armed men hurrying toward the hut. They were covered with blood, and one carried a woman's severed head by the hair. When they saw Yim, they charged. Yim responded with pure rage. Without a second thought, she rushed to meet her attackers. As Yim ran, she heard maniacal laughter that was as bloodthirsty as it was gleeful. It wasn't until she had nearly reached the men that Yim realized the laughter was hers. By then, the men had stopped running. If Yim had paused to think about it, she would have thought they had become strangely passive. But Yim wasn't interested in thinking, only killing. She hacked clumsily at the nearest man, taking several blows to bring him down. Energized by that slaying, she drove her blade deep into the second man's eye, killing him instantly.

Grinning, Yim turned to the man who carried the head.

Like the others, his expression was neither fearful nor angry, merely vacant. Yim swung her sword at his neck, but struck his shoulder. Wrenching out the blade, she swung again and this time struck her mark. The man sprayed blood, toppled to the ground, and died. Nonetheless, Yim continued hacking until she decapitated him. Then she kicked his head into the weeds and replaced it with that of his victim. In an exultant mood, Yim giggled at her gruesome humor, then looked around for someone else to slay.

Seeing no one, Yim felt disappointed. As consolation, she ran her tongue along her blade to savor her victims' blood. The blade felt hot against her icy tongue, making Yim aware of how cold she had become. Then with a shock, Yim realized that it was likely that Hewt and Witha's blood was also on the blade. Her dismay quelled her rage just enough for a memory of Witha to surface. It was from the day they met. Yim recalled the old Wise Woman sitting at the table and the intensity in her milky blue eyes. Yim also remembered what Witha had said: "*Don't feed tha dark. 'Tis stronger than ye think.*"

As soon as Yim had that recollection, rage flared up again. However, this time, she realized its source and struggled against it. It wasn't easy; by killing she had strengthened her inner foe. Yim's mind was in turmoil, but it possessed enough clarity to realize that to overcome her nemesis she had to replace hatred with compassion. Yim saw that she hadn't meted out justice or even wreaked vengeance. Instead, the enemy had helped her murder men it had inflamed. *That's why the men didn't defend themselves; the Devourer gripped them, and it wanted them to die.*

Despite understanding what she must do, Yim felt unable to accomplish it. She couldn't forgive the men who had killed Hewt and Witha. *Hatred is the Devourer's tool*, she told herself. Still, it smoldered in her. The men had brutally slain two good and gentle people. It felt natural to strike back. Moreover, it seemed proper. Nevertheless, it was also a trap. Yim saw her inability to cool her anger as a sign of her weakness and the Devourer's strength.

Complicating matters was Yim's current danger. She was certain that more men would arrive. If she faced them, she'd further strengthen the Devourer's hold on her. Fleeing seemed her only hope. Yim headed toward the hut to gather the necessities for a hurried departure. Even doing that required all her will, and though she tried, she felt unable to abandon her newfound sword. When Yim reached Hewt's body, she dragged it into the hut so he would lie beside Witha. Then she hastily gathered clothes, equipment, and provisions for her journey, all the while blinking tears from her eyes.

When Yim was ready to leave, she took the time to assemble a funeral pyre for Hewt and Witha out of anything inflammable that she could readily find. When it was completed, she dragged her two friends atop the makeshift pile and, uttering a prayer to Karm, lit it. As the flames began to spread, Yim hurried out of the hut. She was burdened with a full pack, three water skins, a hefty sack of grain, and a sword without a scabbard. Moreover, she was fatigued from her long run to the hut, the effort of making a pyre, and the exertion of killing five men. Nevertheless, she moved as rapidly as she could. Yim needed to head south, and that meant crossing the valley.

What Yim feared most was that she would run into more marauding men. That was one reason why she kept the sword. She suspected that there were other reasons as well, darker ones that she couldn't dwell upon in her current state. *That's a struggle for later*, she thought as she glanced about for signs of danger, *first I have to survive this day*.

Yim had ventured onto the valley floor while herding goats, but she had never gone as far as the other side. Generations of grazing had reduced the valley's interior to a meadow of waist-high plants with only a rare tree to break the line of slight. Yim felt dangerously conspicuous, and her apprehension grew the farther she traveled. When that feeling became too great, she dropped to the ground, afraid to continue. Sunset wasn't far off, and Yim weighed her options. The weeds would screen her from a distant viewer, but if someone walked nearby, she'd be seen. Thus she could lie low until dark and risk the enemy finding her, or she could continue fleeing and risk being spotted. Deciding which was riskier seemed a pointless exercise since she knew nothing about her foes—their numbers, position, purpose, or leader.

That's not true, Yim thought. *Their leader must be Froan.* It made perfect sense. Once before, she had encountered men like the five she had just killed. They had been members of Lord Bahl's peasant army. They, too, had seemed dehumanized and enraged. Only one man at a time possessed the power to create such an army, and it was apparent to Yim that the power had passed to her son. *Those men were Froan's creations.* It wasn't only logic that led to Yim's conclusion; it was a mother's certainty that her greatest fear had been realized. Her heart told her it was true, and that persuaded her as much as any evidence.

Yim recalled her terrifying journey to Froan's father and how she had passed through the violent mob under his sway. It had been a nightmare experience but not nearly as terrible as Lord Bahl himself. He had been the wellspring of his army's madness, its malevolent core. Yim assumed that Froan was nearby, driving men to rampage through the valley. *He might be in the burning village or even closer.*

It was ironic. Yim had been preparing for a long and arduous journey to find her son, and instead, he was about to find her. All she needed to do was stay put and rise from her hiding place to be escorted to him. Then Yim envisioned herself standing before her son, red-handed from butchering five men, to lecture him on restraint. With a sinking feeling that bordered on terror, she feared the task was beyond her.

Never had Karm seemed so distant or had the Devourer seemed so strong. *Can I overcome the evil inside me to turn Froan from his path?* Until that afternoon, Yim would have said yes. The frenzied slayings had made her uncertain of that answer and herself: It had felt good to slay those men. She had licked their blood and savored the taste. *This is the moment of my greatest weakness, a time when all I can argue is, "Heed my words, not my deeds."* That seemed an effort doomed to failure.

The long trip to Bahland had one appeal—it postponed the confrontation with Froan. Yim told herself that she wouldn't be running from it, but rather choosing a more fitting place and time. *One when I'll be better prepared.* As soon as she came up with that rationale, she embraced it with enthusiasm that smacked of desperation. It seemed to hint how difficult that confrontation would be and reveal her lack of confidence. Nevertheless, Yim resolved to head south.

That decision brought Yim back to her original dilemma; she had to evade the marauding men. After wavering over what to do, she chose to lie in the weeds and hope for the best. If no one found her, she would head south at nightfall. If men came upon her, she had a sword. Yim was resigned to use it, though she feared the consequences. Yim didn't believe in fate, so it seemed her life's course would be determined by chance. All she could do was wait and learn how it played out.

THIRTY·THREE

MOLI WAS in her wagon, surrounded by what pillaged luxuries the Empty Lands afforded. She lay upon a feather mattress that filled most of the wagon bed. It possessed sheets and coverlets and was piled with all sorts of pillows. The brass oil lamp from the war boat dangled above her. Gowns were strewn about and there was wine—lately, Moli had grown quite fond of it—in a large cask. She drank it from a silver goblet.

The oil lamp was not lit, for the sun's slanting light still filtered through the wagon's canvas covering. The sides of that covering could be rolled up to allow her to view the passing landscape. Currently, they were rolled down, and since they were fastened from the outside, Moli was unable to change that. The air was heavy with smoke, so she knew why the view outside was hidden. *Shadow's keepin' his promise ta me*, she thought, not without irony. In Midgeport, he had told her that she would be spared the sight of death. The sealed covering accomplished that.

While Moli couldn't see the continuing slaughter, she was nevertheless aware of it. The frequent smell of smoke was evidence, and she sometimes heard screams or weeping, which were always cut short. Additionally, there was the daily flow of goods that were always somewhat used. Shadow never spoke of what was done to acquire them, and he apparently forbade the soldiers to do so within her earshot. That didn't prevent Moli from sensing their cost in human suffering. In a way, Shadow's efforts to hide that suffering from her made it loom ever larger in her thoughts. She hoped imagination exaggerated the horrors she envisioned, but she had no way of telling. Thus guilt dampened the pleasure that came from having fine things.

The denseness of the smoke and the sharply winding route the wagon was taking made Moli suspect that she was in a village. All that was lacking was the sound of human voices. Even the soldiers had grown silent. The deathly stillness made Moli imagine atrocities. Horrendous thoughts plagued her until she realized that only the truth would vanquish them. Instead of imagining what lay outside, Moli resolved to actually glimpse it. The wagon's canvas covering obviously had been carefully crafted to prevent her from doing that. It was securely erected and equally well sealed without a single opening that could serve as a peephole. *Then Ah'll just have ta make one.*

Using the pin of a silver brooch, Moli picked at the threads in a seam in the wagon's covering. They were thick and tightly sewn, making the process slow and difficult, but at last she created a gap. It was only the length of her palm and so narrow as to allow only a sliver of a view. Wishing to keep her peephole secret, Moli decided not to enlarge it, so she set aside the brooch and put her eye to the tiny opening.

She saw nothing alarming. In fact, she saw very little, taking in just a thin slice of the world outside that changed slowly as the wagon made its way down a narrow street. For a while, all she glimpsed was a dirt lane and a wattle-and-daub wall. Then she saw a doorway and the smashed remnant of a door. The wagon traveled farther, and Moli glimpsed the bare feet of someone lying in the lane. Next she saw ankles, then calves. Then the folds of a peasant woman's skirt slowly passed before her eyes. The hump of a woman's behind came next. It was followed by nothing except blood and entrails; there was no torso.

Moli had seen nothing that terrible in Midgeport, and despite herself, she screamed as she scrambled away from the peephole. Then she heard the wagon driver's voice through the canvas walls. "M'lady, is something wrong?"

"Nay," said Moli, struggling to keep hysteria from her voice.

"Ye sound upset. Should I send for Lord Shadow?"

"Nay, nay, 'twas only a bad dream, and it has passed. Don't trouble my lord."

"As ye say, m'lady."

Moli crawled over to the wine cask to fill her goblet. Her hands were trembling as she gulped down the wine, causing her to spill it on her pretty blouse that still bore the scent of a strange woman. *What did they do ta her?* she wondered. Then Moli refilled her goblet in an effort to stop wondering.

After downing a third goblet, Moli fell into a stupor that ended when the driver entered the canvas enclosure to light the oil lamp. The wagon had stopped, and Moli caught a brief glimpse of campfires burning in the night. Her head ached. So did her heart. "We've stopped for the night, m'lady," said the driver. "Lord Shadow's with the captain, but he sent word that he'd be here shortly." The driver's eyes went to Moli's wine-stained blouse. "I'll leave ye now, for mayhap ye wish to change."

Moli took the driver's hint after he left, changing into a low-cut shift that was one of Shadow's favorites. Wearing it no longer embarrassed her since the bite marks on her breasts had faded. They were nearly invisible, but even when they had been prominent, they had never repelled Shadow. Neither had her bruised face or missing teeth. Moli felt that he was more enamored with her inside than her outside. He had always been tender to her, and Moli was certain his tenderness was genuine.

That made what she saw in the afternoon all the more disturbing, for it was proof of Shadow's other side. It was the side all the soldiers feared. The side that reaped the flow of plunder. Worst, it was the side that Shadow showed whenever he spoke about his future conquests. If a wagon-load of pretty clothes and soft bedding required the slaughter Moli had glimpsed, she shuddered to think what a palace would necessitate. Moli imagined a river of blood that would stain each beautiful thing and drown every joy.

It seemed to Moli that there were two realities—the one inside the wagon and the one without. Inside the wagon was safety and ease. Outside was brutality and death. That was so because there were two Shadows also—the one who visited the wagon and the one who devastated the country-side. Moli was beginning to wonder if the wagon would always remain safe, or whether someday Shadow would bring the outside world with him.

The clink of chain mail alerted Moli to Shadow's arrival. He always removed it before entering the wagon. While he did, Moli quickly filled two goblets with wine. She did so to hide her earlier drinking, not that Shadow would have scolded her for it. He never scolded her. Goblets filled, Moli rose to a kneeling position and raised them as Shadow lifted the flap to climb into the wagon. He bore a tray of food, for it was his custom to serve her himself.

Shadows eyes were cold, but warmed as soon as they re-garded Moli. His face softened also. "I've been thinking of wine," he said, "but mostly of you. Take a sip, dearest, and let me taste it sweetened by your lips."

Moli smiled. "Fer a fensman, ye sure talk fancy."

"You make me feel that way—fancy." Shadow set the tray down, then sat next to Moli on the mattress and re-moved his high black boots. Afterward, her turned to Moli and kissed her with icy lips. It was a long kiss, and when it was over, he sighed and flopped down on the mattress. "That was the perfect cure for a hard day."

"What made it hard?"

"Five of my men were killed. Brutally, too, by someone with a sick sense of humor."

"What happened?"

"I won't upset you with the details. It's troubling to know what some people are capable of doing."

Why does he talk as if I'm stupid? Moli wondered. She couldn't imagine that he believed she was unaware of events around her. She had witnessed the slaughter at Midgeport. She was traveling with marauders. *Then why does he pretend with me?* Upon reflection, it occurred to Moli that Shadow's pretense was more for his sake than hers, an attempt to keep the world outside the wagon. In her imagination, Moli envisioned the wagon as Shadow must see it at day's end. The oil lamp would make the canvas walls glow in the gathering dark. They would serve as his beacon as he stripped off his armor to join her in the light.

Then Moli saw that she was more than Shadow's woman. She was his means to cleanse himself through tenderness and love. He needed her to be human. The notion both roused her sympathy and increased the burden that she felt.

Yim was still hiding in the meadow when daylight fled the sky and the stars grew bright. The waning moon would rise late, and she intended to take full advantage of the darkness. A brisk pace and Rowena's cloak kept the night's deepening cold at bay, though it did nothing to warm Yim's internal chill. That coldness was proof of how her deeds had strengthened the Devourer, as was her lingering anger.

Yim reached the ridge at the valley's far side without incident. That didn't surprise her. The advancing army had no need to post sentries, for no enemies lay before it—only victims. She climbed the ridge, which wasn't especially steep or high. Unlike its slopes, its summit was devoid of trees, allowing her to peer down at the valley. She saw the enemy's—and her son's—encampment, which had been set up alarmingly close to where she had been hiding. It was marked mainly by campfires. From where she stood, Yim could see little but the flames, which seemed to wink in and out as someone passed in front of them. She did notice one light that was different from the others. It looked like a tent lit from within, except it didn't appear to be resting on the ground. Its soft yellow luminescence was dimmer than that of an exposed flame. For some reason, the sight calmed Yim, and her anger faded. Then she turned south to put as much distance between her and the camp as she was able.

Daven was unable to sleep, so he rose from his mat to toss some kindling upon the embers in the hearth for a bit of warmth and light. The flames illuminated Honus, who was sleeping soundly after a day of hard training. He was thin, but he no longer looked gaunt or haggard. *He's much improved*, Daven thought, *but is he ready?*

Even as Daven asked that question, he understood its futility. A malevolent force was loose in the world, and it cared nothing about readiness. Having received the gift to sense unseen events, Daven had spent the day buffeted by them. The weather had been calm, crisp, and sunny; yet it had felt otherwise to him. Growing foreboding had pushed Daven to the brink of utter despair. By late afternoon, his terror was agonizing, but then it diminished. By dusk, he had the conviction that a disaster had been averted, though he was unable to fathom what it was. All he knew was that its threat had been postponed, not eliminated. The end was inevitable. Daven was certain of that, although he was ignorant how it would unfold and whether its result would be benign or catastrophic.

Tomorrow, he would send Honus to play his part in that end, the runes were clear on that. They were unclear on nearly everything else. Daven didn't know what Honus's part would be or what it would achieve. The markings merely indicated that Honus should venture forth and that Daven would never see him again. The thought of that parting brought tears to his eyes, and since Honus couldn't see them, he let them flow freely.

*   *   *

When Honus rose at first light, Daven was already up. Honus bowed his head, "Good day, Master."

"You won't hunt or train this morn," said Daven. "Today will be devoted to more important things."

Honus bowed his head and waited to hear what those things would be.

"Your training's over. Not completed, but over all the same."

"Have I failed you in some way, Master?"

"No, Honus," replied Daven, his voice softened by affection. "All lives are leaves in a wind. When you arrived, Karm bestowed on me the gift to feel its gusts. Now it's blowing you away."

"To where, Master?"

"Today I'll study your runes to get some sense of it. When a master and Sarf part ways, it's permitted for the Sarf to learn some of what's needled on his back. Didn't Theodus tell you to never bear your own burden?"

"Yes, but he didn't know we were parting ways."

"I think he did. But one thing he didn't know: whose burden you must bear. I believe it's Yim's."

"But I bought her because of what he'd said!"

"The runes spell out an ancient tongue that's often ambiguous. Theodus's interpretation makes sense, but he didn't know what I know. He didn't know about Yim."

"Are you saying everything that happened is due to a mistake?"

"No," replied Daven. "Just because the runes are tattooed into flesh doesn't prevent their meaning from changing. Life and your choices alter their import. That's why a Bearer must study them over and over." Daven rose. "I have an errand this morning. Fast while I'm gone. Cleanse your body. Meditate to clear your mind. When I return, I'll perform your final reading."

THIRTY·FOUR

AFTER DAVEN departed, Honus left the ruined keep and descended the hill it crowned. Beyond the slope's eastern side flowed a clear brook filled with cobblestones. Upon reaching it, Honus hopped from stone to stone until he reached a huge block of cut granite that appeared to have once been part of the castle. It partly blocked the waterway, creating a pool. Honus shed his clothes and entered it. He gasped at the water's coldness, then ignored it as he bathed. Afterward, Honus sat naked upon the stone to dry and meditate.

Ignoring the water's iciness had been easy compared to subduing his tumultuous feelings. Daven's announcement had caught Honus by surprise, and he felt far from ready to be a Sarf again. Age and disuse had dulled his prowess. Moreover, he had come to understand how much that prowess had been the foundation of his confidence. Theodus would have chided him for placing so much faith in his body. "Flesh never endures," he had often said, usually in self-deprecation. Although Honus attempted to be stoic about his decline, having lost his edge, he realized how vital his physical skills had been.

Thus one emotion Honus sought to subdue was fear. He feared that he'd perish before finding Yim. Moreover, he was afraid that he'd fail her if he did. Honus wasn't alone in those concerns. Having regained his ability to gaze into eyes and see beneath appearances, he knew that Daven had the same fears. Honus also knew that his new master was loath to send him away.

It would be a difficult parting, but Honus was bolstered by the prospect of a reunion with Yim. So, besides purging himself of apprehension, he sought to push longing from his mind. This promised to be harder to expel than fear. Every time Honus approached a state of calmness, he envisioned himself embracing Yim. Then memories of her face and body, her touch, her voice, and even her smell would flood back, and he would be momentarily overwhelmed. The possibility that flesh and blood might soon replace memory wasn't conducive to meditation.

In addition to clearing his mind of fear and love, Honus had to face his uncertainty. His many winters of aimless wandering had left him disoriented. He had no idea where he was or where he should go. His sole hope was that Daven would provide a destination after studying the runes on his back, though Honus had little faith the inscriptions would be helpful. They had seldom guided Theodus, and they had never guided Yim. It was a Bearer's role to determine the path, and a Sarf's role to follow it. Once Honus departed, he would be masterless again. He felt ill equipped to be his own guide. His only recourse was to accept that he saw no path to his goal and to believe that it didn't matter. Both went against his nature; yet each was necessary.

Daunted by all he had to overcome, Honus was momentarily tempted to abandon meditation and trance instead. As soon as the impulse arose, he was chagrined by his weakness. Then obtaining calmness became even more imperative. Honus saw it as a test that he mustn't fail. To achieve the proper state of mind, Honus focused solely on the present, where both past and future were nonexistent. He sat perfectly still, perceiving the fullness of the world around him until it filled his mind, leaving no room for

anything else. It wasn't easy, and it took all of Honus's renewed self-discipline to accomplish.

It was late morning before Honus purged himself of fear,
longing, and uncertainty to achieve complete tranquillity.
By then, his goose-pimpled skin was perfectly dry. He
donned his clothes and headed for the keep. The masters
who had trained him in the temple used to say that a clear
mind was like a boy's untattooed back; it was where Karm
transcribed her will. If that was true, then Honus hoped the
goddess wanted him to find Yim.

When Honus arrived at Daven's humble abode within
the ruined castle, he found it empty. Accordingly, he removed his sandals, sat cross-legged on his mat, ignored his
empty stomach, and resumed his meditations. It was late
afternoon when Daven returned bearing a sack. "Honus,"
he said, "have you achieved calmness?"

Honus bowed his head, "Yes, Master."

Daven opened the sack. "Then garb yourself properly
before I read." He removed garments from the sack. They
were made from homespun wool and dyed a darkish shade
of blue that approximated the color worn by Karm's servants. The style of the clothes imitated those worn by Sarfs.
There were leggings, a pair of baggy pants that ended just
below the knee, a long-sleeved shirt, and a cloak, all without ornamentation.

Honus took the clothes. They were obviously of peasant
make, but they were new. It had been over seventeen winters
since he had walked abroad so garbed, and his hard-won
tranquillity diminished as he envisioned doing so again. Nevertheless, he smiled. "You seem to have been preparing this
surprise for a while."

"I have one more," said Daven. From beneath his sleeping mat, he produced a sword and scabbard. It had the
slightly curved blade and two-handed hilt of a Sarf's
weapon. He handed the sheathed sword to Honus, who immediately drew the blade to examine it.

"This isn't temple forged," said Honus. "Where did you get it?"

"A blacksmith dwells two villages over. He makes mostly plows and mattocks, but his knives are sharp."

Honus ran a finger over the sword blade's edge, noting that the steel lacked marbling. "It's certainly that." He slashed it about, and found the sword adequately balanced, but no more than that. He smiled again. "It seems this day was long foreseen."

"I knew it was coming," replied Daven. "But I didn't know when until yesterday. Are you pleased with the sword?"

"Your foresight pleases me. As the saying goes, a naked Sarf always dons his sword first."

"But the sword pleases you less."

"It's a skillful imitation. I doubt a man lives who can forge the traditional blade of my order."

Daven sighed, "The times require us to use what's at hand."

"That's surely true," said Honus. "I'm not much of a Sarf."

"I was thinking of myself. Your part was foreseen long ago. It's needled on your back, though I lack the skill to fully understand it. Put on your new leggings and pants. Don your sword but not your shirt. Then we'll sit in the sunshine, and I'll study what the Seer tattooed."

Soon Honus was sitting outside, feeling Daven's fingers trace the markings on his back. Daven studied the runes for a long while. Then he pondered them even longer. Honus remained motionless throughout. Finally he heard Daven's voice. "This is the clearest guidance I can give you, and I'm uncertain about a word in it. That word is 'tul.' It usually means 'tool,' but it can also mean 'weapon.' The runes say that when you find your proper tul, seek the leader who cannot wield it."

"Thank you, Master."

"Is that any help?"

"Not at the moment, but I'm told time oft reveals meaning."

"Yes, but I was hoping it would make sense to you now. The rest is less specific. I think Yim's seeking someone named Froan. Perhaps she's doing so as we speak; it's hard to tell. So, if you encounter someone by that name, I'd say that's a promising sign. That's all the runes reveal." Daven sighed. "You should leave tomorrow."

"Did you read that also?"

"No, but I feel it in my gut. Where will you go?"

"I'm unsure. Do you know where I am?"

"In the ancient domain of Prensturg, though I daresay none of its inhabitants recall the name. The last of its dukes fell in one of the Luvein wars. I reside in his castle. You're on Luvein's western border, about a half-moon's journey south of Lurwic."

"Then I suppose I'll head for the Western Reach. It's close and where I last saw Yim. At the time, she was planning to head north. So if she's seeking someone, she might pass that way." Honus shook his head. "It'll be like looking for a pea in a gravel pile."

Daven brushed his fingertips over Honus's bare back one last time, stopping at the marks that spelled "Yim." Her name appeared several times within the lengthy text, and was its final entry. "Have faith, Honus. Somehow you'll find her."

After the reading, Honus went hunting. That evening, he broke his fast with Daven, who roasted the pair of pheasants that Honus had bagged. The birds were a rare treat, and they lent a festive air to the meal. "This is a sign of Karm's grace," said Daven between mouthfuls. "I haven't even seen a pheasant all summer."

"Probably because you never looked," replied Honus.

"No, it's Karm's grace, and I should know. I'm a holy man."

"You said you were a hermit."

"Well, you spoiled that, didn't you? A hermit lives alone." Daven, who had been grinning, suddenly grew serious. "When you arrived, I learned the depths of Karm's compassion."

Honus, hoping to steer the conversation back to a lighter mood, asked, "So what's the difference between a hermit and a holy man? Your wardrobe hasn't improved."

"Respect," replied Daven.

"Is that how you got the blacksmith to make my sword?"

"Yes. And the peasant woman to sew and dye your clothes."

"I'm surprised Karm's still honored here."

"Superstition probably played as great a part as faith," said Daven. "Holiness makes people nervous. Besides, I've done some good since I've arrived. They remembered that, too."

"You saved my life as well," said Honus, surrendering to Daven's mood. "I'm grateful."

"You should thank Karm for that, not me," replied Daven. "I know you don't believe me. I see through your show of piety. If we had more time . . . but, well, we don't. I can only hope you'll reconcile with the goddess. She loves you, Honus. And her love will give you strength, but only if you accept it."

"I've submitted to your discipline."

"You did. In that, you were exemplary. Gatt was likewise, and yet he tried to kill Yim. A Sarf needs more than discipline and prowess. He must model the goddess in compassion."

"And what if Karm isn't compassionate?"

"She is, Honus. She is." Then Daven smiled again. "Take the word of a holy man."

* * *

At dawn, Honus rose and ate for the last time with Daven. Afterward, Honus embraced the former Bearer and began his journey. He bore a pack heavy with provisions and other necessities. The weight didn't bother him, but it felt wrong to bear his own burden, for Theodus had admonished him to never do so. Honus's late Bearer had read the same runes that Daven had; yet Daven had come up with contradictory advice. *And Daven claims the runes say I'll find Yim*, thought Honus. *Will they still say that tomorrow?*

When Honus had last been a Sarf, the divine will had always perplexed him. It still did. Despite what Daven had said, he couldn't see how an inscription on his back could mean one thing and then another. It made him doubt everything Daven had told him. As for "when you find your proper tul, seek the leader who cannot wield it," that was gibberish. *Spoken like a Bearer*, thought Honus, reflecting that the guidance of holy ones was often cryptic. *Perhaps it held some meaning for him, but I'm only a Sarf.* He adjusted the burden on his shoulders and continued to trudge westward.

THIRTY·FIVE

As Honus began his journey uncertain where it would take him, Yim resumed hers knowing her destination. It wasn't without irony that she trekked south, for she was convinced that Froan was behind her, not ahead. Though Yim lacked concrete proof that Froan led the men who had killed her friends, all her instincts told her it was so.

Nevertheless, she persisted in journeying toward the Iron Palace.

Ever since Yim fled the marauders, she kept reliving her horrific deeds. The memories of those killings had been worst during the first night, when their freshness and the dark enhanced their vividness. As time passed, the gruesome slayings seemed more like nightmares than things she had actually done. Yet the bloodstained sword she still carried contradicted that. It was proof that she had dreamed none of the horrors.

Yim knew that most people would say the five slayings were justified and commend her for them. They would also think that she was prudent to carry a sword when traveling alone. Yim agreed in part, and she felt unable to forsake the weapon. Nevertheless, she was convinced that violence ultimately served the Devourer and couldn't be used to defeat it.

I must find another tactic, Yim thought. All she could think of was to plead with Froan to resist the evil thing within him. She worried that approach would fail, but it seemed her best chance. *After all, I'm his mother. Besides, I'll have time to polish my arguments.* Yim knew she'd have that time because Froan's army seemed to be heading east, not toward Bahland. Nonetheless, she was certain that he'd arrive at the Iron Palace sooner or later. *By then, I should be ready to confront him.*

Yim intended to prepare for that confrontation by several means. First, she would stay clear of folk for as long as possible. The large sack of grain would allow her to survive on her own for many days. That way, with luck, she'd have no need to use violence to defend herself. Second, she intended to meditate frequently and grapple with her inner foe. She hoped that it would be a means to weaken its hold on her. Finally, Yim prayed that her encounter with Honus on the silver path—whether it had been a vision, a dream, or something else—was prophetic. *Honus said his*

runes foretold that we'd meet again and that he'd help me.
Although it smacked of wishful thinking, Yim clung to the
hope that his promise would be fulfilled. Even though she was
unable to imagine what help Honus could provide, she felt
she'd need it when she faced her son again.

Froan was also on Stregg's mind, though the black priest
thought of him as "the heir" or "Lord Bahl." His conviction that Lord Bahl's missing son was somewhere in the
Empty Lands hadn't faltered, although he had heard nothing to confirm his belief. That was hardly surprising, for
news spread slowly between the scattered settlements. No
traveler had passed through his village in over half a moon,
which was somewhat strange considering the season. Still,
it was deemed more a cause for talk than concern.

Therefore, when Stregg heard frantic knocking on his
door, he was unprepared to find a stranger standing before
him. The man was wild-eyed, disheveled, and surrounded
by a small flock of sheep. The animals that milled about
looked as if they had been driven hard. Then the stranger
spoke over their bleating. "Tha folk here say ye ken make
charms."

"I'm graced by the Devourer," replied Stregg, fingering
the iron pendant that hung from his neck. "Are ye a be-
liever?"

"Aye," replied the man.

Stregg could sense that the man was lying, not that he
cared. The priest also noted the stranger was terrified. That
pleased him, for fear would make the man more pliable.
"What type of charm do ye seek?"

"One that breaks a curse."

Stregg put on a concerned face. "A curse. So 'tis a serious matter. What manner of curse?"

"Ah'm haunted by tha dead."

"A perished loved one? Someone ye killed? Be specific."

" 'Twas none o' those," replied the distraught herdsman.

" 'Twas a whole town o' corpses. They were all rottin', and vile things had been done ta them. Vile, Ah say!" The man shuddered. "And now Ah kennot get them from my thoughts or dreams. Ah'm cursed by what Ah saw. Ye must drive tha visions from me."

Stregg's interest perked, though he maintained a calm appearance. "Was this a dream?"

"Nay, 'twas a real place. Midgeport. Ah oft visit there ta sell mah sheep."

"I know it," said Stregg. " 'Tis on the Turgen, about six day's journey from here."

"Not 'tis, 'twas! There's naught a soul alive there now, only spirits who chase after ye. Ah need a charm to keep them away."

"I'll require a sheep for that," said Stregg.

"A whole sheep!"

"Aye. To sacrifice to the Devourer. Mind ye, once its throat's been cut, the carcass belongs to god." Then, seeing that the man was dismayed by the expense, he added, "The dead want ye to join them. That's why they haunt yer thoughts and dreams. 'Tis good fortune ye found me, for I doubt ye'd have lived much longer." Stregg regarded the flock, then pointed to the choicest ewe. "That one will do."

The man sighed. "Then take it."

Stregg drew a dagger from the folds of his robe, strode over to the ewe, and quickly dispatched it. Then he dipped his index finger in the blood and used it to paint a circle on the stranger's forehead. "Never wash that off," he told the man. "I have something else for ye." Stregg entered his hut and returned shortly with several dried plants. "Each night afore ye sleep, steep two leaves in water that ye've brought to boil. The brew will ease yer dreams."

"So tha dead will trouble me no more?"

"With time, that may be so," replied Stregg. "The important thing is the dead won't slay ye."

The stranger appeared less than satisfied by that news,

but he didn't complain. Instead, he merely bowed his head. "Ah thank ye, Holy One." Afterward, he drove his flock down the lane, looking no less agitated.

Stregg hefted the ewe to drain its blood and butcher it. His mouth watered at the idea of roast mutton, and he was disappointed that so much of it would go to waste. It couldn't be helped. He felt compelled to leave tomorrow morn, for the slaughter in Midgeport seemed the work of someone inspired by the Devourer. *No common brigand would wipe out an entire town, only someone driven to harvest souls.* Once more, Stregg could almost feel the silver chain about his neck.

That evening, the priest stuffed himself on mutton, dried some for his journey, and left the rest outside for scavengers. The next morning, he departed to find the heir. Although Midgeport lay to the northwest, Stregg headed due north. He did so because he assumed that Lord Bahl's son was on the march and most likely heading east, for that's where the greatest plunder lay. If his assumption was correct, then a northern route would eventually cross the heir's trail. If Stregg found nothing by the time he reached the Turgen, he would head to Midgeport and look for clues there.

Stregg departed at sunrise on his quest and traveled through the morning without seeing another soul. That wasn't unexpected, for it was rare to encounter other travelers in the Empty Lands. That was especially true once one left the road. Thus the lone figure approaching Stregg immediately caught his attention. He had just crested a hill when he spied a tiny form crossing the plain below. The priest immediately halted and squatted down to hide his silhouette. He studied the figure a long while before he could discern the traveler was a woman. Soon after he determined that, she sharply changed her course, heading westward rather than due south.

She's seen me, thought Stregg, *and wishes to avoid a meeting.* It was a natural response for a woman traveling alone. It was far more unusual that she had ventured out at all. Assuming that only dire circumstances would force a solitary woman to undertake such a risk, Stregg decided to question her. He retreated partway down the slope, then headed west to intercept the traveler. Later, when he rounded the hill's western side, he spied her again.

She was much closer. He could see that she had dark hair, wore peasant garb, and was burdened with both a pack and a large sack. He was also surprised to see that she carried an unsheathed sword. The weapon didn't frighten the priest. He was confident he could intimidate any woman, even if she was armed. Moreover, he had painted his dagger with a quick-acting poison. Nevertheless, there was something about the woman that gave him pause.

Stregg froze, uncertain what to do. As absurd as it seemed, he felt intimidated. It wasn't the woman's demeanor or her sword that evoked the feeling. It arose from his gut, an indefinable unease that grew stronger as the woman drew nearer. When she was about a hundred paces away, Stregg's unease turned to terror. He bolted and ran back the way he had just come, still puzzled over the cause of his fear. Nonetheless, terror governed him, and he was long gone by the time the woman rounded the hillside and continued south.

Honus had been a wanderer ever since he had renounced the goddess, thus he was no stranger to the road. Nevertheless, it felt different to him, for the road was supposed to take him somewhere. For seventeen winters, Honus had been a traveler without a destination, a man who spent nearly as much time upon the Dark Path as walking the living world. Suddenly he had a place to go, only he didn't know where it was.

Others in his situation might have ambled leisurely, but Honus felt spurred by his uncertainty. He strode with a vigorous pace as if somehow speed would aid in unraveling the mystery ahead. His primary hope was that he would chance upon someone or something that would guide him or serve as a sign. For three days he traveled west, sleeping outdoors and eating porridge that he cooked—and burnt—in a small pot. As evening approached on the fourth day of his journey, he decided to seek hospitality. That, too, was something he hadn't done since he had traveled with Yim. Spying a rude hut a short distance from the dirt lane, he approached it.

The hut was built of sod, and its roof resembled a meadow. As Honus approached the dwelling, a man bearing a mattock emerged from it. Though the peasant held the tool like a weapon, Honus didn't slow his steps until he was but a few paces from him. Then he halted and calmly bowed before he spoke. "Greetings, Father. I request shelter and food in respect for the goddess." The phrase felt strange to utter after so many winters.

"And what goddess is that?"

"Karm, the Goddess of Compassion. I'm her servant."

"Ye are? Well, if she's so kindly, why does her servant bear such an angry face?"

"My tattoos show her wrath toward evildoers, not innocent folk like you."

The peasant glanced nervously at Honus's sword. "Still, who would dare refuse ye?"

Honus knew the appropriate response was, "I'll take nothing you don't give freely," but instead he replied by saying, "I mean you no harm."

The peasant slowly lowered the mattock. "Then sup and stay with us if ye wish. We can offer but roots and tha floor near our hearth. Ah hope that suits ye."

Honus bowed. "Karm sees your kindness, and I'm grateful for your hospitality."

The peasant called into the hut, "Wife, we have a guest."

A young woman appeared in the doorway. She was barefoot and ragged, as was her husband, and her face appeared prematurely worn. About her shirt clung three small children. Like their mother, they stared at Honus fearfully. Aware of their trepidation, Honus smiled and bowed. "I serve the goddess Karm, who sees your kindness."

"Karm?" said the woman. "My grandmam prayed ta her." Then she shrank back as Honus followed her husband into the hut.

The tiny dwelling contained a hearth, a crude table, a pair of equally crude benches, a single mattress made from bundled straw, farm implements, and the family's meager possessions. The latter lay about the dirt floor or hung from sticks pushed into the sod walls. A crockery pot containing boiled roots sat on the table, along with five small wooden bowls. Each of these contained cloudy liquid and a half-eaten root.

The woman scurried to a corner, brought another bowl to the table, placed a root in it, and then filled the bowl with liquid from the pot. "Have a seat, sire. 'Tis lowly fare, but 'tis all we have."

"Lowly fare suits my station," replied Honus. "I'm but a servant, so you should call me Honus, not sire." Honus sat down upon the bench.

"Sit, children," said the woman, "and finish your evemeal."

The children bunched together on the bench where Honus sat, keeping as distant from him as possible without falling off the end. The eldest child was a girl of about four winters. She regarded him with a mixture of fright and fascination. Finally, the latter seemed to gain the upper hand, for she spoke. "Why's yer face so dirty?"

Honus smiled. "That's not dirt. Those are tattoos."

"Atoos?"

"Marks made by needles so they won't come off. You can touch them if you'd like."

The girl hesitantly reached up, then quickly brushed Honus's cheek. Afterward, she examined her fingers for stains. Finding none, she asked, "Did it hurt?"

"Yes," replied Honus, "but that was long ago. It doesn't hurt anymore."

"Ah've nary seen yer like afore," said the child's father. "What brings ye here?"

"I'm searching for a woman. She may have traveled this way. She's comely with dark hair and eyes. Have you seen her like?"

"We seldom see travelers and none like her," said the man. "What of her companions?"

"I think she has none."

"Then she's foolish and won't get far."

"Pray neither's true," replied Honus, "for she's meant to save the world."

Honus's host grinned, as if the Sarf had made a jest. "A lass save tha world? Then we're in sore peril."

THIRTY-SIX

HONUS DIDN'T respond to his host's comment, except by his silence and grim countenance. That was sufficient, and the smile slowly faded from the peasant's face. "So ye say our fates lie with tha lass?"

"I'm certain of it."

"Small wonder yer seekin' her," said the man, adopting Honus's somber mood. "Why do ye think she'd come this way?"

"I've no reason to believe she would. I'm only guessing that she's passing through the Reach."

The peasant shook his head. "'Tis a wide place. She could be anywhere."

"I know," said Honus. "I'm hoping some traveler has seen her."

"If ye want ta speak ta travelers, ye'd best walk toward tha sunrise half a day till ye reach a rutted road. Turn left, and 'twill lead ye ta a height. Ye'll find a town there. Been there mahself once. 'Tis a place travelers stop, fer it has taverns aplenty."

Honus thanked his host for that advice, and then settled into silence. It was dark by the time the family finished its meal and retired to sleep in a tangled mass upon the single mattress. Honus wrapped himself in his cloak and slept near the hearth. In the morning, he thanked the family and departed. Having no better idea where to go, he headed for the town his host had described.

The landscape through which Honus strode gradually flattened until there were no hills at all, just a featureless, grassy plain that extended to the horizon. It underscored both the vastness and the emptiness of the Western Reach and made Honus despair of ever finding Yim. A little past noon, he encountered a place where the ground was cut and scored by wagon wheels. It was the road that his host had mentioned. Honus turned left and south to follow it. By late afternoon, he could see the road was heading toward a bump on the horizon. As Honus continued walking, the bump grew in prominence until it became a hill approaching the size of a tiny mountain. It dominated the flat landscape, being the sole vertical element. An assortment of buildings had sprung up on its eastern slope like mushrooms on a log.

Honus recognized the place from his earliest travels with Theodus, though he hadn't seen it for thirty winters. The town was called Cuprick, named for the copper that was mined in the hill. Bahland's armies had devastated it more than once, but the town had always sprung up anew due to the ore buried in the hill. It was dusk when Honus arrived there. The majority of the town's buildings had a temporary look, seeming to have been built with a minimum of material and effort. Most were framed with slender timbers and finished with wattle-and-daub walls. The town's dirt lanes had been so churned by hoofs and wheels that a film of dust was on everything. Honus recalled it as a home to few women and many rough men. Thus, as he strode its dusty streets, he took on a calm but menacing air.

Yim would avoid such a place, Honus thought. But Cuprick had been a way station for north and south traffic and it probably still was. That made it a promising site for questioning travelers. There were ample places to do so. Honus had already passed two taverns when he glanced up the lane and spied three more. He entered the nearest one to begin making inquiries. The interior was what he expected—poorly lit, crowded, and dirty. It had been noisy until he entered. Honus spoke to the hushed room. "I'm seeking a woman."

"Well, aren't we all," quipped a man. No one laughed.

"It's important I find her," continued Honus. "She has dark hair and eyes and a comely face. Most like, she's traveling alone. Has anyone seen her?"

A few men said nay and the rest merely shook their heads. Regardless, Honus stayed until he had looked each man in the eye. He detected hostility in some, but since he found no deception, he left. Honus visited two more taverns with similar results before he entered an inn. Its common room, though crudely built and furnished, was large and more inviting than any of the taverns. Before he could say anything, Honus heard music coming from plucked strings. The notes silenced the room, for even in Cuprick no one spoke when a bard performed. At the far end of the room rose a man dressed in weatherworn finery who began to sing as he accompanied himself on a small harp.

"Thirteen clans in Averen fair
  Name sons as their chieftain's heir.
  The Urkzimdi are alone
  In placing maids upon their throne."

It's a ballad about Cara's clan, thought Honus, turning to listen to the bard. The song began according to form, with stanzas that described the protagonist's lineage without ever mentioning him or her. The bard had just finished an account of Dar Beard Chin and was describing her daughter when someone tapped Honus's shoulder. A man wearing an innkeeper's apron gestured that he wanted to talk. Honus followed him outside.

"There's lads who wish a word with ye," said the innkeeper, pointing toward three men who stood a short way up the unlit street. When he spoke next, it was obvious that he was addressing those men, not Honus. "There. I gave him yer message. He ken do as he wills with it." Then the innkeeper returned to his establishment.

Honus glanced at the men. All he could see was their silhouettes. The dark figures were bulky and had youthful stances.

"Someone said ye're lookin' fer a lass," said one.

"Aye, a pretty birdie," said another.

"With dark eyes and hair," said the third.

"Have you seen her?" asked Honus.

"Nay," said the first man. "But mayhap a friend o' ours has. He lives up tha hill a bit."

"How did you know I was looking for her?"

"Word travels fast," said the first man. "A Sarf in Cuprick? That's news indeed."

"Aye, even an old Sarf," added his companion.

"Is there any other kind?" asked the third.

"Old, but quick," said the first. "Don't ye ferget it."

"Your friend," said Honus, "what did he say about the woman?"

"Not much," replied the first man. "Best ye ask him yerself. Come, we'll take ye ta him."

Before Honus could respond, the men started walking up the dark street. Honus hesitated to follow them, for their manner alerted his suspicions. *But they may have news of Yim*, he thought, *and there are only three of them.* After only an instant of indecision, Honus strode after the men, although he kept a short distance between them and himself.

Honus's guides didn't speak as they made their way uphill. Soon they were passing among hovels shuttered for the night. The rude dwellings flanked a narrow lane that was little wider than an alleyway. The only light came from the night sky or from firelight that glowed feebly through cracks. Suddenly, one the men cried out as if bursting from suppressed excitement. "A Sarf! A tuppin' Sarf!"

"Shut up!" said one of his companions.

Honus heard a door open and close. Then there were six men in the lane besides himself—three in front and three behind. None of them were moving. Honus's hand went to his sword hilt. "Does your friend live here?" he asked.

"Mayhap," replied one of the silhouetted men.

"Mayhap not," said another.

Honus performed a quick turn, slipping off his pack while determining where each man stood and who was closest. "I didn't come to fight."

"Then 'tis a pity, for 'twill spoil all the fun."

Honus turned toward the voice and saw movement and the glint of steel reflecting starlight. He darted to one side as he drew his sword. A blade whispered through the air and struck the dirt near his feet. Honus swung his sword and it bit into his assailant's neck. Warm liquid spattered on his hand as the man fell without uttering a sound. Honus leapt over the prostrate body, glancing about as he did. The other men had neither advanced nor retreated. "What's the sense in this?" Honus asked.

"How many men ken say he bested a Sarf?" said a man. "Well, Ah ken."

"Aye," said another. "Folk still talk 'bout it."

Then, as Honus expected, all the men attacked at once. By that time, he had backed against a wall. This not only prevented his attackers from surrounding him, but also forced them to crowd together, which hampered their movements. In the dark, they appeared to Honus as a confusing knot of faceless bodies and flailing arms. Only one man bore a sword; the rest gripped clubs. Honus fought defensively, keeping his assailants at bay while looking for an opening to attack. Though his opponents were only ruffians, he was well past his prime. Moreover, he was rusty, so his defense had a slightly desperate quality.

Despite their numbers, Honus's assailants seemed hesitant to risk their lives by pressing him too aggressively. Instead, they used their numerical advantage to harry him, waiting for exhaustion to slow his parries. Fighting became a contest that Honus must win five times and never lose. As it drew out, its commotion attracted attention. Shutters flew open as folk peered into the night to witness what was going on. Firelight spilled from the open windows, and Honus could see his attackers' faces for the first time. They were young and battered, with the cold, vicious look of bullies.

For a long while, Honus was taxed just to fend off the assaults, and his arm began to tire from the effort. Sensing the contest was turning in their favor, his adversaries grew more aggressive and moved in closer. That was when Honus saw an opening and thrust at the swordsman's chest. His blade point pierced flesh and scraped bone as it passed between ribs to find the heart. The swordsman dropped his weapon, and the flailing arms briefly froze as his companions learned that their sport had claimed yet another victim.

The dying man began to slump. As Honus withdrew his sword, a club struck it. His blade snapped. Then Honus was left grasping a hilt with a short, flat stub of steel at its end. The remnants of his sword remained in his opponent's chest or lay in shards upon the dirt lane.

The skewered man made a rasping sound. Then he toppled to the ground and didn't move again. For a moment, there was only silence. Then a harsh voice broke the stillness. "Well, lads, let's send this tattooed prick ta tha Dark Path."

THIRTY-SEVEN

DARKNESS. PAIN. A putrescent stench. Those were Honus's first sensations. The pain suddenly grew sharper. Something was biting his leg and shaking it. Honus kicked with his free foot, and it struck his tormentor. It yelped and released his leg. Honus opened his eyes. It was still dark, but slightly less so. Something was growling. A shadowy form moved toward him with stealthy, hesitant steps.

A dog, thought Honus. "Shoo!" he shouted.

The dog jumped back, then started barking. Honus groped for something to throw at it and felt a bone. He tried to lift it, but the bone wasn't loose. Things were attached to it—sinews, shreds of flesh, a hand, and an upper arm. Honus realized that he was lying on a corpse, and not a recent one. It was the source of the stench.

Honus tried to rise to his feet, but the effort made him nauseous and dizzy. The best he could manage was to crawl. The dog kept barking. "Was I supposed to be your breakfast?" asked Honus. "Or perhaps it's your dinnertime." Either seemed possible to him, for he had no idea how long he had been unconscious. Neither did he know where he was, other than somewhere dark, wet, and muddy. He remembered being struck by clubs. His aching head and body were evidence of that. The rain of blows had seemed short before the dark had swallowed him. *And now I'm here.*

Where's that? It hurt Honus to move his head, but he did so anyway. Looking up, he saw a small and irregular patch of sky surrounded by stone. The sky was dark, but it seemed to be growing brighter. Honus lay back in the mud to watch it. The blue-gray patch gradually lightened and took on a pinkish shade. *Dawn,* he thought.

Honus felt teeth nip his ankle. He kicked again and sat up. By then, it had grown bright enough for him to see his nemesis. The dog was midsize and scruffy, but it didn't look starving. It bared its teeth and growled at Honus but kept its distance. The dislike was mutual. Honus groped for a stone, found one, and let it fly. The stone grazed the animal's flank hard enough that it yelped and ran off. Assuming that the dog had merely retreated into some dark corner, Honus grabbed another stone and waited for it to return.

While he waited, Honus surveyed his surroundings, which were increasingly visible as the illumination grew brighter. He was in a dome-shaped chamber. Honus assumed it was the result of mining, though he didn't know its function. It certainly wasn't a mine shaft, for its stone walls curved inward to an opening that appeared unreachable without an extremely long ladder. It was hard for Honus to judge how far above him the opening was, but the distance seemed at least the height of three men.

Honus turned his gaze downward to the chamber's floor. A stream flowed across it, originating in the dark and disappearing into it also. It apparently had deposited the thick layer of mud that covered most of the stone floor. Whatever its original purpose, the chamber had become a dumping place. In addition to assorted refuse, bones of horses lay strewn about as well as several equine carcasses in various states of decay. Human remains mingled with those of animals. Besides the bloated corpse that had broken his fall, Honus spied two other decomposing bodies. One was nearly a skeleton.

Honus was less surprised that he had been dumped into such a place than that he had been dumped into it alive and intact. His assailants had been out for blood, yet they hadn't killed him when they'd had the chance. That seemed far more improbable to him than surviving his fall. *Perhaps they intend to come back for me.* Honus was unsure if that was likely or even possible, but the chance of it spurred him to seek a means of defense.

A leg bone would make a good weapon, so Honus looked for one. He had just begun his search when sunlight from above reached the nearly skeletonized corpse and revealed that it was garbed in dark blue. The clothing had been reduced to tattered rags, but its color was unmistakable: it was the shade worn by Karm's servants. Honus went over for a closer look.

A scrap of gray flesh clinging to the skull had a line tattooed upon it; the rest of the face was gone. *So this was the Sarf my attackers claim they killed*, thought Honus. He wondered if he had known the man. He also wondered if the Sarf had remained faithful to the goddess, and if so, how he had conducted his life without a Bearer. Honus made the Sign of the Balance over the remains, and was about to resume his search when he saw a sword hilt projecting from the mud. He recognized the style immediately as distinctive to his order. He pulled the weapon from the muck. It was still in its scabbard. Honus brought it into the light and examined it. The braided wire that wrapped the hilt was green with corrosion. Honus drew the blade, fearing it would be ruined by rust.

The blade was in perfect condition, for a Sarf's scabbard

was as meticulously crafted as the sword it held. An oiled leather gasket had kept any moisture out. Honus admired the marbling of the temple-forged blade, which gave it resilience that the village blacksmith's sword had lacked. *I wouldn't be here if I had this when I was attacked*, Honus thought, reflecting on the irony of his situation. *I finally have a proper sword, and it's no use to me.*

Honus retreated from the sunlight because it hurt his throbbing head and he didn't want to be seen from above. If men were coming for him, he wanted to be ready. The first thing he needed to do was determine where they'd come from. He glanced about the chamber walls, which were still wrapped in shadow, and looked for an entrance. He couldn't see any, so he made a slow circuit to feel the walls for openings. He found no doorways, only two crevices through which the stream entered and exited the chamber. The openings were fairly broad, but low. *A man might slither through there, but it'd be a tight squeeze.* Honus assumed any attackers would choose to lower themselves through the hole in the ceiling.

Taxed by the effort of his explorations, Honus leaned against the wall to rest. He quickly dozed off. When someone threw a dead dog from above, he woke with a start but soon fell asleep again. The next time Honus woke, it was pitch-black. He groped his way to the stream and drank before crawling back to the wall. His stomach had settled and was racked by hunger. When morning came, it would be at least two days since he had eaten, perhaps more. It occurred to him that his assailants might have left him alive on purpose. His fate would be gruesome enough to satisfy the most vindictive. He wondered if they believed he'd become like the dog, reduced to eating corpses.

Thinking of the dog led Honus to reflect that it would be edible. That, in turn, made him wonder where it was. *Has it been hiding all this time?* Honus thought that was unlikely. *Perhaps it has a way out of here!* Before his hopes rose,

Honus realized that if such a passageway existed, it might be large enough only for a dog. Whatever the case, it was too dark to look for it, so Honus slept again.

Teeth roused Honus. They gripped his leg. Dawn's light filtered from above, and with it, the dog had returned. This time, Honus was ready with a supply of rocks. The first one he threw hit its mark, sending the dog scampering. It dashed up the stream and disappeared into the shadows. Honus walked over to the crevice. Kneeling in the dark, he felt about the muck with his hands. His fingertips detected paw prints and the slight depression of a well-used pathway. Honus bent his head to peer into the crevice. It was absolutely black. The crevice might lead to the world above or to a horrible death, and there was no way of discovering which without venturing into the darkness.

Honus knew that if he wished to live he must escape the pit. It seemed that his sole chance to accomplish that required entering the low opening, although he dreaded doing it. Honus had always felt uneasy in cramped spaces, and the pitch-black crevice was the realization of his deepest fears. *This is the only way to Yim*, he told himself. *Think of it as Karm's path*. In preparation, Honus removed his newfound sword from his belt to prevent it from getting hung up on some obstruction. Handling the sword made Honus recall the guidance of the runes: *"When you find your proper tul, seek the leader who cannot wield it."* Daven had said that "tul" might mean "weapon." If that was so, then finding the sword was part of finding Yim.

That thought spurred Honus to enter the cramped, dark space. He had to do so on his belly, for there was insufficient space to crawl. If his raised himself only slightly above the mud, his head or his back touched the crevice's ceiling. He was thankful that the mud made it easier to slide along and that the stream didn't flow across the entire width of the passageway. His progress was impossible to gauge in the absolute darkness. The way slanted upward, but since the hole was probably on a slope, Honus might be no closer to the surface. As he slowly advanced, the crevice walls grew closer. Honus could tell because he used his sheathed sword like a cane to feel the way ahead.

Time became meaningless. There was only the present; and it was dark, wet, and fearful. Eventually, the crevice became so narrow that water flowed across its entire breadth. Then Honus slid over bare rock as the current pushed against him. The farther he went, the narrower the passage became. His body partly blocked the stream, causing its water level to rise until he was forced to lift his head each time he took a breath. Every time he did, he bumped the ceiling.

Feeling the way before him with his scabbard, Honus could tell that the crevice shrank to the width of his shoulders. The ceiling became equally cramped. It is what he had dreaded—a place where he could become wedged. While his scabbard told him the way ahead grew narrower, it couldn't tell him if the crevice ever widened again. There was only one way to find out.

Honus stretched his arms forward and pushed against the cramped walls with his feet to advance. As his body blocked the crevice, the water flowed over his head and down his back. The current fought his progress as it sought to drown him. Scraping both sides of his torso against stone walls, Honus struggled to find air. His lungs felt about to gasp in liquid when his hands no longer touched stone walls. Honus gave one last push with his feet; then he was able to move his arms and elbows outward. Reaching back, he pushed against the sides of an opening and his head broke the water's surface. He gasped for breath, thankful to be alive.

Despite squeezing through the crevice, Honus remained trapped in perfect darkness. He felt about with his sword and free hand. He seemed to be in a cavity containing a shallow pool. It was so wide that he had to move before he touched a wall. Honus rested awhile, then followed the sound of running water into a new crevice. It was almost as narrow as the one he had just exited, but it was high enough for him to crawl. After what he had been through, crawling in the dark seemed easy. Honus groped his way for a long while before he saw dim light ahead. Encouraged by the sight, he moved quicker. The light grew brighter. Then sunlight poured in from a crack above. It was blinding for a moment.

When Honus's eyes adjusted, he saw how he could climb up the crevice and escape. His empty stomach urged him to do so immediately, but he thought that it would be wiser to make his reappearance at night. Thus he crawled a short distance back the way he had come and waited for dusk.

When Honus finally climbed out of the crevice, he found himself standing on the slope above Cuprick. He couldn't see the hole into which he had been dumped, just a squalid jumble of hovels, and below them, the town proper. As Honus descended the hillside, he gave wide berth to the hovels and made sure that few saw him until he returned to the inn. There, everyone hushed when he stepped into the common room, and men cleared out of Honus's way as he strode up to the innkeeper. The unfortunate man stood paralyzed, his face pale with terror.

"You gave me a message a while ago," said Honus in a hard voice. "An invitation to a trap."

The innkeeper merely nodded.

"I suppose you acted out of cowardice," said Honus, "thinking my attackers posed a greater threat than I." Honus grinned in a way that caused the innkeeper to start trembling. "That was a mistake."

"Please, sire, spare my life!"

"I'll consider it," replied Honus. "While I do, perhaps food and lodging would sway my judgment."

A relieved look crept over the innkeeper's face. "Oh thank ye, sire. I wronged ye, and I'll gladly make amends. Stay for as long as ye wish and sup freely with no mind toward payment. Yer forbearance is coin enough for me." Then, bowing frequently, the innkeeper led Honus to a vacant table before rushing off to bring food and drink.

As Honus sat waiting for his meal, the common room returned to a semblance of normality. Nevertheless, Honus felt conspicuous, for while the inn's patrons kept their distance, they glanced at him surreptitiously. The exception was the bard, who stared at Honus with unabashed fascination. After some hesitation, he picked up his ale mug, rose from his place, strolled over to Honus's table, and bowed. "I'm Frodoric of Bremven, Karmamatus. As a devotee and chronicler of valiant deeds, may I join you? It would be an honor to drink with one worthy of a ballad."

"I'm not seeking renown, only a woman."

The bard pulled out a chair and settled into it. "Of course! Of course! The ideal hero never cares for reputation. That's a bard's task. But take my word for it, you're prime material. Granted, your dealings with the innkeep could have gone better. They started with such promise. That line about an invitation to a trap; well, that was nearly perfect. But the ending—pah! Meals and a bed? A decapitation would have served drama better:

His flashing sword spelt the coward's doom
In ruby droplets that sprayed the room.

Now, *that's* a proper ending!"

"Mine was more practical," said Honus. "And I think our host prefers it."

"Pah! Ruby droplets possess more flair. Trust me, I sing for my living. But in your case, they're just an ending flourish. I'm more interested in the woman."

"I believe she's traveling alone and—".

"No, not that one! The one who stopped the fight, at least by most accounts. Some say she was flesh and blood—a witness who squelched your foes' courage. Others swear she is a spirit. There's even talk that she was Karm herself, though few in Cuprick still worship her. So tell me . . . which version's true?"

"I saw no woman," said Honus, "only clubs and then nothing more until I woke up in a pit."

Frodoric looked disappointed. "Ah, yes. I already know about the pit. I thought it was the end of you. Nevertheless, it was a sign of respect that you didn't go in naked. That's a high degree of charity for Cuprick. But if it makes you feel better, folks thought you were dead."

"They didn't try very hard to make sure!" said Honus.

Frodoric shrugged. "They seldom do. May I ask how you got out?"

"I followed a dog."

"A dog!" Frodoric sighed dramatically. "Couldn't you have followed the woman?"

"The woman I didn't see? By the time you're done, I'm certain your license will place her there."

"You mistake my craft. My lays are historical, not fanciful. So tell me your name that I may get it right."

"Honus."

Frodoric shook his head. "Which only rhymes with 'bonus.' Oh dear!" He sighed again, this time with even greater drama. "Art's always a struggle."

"I heard part of one of your songs. It was about the Urkzimdi clan. Was that one historic or artistic?"

"You mean 'The Ballad of Cara One Arm'? Every bit is fact. The fairies took her arm in payment for saving her clan during the Summer of Feuds."

"I know Cara, and the last time I saw her she possessed two arms."

"Then you haven't seen her for a very long while. Yet I'm surprised you haven't heard the ballad. It's quite well known. An Averen bard composed the lay, but I've improved it. In all modesty, my final stanza is masterful:

> A chieftain's might springs from her brain.
> Though I can't wield a sword again,
> My foes will learn to fear my wit
> As long as on this throne I sit.

Though I've never met the lady, by all accounts, my ending suits her perfectly."

"So Cara's the leader who cannot wield a sword!"

Frodoric looked surprised by Honus's excitement. "Perhaps if she were left-handed she could, but I'm told she's not."

By then, Honus was grinning broadly. "Frodoric of Bremven, you're more that a bard; you're Karm's own tongue!"

Frodoric smiled. "A well-turned phrase, but a mite flamboyant."

Honus didn't reply, for his mind was far elsewhere. He had learned his destination at last. It was Cara's hall, and all his thoughts were focused on getting there as quickly as possible.

THIRTY·EIGHT

HONUS REMAINED absorbed in planning his next move until the innkeeper brought out his meal. It consisted of a partial loaf of bread, a hunk of cheese, and a meaty mutton bone, all served on a wooden platter. He also brought out a ceramic mug with a broken handle and a jug of ale to fill it. The sight of food awoke Honus's hunger and briefly banished thoughts of the journey ahead.

Frodoric smiled as he watched Honus dig in. "Our host washed your plate! You must have terrorized him indeed." While the Sarf chewed, the bard replenished his mug from the ale jug. "No doubt our host will refill this jug as many times as you wish."

Honus swallowed his food. "I'd think art suffers when drinking and singing mix."

"I shan't sing tonight," replied Frodoric. "It's a problem of repertory. Cuprick's denizens favor novelty over artistry and dislike hearing the same ballad twice."

"So why not sing in another inn?"

"This is the town's most elegant establishment, such as it is. I have my standards. Elsewhere, 'The Randy Plowman' or 'The Maiden's Mistake' are the favored lays. wouldn't sing such drivel even if I knew the verses. Bu 'The Ballad of Honus,' now there's a—"

"Forget it," said Honus. "I'm leaving as soon as I can."

"And walk away from a never-empty ale jug? I don't understand you."

"All the more reason not to sing about me."

Honus resumed eating. Frodoric sighed, then drained his mug and refilled it. When he saw the innkeeper enter the room, he signaled him to come over. Upon the man's arrival, Frodoric handed him the empty ale jug. "I believe th Sarf would like some more," he said. As the innkeeper hurried off to fill the jug, Honus flashed the bard a disapproving look. Frodoric bowed his head, partly to hide his smile "I know you wanted more but were too shy to ask."

"I've barely touched my first mug," replied Honus.

"Oh, you needn't set an example. I'm beyond saving."

"Evidently so."

"So which version do you believe?"

"Version of what?"

"The fight's ending. I know the reputation of those men. You should be dead."

"I suppose the goddess saved me," said Honus.

"Why say 'suppose'? Karm loves you."

Honus glazed at Frodoric in surprise.

"After all," said the bard, " 'Karmamatus' means 'Karm's beloved.' "

"My life is none of your business."

"Of course it's my business. I'm a bard!"

"And a tiresome one at that." Honus spotted the innkeeper and called him over. The man rushed to the table, bowing several times along the way. This time, Honus greeted him more amiably. "I've enjoyed your fare. Now I'd like to rest."

"Certainly, sire. The sleeping chamber's upstairs, and there's a covered bucket for yer convenience."

"It's a large room with no beds," whispered Frodoric. "Everyone sleeps on the floor. Several dozen every night."

"And do you reside on the premises?" asked Honus.

"Aye, sire."

"Good," replied Honus. "Then I'll stay in your quarters."

The innkeeper's face fell. "Very well, sire. May I ask how long ye plan to stay?"

"Of course, you may," replied Honus. Then he raised his voice so all might hear. "I wish to leave tomorrow morn. But to do that, I'll need my pack, its contents, plus a horse, bridle, and saddle. Until I receive them, I'll stay here and employ my idle time in hunting all who wronged me. Let it be known that I'll drag each man to the pit alive and toss him down in tiny bits. I've the skill to make the cutting last a half day at least."

Frodoric clapped his hands with enthusiasm "Now *that* would make a ballad!"

Lulled by the comfort of a feather mattress, Honus slept late. It was past sunrise when he heard timid knocking on the door. Honus rose and opened it to find the innkeeper with his displaced family bunched behind him. The innkeeper was holding Honus's pack and attempting to smile. After handing the pack to Honus, he bowed. "Sire, a saddled horse awaits ye outside."

Honus was relieved that his threats had worked, for he had no stomach for revenge. He hoped that his attackers—and not his host—had provided the horse; but as he went out to examine it, Honus didn't inquire about the animal's source. The steed was tied outside the inn's back entrance and appeared to be a serviceable mount. After a thorough inspection, Honus turned to his host and flashed him a sincere smile. "Though your hospitality was coerced, it has honored Karm. In addition to her grace, you have my gratitude."

The innkeeper smiled with relief. "Come eat, sire, before your departure."

Honus followed the man back into the inn. The common room was less full than on the previous night, but the bard was there. He rose when Honus entered, and when the Sarf was seated, he joined him without leave. Honus raised an amused eyebrow. "I regret to disappoint you, but my stay won't have a bloody ending."

"I know," replied Frodoric. "I saw the horse. I counsel riding off quickly. The four that brought it here most likely stole it."

"You should probably leave also," said Honus. "When foes can't harm a man, they oft hurt his friends."

Frodoric smiled. "Are you naming me a friend?"

"Only in the poetic sense, but I think my foes will be more literal."

"But what reason would they have to harm me?"

"It's my experience that malice is unconcerned with reason."

"Well, Cuprick has become wearing," said the bard. "Such an unrefined audience. A change might suit me. Indeed, I'm certain of it. So, where are we going?"

"I'm going to Averen, and I intend to go alone."

"Averen! Where everyone speaks like sheep? Na this and na that. Why go there?"

"To visit the subject of your ballad."

"You mean Cara One Arm? Do you *really* know her?"

"Since she was a child. I left her behind during what you called the Summer of Feuds to fight alongside her brother. I was with him when he died, but I never saw her again."

"What happened?"

Honus glanced at Frodoric and saw that the bard was regarding him with keen interest. The look made Honus aware that his voice had betrayed the depth of his feelings. "That tale, Frodoric of Bremven, would indeed be worthy of a ballad. Yet I've neither the time nor the heart to relate it. Moreover, it's not yet finished."

Frodoric exhaled one of his theatrical sighs. "If you were a maid, I'd name you flirt, not friend," he said. "But can we leave together, at least?" He lowered his voice. "My journey will begin more safely if your foes believe I'm under your protection. Please, Karmamatus. Just a little way together. I'm quite entertaining."

Honus gave in to the bard's wheedling, and the two men departed Cuprick soon afterward. They shared the saddle, with Frodoric in front so he might strum his harp as he sang "The Ballad of Cara One Arm" for Honus. The ballad enchanted Honus, and though he doubted the truth of its particulars, he felt the lay captured the spunk and courage of the young woman he had known. When Frodoric finished the lengthy piece, Honus asked him to sing it again, which the bard did. Thus it wasn't until noon that the two men parted ways.

As soon as Frodoric dismounted, Honus spurred his horse south toward Averen. The mare wasn't up to a prolonged gallop, and Honus soon slowed her to a more sustainable trot. The pace didn't suit his impatience, but a lame horse would slow him far more. Reflecting upon Cara's ballad, he felt that he was in one also—a lay where Karm composed the lines. Theodus had always denied that fate existed, saying the goddess never foreordained one's life. Honus's late Bearer had claimed that Karm provided chances for each person to make choices. Nonetheless, Honus felt that the chances in his life were set toward some purpose he couldn't understand. He could perceive no grand scheme, and without that understanding, his only guidance had been his love for Yim. He had even renounced the goddess because of her. *And now I've reconciled with Karm for Yim's sake.*

When Honus considered his visit to Cuprick, he saw the goddess's hand in almost everything that had happened. He believed that Karm had saved him so he might find the sword. *Yet if that's true, then the other Sarf died so I could find it.* Such reflections made it difficult to believe in Karm's benevolence, and he tried to push them from his thoughts. Instead, he focused on recollections of Yim. They made him hurry his horse's pace toward Averen, where he hoped to exchange memory's phantoms for flesh and blood.

As Honus rode south, guided by love and an inscription on his back, Stregg trekked east, guided by ambition and carnage. As he had suspected, a trip to Midgeport had been unnecessary. After three days of traveling north, he encountered a burnt-out hut that entombed a butchered family. Tales from his childhood made Stregg well aware of how men behaved when inflamed by the Devourer, so he recognized their handiwork. The destruction appeared wanton, and the killings reflected excessive savagery.

Stregg's god was empowered by traumatic death, and the potency of its servants increased along with that of their master. Therefore, after the priest turned eastward, he was guided by more than trampled ground, ruins, and corpses; he felt his powers expanding as he neared their source. Both Stregg's father and grandfather had spoken of the phenomenon. When Lord Bahl was at his zenith, both priests had been able to dominate all but the most forceful individuals. *Soon it'll be my turn to garner fear and respect*, thought Stregg, *and see folk quake as they obey me. And as the More Holy One, my turn will last forever*. Since he hadn't encountered a living soul after heading eastward, his power was more a feeling than a proven fact. Nevertheless, Stregg never doubted its reality.

Day's end approached without any glimpse of those who had wrought the destruction. Stregg wasn't surprised, for none of the corpses that he found had been fresh. As the sun set, he spotted the burnt remnant of yet another peasant hut and headed for it. He had no intention of camping there, for such places usually reeked of putrescence. But armies seldom plundered gardens, and Stregg hoped to find something edible. When he located the trampled vegetable plot, he found a stick and began to dig for roots. After gathering enough for a meal, Stregg moved away from death's stench to roast his find and sleep.

It was dark by the time he set up a simple camp and got a fire blazing. The clear night threatened to be a chilly one, and there was already a nip in the air. When the fire had produced sufficient embers, Stregg raked some aside and threw the roots upon them to roast. While they cooked, he sat on a log and contentedly warmed himself.

The child was so sooty that, at first, all Stregg saw were eyes in the night. Once he spotted them at the farthest reach of the firelight, he saw the rest of the girl. Silent, still, and ragged, her small, thin form was easy to miss in the dark. However, her eyes stood out. They had the haunted stare of one who had gazed upon things impossible to forget and too terrible to utter.

Stregg surmised that she had somehow survived the attack and had hidden among the ashes of the hut. The girl's shift was a skimpy rag that didn't cover her arms or most of her skinny legs. The fire could have drawn her or the smell of food or the sight of another living person, but as the priest regarded the girl, she appeared too terrified to come any closer. Stregg decided to test his power. "Come here!" he said in a stern and authoritative tone.

Rendered mute by fear, the girl advanced like a sleep-walker, her bare feet making no sound as she advanced toward the priest. Stregg sensed that she made each step unwillingly, acting solely because he had compelled her. That understanding gave him a delicious sense of control. When the girl halted before him, she was close enough to touch. In the firelight, Stregg could see her better. She appeared only five or six winters old, and her dark hair was actually blond beneath the ashes. Stregg didn't question the frightened child because he was uninterested. To him, her name and her tragedy were inconsequential, and the girl's only significance was as a means to test his growing abilities.

"Stay perfectly still!" commanded Stregg. The girl stiff-ened. The priest bent down and picked up the knife that he planned to use for peeling the roots. Its blade was only the length of his slender thumb. He smiled as he held its point against the child's thin chest and saw her eyes widen. Stregg reached around the girl and pressed his left hand against her scrawny upper back. He could feel her trembling. The silence of the moment made it all the more exquisite. It seemed both a token of his power and his victim's helpless-ness.

The priest felt that he had become a lord of life and death. To enjoy that sensation to its utmost, he pushed the knife in as slowly at he could. The sternum offered some resistance, but it was softer than an adult's. Once past it, Stregg was cer-tain that he could feel the girl's pounding heartbeats through the blade. He was reluctant to make the final push that would stop them, so he paused to gaze into his victim's eyes and relish their terror. *Does she think this is only a night-mare?* he wondered. Stregg hoped not. "Speak!" he com-manded.

"Please," said a tiny voice so softly that he could barely hear the word.

"Please what?"

"Please don't."

Satisfied that the girl knew she was being murdered, he plunged the knife in the rest of the way. There was surprisingly little blood. The girl's mouth flew open as if to cry out, but she made no sound. Instead, to Stregg's great disappointment, her features relaxed and took on a peaceful cast. Then her body went limp. Stregg lowered the little corpse to the ground and stared it for a long while. Although he had poisoned a few people, slaying with a knife felt more visceral and produced a superior sense of accomplishment. The black priest was certain that he had increased his master's power, and accordingly, his power also.

Caught up in savoring his deed, Stregg neglected the roots he had been cooking. When he finally pulled them from the embers, they were charred throughout. He gazed at his ruined meal and shrugged. "So what if I eat no vegetables tonight," he said to the surrounding darkness. "I have meat."

THIRTY·NINE

THE NEXT day, Stregg continued to follow the trail of destruction, convinced that Lord Bahl's son led those who had wrought it. All the while, he worried that another priest might find the heir first and snatch away the prize he had come to regard as his. That concern hastened his steps and spurred him to wake at daybreak and hike as long as there was light to see. The priest followed that grueling

routine for five days before he was rewarded by the sight of
smoke on the horizon. Though weary and footsore, he
picked up his pace.

It was nearly dusk when Stregg crested a small rise and
glimpsed the still-smoldering village. The tiny settlement
would have seemed unimpressive even when it had been intact. In its ravaged state, it scarcely seemed a village at all.
A single hut remained standing. All other structures had
been reduced to a few charred timbers poking up from
blackened mounds of smoking rubble. There were less than
two dozen mounds in all.

The priest had grown used to destruction and was blasé
about it. What roused him was the sight of the men who had
perpetrated it. They seemed to be of two types—a small unit
of soldiers and a mob of agitated men. The soldiers were
engaged in setting up a camp and loading goods into wagons.
The mob was more numerous, and its men paced about aimlessly or hacked at corpses. The scene reminded Stregg of his
father and grandfather's tales of Lord Bahl's campaigns. The
soldiers resembled the Iron Guard, while the mob likened to
Bahl's peasant troops. In fact, the similarities heightened
Stregg's fears that some other priest had found Bahl's son and
instructed him on his father's tactics.

In an attempt to assess the situation, Stregg continued
his observations. A wagon with a canvas covering drove
over to the intact hut. Its driver climbed down to help a
woman from the vehicle and escort her into the hut. The
woman didn't reappear, but the driver did. After unloading
some items into the tiny dwelling, he drove the wagon off.
A short while later, a different man entered the hut and remained there. Stregg continued to observe the village until
the light began to fail, but he was too distant to gather
much additional information. To his relief, he saw no one
wearing the black robes of a priest. That seemed promising. Nevertheless, Stregg remained put.

With his goal in sight, Stregg felt the full enormity of

what he was about to do. He had little doubt it would change the world, and his life would be divided forever into before and after he entered the burnt-out village. He sensed the same would be true for nearly everyone alive. Stregg told himself that he had no reason to fear the future he was about to unleash; yet a part of him did. His trepidations were instinctive and vague, but they held him back until he rationalized them away. That done, the black priest hurried to fulfill his role.

Though the hut was small and rudely furnished, it was more comfortable than the wagon in cold weather. Moli huddled by the hearth to warm herself, while Froan silently paced the tiny room. His restless movements, which had nothing to do with generating warmth, quickly caught Moli's attention. "Shadow," she said after he completed yet another circuit, "is somethin' wrong?"

"No."

"Ye seem angry."

"Well, just look at this place!"

"It reminds me of home," said Moli, her voice soft and humble.

Moli's reply only increased Froan's irritation. "It reminds me of home, too. It's as miserable as the hole I fled."

" 'Tisn't so bad."

"Pah! It is, and each night's stopping place is worse than the last one. I feel all I'm doing is filling my men's bellies. For what? So I can do it again tomorrow! We should be living like a lord and his lady, not like peasants."

"Ah *am* a peasant, Shadow."

"No, you're not. You're my woman."

Moli rose from the fireside and went over to kiss Froan. "And Ah'll be that whether we sleep here or someplace grand. If ye don't like this life, send yer men away. What has all their killin' gained ye?"

"You don't understand."

"Ah'm sorry, Shadow. Ah don't. Ah'm scared."

"Of what? Me?"

"Nay, never of ye, dearest. Jus' o' all tha death 'bout us."

"It'll end someday," said Froan, though he couldn't foresee when. He only had a feeling that it wouldn't be anytime soon.

"Ah'll be glad when it does," said Moli.

Froan heard a knock on the door. "Enter," he said, expecting it to be a soldier bringing food. Instead it was Captain Wuulf. Trailing behind him was a stranger dressed in black robes.

Wuulf bowed his head to his commander. "Lord Shadow, this priest strolled into camp and demanded to see ye."

Froan glared at the stranger. "Demanded?" When the black-clad man met his glance, Froan had two contradictory reactions. Part of him felt revulsion, while another part saw a kindred spirit. Those impressions warred within Froan, reducing him to a state of passivity.

Meanwhile, the man approached, dropped to his knees, and bowed his head. "My most august and powerful lord, long have I searched for ye. I bring news of yer parentage, and the great honor of yer line."

Those words caused Froan to recall the visitation from his father's spirit. Furthermore, they piqued his curiosity. His revulsion faded as growing expectation replaced it. "Who sent you?"

"The holiest of my order and yer father's most devoted servant. He is the Most Holy Gorm, and he has sent forth priests to comb the world for his lord's son, who was stolen upon his conception. Your realm awaits ye. A great destiny awaits ye also, for all the world knows yer name."

"And it's neither Shadow nor Froan?"

"Nay, yer lordship. May I kiss yer hand?"

Intrigued, Froan extended it.

" 'Tis my everlasting honor to be the first to call ye Lord Bahl."

Froan appreciated the gravity of the announcement by its effect on Moli and Captain Wuulf. The captain, though stern and battle hardened, appeared completely stunned. Moli's face had gone perfectly white, and for the first time, she regarded him with a hint of fear. What surprised him most was that neither Moli nor the captain seemed to doubt the priest's declaration. It was as though its truth was so evident that, once revealed, it couldn't be denied. Froan, too, believed the priest whose announcement fit so perfectly with what the spirit had said. Nevertheless, he asked, "What makes you name me thus?"

"My devotion to god. Ye, of all men, are most graced by the Devourer. I felt its strength within ye and was drawn to it. Cannot ye easily sway others to yer will? Don't they die readily for ye? Such power is unique to yer line, and it always passes from father to son. 'Tis what makes ye my rightful lord."

I'm Lord Bahl! thought Froan, recalling with amusement that his mother had said the man was merely a myth. The priest's revelation was the realization of all his fondest hopes and dreams: He wasn't the son of a lowly goatherd. He was someone grand and mighty. The concept was intoxicating, and Froan enthusiastically embraced it. Summoning a newfound sense of gravity, he spoke. "Rise, priest. What is your name?"

As the priest stood, Froan wondered why he had ever found him repellent. Once on his feet, the man bowed low. "I'm Stregg, yer lordship."

"As I rejoice in this day, so shall you," said Froan. He turned to Captain Wuulf. "Order the cooks to prepare the finest feast they can and bring it here. Then join me in the festivities. There's a man in your troop named Bog Rat. Bring him with you."

"Is he the one who now calls himself Telk?"

"Yes, the very one." As Wuulf departed, Froan turned again to Stregg. "So tell me more about my realm."

"'Tis called Bahland, my lord, and it lies many days journey to the south and west. The seat of your domain is the Iron Palace, a grand and mighty edifice on the seacoast. There, your army awaits you, for 'tis foretold that ye'll ride forth to conquer all the world."

Froan turned to Moli and beamed. "Everything I told you shall come to pass. Soon, you'll be living in a palace!"

Moli smiled, but there was no gladness in her eyes. Froan didn't notice, for he had already turned to Štregg to ply him with questions about his palace, his realm, his army, and his destiny.

FORTY

MOLI FELT ignored while the two men talked as they waited for the feast to arrive. The priest was a total stranger, and her lover was becoming one. Moli didn't even know what to call him—Shadow or Lord Bahl. She feared it would be Lord Bahl. *Ah called him "dearest" jus' afore tha priest came*, she thought. Moli wondered if she'd ever do so again. Somehow, it no longer seemed appropriate.

Like everyone raised in the Empty Lands, Moli knew the name of Bahl. For generations, his lordship's armies had pillaged the countryside. They had given the Empty Lands their name by eradicating towns and villages, their folk, and hope. No one distinguished one Lord Bahl from another, for they all seemed identical—deadly tyrants without a shred of mercy or restraint.

As Moli reflected upon Lord Bahl's legendary harshness, she felt it was overwhelming her tender Shadow. The part of him that she loved seemed to be falling away. To her thinking, it was as if Lord Bahl had always been within him, like a seed beneath soil. The priest's revelation was the water that had caused it to sprout. Nor was the change merely a matter of conception: it appeared physical as well.

Shadow's eyes, which always had softened when they gazed at her, remained sharp and cold. In fact, Moli had never seen them so cold before. Though she wondered if it might be only her imagination, his eyes appeared to have grown paler. The alteration made the black pupils all the more piercing. Shadow's voice had become harder also. A certain haughtiness had crept into it, and he spoke to the fawning priest as if he were speaking from a throne and not a crude wooden bench. Lastly, the chill that always clung to him had intensified. It caused Moli to put more wood on the fire and to shiver at the thought of lying naked beneath so icy a man.

While Moli had those dismal reflections, Shadow's attention was directed elsewhere. In effect, she was invisible. "So tell me," he said to the priest, "is my palace truly made of iron?"

"Its towers and outer walls are covered with thick plates of it, my lord. Yer subjects keep it oiled, so 'tis black and shiny."

"And you say the place is large?"

"It has no rival in this world. Not even the emperor in Bremven can boast of so grand a dwelling. Many hundreds of huts this size could fit in its great hall."

"It sounds like a fitting abode," said Shadow. "And you've seen this place?"

"Aye, yer lordship. I was there recently for an audience with the Most Holy One."

"Speak of this man."

"His name is Gorm. He's a wise and loyal counselor who's skilled in the magic arts."

"A sorcerer?"

"Nay, a holy one. He's head of my order, and his powers come from the grace of god."

"You mean the Devourer."

"Aye, the mighty one who has guided ye. Ye know its strength."

"Yes, I know it, though I called it by another name. When I was little, I named it my shadow."

The priest smiled. "And then ye were its namesake for a while. How prophetic."

Even when Stregg smiled, Moli could detect no humanity in his hatchet face. Likewise, his oily voice was cold even when his words were courteous. Already, she detested the man and instinctively saw him as her enemy. Moli could tell that he wanted to drive her out. While he did nothing overt, he didn't include her in his conversation or even acknowledge her presence. Instead, all his attention was on her man, who seemed thoroughly pleased by it.

Just then, the captain returned with Bog Rat. Moli remembered the tall fensman as Shadow's companion and friend. That was when the pair first joined the pirate band. After Shadow took over, she saw little of Bog Rat, who had become one of Captain Wuulf's men. Moli didn't even know that he had a different name, and she was surprised that he was included in the feast. Unlike his captain, who had regained his composure, he seemed dumbfounded by the turn of events.

Shadow grinned at the sight of him. "Telk! Didn't I say that I was destined for great things?"

"Froan, they say ya're Lord Bahl now." Moli noted fear in Telk's voice.

"I was always Lord Bahl, only Mam hid the truth from me. But all has been revealed. Now aren't you pleased you came with me?"

"Aye," said Telk without enthusiasm.

"Henceforth, should we call ye Lord Bahl?" asked Captain Wuulf.

"Of course," replied Shadow. "Or 'my lord' or 'your lordship.' Now, when will the feast be ready?"

"Soon, my lord. 'Tisn't palace fare, but at least there'll be wine." A knock was heard. "That should be the wine now."

"Enter," said Shadow.

A soldier opened the door and brought in a small wine cask. He was followed by a second soldier bearing two goblets and some wooden bowls. It was obvious by the soldiers' uneasy manner that the news of their commander's true identity had spread. The cask was opened, and the drinking vessels were filled. Naturally, Shadow was served first. Moli noted that the soldier's hand trembled as he presented the goblet. The man then held out the remaining goblet to her, only to spill half its contents when Shadow commanded him to give it to the priest instead.

Moli gulped her wine from a wooden bowl that night. No one noticed how much she drank. Shadow and the priest seemed oblivious of all the others. Telk appeared withdrawn, miserable, and perhaps a little mad. When Moli gazed at Captain Wuulf, he seemed to be weighing his change of fortune. He drank sparingly, said little, and closely watched Shadow and the priest. *He wants ta see if there's a place fer him*, thought Moli. She could sympathize with his plight. Lord Bahl already had an army. Moli knew little of such things, but she imagined it was full of captains who owned proper armor and had finer backgrounds.

Moli thought that her prospects were even bleaker than the captain's. As Lord Bahl, Shadow would have his pick of women. Moli doubted he would choose a whore with missing teeth and a peasant's sun-darkened complexion and work-calloused hands. Moreover, Moli sensed that her lover was beginning to forsake human feelings altogether. It was just an impression, but her instincts were seldom wrong.

When the roast mutton, boiled roots, and grain porridge had been consumed and the wine cask was empty, Shadow rose. "Captain," he said, "tomorrow we will alter course and head for Bahland. Why conquer a realm when one awaits us?"

"As ye command, my lord."

"Have the men ready to march at dawn."

"Aye, yer lordship."

"Priest Stregg," said Shadow, "this hut is a lowly place but warmer than sleeping on the ground. Stay here tonight."

Stregg bowed. "Ye honor me, my lord. But I don't wish to intrude upon yer privacy."

Shadow smiled. "Privacy means naught in the field, so don't decline this honor. Besides, my woman's a pirate wench and used to tupping in front of others."

The march began shortly after dawn, and though it headed southwest, in many ways it seemed little different from previous marches. Shadow and Captain Wuulf rode on horseback at the head of a small column of soldiers. To the front and the sides were the men Shadow had inflamed, roving like foraging ants. Ragged, ill armed, and mostly mad, they wrought most of the destruction. Whether the band of soldiers and hapless peasants were Shadow's men bent on conquest or Lord Bahl's men heading homeward, they still needed to live off the land. Thus they pillaged everything in their path.

The canvas sides of Moli's wagon were raised, and even though the vehicle brought up the rear, she noted changes in the march. For one, the soldiers seemed grimmer. Moli suspected that was because their prospects had diminished. None of them could expect to grow rich on booty; that would go to Lord Bahl's coffers. Also, it was apparent that Shadow had withdrawn his order that she be shielded from gruesome sights. His men's victims were left in view; whereas before, the soldiers had whisked them away before the wagon passed. Finally, the wagon was no longer her sanctuary. To her dismay, Shadow had offered Stregg a place in it. She was relieved that the priest had declined to ride, saying he preferred to march with the men. Moli occasionally spotted him talking to the soldiers. She had no idea what he was saying, but the conversations didn't appear casual.

Early in the afternoon, Moli looked ahead and saw that the road would soon pass between wooded hills. The sight of them set her heart pounding, for all day she had been looking for an opportunity to escape. Moli felt it was her only hope. She no longer believed that she had a future with Shadow, although she doubted that he would release her. While Moli thought a part of him still cared for her, that part was rapidly fading. Shadow might need her, but Lord Bahl didn't. Every tale she'd ever heard served up this warning: Lord Bahl was never stayed by sentiment. When she became useless to him, he'd destroy her.

Moli crawled under the coverlet to dress in her most practical clothes. She would have preferred peasant garb, but all she had was finery. In the end, she chose a sky-blue cloak of lightweight wool, and an equally thin wool shift. For footwear, she had to settle for dainty slippers. She remained under the coverlet after she dressed, peeking out occasionally to gauge the wagon's progress. At last, it entered the trees.

As Moli had hoped, the lane was narrow and hemmed by scrub and undergrowth. The men afoot were ahead, and the wagons dropped behind as their drivers struggled to guide their teams through the difficult way. Since the horses had her driver's full attention, Moli was able to gather a body-shaped mound of clothes and pillows beneath the coverlet. That done, she crawled to the wagon's rear, dropped over its end, and dove into the surrounding bushes.

Afterward, she anxiously listened for some sign that her departure had been noted. If someone spotted her, she planned to say she was tending to a female problem—that usually silenced men, even soldiers.

The ploy proved unnecessary. The sounds of wagon wheels, hoofbeats, and marching feet gradually faded into silence. Moli was alone. She was also free for the first time since the pirates took her. As a dishonored woman, she could never return home, even if she knew the way. Therefore, Moli was well aware of the risk she was taking. She was lost in a desolate land. She had no food or water and was inadequately dressed. Nevertheless, she hoped to find a refuge. With luck, she might even become a wife, for the world was full of needy men.

FORTY·ONE

TOWARD THE middle of the afternoon, Lord Bahl's forces encountered an obstacle. Upon rounding a curve, the men discovered that a stream had cut a gully across the road. Captain Wuulf rode up to it for a closer look. Gazing down the lane, he could see that the trees thinned in the distance and the way ahead was clear, but that didn't solve his immediate problem. He paused to study the terrain awhile, then rode back to Lord Bahl. "Yer lordship," he said, "the gully is no barrier to men or horses, but we can't drive a wagon across its gap." Wuulf watched his commander's face redden, and for the first time, it frightened him.

"So we must turn around and waste a day!"

"If we empty the wagons, the men could carry them down and up the gully. That will take time, but less than a detour."

"Then do it."

Wuulf called his sergeants over and told them his plan. Afterward, they immediately set their squads to work. First, the wagons were driven as close as possible to the obstacle. Then the horses were unhitched and led through the woods to cross at a place where the gully's sides sloped gently. Meanwhile, the supply wagons were emptied and their contents carried to the far side of the gap. All this went smoothly until it was time to empty Moli's wagon. Captain Wuulf sensed something was amiss when he saw the wagon driver walking up with the reluctant pace and fearful expression of one bearing bad news.

"Captain," said the frightened man. "Captain."

"What is it, soldier? Speak up."

"She's gone, sir! Lord Sha— Lord Bahl's lady! I thought she was sleeping, but . . ."

"Have ye looked for her? She might be strolling about."

"I did, sir, and I couldn't find her."

Captain Wuulf spotted a sergeant and called him over. "I want yer squad to make a quick search for our lordship's lady. Before I tell Lord Bahl she's missing, I want to be certain she is."

The mere mention of Lord Bahl spurred the sergeant and his men into action. As Wuulf watched them hurry off, he reflected on the power of that name. He wondered if its fearsome reputation was the reason that Shadow seemed transformed, but he suspected a more arcane power was at work. *Something to do with the priest and his god.* Even thinking about it made him uneasy. *Shadow's become less a man and more a monster. If his woman's fled, I don't blame her.*

A short while later, the sergeant reported back. "She's

not here, sir. I think she ran off, for she piled clothing under her blanket to fool her driver."

"Thank ye, Sergeant. Resume moving the wagons."

Wuulf rode off to speak to Lord Bahl, who had remained mounted to better watch the soldiers work. The captain had a tight feeling in his gut, which became even stronger when he noted that the priest was with Bahl. Wuulf reined his horse to a stop, then bowed from the saddle. "My lord, I bring ill tidings. Yer lady has disappeared."

"What! How?"

"I believe she's taken leave."

"Bring me her driver," said Lord Bahl. "I wish to question him."

Wuulf soon returned with the young soldier. When the pair arrived, they found Lord Bahl on foot. The captain quickly dismounted so as not to tower over his superior, who was smiling coldly as he approached the soldier. "I'm told you have some news for me."

All the color left the soldier's face. "She sleeps a lot, sir, I mean, yer lordship. I thought that's what she was doing. Sleeping."

"And?"

"So when it was time to unload the wagon, I went to wake her, and when I shook her covers . . . well, there was nothing under them. Only clothes and stuff. I looked for her. I really did. Hard, too. But she was gone."

Captain Wuulf expected Lord Bahl to question the driver further, but he merely gazed into the man's eyes. The soldier's features and body became rigid, and remained that way until Bahl broke eye contact and smiled. "My woman has disappeared, but that's her doing, not yours. You weren't an accomplice."

The soldier looked relieved until Bahl's dagger pierced his belly. It happened so quickly that even Wuulf didn't see the weapon being drawn. "Nevertheless," said Bahl, his voice seemingly calm, "you were careless, and those who serve me are held to a high standard." Bahl's expression matched his voice, as though he were giving the man a mild rebuke. "You didn't meet that standard." He twisted his blade before withdrawing it. Then he pointed to a nearby soldier. "You! Come here!" The man rushed over. By then, the driver was doubled over, clutching his bloody gut. Bahl turned to the newcomer. "Set this man by the roadside and let no one tend him while he dies. Fail in this, you'll suffer as he does. Now go."

Bahl turned to the captain. "I want her back."

Wuulf felt that he might soon share the driver's fate, and strangely, the prospect of death heightened his courage. He bowed low, then spoke. "I'll get her if ye command. But first, my lord, consider this: Some lasses liken to wildflowers. They're comely in a rough setting but soon wither when plucked from their roots. Moli won't thrive in yer iron house. 'Twill kill her. She knew that, and so she left. Though I may fetch her, ye won't have her—not for long. Recall yer tenderness toward Moli, and let her go so she might live."

Wuulf gazed at Lord Bahl, half expecting to feel his blade. Instead, he saw tears welling in his commander's eyes. The hardness was gone from them, and when his lordship spoke, his voice had thawed. "I'd never harm her." He paused a moment, and his face grew sad. "Continue moving the wagons, Captain. I'll let her go her way."

As Captain Wuulf mounted and rode off, Stregg lifted his eyes from the dying soldier to gaze at Lord Bahl's face. He was alarmed to see tears there. As evidence of sentiment, they betrayed a weakness that must be stemmed. He pondered a moment on which tactic to use. Then he spoke. "I think your captain is perceptive. The wench wasn't suited for palace life. Ye acted wisely."

Lord Bahl sighed heavily. "I guess so."

"Yet I fear yer men will see weakness instead of wisdom," said the priest. "Although ye were stern with the man, they'll think ye let a wench flout ye."

"It can't be helped."

"It might be better to grant her leave before everyone. Then her freedom would arise from yer generosity, not her disobedience." Stregg paused a moment, as if considering his idea. "But of course, ye'd have to fetch her to do that."

"It would serve her ill to drag her back."

"More likely 'twould help her. I suspect she lacks provisions. Besides, ye could say proper farewells."

"You're right," said Lord Bahl. "I'll have the captain find her."

"No need to do that, yer lordship. Using him will delay the march. I'll speak with yer friend Telk. He can be trusted with the task. And I'll ask another to aid him."

"Thank you, Stregg. You've lightened my heart."

The priest hurried off. Lord Bahl mounted his horse, and watched as his men struggled to lift the first of the wagons over the far edge of the gully.

There was still enough daylight left to resume the march when the wagons were moved and their teams hitched up. Captain Wuulf was making his final checks when one of his sergeants approached him. "Sir, I've two men who haven't returned. Should I post a man to wait fer them?"

"Haven't returned? Where did they go?"

"On some business fer his lordship. The priest sent them."

"And who were the men?"

"Telk and Chopper."

"Don't post a man, Sergeant. I'll look into this." Upon saying that, Wuulf rode off to find Stregg. When he did, he reined his horse just short of trampling the man, and then glared down at him. "Before I tell Lord Bahl the march is delayed, I'd best know the reason why!"

Stregg looked up with an innocent expression. "Delayed?"

"Because ye sent two men somewhere. Why?"

"*I* didn't send them anywhere. 'Twas Lord Bahl. He changed his mind about fetching the wench."

"And ye asked Chopper to do it? The man's a rabid dog."

The priest maintained his innocent expression. "And how was I to know that?"

"Because ye've two eyes and mayhap a bit of brain. When did they leave?"

"A while ago."

Wuulf spurred his horse down the road to find the two men. He considered Chopper a lunatic, but Telk was observant and accustomed to the wild, which potentially made him a good tracker. The men would be seeking Moli, and he was seeking them. Thus it seemed his best chance to find the men was to look for Moli. Since her wagon was at the rear of the march, her trail should be undisturbed. He rode slowly down the dusty road, gazing at its surface and the vegetation that flanked it. Toward the border of the woods he found something. It wasn't Moli's trail, but that of her pursuers. Since they had no reason for stealth, it was easy to follow. Wuulf dismounted and led his horse along a path marked by trampled undergrowth, broken twigs and branches, and the deep footprints left by hurrying men. He had traveled only a short way before he heard someone coming.

Soon a figure appeared among the trees. Wuulf recognized the man from his scarred nose and manic gaze. "Chopper! What are ye about?"

"The master's business, Cap. She took it."

As Chopper came nearer, Wuulf noticed a change in him. The man's madness had blossomed. His face twitched, drool bathed his chin, and his eyes were bright and agitated. It made the captain wonder what Stregg had said or done to him. "What did she take?"

"Somethin' the master wants. Somethin' he needs back."

"What are ye babbling about?"

Chopper reached into a pocket and pulled out a lump of bloody flesh. "Our master's heart. Hid it in her chest, she did. But Ah chopped and chopped and chopped it out." Chopper grinned broadly, but the smile didn't reach his troubled eyes.

Wuulf gripped his sword hilt, but stayed his hand. *What's the point?* he thought. *Lord Bahl will serve him worse.* Instead of slaying Chopper, he asked, "Where's Telk?"

Chopper shrugged. "Back there."

"Alive?"

Chopper shrugged again. "Master wants his heart."

"Then ye should give it to him."

Chopper ambled off as Wuulf mounted his horse. Following Chopper's trail, the captain eventually encountered Telk. He was using his hands to dig in the loam while weeping. Moli lay nearby, her chest and face covered with a sky-blue cloak. "Telk?"

Telk didn't look up; he just continued digging and sobbing. Wuulf dismounted and drew his sword. He walked over to the weeping man and began to use his blade to enlarge the hole. The two dug wordlessly together until the sky began to grow dark. By then, they had excavated a shallow grave and Telk had stopped crying. Finally, the captain broke the silence. "We should get her in the ground. They may come looking for us."

"She didn't deserve ta die like that."

"Nay, she didn't."

"She loved him, and I think he loved her."

"That's why the black priest wanted her dead," said Wuulf. "I see his game now. Ye shouldn't go back. He'll slay ye, too."

"Why?"

"Because ye're Shadow's friend."

"But where can I go?"

"Anywhere but back, if ye value yer soul. I can give ye a ride awhile, for I'm not returning." Captain Wuulf gazed at his dirt-covered blade and reflected that digging was the only worthy use he had put it to for a long time. "I'm a hard man, Telk. But not so hard that I'll serve Lord Bahl. For that's what yer friend will be. Not just in name, but in spirit. The priest will see to that."

"I don't know if I can leave him."

"I know he has a hold on ye. I can see it in yer eyes. Mayhap that hold will break when yer far enough away from him. Ride with me and find out. Think on it while we put yer friend's love to rest."

The two men dragged Moli to her shallow grave and covered her as best they could. Then they rode off together.

It took a while for Stregg to realize just how well things had turned out. Having engineered the wench's slaying, he had anticipated Chopper's return and execution. Though love had fueled Lord Bahl's rage, it was rage nonetheless and therefore served the Devourer. The captain's and Telk's desertions were unexpected boons. Their departure saved the need for further plots. After just a single day, Stregg had managed to get the heir all to himself. On the long trip to Bahland, he would use that opportunity to become his lordship's mentor. The priest smiled, seeing the prospect as a sign of the Devourer's grace. It seemed but the first of many blessings to come.

FORTY·TWO

For Honus, the days of travel blended together until he lost count. Over time, the landscape altered, and mountains rose on the horizon. The trees began to shed their leaves as the days and nights turned cool and then cold. But these changes were significant to Honus only as far as they marked progress toward his destination. It was his entire focus; comfort, rest, and even food seemed of little importance. When he reached Averen, the terrain turned rugged, and on a stony mountain trail his mare slipped and broke her leg. The only way Honus could ease the horse's suffering was by ending her life. He did it reluctantly with a single swipe of his sword and then continued onward.

Eventually, he was greeted by a sight that he hadn't seen for eighteen winters, the Lake of the Urkzimdi. His path hugged the northwestern shore, and the lake stretched out before him, steel gray beneath an overcast sky. Low mountains formed a backdrop, their sides dark green with pine and spruce or gray and brown with leafless maple and winter oak. To the east lay fields, orchards, and in the distance, Cara's hall. Honus noted some changes since he had seen it last. The village had enlarged, and the walls surrounding the manor house had sprouted a strange, stumpy tower. It appeared to have a tree growing from its top.

As Honus stared at the tower, he heard a voice behind him. "Greetings, Karmamatus. She's na yet arrived."

Honus turned and beheld a bizarre young girl. From her boyish frame, he judged her nine or ten winters old. A length of vine was wrapped several times around her thin waist. It held long leaves that formed a sort of skirt, which barely met the needs of modesty. The vine and leaves were all she wore despite the chill weather. Stranger yet, she was soaking wet. Her long blond hair was plastered to her goose-pimpled skin. Nevertheless, her face was perfectly serene, showing no hint of discomfort.

"Who hasn't arrived?" asked Honus, too surprised to say anything else.

"Mother."

"Your mother?"

"Nay." The girl smiled. "And yes." Her moon-pale skin and sky-colored eyes seemed reminiscent of someone Honus had met, but at the moment, he couldn't recall whom. Puzzled by the girl's reply, Honus asked a question that might get a more straightforward answer. "Were you swimming in the lake?"

"Aye."

"Why? The water's deadly cold this time of year."

"To meet you." The girl gazed at Honus awhile, seeming to study him before she spoke again. "Your iron stick has served its purpose. Best be rid of it."

"I thank you for that counsel," replied Honus, not knowing what to make of the nonsensical advice or the girl who gave it. His only certainty was that she made him uneasy. Thus he smiled courteously and said, "I must take your leave, for I'm in haste to get to the hall."

"Of course," the girl replied and headed in that direction.

Honus resumed walking. Without ever looking back, the girl maintained a pace that kept her in front. It seemed to be a game to her, for whenever Honus sped or slowed his steps, the girl adjusted hers so that anyone who saw the pair would have thought the Sarf was being led. When they entered the village, Honus was surprised to find the dirt lane to the hall had been paved with fitted stones. The buildings that flanked it seemed to mark prosperous times. There was a proper inn in addition to other new structures, and many of the older ones had a story added or other improvements.

The gates in the clan hall's outer wall looked unchanged except that a new door had been inset within one of them. It flew open even before the girl reached it, and a young woman emerged. She appeared to be a servant and bore a dull brown cloak, which she wrapped about the girl. "Thistle!" she said, "why are you about?"

"Mother's coming. Karmamatus is already here."

The woman looked up and seemed to notice Honus for the first time. She bowed, then said, "Greetings, Karmamatus. Our clan mother welcomes all Karm's servants to her hall."

As Honus returned the bow, Thistle slipped through the open door and disappeared. "Your chieftain's hospitality is known to me," said Honus, "for we're old friends."

The woman looked surprised. "You are?"

"From the days when Cronin was alive."

"Clan Mother's slain brother? Then na wonder I do na know you, for I was but a lass during the Troubles." The woman bowed again. "Karmamatus, please come inside and tell me your name so I might say it to Clan Mother."

"Tell her Honus has returned."

Honus followed the woman through the doorway. The pair then passed through a small, cobbled courtyard and into the hall of the Urkzimdi clan. The wood-paneled entrance hall matched Honus's recollections. Upon entering it, his guide turned to him. "You seem travel worn. Perhaps you'd like some refreshments and a chance to rest."

"Those things matter little to me," replied Honus. "I'm more eager to speak with your clan mother."

"Then I bid you wait in the great hall while I tell her that you're here."

The woman escorted Honus to the empty room and then departed. Honus gazed about the hall, which was the site of banquets and important occasions. Everything he saw evoked memories of his last visit. He recalled the evening Yim and he arrived. At the banquet, Yim had told Cronin that his true enemy was the Devourer and that he couldn't fight a god. *Cronin stormed out of the hall, but what she said proved true.* Honus reflected that it remained true, and although Lord Bahl had lost his power, it had merely passed to another. *The foe remains the same, and we're still powerless against it.* Then Honus's musings were interrupted by the echoing sound of rapid footsteps. He turned and saw Cara running toward him.

"Honus! Oh, zounds, is it truly you? I've thought you were dead for nigh on eighteen winters! And who would na? Havren said you went to fight Lord Bahl alone. And then na a peep from you since then. I'm displeased, Honus, I truly am."

Honus smiled. "Then I throw myself on your mercy."

"Well, 'tis in short supply. My children have used it up. I have five, na that you'd know. Where have you been? Under some rock? And what of Yim?"

"It's a long tale, Cara."

"And I want to hear every word of it," replied Cara. " 'Tis clear you've na led an easy life. Zounds, Honus, you look awful!"

"And you look just the opposite," said Honus. "You seem little changed since we parted."

"Pah, Honus! When did you learn flattery? I'm thicker in the middle—children do that to you—and short one arm, in case you have na noticed. But 'tis . . ." Cara's eyes welled with tears, and she threw her arm around Honus. "Oh 'tis *so* good to see you! So . . . so very good."

Honus felt his own eyes tear up as he returned Cara's embrace. They stood that way awhile, neither speaking, until Cara finally broke the silence. "Now tell me something, Honus. What happened at Tor's Gate? I know that Yim arrived, for Havren told me so. He also said she left the same night and did something that changed all our fortunes and that you went to find her."

"He promised silence concerning my plans."

"Oh, zounds, Honus, I *married* him. So naturally, he told me everything. He did na have a choice."

Honus smiled. "I can readily see that. Well, here's a shortened version of my tale. Yim arrived, convinced that she was supposed to bear my child."

Cara grinned. "I did that!"

"But I had to position my troops before she and I could lie together. While I was gone, Karm came to Yim and revealed who must father her child."

"It wasn't you?"

"No."

"Then who?"

"Lord Bahl."

Cara stared at Honus, shocked into silence for once.

"When Yim conceived with Bahl," continued Honus, "his powers went to his unborn child. Yim's sacrifice brought us this current stretch of peace."

"But who told you that? Yim left you."

"Yim herself. I freed her from Lord Bahl's soldiers. I would have gone anywhere with her, but she said that we must part. She went north to raise the child alone and I . . ." As Honus paused to calm himself, he thought of how Cara had married, borne children, and governed a clan, while he had become self-absorbed with his misery. The comparison chagrined him. "I didn't take it well. I blamed Karm for tearing us apart and despised her for it. In my rage, I renounced her. I became a derelict who tranced to seek the forgotten joys of the dead."

"Oh, Honus, why did na you come here instead?"

"My entire life was dedicated to the goddess. After renouncing Karm, I lacked purpose. Moreover, anything that reminded me of Yim heightened my pain. I couldn't come here. I found happiness only on the Dark Path, though it was never truly mine."

"So what changed?"

"A former Bearer plucked me from my errant path by giving me hope and a purpose. He said Yim needs me."

"Then why come here? I'm pleased you did, but puzzled."

"It was the guidance of my runes. They said to seek you out."

"So now what? Yim's na here. I've heard na more from her than you. I thought both of you were dead."

"Regardless, my runes directed me here," said Honus. "Now all I can do is wait."

"And you're more than welcome to do so. We can grow old together, though it seems you've got a big head start. Zounds, Honus, those runes were tattooed on your back when you were just a child! They've been saying the same thing for what? Forty winters?"

"Actually, a bit longer."

"So what makes you think Yim will show up anytime soon? I hope to Karm she does. But, face it, it does na seem likely."

"I'm surprised to hear you say that," replied Honus. "You used to be such a romantic."

"I still am. But I've seen a lot since we last spoke. Too much, *that's* for sure! And I so wanted Yim and you to . . . oh, well . . . at least *you've* come back. I'm glad for that."

"Now you must tell me about your life," said Honus, "though I'm not entirely unenlightened." He smiled. "You're quite renowned. I've even learned from a ballad that faeries took your arm."

Cara rolled her eyes. "So you heard that version. Na the one where a great fish bites it off? Myself, I prefer the ballad in which I take up my severed arm and club my foes to death."

"So what really happened?"

"My steward betrayed me, and the hall was attacked. Yim and I escaped, but were caught outside the walls. A man with a scythe did this," said Cara, pointing to her stump. "Yim saved me by rowing us to the faerie dell, where the Old Ones healed me in a single night. The next day was the last I ever spent with Yim."

"So you've met the Old Ones?"

"Only that one time."

"What are they like?"

"They were the size of children and covered with fur. Though they looked a bit like animals, I thought they were kindly and wise. That's before I learned about Dar's Gift."

Honus was puzzled. "You mean the cheese?"

Cara laughed with a hint of bitterness. "That's what we called that ball of cheese. We called it Dar's Gift for generations. The clan mother and her eldest daughter took the cheese to the dell each fall when the tree turned gold. But the cheese was never truly the gift."

"Then what was?"

"I learned *that* the hard way! My first born were twin girls, Rose and Violet, so much alike that the midwife confused them and couldn't say who was birthed first. So to keep with tradition, both accompanied me when I took Dar's Gift to the dell. There, you place the cheese on a certain stone, the same one where Dar Beard Chin made the first offering. And then it seems you only blink your eyes, but the day is gone and so is the gift. But the fourth time I took the twins with me, when I opened my eyes, more than the cheese was gone. Violet was, too!"

"You mean the Old Ones stole your daughter?"

"I thought as much, though I dared na search the dell for her. Besides, 'twould have been pointless as well as perilous. But in the spring, Violet came home on her own, seeming na a day older than when I last saw her. She said she'd been faerie-kissed."

Honus recalled the faerie-kissed girl that he and Yim

had encountered on their journey. Her name had been Lila, and he realized that Lila was the one whom the strange girl resembled. "Do the Old Ones do this often?" Honus asked. "On the road today, I met a girl named Thistle who also seemed faerie-kissed."

"Then you saw Violet, for Thistle's the name she's taken. Was she naked?"

"No," replied Honus. "She wore a skirt of leaves."

"Well, thank Karm for that! I swear that— Nay, I will na go into it. Yet 'tis strange you met her, for 'tis the season when she sleeps with the Old Ones. Sleeps like a bear through winter in their burrows. She does na age then, only when she bides with us. 'Tis a strain on me, there's na denying it. Rose has entered womanhood, and her twin remains a child. But a child who seems older than anyone I know. And odder, too. Zounds, *that's* Karm's truth. Na doubt you saw her tower. I had it built when she could na longer abide the manor. Did you see that tree? 'Tis an oak with a trunk thicker than a man. Well, it grew in just one season." Cara shook her head. "The Old Ones saved my life, but took my daughter. And you know what, Honus? There's many a day that, if given a chance, I'd work that bargain the other way. I swear by Karm, Violet's stranger each time she returns from the dell. She's taken to giving things different names and insisting they're the right ones. Thistle, for one. She'll na answer to Violet, though I keep trying."

"Does she call a sword an iron stick?"

"Aye. Why do you ask?"

"She told me to get rid of mine. She said it had served its purpose."

"Then you see what I put up with—a string of nonsense."

"I'm not so sure it's nonsense," replied Honus.

"Zounds, Honus! Do na start with me! What would you know about it?"

"Yim and I encountered a mother and daughter who were both faerie-kissed."

"Yim never mentioned that."

"I'm not surprised," said Honus. "There was something otherworldly about the pair, as if they spoke only secrets." Honus paused. "I just recalled something—both of them called Yim 'Mother.' I think your daughter did the same today. She greeted me on the road and said, 'She's not yet arrived.' When I asked who hadn't arrived, she said 'Mother.' And she told a servant 'Mother's coming.' "

"So?"

"I think Thistle was telling me that Yim's coming. I believe she's far wiser than you credit. Why wouldn't she be? After all, Thistle's your daughter."

"I'd prefer you call her Violet, and na that weed. Zounds, the trials one's children put one through! You should thank Karm that you didn't beget a child!" Cara, put her only hand to her mouth, "Oh sorry, Honus, I should na have said that! How stupid! Please forgive me."

Honus smiled, albeit somewhat sadly. "I do, Cara. But before you complain about Violet again, remember Yim and *her* child."

FORTY-THREE

HONUS AND Cara lingered in the great hall, speaking together for a long while. As usual, Cara did most of the talking. Honus heard of Havren's return from Tor's Gate, bearing tidings of Cronin's death and how Havren's kindness tempered Cara's grief. She told how their love blossomed in the aftermath of the Troubles, and she shared stories of their courtship, wedding, and marriage. Cara spoke of all her children, not just Violet. Rose—like her twin—was nearing her sixteenth winter. She had already become renowned for her beauty and courtly manners. Young Cronin, Cara's eldest son, had the looks and strong personality of his namesake. At fourteen, he was sturdily built and a natural leader. Holden, the middle son, was the quiet and thoughtful one, while Torald emulated his eldest brother. Cara also spoke of politics, her trips to Bremven, her current building project, the fall's harvest, and whatever else popped into her mind, enlivening her accounts with all manner of gossip. None of it was mean-spirited, for true to her word, Cara remained a romantic.

Honus gave only terse descriptions of his doings and would have been content merely to listen to Cara if she had permitted him. At her insistence, he spoke of his winter siege of Bahl's stronghold and how he had rescued Yim. He said little about their parting, and next to nothing about the long, empty stretch of winters that followed. In truth, he remembered little of that time. Although he spoke of Daven and the incidents in Cuprick, he kept his otherworldly encounter with Yim to himself. Through his calm and matter-of-fact tone, Honus tried to hide the depths of his feelings, but Cara sensed them nonetheless.

"And you still love Yim after all this time," said Cara, her eyes alight.

"Yes," admitted Honus, "though that love oft seems like torment."

"When I first saw you two, I knew nothing about love's pain," said Cara. "Then, it seemed all about living happily ever after. Yet even then I was clever enough to see that you were smitten, though you denied it. And to think you thought Yim was your slave! Zounds, she sure turned *that* around!"

Honus sighed. "She certainly did."

"This is going to end well, Honus. I do na know how, or why, but I think it will. I certainly *hope* so!"

Cara would have liked to have wiled away the afternoon with Honus, but she had to sit in judgment over a dispute. She left him in the care of Freenla, the same young woman who had met him at the door. "Clan Mother says you're to have a room to yourself," said Freenla, unable to conceal her puzzlement. " 'Tis a high honor."

"Especially for a worn-out and ragged derelict."

"You look fine, Karmamatus."

"And you're a gracious liar," said Honus. He silently followed Freenla through the corridors awhile before asking, "Do you know Violet well?"

"Aye. And she's Thistle, never mind what her mother says. I tend Thistle during her season with us. That is, what little tending she needs."

"But according to Lady Cara, this is the season when she sleeps in the dell. Was it just happenstance that you met her at the door?"

"There's na such thing where Thistle is concerned. She dreamed to me so I'd be waiting."

"Dreamed to you? What does that mean?"

"She can enter dreams as a way of speaking."

"Yet you seemed to not know why she came."

"Aye, Thistle keeps much to herself."

"Does she say anything about the one she calls Mother?"

Freenla bowed her head. "Begging your pardon, Karmamatus, but 'tis a matter between you and Thistle, na the likes of me."

"You seem to hold the girl in high regard," said Honus, "higher than her mother does."

"Karmamatus, my husband's an Urkzimdi, but I'm a Dolbane. I'm alive because of Lady Cara. When my da and mam were slain in the feuding, my brother brought me here. Lady Cara protected us and provided as best she could. All the food we ate came from her hands, so I'll na speak ill of her. But Thistle is beyond her ken. And mine, too."

By then, the pair had reached the upper floor of the

manor house. Freenla led Honus down a narrow corridor and into a room tucked under the eaves. Its slanting ceiling was broken by a dormer that faced the low mountains nearby to the north and the road Cronin's army had taken to Tor's Gate. The room appeared seldom used, and its floor was strewn with flowers that had withered to shades of beige and brown. Nonetheless, it was a pleasant chamber with wood-paneled walls carved with floral designs, a large feather bed, and a small fireplace. A fire had been lit to warm the room, and nearby was a basin and an ewer of water. Upon a small table was a loaf of bread, a large piece of cheese, an ale jug, and a goblet.

After Freenla left, Honus realized how hungry and tired he was. All the drive that had brought him to his destination dissipated, and he became aware of how great a toll his journey had exacted. The bed looked inviting, but so did the food. For a moment, Honus's fatigue battled his hunger. Hunger won. Honus bit into the cheese and tore off a large hunk from the loaf. As he chewed, he walked over to the window. From it, he could view the tower Cara had built for her faerie-kissed daughter. It seemed a large undertaking for the sake of a child, a concrete testament of maternal devotion.

Honus peered at the structure with interest. It rose slightly higher than the hall's surrounding wall, but not as high as the manor itself. It was an open-topped cylinder that tapered slightly from its base. The structure was starkly functional, and its stonework gave the impression that it had been hastily erected. Its top, which was about ten paces in diameter, lacked crenellations. From his viewpoint, Honus could see nothing of what lay inside the tower's open top except the tree. It rose to form a roof of sorts. Since the tree was an oak, it had retained most of its brown autumn leaves. They were whipped about by a brisk wind that had suddenly filled with snowflakes.

As Honus gazed at the tree, he spotted Thistle sitting

high among its branches. She was still wrapped in the brown cloak that Freenla had given her, which made her blend with the dry leaves. Her bare legs and feet dangled in the wind, appearing almost as white as the falling snow. She swayed with the branch on which she perched but was otherwise perfectly still. Thistle stared northward. Even from his removed vantage point, Honus sensed the intensity of her gaze and concluded that she was waiting for something important to happen.

Settlements were few and far between in the Western Reach, so it wasn't uncommon for Frodoric to be caught outdoors by nightfall when he traveled. Halfway between two distant and tiny villages, the bard scanned the darkening landscape for any sight of firelight. When he saw none, he sighed and spoke to the only one present—himself. "By Karm's icy feet, another night 'neath her starry roof. And winter nipping at my buns. But there's naught to do about it, other than gather firewood. Best seek some while there's yet light." He set down his pack and harp to go looking for wood.

By the time it was dark, he had a small blaze going. After he brewed some herb water in a small pot, he pulled out his only income from the previous night's singing—a small loaf of brown bread. He broke it in two with difficulty, then dunked an end into the herb water to soften its crust. After consuming half the loaf, the bard took out his harp and strummed it. Music helped make the night feel less lonely. He continued playing until he thought he heard footsteps in the dry grass. Frodoric stopped strumming and listened. He heard a couple of footsteps, then nothing more. Peering about, he saw only black beyond the light cast by his fire.

"Hallo! Is anyone about? I'm but a traveling bard, poor in everything but songs. Come, and I'll share one with you."

Frodoric waited. For what seemed a long while, he heard

and saw no sign of another person. "Come, friend," he said. "I'm sure you mean no harm, for I've nothing worth taking."

After an additional spell of silence, he heard the rustle of footsteps in the grass. Their slow cadence gave the impression of a cautious approach. Frodoric peered in the direction of the sound. Eventually he saw a shadowy form. As it drew nearer, the form became a hooded figure carrying a stick in one hand. Then the firelight illuminated the figure better and the "stick" turned out to be an unsheathed sword, its blade coated with dried blood.

Frodoric's heart sank, and he made the Sign of the Balance. "For Karm's sake, please don't hurt me!"

The stranger spoke with a woman's voice. "I only want directions. Do you know these parts?"

"As well as any man, better than most," replied Frodoric, feeling somewhat relieved but still cautious.

"Then how do I get to Bahland?"

"Why in the name of mercy would you wish to go there?"

"I have a relative in the Iron Palace."

"I have relatives on the Dark Path, but I've no wish to visit them."

The woman stepped closer to the light. She looked weary and melancholy. Frodoric noted that she had an ugly scar across her throat. "Will you help me or not?" she asked.

"I'll help you," replied the bard, "by warning you to stay clear of that place. Its folk are hostile to strangers, and quick to do them harm. Many a traveler has been snared by their harsh laws, which are enforced with hot irons, the gibbet, and the chopping block."

"Yet it's my doom to go there," replied the woman.

Her resigned manner calmed Frodoric's fear and awoke his sympathy. "That's no gentle fate," he said.

"There's no such thing as fate," replied the stranger. "It's my choice."

"Well, it's an unfortunate one."

The woman sighed. "So you don't know the way?"

"Only what I've learned from song. Bahland lies to the west, and the Iron Palace overlooks the ocean from a high cliff at the head of a bay."

"I already knew that, but thank you anyway," said the woman, who seemed about to leave.

"You're not a sorceress are you?"

The woman smiled at the question. "No," she replied.

"If you can't conjure up your dinner, then dine on this." Frodoric held out what remained of his loaf. "It's a rare thing to meet a woman traveling alone." As soon as the bard said that, he thought of Honus's search. He was about to mention it when he recalled that the Sarf had gone to Averen. Therefore, he simply stated that he was Frodoric of Bremven.

"I'm Mirien of Nowhere."

"Ah," said the bard, "a locale of high repute. I'm told many folk are headed there. In fact, I'm oft told that I'm going there myself. Are you a native? Mayhap you could acquaint me with its inns."

The woman smiled. "No one runs a fine establishment."

"Excellent news! No one has been good to me before."

"Then, no doubt, no one will be good to you again."

Frodoric grinned. "Such fine repartee! Mirien, would you mind pulling back your hood?" When she complied, he appraised her face. "I know this will sound forward, but my intentions are entirely commercial. Forget your trip to Bahland and accompany me instead to pass my hat while I sing. We could make a fortune. My art matched with your wit and comely looks would be a lucrative combination."

"You should be more cautious about whom you invite as a partner," replied the woman, "for I'm not alone."

Frodoric started and fearfully scanned the surrounding darkness.

"My companion is not in the darkness without," said

the woman in response to the bard's fearful peering. "It's the darkness within. I struggle with it daily."

Her reply confused Frodoric and did little to calm his apprehension. "And do you win those struggles?"

"I've yet to lick the blood from my sword, and I haven't slain anyone for a while."

Frodoric swallowed hard, regretting his invitation. "You talk as if it's a temptation."

"As I said, it's a struggle. I've grown stronger, but so has my foe."

Frodoric impulsively pressed the bread into the woman's hand. "Then eat and build your strength. There's herb water in the pot. It helps with the chewing. While you eat, I'll sing something calming. I trust you're not a friend of Lord Bahl."

A hint of a wry smile briefly passed over the woman's lips. "No. Not a friend."

"Then I know a ballad that should please you. It's based on recent history and tells how a heroic young man joins Bahl's army and subdues his power. It's an uplifting song, though its ending's sad."

"As many endings are," said the woman. "What's it called?"

" 'The Lay of Count Yaun.' "

"Count Yaun! That nasty toad!"

"You must be confused."

"Did he die at Tor's Gate?"

"Yes, quite heroically."

"I know all about the man's end, for I was there. Believe me, he was no hero. To call him a pig is an insult to pigs."

Frodoric threw up his hands. "Lately, it seems everywhere I go I meet someone who claims to know the subject of my ballad. First the Sarf, now you."

"What about the Sarf?" asked the woman, looking intrigued.

"He claimed he knew Cara One Arm when she was but a child."

"What was his name?"

"Honus. He named me Karm's Own Tongue."

"When?"

"Just half a moon ago, in Cuprick."

The woman grew excited. "Where's that? Is it far? Can you take me there?"

"If you're looking for him, he isn't there. He went to visit the Cara of the ballad."

"Do you know the way to her hall? If you'll be my guide, I'll help you with the hat and you can keep all that goes into it."

Frodoric was tempted, but wary. "What of your inner darkness?"

The woman raised her sword, swung it around her head, and hurled it into the darkness. "You're the sign that I may triumph yet. Now will you be my guide? Please. Please!"

"I can take you part of the way," said Frodoric. "I'm headed for Vinden and will pass close to Averen's northern border. I can get you that far and set you on the road to Cara One Arm's hall. Mind you, the way through Averen is hard traveling this time of year."

"I've trod far harder paths."

"Truly?" said the bard. "Any worth a ballad?"

The woman didn't reply, for her thoughts were obviously elsewhere. Her fatigue and sorrow fell away, and she beamed in a way that vanquished Frodoric's lingering fears. Then, for a moment, her face took on such radiance that she befitted the old saying and looked "as lovely as the goddess." The moment passed, and it seemed to Frodoric that the woman's inner darkness had risen up to subdue her joy. If that was so, the bard thought she might be a fitting subject for a ballad, though its ending would likely be a sad one.

FORTY·FOUR

HONUS WOKE in his room well past sunrise, which was unusually late for him. It was as if his body understood that he had no place to go and nothing to do and so surrendered to exhaustion. Despite his long sleep, he felt tired and fuzzy-headed. Nevertheless, he rose and looked out the window. The fields and the mountains beyond them were snow covered, and flakes were still falling from a gray sky. Honus thought of Yim, trudging somewhere out in the cold.

She could be anywhere, he thought. Ever since his stay in Cuprick, he'd been expecting to find Yim waiting for him at Cara's. Gazing at the empty and wintry landscape, Honus felt the full weight of his disappointment. He worried that Cara might be right, and he'd grow old waiting for Yim. *I feel old already.*

Thistle's cryptic talk of "Mother" gave Honus his only hope. He had planned to question her about it at last evening's meal, but she hadn't shown up. Cara's other children had been there, and he had met each of them. Rose had made the strongest impression, for she was strikingly similar to Thistle and different at the same time. Despite the two girls' seeming disparity in ages, Rose was clearly Thistle's twin. She had the same golden hair, blue eyes, and finely formed features; although Rose's complexion was ruddy, not pale, and her countenance was animated rather than serene. However, the principal difference was that Rose had grown without interruptions and had entered womanhood. As such, she was singularly beautiful and possessed the poise of a young lady well aware of her powers of attraction.

When Honus had asked Rose where her twin was, her face briefly lost some of its prettiness. "She's off sleeping naked with bears," she replied.

"But I saw her just this morning."

"Then you know more of her whereabouts than I. I thought she had disappeared till spring." Rose lifted her hands in a graceful gesture of despair. "She's such a wild little thing, I can't keep track of her."

Honus had made no more inquiries, and had spent the remainder of the evening attempting to be a cordial guest at a typical clan hall dinner, which included more than two dozen diners. It was a role he hadn't played for ages, and he had felt uncomfortable in it. He had been a failure as a conversationalist, for there was little about his recent history that he cared to remember, much less relate. As for his life before Yim's departure, it seemed to him the tale of a different man, one who had become a stranger. Cara had sensed Honus's unease and shushed young Cronin's and Torald's pleas for tales of battle. Nevertheless, Honus couldn't politely evade Havren's inquiries, and he had given a terse account of his one-man siege of Bahl's stronghold and the pursuit of Yim's captors that led to her rescue. Otherwise, he had eaten in silence, and departed as soon as courtesy allowed.

Honus's late rising meant that the hall's daily activity was well under way by the time he left his room. He went down to the chamber off the kitchen where the household ate their morning porridge. Due to his tardiness, he expected the porridge to be cold, and it was. Honus also expected the room to be empty. Instead, Cara was waiting for him.

"Good morn, Honus," she said cheerily. "I trust your bed was softer than the frozen ground, and the room warmer than a snowbank."

"Yes, it exceeded all expectations," replied Honus. "It

was even strewn with flowers in shades appropriate to the season."

"The room was last used by newlyweds," replied Cara. "Hence the flowers."

"If it's a love nest, then I'm out of place."

" 'Twas na you I was thinking about," replied Cara with a twinkle in her eye. "Who knows? Perhaps Yim will turn up. One can always hope."

"Only yesterday, you seemed to caution against hope."

"Perhaps I've been encouraged by this morning's miracle, for it seems you've grown a new tongue. You were quite the lump at last night's dinner."

"I've grown unused to dining with others. So, it seems, has your other daughter. I missed her last night."

"You mean Violet?"

"Yes. I wished to speak to her about Yim."

"Well, there's little point in waiting for her at meals. She seldom shows up. Better to go to her tower. She stays in a burrow beneath the tree. If she chooses to speak with you, she'll pop out of it. Otherwise, she'll na appear. If so, let her be. 'Tis unwise to trifle with her."

"She's but a girl."

"Do na be fooled by appearances. Provoke her, and you provoke the Old Ones. And they make fell enemies."

"All I want to do is talk. I doubt that will offend her."

"Well, there's a log that runs from the outer wall to an opening high in the tower's side. 'Tis the only entrance and treacherous footing in icy weather. After all your journeying, 'twould na do for you to slip and break your neck, so take care. Oh . . . and have na iron upon your person. That's all the advice I can give, except to counsel talking more at dinner. You were na so shy with me yesterday, thank Karm for that!"

"That's because we're old friends."

"Oh, we're na old. At least, I'm na. Neither are you, just weather-beaten. You've left yourself outdoors too long. It has na served you well, but never mind. A rest will mend you. Well, I must be off. A clan mother heads a large family indeed, and they save their squabbles for the wintry moons. Today, it's over oat fields and roving sheep. Serious business, Honus. Trust me, *very serious*. May Karm give me strength!"

Cara hurried off, leaving Honus to eat his cold porridge. When he finished, he returned to his room. There he checked his pockets for anything made of iron, then donned his cloak and headed for Thistle's tower. The log that Cara mentioned bridged a three-pace gap between the tower and the clan hall's surrounding wall. It was no thicker that a man's thigh, so it functioned as an obstacle as well as a bridge. The snow on its surface was undisturbed, a thin line of white contrasting with the tower's dark stone. Honus stepped onto it and made a hasty crossing to the low opening on the far side. He had to duck to enter it.

Once inside the tower, it seemed as if he were standing in a brown meadow surrounded by a circular wall that shut out the view of everything except the sky. A winding path had been trampled through the waist-high plants, and it led to the tree in the center of the enclosure. The oak grew atop a small mound and its gnarled roots surrounded the opening to the burrow that Cara had mentioned. Honus strode up to the hole and called down the dark opening. "Greetings, Thistle. Will you speak with me?"

Honus waited, but he heard no reply or sound of any sort.

"Thistle?"

Again, there was no sound. After standing in the snow awhile, Honus concluded that he should return to the hall. He was about to cross the log again when he heard a voice call, "Karmamatus!" Honus turned and saw Thistle sitting cross-legged on the snow in front of her burrow. She possessed such a presence that Honus bowed before walking back and squatting before her.

Thistle wore the same cloak that Freenla had given her. Close up, it appeared woven out of grass and vines, a rough garment that didn't look warm. Thistle had tucked the rear of the cloak beneath her to avoid sitting directly on the snow. It was her only concession to the cold; beneath the cloak she wore only her skirt of leaves, and her pale skin had taken on a bluish cast. It made Honus pity her suffering.

As if she had read his thoughts, Thistle smiled and said. "I'm merely one with the season, though at times I miss my bear. Despite what Little Sister said, I only sleep with one."

"So you don't mind the cold?"

"Does the snow mind it? But you did na come to ask me that. Speak what's on your mind."

"When you met me, you spoke of one you called Mother."

"You know of whom I speak."

"Yim?"

Thistle smiled. "Mother."

"You told Freenla that she's coming. Is she coming soon?"

"Mother gathers coins as she walks. It slows her pace. But I'll be winter hued when she and I speak." Thistle smiled as if Honus had said something funny. " 'Tis na so strange to come to me for answers. I'm older than my sister, and wiser, too." With that last remark, it seemed to Honus that the girl's tranquil expression turned sad. But it was only a passing change, and Thistle was placid when she spoke again. "Karmamatus, we two are alike—'tis our lot to wait and help as best we can. Build your strength, and your inner strength most of all. Ere long, 'twill be tested."

Once again, Honus felt that he should bow. He did, and when he raised his head, the only sign of Thistle was a slight impression in the snow. He rose, crossed the slender bridge, and made his way back into the warmth of the hall. All the while, he kept thinking of Thistle. It seemed to him that her lot was particularly hard, for Rose showed what her life would have been had the faeries not taken her. *Did the Old Ones bless or curse Thistle?* Honus couldn't decide which, any more than he could decide if his love for Yim was a blessing or a curse. Either way, he felt bound by it.

Although Honus's interview with Thistle wasn't entirely satisfactory, it gave him hope that he would be reunited with Yim before the winter was out. Since his role was to wait, he resolved to become good at it. He became more sociable. He trained during the day or participated in the frequent hunts. He devoted his evenings to Cara's children, relating his adventures with their late uncle whom they had never known. He visited Thistle's tower several more times, but she never came out when he called. Since she made no appearances in the hall, Honus believed that she had returned to the faerie dell until Freenla told him otherwise.

"Doesn't she eat?" Honus asked. "No one takes food to her tower."

"The mice do that," replied Freenla.

Honus thought that she was jesting until he remembered that owls had brought food to Lila. Afterward, Honus noted tiny trails in the snow leading to a narrow crack in the tower's base. Once, he even spied a rodent convoy, traveling single file and unmolested by the cat that watched it. It made him think of Thistle, high in her tower and yet underground. He empathized with her loneliness, for he had lived apart from others also. However, he had frequented the Dark Path, while Thistle seemed to travel in different realms. Honus had no idea what they might be. Neither could he fathom how she lived, nor what things—if any—brought her joy. Yet he knew what she was doing. Like him, she was waiting. He wondered if she foresaw what would happen when the wait was over. He certainly didn't

FORTY-FIVE

THE COMMON room was perfectly silent except for Frodoric's frenzied strumming. Yim prepared to rise, knowing that the ballad was about to end. Then the bard accompanied his harp playing by singing in a high falsetto:

"A chieftain's might springs from her brain.
  Though I can't wield a sword again,
  My foes will learn to fear my wit
  As long as on this throne I sit."

Frodoric played the final chord, and as its echoes died, he bowed. While his audience clapped and shouted, Yim rose to whisk the bard's floppy, feathered cap from his head and gracefully move about the room. As she held out the sacklike hat to receive donations, she looked like a woman enraptured by song. There was nothing beggarly about her demeanor; yet each time a man threw a coin into the cap, she smiled so warmly at him that he often tossed in a second one and sometimes even a third. Yim seemed to pay no mind whether the coin was copper or the far rarer silver, but she kept track nonetheless.

After making her rounds, Yim deftly whisked the coins into the large pocket at the front of her woolen skirt, holding back a few to pay for Frodoric's ale. She obtained a large mug and brought it over to the bard, who was surrounded by rustic admirers. Frodoric smiled when she handed him the ale. "Thank you, Mirien. Singing's thirsty work." He took a deep swallow. "What did you think of tonight's rendition?"

"Oh, Frodoric, it was your best yet! I don't know how you did it, but this night you surpassed your performance for the emperor. When the faeries demanded Cara's arm and you sang 'This hand will ne'er my firstborn hold,' I—I—" Yim began to sob. Frodoric seemed forced to reach out and pat her hand before she could continue. "I—I was just so moved. I love that ballad and never tire of it."

Frodoric smiled. "I know." He turned to his audience. "Mirien was betrothed to a count, but my art ensnared her, and she forsook him to lead our vagabond life. I oft feel guilty over it."

"Pray don't, my sweet," said Yim. "What are jewels and manor houses compared to truth and beauty?" Then she grabbed Frodoric's mug and took a long swig from it before settling into a chair and assuming a blissful expression. It was a convincing performance, and none in the room—not even Frodoric—guessed how thoroughly sick Yim was of "The Ballad of Cara One Arm." She knew every word by heart, and having lived through the events that they purportedly recounted, she was irritated by their falsehood. As far as Yim was concerned, all the ballad got right was Rodric's betrayal and a reasonable approximation of Cara's fortitude and bravery. The rest was goat dung in her estimation, and she was heartily glad that there was no mention of her in the song whatsoever.

Frodoric knew that Yim was tired of the ballad, but he knew nothing about her role in its actual events. That was because Yim had taken care to remain a mystery. She was still Mirien to Frodoric—witty, useful, and aloof. In large part, she was as contented with their arrangement as he was. Traveling with Frodoric provided a modicum of safety, not only because a man accompanied her but also because bards were valued entertainers. Moreover, Frodoric knew the roads, and they usually slept indoors.

The price for those advantages was traveling slowly. The bard never passed any village that held the slightest promise, and the farther south they went, the shorter were the distances between settlements. Although Frodoric hadn't mentioned it, Yim knew that they were approaching Averen. It had taken them nearly two moons to get that far, and the closer they got to her goal, the slower they went. Yim was convinced that was intentional on Frodoric's part.

While the bard was enjoying his ale and adulation, Yim saw the innkeeper and gave him three extra coppers so that their room would be a private one. Then she took a rush candle and retired to it.

The chamber was small, and contained only one bed. That was also small, but at least it had a cover. Augmented by her cloak, it would make for warm sleeping. Yim spread her cloak over the tattered cover, took off her boots, and slipped into bed, otherwise fully clothed. She wasn't tired, for they had traveled only part of the morning, but it was warmer to wait in bed until Frodoric finished drinking.

It was late when the bard entered the room, humming softly to himself. "When the innkeeper told me about the change of rooms," he said, "I had hoped to find you naked."

"Then the power of your optimism is exceeded only by your imagination," replied Yim.

"A man can dream, can't he?"

"Dreaming's permissible, but only that."

Frodoric shucked his boots, removed his multicolored jerkin, and then pulled off his striped trousers, so that he was dressed only in his hole-riddled socks and a long linen blouse. "Move over, Mirien."

"What?" replied Yim. "I, a count's betrothed, share a bed? Fie! Haven't I already abandoned my jewels and manor houses?"

Frodoric laughed. "That was a nice touch, as was 'my sweet.' Now move over."

Yim shifted toward the wall. As Frodoric climbed

beneath the covers, he frowned. "Must you wear all your clothes to bed?"

"Yes, as a prevention for temptation. Besides, I'm always cold."

"Mayhap, but your clothes are getting ripe."

"No riper than our patrons'."

"I should warn you that, unlike me, peasants favor musky women."

Yim laughed. "I doubt it'll be a problem."

"So what of tonight's accounts?" asked Frodoric.

"Nineteen coppers and one silver. Nine coppers for room, meals, and ale. One silver for provisions. That leaves ten coppers."

"Ten coppers for the night? I'd thought I'd do better."

"You'd be surprised what ten coppers can buy," said Yim.

"But what about the silver? What provisions did you buy with that?"

"Those were for me," said Yim in a quiet voice. "Tomorrow, I leave for Averen."

Frodoric was quiet awhile as the news sank in. At last he said, "Don't go, Mirien."

Yim rolled onto her side and lightly touched his shoulder. "You knew this time would come. I must go."

Frodoric simply stared at the cracked ceiling as his eyes began to glisten. When he spoke again, his voice had none of its jocularity or bravado. "Come to Vinden, and forsake this thing you plan to do. I don't know your intentions, but an artist oft feels things he cannot understand. A doom hangs o'er your undertaking. Mirien, if that's your name—which I doubt it is—turn away from it. Travel with me. Gather whatever my singing brings, pay for my ale and board, and keep the rest for yourself. Just don't walk into the dark."

For the first time ever, Yim kissed Frodoric's cheek. "Would you walk away from your songs and art for the security of plowing another man's fields?" Then she answered for him. "No. Though your path is often hard like mine, it's *your* path. And there's satisfaction in following one's road to its end."

"Then take my earnings for your trip," said the bard. "They were always more yours than mine, anyway."

Yim smiled. "I've purchased all I need, except for directions to Cara's hall. I'm hoping you'll give me those."

It was snowing lightly when Yim left the inn the following morning. A cold northern wind swept most of the flakes from the road, which was an old imperial highway. It still retained most of its paving, but due to generations of neglect, many of the ancient stones had heaved up to work mischief on unwary feet. The road reminded Yim of the one she and Honus had traveled along the Yorvern. In fact, it was part of the same highway.

To the south, a series of low mountains rose like waves on a pond turned to stone. They were shades of gray frosted with white. According to Frodoric's directions, two days of hard walking would take her to the place where she would leave the ancient highway for a more rugged road into the mountains. That route would bring her to Cara's hall in six days, if the weather was favorable. The bard had even purchased a scrap of parchment and inked her a crude map. That and his striped scarf were his parting gifts, which he bestowed on her with teary eyes and many wishes for a safe journey.

Yim felt uneasy traveling alone, and at times wished that she hadn't discarded the sword. Though she was unarmed, except for a small sheath knife that she used in cooking, the harsh weather protected her. It cleared the highway of all but those on urgent business. Thus Yim encountered few travelers, and they were hunched against the icy wind and anxious to get out of it. Those inclined to prey on others apparently were waiting for milder days.

Toward noon, Yim crossed the western branch of the

Yorvern River via an ancient bridge. The frozen waterway seemed little more than an overgrown brook compared to what it would become, and the stone structure required but a single arch to span it. Afterward, the highway followed the river east, and Yim occasionally spied a hut built on stone pilings in the manner of river folk. Although the shanties appeared maintained, she saw no signs of occupation, causing her to assume that they were seasonal dwellings.

As dusk arrived, Yim considered staying in an empty hut until she saw a light in the distance. Recalling the hospitality that Maryen had shown her and Honus long ago, Yim decided to ask whomever dwelt there for shelter. The elderly couple that came to the door seemed reluctant to take her in until she said that she knew "The Ballad of Cara One Arm." Then Yim was welcomed. After a hearty meal of smoked fish stew, she sang the ballad in its entirety, and then repeated the couple's favorite parts. Afterward, they insisted that she share their bed. Yim accepted the offer gratefully, for it was a frigid night.

Late on the following day, Yim left the highway for the road into the mountains. At first, it was easy to follow, but as she began to climb higher, the snow covered the roadway. Soon Yim encountered places where it was difficult to distinguish the road from the surrounding terrain. A few times she strayed from her route, but after blundering about awhile, she always found it again.

Yim came across no dwellings, and that night was the first she spent outdoors in a long time. She found a sheltered hollow on the mountainside, broke off dead tree branches for firewood, made a crude shelter from pine boughs, and lit a campfire. Yim cooked porridge, then built up the fire and went to sleep.

Though the night was frigid, Yim's inner chill made her accustomed to cold. Thus the winter weather was tolerable. That tolerance was the only benefit of the dark thing within her, a thing that had increased in strength as she had journeyed south. Aware of its growing power, Yim had been ever vigilant against sudden rages and murderous impulses. She had experienced more than a few. Their only outward manifestation was Yim's expression of grim concentration as she suppressed them. Yim suspected that Frodoric had been aware of her bouts. She never knew how much he understood their nature, but he was always timid after one of them.

When the sun rose behind heavy clouds, Yim rose with it, chilled, stiff, and tired. After cooking some porridge, she continued her journey. Trudging through snowy mountains was tedious, and the following days were much the same: The sky was always gray, and it was always cold. The snowfall varied from an occasional flake to a steady stream of white, but it never ceased. Yim often lost the road, but the mountains helped her find her way. Unlike the snow-choked roadway, the peaks were impossible to miss, and Frodoric's map depicted them well enough that she could recognize them. Apparently, the bard was as good at memorizing topography as he was at memorizing ballads. The main variations in Yim's monotonous existence were how much snow fell and whether she slept outdoors or found hospitality. Twice, she sang for her supper; the other nights she camped.

Yim's sixth day in the mountains began with promise, for when she crested a ridge in midmorning, she spied the pair of low mountains that lay to the north of Cara's hall. Yim recalled standing atop the manor's walls to watch Cronin's army march between those peaks on its way to battle. The mountains were pale gray shapes, not close but certainly reachable before dusk. Cara's hall was only a short distance beyond them. If Yim pushed herself, she'd be dining that night with her friend.

Between Yim and the mountains was a broad valley that was forested only around its edges. Its center was a large, featureless expanse of snow. Yim thought that there was something special about the valley, so she pulled out Frodoric's parchment. It was uninformative. Numerous viewings in falling snow had caused its ink to run in many places. A gray stain marked the valley, nothing else, and the mountains' smeared outlines were as blurry as they appeared in the falling snow.

Yim tucked the map away and headed onward, determined to reach Cara's hall before nightfall. Initially, she made good progress, although the snow fell ever more heavily. Occasionally, all she could see ahead was white. Nevertheless, she saw the mountains often enough to keep headed in the right direction. By noon, she had descended from the ridge, had passed through a grove of trees, and was traveling over the broad plain in the valley's center, heading straight for the pass between the two mountains.

The walking was fairly easy. Although the snow often rose higher that Yim's boot tops, the footing beneath it was smooth and regular. The greatest problem was the wind, which having nothing to break it, whipped across the plain with biting force. Focused on her goal, Yim advanced halfway into the plain before its perfect evenness began to worry her. She hadn't encountered as much as a single bush or clump of grass.

With a surge of panic, Yim realized why that was so. *I'm walking on a frozen lake!* She halted and pulled out the bard's water-blurred map again. *That's what was marked in the valley—a lake.* She was angry with herself for recalling it too late. *The road skirted it.* Yim looked around, wondering if she should turn back. Gazing at the tracks she had made, she saw that all but the closest ones had been erased by the wind. Not only had the wind picked up, the snowfall had also. *I've made it this far safely*, she reasoned. *If I backtrack, I'll end up camping in a blizzard.*

With her journey's end so close, Yim decided to continue onward. While she was nervous about encountering thin ice, she also feared that the blizzard would obscure the way ahead. A band of trees marked dry land on the far shore; sometimes she could see it but often not. Whenever she could view her goal, she dashed in its direction. She was running when the ice before her suddenly tilted downward. There was no sound, but the snow ahead darkened as water poured over it. Yim halted and darted away from the advancing water. She made a few steps in the opposite direction before the ice tilted again and water began to well up through the snow ahead of her. This time, Yim didn't stop moving. She took two more bounds and then launched herself forward, hoping to leap over the crack.

Yim's experience in the fens had taught her to distribute her weight over unstable surfaces. Thus she didn't try to land on her feet, but on her chest. Perhaps that saved her life, for she slid through the wet slush instead of plunging through it. Yim clawed at the snow with her hands to pull herself farther way from the wet, frigid trap that had nearly swallowed her. She moved that way for a dozen paces before feeling secure enough to rise to her feet. Then she stood shivering from cold and terror.

The front of Yim's clothing was soaked with icy slush and the edges of her cloak were already stiffening as they froze. Yim looked back at the trees that were so close but apparently unreachable. She might have been merely unlucky, stumbling upon a rare thin spot, or the entire shoreline might be one long death trap. Yim didn't have the nerve to find out which. Her only safe option was to return to the other side of the valley, build a fire to warm herself, and then trek around the lake the following day. Yim glanced at her former destination. It was only a pale gray band in a wall of white. The grove of trees that she had passed through to reach the lake was invisible in the storm. Nevertheless, she headed in what she assumed was its direction.

Though Yim was terribly cold, walking helped warm her, and the thought of a fire spurred her efforts. She kept hoping that the snow would let up and give her a sight of her surroundings. After a long while it did, and she could see the

vague shapes of trees ahead. The sight cheered her until the
snowfall lessened even more and she could see mountains
behind the trees. They were the low, twin mountains north
of Cara's hall: she had circled back in the storm.

As Yim weighed her situation, the mountains grew ever
fainter. Then they were gone, and she stood in a white void.
Its only features were her tracks, and they were disappearing
as she watched. Every direction seemed the same. Yim realized that if she resumed walking, she'd likely travel in yet another circle. *And fall through the ice*, she thought. The only
safe thing to do was to stay put until she could see where she
was headed. Yim crouched down so the wind would be less
punishing and waited for a break in the weather.

The snow fell more heavily instead. The wind piled it into
a drift around Yim, transforming her into the sole landmark
in a white world that was otherwise perfectly featureless.
Yim continued to wait for a change, and the waiting dragged
on and on. Finally, something did change. The white void
slowly turned gray. Behind the heavy clouds, the sun was
leaving the sky. The gray darkened as dusk arrived.

The night was especially dark. The blizzard slackened,
but it was too late. Darkness obscured Yim's surroundings
as well as the falling snow had done. The starless sky was
black, and the snowbound landscape was so dark that it
seemed little different from the sky. Yim thought of the irony
of having faced so many perils only to perish crouching in
the cold. She decided that if she was going to die, she
wouldn't do it passively. Yim rose to walk in the hope that
she might get lucky and survive. *If I break through the ice, at
least I'll die more quickly then freezing.* Yim stumbled off
without deliberation. When all directions looked alike, one
was as good as any other.

Half-frozen and stretched to her limit, Yim had difficulty
thinking coherently. Existence took on the unreal quality of
a dream. After a while, there seemed to be a wavering pale-

ness in the dark. It was only a tiny point, but since it stood out in the night, Yim headed toward it. She didn't care if it was an illusion; it provided a direction.

When Yim moved toward the paleness, it moved toward her. As it did, it changed. Over time, it assumed the form of a young girl with long pale hair that the wind whipped about. Except for a short skirt of leaves, she was exposed to the elements. The girl came closer. Yim was wondering how a child could endure walking barefoot through snow, when she saw that the snow was actually a field of wildflowers. Yim thought it strange that she hadn't noticed before. The flowers were faerie lace, which grew so thickly that their white blossoms merged into an unbroken expanse of white.

The wind no longer felt cold. Then Yim realized that she was also walking through flowers. The girl came close enough for Yim to see her face. It was serene, and there was a twinkle in her sky-blue eyes. She knelt before Yim, grasped her hand, and kissed it. "Greetings, Mother. Long have I awaited you."

Yim smiled. "This is a dream."

"But it's a good dream," said the girl. "Drop your heavy pack and run with me."

"Where?"

"To Dar Beard Chin's hall. Your bear waits for you."

"Gruwff?"

"Na her. A he bear."

Since it was a dream, Yim did as she was asked. When the girl dashed off, Yim followed close behind. It felt good to run. The flowers released their perfume as she crushed them beneath her feet. *This certainly is a fine dream*, she thought. The girl looked back over her shoulder and grinned in agreement.

The flowers parted to reveal a road that wound between two mountains. Yim continued to lope behind the girl. It was effortless. Her breathing was easy and her legs weren't

tired at all. Above, the clouds gave way. A full moon hung
in a starry sky. Thus when the pair rounded a bend and
viewed the valley beyond, Cara's hall and its surrounding
village were silhouetted against the silver of a moonlit lake.

The girl increased her pace, and Yim matched it. She felt
like wind rushing down the road, unburdened and free. *My
bear awaits*, thought Yim, envisioning strong furry arms
wrapped about her. It was only when they had passed
through the sleeping village that Yim began to feel cold
again. Suddenly her breath came in gasps and her throat was
raw. Her legs turned leaden and her face and fingers stung.
Yim slowed. Then she cramped and nearly doubled over in
pain. She felt incapable of taking another step. Her clothes
were caked with snow. Parts were wet, while other parts
were frozen. Glancing back at the countryside, Yim saw only
darkness, ice, and snow.

The girl grabbed her arm, tugging it urgently. "Come inside, Mother. Do na stop now. Remember your bear."

"What bear?"

The girl didn't reply. Instead, she tugged at Yim, forcing
her to take a painful step. The girl tugged again. Yim took
another step. By this means, she was pulled through a door
within a gate, across a courtyard paved with ice-covered
cobbles, and into a manor hall. It was warmer in the hall,
but so dark that Yim could barely see. The girl helped her
pull off her wet, snow-caked boots. Yim left them lying in
the entrance hall along with her dripping socks as the girl
took her hand and guided her away. Their bare feet made
no sound as they walked down a corridor, climbed several
flights of stairs, and passed down a hallway. The girl
stopped in front of a closed door. "Your bear waits inside.
It's winter, so let him sleep."

"Am I still dreaming?" asked Yim.

"Partly," replied the girl. "Come inside. I'll help you out
of your wet things."

Yim nodded wearily. The girl opened the door and pushed her into a paneled room that smelled of ancient flowers. It had a window that overlooked a winter landscape. By its dim light, Yim saw the shadowy form of the bear. He lay on a bed and was sleeping, just as the girl said he would be.

The girl undressed her. One by one, Yim's garments fell to the floor with a wet flop. Concerned that the sound would wake the bear, Yim glanced in his direction. Then she squinted her eyes, for it seemed that the bear was a man asleep beneath a cover. Then he was a bear again. The girl pushed Yim's sodden clothes aside. Then she lifted the cover to reveal the bear. He was a small bear. "Small, but warm," said the girl. She patted the bed. "Come crawl beside him."

Yim did. The girl vanished. The bear stirred in his sleep. When Yim nestled against his warmth, he wrapped an arm around her in a way that seemed almost human. The gesture scarcely registered on Yim's consciousness. She was slipping from one dream into another.

FORTY·SIX

IT WAS a dream, but it contained truths. Honus was lost on the Dark Path, traveling over cold, stone hills and through misty, yet dry, rocky valleys. He had been doing it for so long that time had lost all meaning; there was only stone, mist, and emptiness. Then Honus crested a hill and beheld a valley filled with white flowers. Descending among them, he felt warm for the first time in ages. The blossoms overflowed the valley, extending to the horizon. The air was thick with their fragrance. A young woman stood in their midst, her long golden hair stirred by a soft breeze.

At first, Honus thought that the young woman was Rose. Then he drew nearer and saw that her gown was made of violets and her tranquil face shone with wisdom. "Thistle?" he said.

Thistle smiled. "Karmamatus."

"You've grown up."

"Nay, but I'm nearing my sixteenth winter." Thistle whirled gracefully on bare feet, the hem of her floral gown flaring out. When she stopped spinning, Honus noticed that she held a honeycomb in one hand. His mouth watered at the sight of it. He was on all fours, so instead of reaching for it, he simply tried to bite it. Thistle pulled back her hand, and Honus's snout snapped closed on empty air.

Thistle giggled and skipped off through the flowers, the tantalizing treat still in her hand. Honus loped after her. As he did, he wondered how long he had been a bear. *Perhaps I've always been one and just didn't know.* Honus briefly wondered if that could be possible before turning his thoughts toward a sweeter concern. There was honey ahead, and he longed for it.

As fast as Honus ran, Thistle ran faster. She always stayed a few steps in front of him. Although Thistle didn't seem to tire, Honus did. He was growing sleepy. That wasn't the only change: The blossoms on Thistle's gown were fading to shades of brown and beige. The flowers in the fields were becoming snow. It was getting dark.

Then it was night. Ahead, surrounded by a sleeping village, was Cara's hall. Thistle ran up to its outer gates before she halted. She lifted a finger to her lips, so Honus whispered rather than spoke. "Where's the honey?" he asked.

"I've something sweeter," whispered Thistle.

"What?"

"A she cub to share your slumber."

"Cubs sleep with their mothers."

"This cub's already a mother. She needs something else." Thistle's face turned serious, almost stern. "She needs your strength—the kind that springs from gentleness, not the false might of an iron stick. As you well know, such sticks break. Now go and sleep. When you awake, show your strength."

Then Honus was in his den. Thistle was gone, but he wasn't alone. A cub was in his sleeping space. She lacked fur and felt cold. Honus reached out and pulled her against his warmth. He was confused and fatigued; and since it was winter, he decided to sleep until spring. When he woke, he could try to understand his dream and sort out what was true and what was not.

The dream somewhat prepared Honus for the shock of finding Yim naked in his bed. The discovery was so unexpected and inexplicable that only illogic helped him comprehend it. Yim was sleeping peacefully beside him, her bare skin cool to the touch. Honus ignored questions of how and why she had arrived. Instead, he basked in the glorious wonder that she was there. He did nothing to disturb her, for despite the confirmation of his senses that Yim was real, he feared that she might vanish as mysteriously as she had appeared. Thus Honus remained perfectly still, with one arm wrapped around his love, as silent tears streamed down his face.

They might have remained that way all morning had there not been knocking on the door. It was accompanied by Cara's voice. "Honus, you slugabed! 'Tis bears that sleep through winter, na men! You promised—"

Yim woke with a start, uttering a little yelp. Then she sat up in bed, stared at Honus with wide eyes and uttered a second, much louder yelp.

"Honus?" called Cara's voice. "Who's in there? What's going on?"

Yim was staring at him, her face registering so many emotions that he found it impossible to sort them out. Yim seemed incapable of speech. Honus thought it might be due to the purple scar that crossed her throat. He called back to Cara. "I don't know what's going on."

The door flung open. "Zounds, Honus, I— Oh—oh, Holy Mother Karm! Nay, it can na be! Yim! Are you truly here?"

"No. I think I'm frozen in some snowbank," replied Yim in a distant, puzzled tone. "Or at the bottom of a lake."

"Oh, zounds, nay! You're here! Without a stitch in Honus's bed!"

Yim grabbed the cover and pulled it around her.

Cara glanced at the sodden clothes on the floor. "So those were your boots and socks in the entrance hall."

"I don't know how they got there, or I here," said Yim. "I've no idea at all. I was lost in a storm at night, and then I dreamed of a child wearing only leaves who—"

"Thistle!" said Honus as Cara simultaneously said "Violet!"

"Who?" asked Yim.

"My daughter, Violet," said Cara. " 'Tis a long story."

"She said she'd take me to my bear," said Yim.

"I was a bear!" exclaimed Honus.

"And I'm a lunatic," said Cara, "or soon will be. If you do na know how you got into my hall, how did you find Honus's room?"

"The girl brought me. Only last night it wasn't Honus's room. She said I'd sleep with my bear."

Cara shook her head. "Aye, that sounds like Violet, all right. Well, Yim, have you adopted her lack of dress or shall I get you some dry clothes?" Cara beamed. "Or mayhap, I was interrupting something."

"Dry clothes would be very nice," replied Yim.

Cara looked somewhat disappointed. "Then I'll get

them for you myself. While I do, mayhap you could please figure out what has happened. I'm dying to know. Zounds, absolutely dying! But I'll leave your dry frock outside the door, in case . . . Well, in case of whatever." Cara left, closing the door behind her.

As soon as the door shut, Yim turned to Honus. "You've been weeping."

"They were tears of joy."

Yim reached out to tenderly stroke the contours of his furrowed face. To Honus, her expression resembled that of someone examining wounds. "Oh, Honus, life has been hard to you!"

"That was my fault."

Yim's eyes welled with tears. "I don't believe that."

In an attempt to change the conversation, Honus leaned over and softly kissed Yim's cheek. "You're exactly as I remember, except for the scar."

"A fensman did that. It was an accident."

Honus suspected otherwise, but he said, "And did you bear the child?"

"Yes, a son. His name's Froan."

"Froan?" Honus felt a sudden chill in the pit of his stomach. "That name's mentioned in my runes."

"How do you know that? I thought that Sarfs . . . Do you have a new Bearer?"

"No, but I stayed with one before I came here. He saved my life and gave me guidance. He said that my runes told of three intertwined fates—yours, mine, and Froan's." Honus watched Yim's eyes widen. "You seem surprised to hear that."

"I suppose I shouldn't be," replied Yim. "After all, I had a dream—or perhaps a vision—of you. You said your runes foretold you'd help me." Yim sighed. "And, Honus, I need help. I worry that what I must do is beyond my strength."

"I believe I had the same dream," said Honus. "We met

at night in a lonely place. I recall saying I'd help you and that we'd meet again."

"And then I rushed to embrace you."

"Yes!"

"But you vanished before I could."

"Yes!"

"All I did was brush your face." Yim reached out to duplicate the gesture. As soon as she did, Yim completed what she had begun in her dream. She embraced Honus as fervently as she had in the clearing after restoring his life. He wept, overcome by emotion so powerful that it mingled joy with grief, and she wept also. Honus's mouth found Yim's. Her lips were cool, but her response wasn't. It seemed to mirror his passion.

Honus tugged the cover so it fell away, allowing him to caress Yim's bare skin. He thrilled at the touch of her flesh after so many winters of emptiness and longing. His hands traveled up and down Yim's back before seeking the softness of her breasts. As they did, Honus felt Yim stiffen. Then, she gently pushed him away and pulled the cover around her body.

Honus gazed at Yim at a loss for words, sensing for the first time the gap created by their long separation and wondering how he could bridge it. The possibility that he couldn't suddenly filled him with panic. He worried that, driven by pent-up desire, he might have ruined the moment he had longed for.

Yim was also silent, and she looked equally uncomfortable. Nevertheless, she spoke first. "Honus, I can't. Not yet. I'm still confused, and I'm afraid to rush into anything."

"I'm sorry. I know it's been a long time."

"It has, Honus, and I'm different from the woman you knew."

"How?"

"When I conceived Froan, the Devourer entered me. It's

never left. Not entirely. And I struggle with it all the time. I'm capable of . . . of . . . horrid things."

"Perhaps my love will cure that."

Yim appeared dubious. "Maybe you're right. I don't know. But I didn't leave the Grey Fens seeking love. Froan ran away, and I left to save him."

"Then I'll help," said Honus, hoping he didn't sound desperate.

"Before you make that promise, you should know what you'll face."

Honus gazed into Yim's eyes and saw a depth of despair that made him uneasy. "What is it?"

"Froan is Lord Bahl."

Honus felt he shouldn't have been surprised. Nevertheless, Yim's statement took him aback, and it made her goal seem nonsensical. "Why talk of saving Lord Bahl? It's the world that needs saving."

"Saving the world's beyond me," said Yim. "I can only do what I'm able."

"And you're capable of saving your son, no matter what he's become?"

"I think I'm capable of trying, though trying may be all I can do."

Honus recalled his dream of the previous night. *Thistle said Yim needs my strength.* It seemed absurd to act upon a dream, and Honus realized that he couldn't. Instead, he would act because of love. "If you attempt to save Lord Bahl, you won't do it alone."

FORTY·SEVEN

"ZOUNDS, YIM!" said Cara, shaking her head. "And to think they make up ballads about *my* life!" She refilled her and Yim's goblets with falfhissi, and took another swallow of the dark liquor. It was evening, and the two women were in "Dar's room," the clan mother's bedchamber. The remnants of their private dinner lay on a nearby table, and they were sitting on Cara's bed. Yim, still fragrant from her first bath in moons, wore one of Cara's long-sleeved woolen gowns. "Aye," said Cara, "what a fine time the bards would have with you! You're both Lord Bahl's lover *and* his mother."

"I was never his lover," replied Yim, shuddering at the memory. "Love had nothing to do with it."

"I disagree. If you had na loved Karm so much, you never would have gone to Bahl. The Chosen, indeed! Chosen for a life of torment. Oh, you poor thing. I can na imagine! What you endured sounds worse than any nightmare. And then to sleep through a winter with a bear—just like my Violet—and birth your babe in a bog and raise him there and have your throat cut and then journey here on foot, slaying five men on the way! Why, 'tis nigh impossible to understand how you lived through any of it, much less all of it! Does Honus know about your trials?"

"I've told him very little," replied Yim. "He knows that Froan's Lord Bahl's son, of course. And that Froan's the new Lord Bahl."

"Are you sure he is? I've heard na news of that."

"It's something I sense without the need of tidings."

Cara took another swallow of falfhissi. "So all our tribulations could start over again. I barely survived Bahl's first invasion, and I was younger then. This time, 'twill be five times worse because of my children. I fear more for them than myself."

"Then you understand why I must go."

"Nay, I do na," said Cara. "When the faeries stole Violet, I did na go searching about their dell. 'Twould have been rash indeed, and there's such a thing as prudence. The stronghold at Tor's Gate was naething—naething at all—compared to the Iron Palace. You might as well kill yourself here and save the trip. Anyway, what could you possibly do if you got there?"

"Talk to Froan."

"Talk? Zounds! Well, *that's* a clever plan for sure. Yim, I talk to Violet till my tongue goes numb, yet she still does whatever she pleases. And she's na Lord Bahl. I've heard na rumors that he's a listener. And you, of all people, know how vile he is. Everyone who bears that name's a monster with na a speck of mercy in him."

"Froan's no monster—the thing inside him is."

"That may seem a fine distinction when he tortures you to death. Look, you've done everything Karm told you to do. You've borne the child. Now snatch some happiness with Honus. You both deserve it."

"You're a mother," said Yim. "I thought you'd understand. You don't stop loving a child because he falls ill; you love him all the more for his suffering. Froan didn't choose to be afflicted by that evil thing. When he was young, he called it his shadow." Yim's eyes took on a wistful look as they welled with tears. "He fought against it, Cara. He fought against it and won. And afterward, he was a sweet and loving child. If he could beat his shadow then, he can beat it now."

"Mayhap he na longer wants to beat it. Mayhap he'd

rather be a lord than herd goats in a bog. Men put on black robes for far less than what Froan will gain."

"He needs me," said Yim, beginning to sob. "I won't forsake him. I can't."

Cara sighed, then embraced Yim and held her. "There, there," she cooed. "Of course, you can't, Karm help you. So do na listen to me. I'm just a timid homebody."

Yim paused between sobs to utter "Ha!"

"'Tis true. I'm quite content to stay at home. I have na been to Bremven for three winters, and I do na miss it. And of course, Violet's a handful, and I've only got one hand. But I'll never complain again after hearing *your* troubles! My burden's light compared to yours."

Cara grew quiet and continued to hug Yim until she calmed. Then she poured some more falfhissi into Yim's goblet. "I can see you're going, na matter what I say," she said, "and I guess I can understand why. It does na make me happy. *That's* for sure! But seeing how you said the Old Ones helped you before with the crow and the bear and the horse and all, mayhap you should talk to my faerie-kissed daughter. I never thought I'd say *that* to anyone! But you've dreamt of her already, and that certainly worked out. So mayhap it'd be wise to visit Violet's tower. Of course, you'll have to call her Thistle." Cara sighed. "Mayhap, I should start doing so myself."

It was late when Yim finally returned to Honus's room, and she was more than a little drunk. Honus knew the instant she staggered in. "I see Cara's led you astray."

Yim rushed over to Honus and covered his face with kisses. "Oh, bless you, Honus! Thank you for helping! You're so, so good to me!" Yim flopped down on his bed. "Please hold me tonight. I've longed to sleep in your arms for oh so many winters. I'm sorry I'm chilly. I can't help it. It's because . . . well, you know. I hope it doesn't bother you too much! I'll keep my gown on, so you won't freeze."

"You needn't keep it on for my sake," said Honus.

"Oh, it's all right. I don't mind."

Yim rolled on her side as Honus blew out the candle and climbed in bed beside her. He wrapped an arm around her and pressed his face into her hair. "What have you been drinking?" he whispered.

"Falfhissi," replied Yim. "Cara says it means 'laughing water.'" Then she started to weep.

Honus simply held Yim, partly because he had no idea what to say and partly because he felt that was what she needed. Yim dropped off to sleep quickly, leaving Honus to ponder the strange twist his life had taken. As always, he was unable to discern any pattern or purpose in it, but he felt that Daven had spoken truly when he declared that Karm loved him. Honus held the proof in his arms.

Yim's head throbbed throughout the following morning. Honus had joined Havren's hunting party, which was procuring game for the night's banquet. It was Midwinter's Night Eve, and Cara planned to transform the traditional feast into one honoring Yim. Thus Yim was left to the mercies of the seamstress and cobbler whom Cara had charged with outfitting her. Harried over making a gown and a pair of shoes in a single day, they were politely overbearing. Their fuss compounded Yim's unease over the banquet, but there was little she could do about it. Cara was determined to celebrate her arrival. She had always been a forceful personality, and her tenure as chieftain had enhanced the trait.

There was one benefit to being the center of hectic activity; it gave Yim a reason for postponing her visit to Violet's tower. She suspected that the Old Ones would use the girl as their messenger. Though their counsels might prove useful, Yim wasn't particularly anxious to hear them. It unnerved her to know that the faeries—like Karm's Seers—had known about her even before she was born. It made her feel impotent, a playing piece moved by an unseen hand in a game where she didn't know the rules.

What if she tells me all my hopes are baseless? Yim asked herself. It seemed a real possibility. *If so, should I abandon them?* Yim had to admit that such a surrender would come as a relief. The journey to Bahland seemed more terrifying than ever. She had headed south to postpone a confrontation with her son, and going to Cara's had allowed her to postpone it further. Yet putting it off had done nothing to make it seem easier. On the contrary, Yim sensed that the Devourer had grown more formidable over the intervening time, decreasing her chance of success.

Yim's gloomy mood didn't dampen the frantic but celebratory mood that permeated the hall. Everyone knew of Yim's heroics on the night their clan mother had lost her arm. Thus Yim's sudden appearance after a long and mysterious absence seemed a good omen, one certainly worthy of a celebration. Cara's short notice only heightened the excitement. By the time it was dark, the last seam was sewn, the great hall was lit and decorated, the feast was prepared, and all the guests were assembled.

As Yim and Cara entered the great hall together, everyone bowed. Cara, dressed in a grayish green gown, was crowned with the thin gold circlet of the clan mother and wore the dark green plaid sash and the golden tree brooch of the Urkzimdi clan. Yim wore a long-sleeved gown of dark blue. The two women walked slowly to the head table, which was on a raised platform at the end of the hall. Cara's thronelike wooden chair occupied the center of the long table. Her family, Honus, and the ranking guests stood behind the places where they would sit, arranged according to precedence. Yim would sit in the honored spot on Cara's right, and Rose, as Cara's heir, would sit to the right of Yim. Yim noted an empty spot next to Rose. The place, marked by a simple wooden bowl, was apparently symbolic of Rose's absent twin.

When Cara reached her chair, she didn't sit down. Instead, a servant brought her a goblet. Afterward, servers brought all the guests goblets or drinking bowls. When everyone had a drink in hand, Cara raised her goblet. "A toast!" she shouted. " 'Tis the longest night, the darkest time in a dark season. Yet it also marks the sun's return, a portent of brighter days. There can be na more fitting time to mark Yim's return." She raised her goblet higher. "To Yim!"

The entire company in the hall was about to shout "To Yim" when a blast of wind blew open the great doors that had been shut after the clan mother and her honored guest had entered. The same gust extinguished most of the torches, plunging the hall into semidarkness. The remaining torches illuminated a small figure garbed in a white gown that was as dazzling in the dim light as if a sunbeam shone on it. Yim recognized the girl in white from her dream. Like everyone else in the hall, Yim was transfixed by the sight of Thistle, who moved toward the high table with a stately grace that wasn't remotely childlike.

She wore a crown of thistles in her golden hair. Their spiny leaves and blossoms appeared as fresh as if they had been picked on a dewy summer morn. The girl advanced without a sound, for despite her elegant sleeveless gown, she was barefoot. The gown had a long train, the trailing edge of which shed blossoms. That made Yim aware that the entire gown was made of flowers. When Thistle ascended the platform, Yim could distinguish white violets, faerie lace, bluets, yarrow, anemones, and roses. Every blossom looked perfectly fresh.

Thistle bowed low to Yim. "Greetings, Mother. I bring the Old Ones' love and mine also." Then she bowed to Cara. "Hello, Mama. I would na miss so fitting a feast, and I'm glad you prepared a place for me."

Then Freenla rushed up to Thistle and handed her a wooden drinking bowl. The girl raised it, and with that gesture, everyone suddenly recalled that they had been toasting

Yim. As if the interruption had never happened, all shouted "To Yim" and drank.

Yim watched Thistle during the toast and noted she had mouthed "To Mother." Afterward, the girl made her way to the bench and whispered to Rose, "Sister, you're in my place."

Rose's face flushed red; nonetheless, she moved so Thistle could sit immediately to Yim's right. Then Cara took her chair, and everyone sat down. That required Yim, Thistle, and Rose to step over the bench to sit, and the two girls did it far more gracefully in their gowns than Yim managed. As servants scurried to relight torches, other servants brought out food. There was roast boar and venison, three kinds of fowl, sturgeon and pike, roast whiteroot, groundnuts stewed in wine, onion tarts, differing kinds of bread—both stuffed and plain, five kinds of cheeses, several stews, candied fruit, ale, and wine. Thistle's fare, which was served to her by Freenla, was different from everyone else's. None of it was cooked, and it consisted of roots, seeds, nuts, and—most strangely—fresh wild strawberries and blackberries. Thistle ate everything with her hands. The fragrant liquid in her drinking bowl was neither ale nor wine nor any kind of tea Yim knew.

For a while, everyone was preoccupied with food and drink, and the hall was quiet except for the sounds of feasting. But when appetites were blunted, conversation commenced. Cara turned and smiled at her faerie-kissed daughter. "Vio—Thistle, I'm glad you joined us. 'Tis a rare treat for me."

"Na less for me, Mama. And I'm glad you counseled Mother to visit me. Though she dreads what I might say, she trusts your wisdom."

Yim regarded Thistle. Her floral gown looked thin and chilly. It was already starting to fall apart in places, and Yim wondered if it would last the evening. She also noted that the girl's forehead was scratched and bleeding from her spiny garland. Thistle caught her glance and smiled serenely. "Aye, Mother, it pains me."

"Then why wear it?" asked Yim. "I doubt it's from vanity."

"My attire lets all know that I honor you and calls to mind that even goodly things oft come with suffering."

"I know that all too well," said Yim.

"Then visit me and learn other things."

"You spoke to your mother of my dread. Is it justified?"

"Come speak with me tomorrow and judge for yourself."

FORTY-EIGHT

HONUS'S HAND was on Yim's breast. He was asleep and she wore a gown, so its placement seemed innocent to her. Nevertheless, it felt wonderfully intimate at the same time. Honus's touch stirred feelings in her that had lain long dormant and worries also. *I tupped with Lord Bahl only once, and the Devourer entered me*, she thought. *What would happen if I tupped with Honus?* The chilling possibilities quenched her ardor. *The Devourer might enter him or I might conceive a second Lord Bahl.* Yim gently pushed Honus's hand to her waist; it seemed the prudent thing to do.

Though Yim was awake, she didn't rise. She wanted to relish being held and to feel Honus's warmth, knowing that their closeness brought as much comfort to him as it did to her. Yim glanced at the hand that rested on her waist. It seemed like an old man's hand, although she knew that Honus was still well short of fifty winters. Honus had said little of the time that they were apart, but Yim could readily see its toll. It made her feel guilty over her decision to leave him and raise Froan alone. Considering how it had turned out, she felt it had been a mistake.

Honus stirred, and Yim twisted around so she could kiss him. He smiled and said, "This is a pleasant way to wake up."

Yim smiled back. "I'd hoped you'd say that." She kissed him again. "This feels so natural, though I don't know why it should. How many moons did we spend together?"

"Not many," replied Honus. "Maybe five in all, but we packed a lot into them."

And I lived your entire life when our souls merged on the Dark Path, thought Yim. "We certainly did. I remember . . ." Her voice trailed off, and she sat up to slip on her new shoes.

"You remember what?"

"Why talk of memories?" said Yim. "Can you remember a single one that isn't mingled with sorrow?"

"I can," replied Honus. "Right after you—" He stopped, for he was about to say "restored my life." Instead, he said, "awoke on the dawn after I slew Gatt."

"Yes," said Yim, recalling her single morning of unclouded passion. "That was just before I told you what being the Chosen truly meant."

"Now that you've fulfilled your obligation, perhaps we'll forge new memories."

Yim understood Honus's implication and quickly changed the subject. "Cara thinks I should visit Thistle's tower. I thought I might do so this morning."

"That sounds like a good idea," said Honus. "Thistle has foresight. She knew you were coming and told me as much when we first met. Though, in truth, I didn't understand her."

"Perhaps I won't understand her either," said Yim.

*   *   *

Yim found reasons for putting off going to the tower until late in the morning. When she finally climbed the wall and gazed at the slender log leading to Thistle's abode, she was even more dubious about the visit. The frigid day was gusty, making the "bridge" seem especially precarious. "Come on," Yim said to herself. "You've trekked all through the fens. Surely you can walk across a log."

Yim made the crossing quickly. Once inside the tower's walls, she walked through what seemed a patch of brown meadow to call down the hole at the base of the oak. "Thistle?"

"Enter pelt-clad, Mother."

Yim felt even more dubious than when she had stood before the log. She had expected Thistle to come to her, not the other way around. The dark hole looked narrow and cold. Moreover, "pelt-clad" was the faerie term for "unclothed." The prospect of sliding down the hole naked was distinctly uninviting. Thistle's voice wafted up from the dark. "Come, Mother. 'Tis warm, safe, and secret."

After some hesitation, Yim quickly stripped, placed her gown and shoes upon a low tree branch, and slithered into the hole like a snake. At first, the burrow's sides felt shockingly cold against her bare flesh. The hole curved like a corkscrew, so all trace of daylight quickly faded. Partway into the second turn, Yim saw a faint light ahead. Soon she emerged into a warm cavity with a floor covered with a thick layer of thistledown. It was illuminated by a misty sphere of light that was the size of a child's fist. It floated near a ceiling that was formed by intertwined roots. The light it cast was the same rosy shade as dawn. Thistle sat cross-legged on the down, her lap covered by so many rabbits that "pelt-clad" took on a new meaning.

She smiled and bowed her head low enough to nearly touch the down. "We welcome you, Mother, and are honored that you came."

"I take it, when you say 'we,' you're not speaking for the rabbits."

"They welcome you, too, but I speak for the Old Ones."

"And that's why they stole you from your mother?"

"They did na steal me. Dar Beard Chin made a gift. 'Twas na a cheese, but a promise to help in the time of need. To the Old Ones, I'm Dar." Thistle smiled, seeming to understand Yim's confusion. "So is Mama. And her mama, and all the other clan mothers. Time and death are different for the faeries. Dar's blood flows in me, and that's what they see."

"Still, I don't see why they need you to speak for them. They didn't before."

"They're now constrained and can aid in only little ways."

"Why?"

"This was decreed at the world's beginning, and they're bound by it. Even Karm is likewise bound. Do na look to her for guidance. Your will must become her will."

Yim sighed heavily, already despairing of learning anything useful. "Then tell me whatever you can."

"We cannot enter the spider's web, yet it's attached to living things. When the spider moves, it shakes them and we know." Thistle's face grew sad. "A little boy is bound hand and foot. The evil one will spill his life this night in order to gaze about. He's looking for you. Yet he can na peer into here."

Yim felt a chill in her stomach. "What evil one? Are you talking of my son?"

"Nay, na him. Evil is a choice he has yet to make, though he may soon."

Yim's chill somewhat abated. "So there's hope?"

"Aye, a little."

"What must I do?"

"Hold fast to the shadow," replied Thistle. Though her voice sounded calm, her eyes seemed anxious.

"I don't know what that means."

"You may when the time comes."

"May? That doesn't sound hopeful."

"Hope is all we may do, Mother," replied Thistle. "Yet you're free to make a different choice."

The "counsel" proved as cryptic as Yim had feared it would be. "Can the Old Ones tell me anything more?"

"Aye. Enter death's domain when life's renewed."

"You mean in springtime?"

Thistle smiled. "When life's renewed." She held out something in her hand. "And wear this in your hair."

Yim took the object. It was a small hair comb carved from walnut the exact shade of her hair. She noted that there were small walnut-colored spheres attached to its surface.

"Those are neigin seeds, Mother. The plants grow only in the dell."

"What's their purpose?"

"Swallow them, and though you eat and drink, 'twill be the same as if you fasted."

"So they're poison. I'd die of thirst and hunger."

"When the seeds pass through you, their power will pass also."

Like the Old Ones' counsel, the comb seemed a puzzling gift of dubious value. Nevertheless, Yim thanked Thistle for it.

"Nay, we thank *you*, Mother." Thistle bowed low again. Afterward, she gazed at Yim as if she were debating something in her mind. After a long moment, she spoke. "This I say only from myself: Do na mistake the Old Ones' counsel about the shadow. You need not fear to lie with Karmamatus."

"You mean Honus?"

"Aye, Karmamatus. The shadow can na enter him or any child." Thistle smiled. "I thought it would please you to know that."

"Yes," replied Yim, realizing that she was talking with

another woman and not a child. "I suspect you know just how much."

Thistle's smile grew earthy. "I do. So, why na nap awhile afore the night? 'Tis cozy here, and rest heightens the senses."

Yim hadn't felt sleepy until Thistle mentioned napping. Then her eyelids suddenly felt heavy. As if they had been given a command, the rabbits hopped from the girl's lap and began to nuzzle against Yim. The soft fur and warm bodies against her skin increased Yim's drowsiness. She yawned. The down looked inviting. "A short nap sounds nice." Yim reclined onto the chamber's soft floor. As soon as she did, the rabbits snuggled against her as Thistle lay with her back against Yim's chest. Yim threw an arm over the girl and hugged her close. Thistle sighed contentedly. Yim closed her eyes. *Just a short nap*, she thought. *Then I'll be ready for my night with Honus.*

Honus only picked at his food. Throughout the meal, he kept glancing down the head table toward Yim's empty place. Since seating was set by protocol even at informal dinners, he had to gaze past Havren and Cara to the spot. Cara eventually noticed Honus's glances, and silently shrugged. Havren, caught up in describing the day's encounter with a white stag, didn't notice Honus's anxiousness. Honus, in turn, scarcely heard a thing Havren said.

When the meal was over and Cara rose from her chair, Honus hurried over to her. "Where is she?" he whispered.

"You said she went to talk to Violet," replied Cara.

"Yes, but that was this morning!"

"Violet reckons time differently from other folk."

"You mean the two could still be gabbing? That's a lot of talk."

"Mayhap," said Cara, "or they may have only started. I think that tower has become like the dell. Time moves differently there. Remember that I said the oak grew in just one season?"

"Yes."

"Well, it shed its leaves and sprouted new ones near a hundred times that summer. I know because I counted."

"So what are you telling me?"

"Yim's na tardy, so do na fret. She'll return in time, whatever that time is. So do na go looking for her, *especially* in the tower. I mean it, Honus. You'll stir up things best left alone."

Just as Thistle had foreseen, the Most Holy Gorm ascended his ironclad tower and prepared for necromancy by drawing a knife across a little throat. He painted the bloody circle on the floor and took the magic bones from their ancient rune-stitched bag. They felt exceptionally icy in his hand, an auspicious sign. The bones' powers for divination had increased as the heir's power had grown. Even though Lord Bahl's throne was still vacant, Gorm knew the young man who would fill it would soon arrive. He had known it even before Stregg's messenger brought the news. The bones had told him.

Bahland was already preparing for its new lord. The armories were busy. The Iron Guard was conscripting men. Ceremonies were being planned and arrests were being made. Both Stregg's reports and the bones' portents indicated an heir of exceptional promise. Nevertheless, Gorm—and Gorm alone—knew that one vital ingredient was missing. It was the heir's mother. Only after her son had consumed her blood would the Devourer be reunited in a single body. All signs indicated that it would be the last body the Devourer would ever need.

Gorm tossed the bones to discover the mother's whereabouts. Despite eighteen years of fruitless searching, he was confident of receiving useful clues. Lately, whatever had hidden the missing woman had weakened, or the Devourer within her had grown strong enough to aid in her discovery. Regardless which, Gorm had been able to discern that the heir's mother was on the move. *Last time, there were signs that she was heading south,* he recalled. *Perhaps this time, I'll learn enough to capture her.*

The bones bounced over the black stone floor and settled into place. Gorm studied them with an air of expectation. Centuries of practice had taught him to catch the subtlest of signs, although recently the portents had been easy to spot. The Most Holy One anticipated the same with the current session, and he wasn't disappointed. Almost immediately, he spied two vertebrae that together formed the runes for "mother." A blackened rib pointed in their direction, leaving no doubt that the mother in question was Lord Bahl's. Gorm followed the shadows cast by the two vertebrae. They passed over a second rib, shading one of the runes inscribed into it. The Most Holy One glared at the rune with growing fury, as if his malice could erase the symbol. He would have liked to have stomped the bone to powder, but stepping outside the circle would have risked his life without changing the bone's message.

According to the rib, the heir's mother had vanished. Nothing would change that fact. Gorm remained in place, and gradually his fury cooled. "The heir vanished also," he said to the frigid dark, "and he's now found." Gorm studied the bones further. The more he studied, the more pleased he became. Although the mother had vanished, it would be for only a short while. Better yet, when she reappeared, Gorm wouldn't have to search for her. She would come to him. The Most Holy One flashed a malevolent grin. "When she does, I'll be ready. More than ready."

FORTY·NINE

THE JOURNEY to Bahland was taking much longer than Froan had expected. That was mainly because Stregg had instructed him on the need to "harvest souls" for god. God, of course, was the Devourer, the same divinity that bestowed power upon him. With the black priest's arrival, Froan had learned to think in more religious terms. The invigorating surge he felt after each violent death and the resulting increase in his power was called "grace." The fear he inspired and his ability to inflame men with hate were its manifestations. Thus, according to Stregg, the devastation he wrought on the march to his domain—although it slowed his progress—not only made him more powerful but also more holy.

Froan wasn't entirely convinced. There were still occasions when he felt like a butcher, not a lord. Then, instead of feeling powerful, he felt like a prisoner—a captive of circumstance, of others' expectations, and most of all, of "his shadow." When such a mood was on him, Stregg's flattery rang false and plundered luxuries brought him no satisfaction. It was at those times that Froan would wistfully recall lying in the woods with Moli. In his recollection, everything was simpler: She was just a stolen wench, and he was only a lad plucked from the river who possessed little more than Moli's love. Yet, in ways, he had felt richer than he did as a lord. The mood always passed. But while it persisted, it exposed the depths of his emptiness.

Although Froan missed Moli, it wasn't because he lacked

for women. Stregg procured them along with other spoils. They were either whores or dead men's wives, never virgins. All were clean and pretty, and none was missing a single tooth. Moreover, they were eager to please. Yet after every carnal session, Froan thought that "desperate to please" was a more apt description. Sometimes, when he caught a partner in an unguarded moment, he spied fear in her eyes. One unlucky woman had even shown revulsion, a fatal slip. After his rage had cooled, Froan regretted what he'd done, although Stregg had said it was "no less than the bitch deserved."

The priest counseled that regret was a weakness and unbecoming in a great lord. Despite his sporadic bouts of skepticism, Froan saw Stregg's point. Remorse seemed to be worse than useless. An army needed supplies and loot to sustain and reward its men. Regretting the deeds that were done to obtain them didn't lessen their necessity. A conscience seemed equally without benefit. The priest endorsed that philosophy, and Froan's men concurred—at least those still capable of logic. As for the rest, Froan had so inflamed them that they slew without reflection. When they didn't have a foe to kill, they often slew one another.

Most of the crazed men came from Cuprick. Its destruction dwarfed that of Midgeport. It had taken several days to accomplish, and it was the first time that Froan had used his powers to turn defenders against one another. The feat—evidence of his increased power—had felt easy and resulted in turning an evenly fought battle into a massacre.

Afterward, the name Shadow was forgotten, and Froan became accustomed to being called Lord Bahl. The name aided his transformation. Thoughts of Moli came less frequently, as did the bouts of regret and conscience. His voice grew colder and harder. Men listened carefully when he spoke, as if afraid to misunderstand a single word. He grew used to obedience and ceased restraining his temper.

When Froan neared the border of his future domain,

messengers began to scurry back and forth from the Iron Palace. They often brought gifts. One appeared with a magnificent stallion. The steed was huge, pitch-black, and fiery eyed. Soon after another messenger took all of Froan's measurements, clothing began to arrive. Having grown up wearing goatskin, Froan made his acquaintance with velvet, gold embroidery, and tooled polished leather. Armor arrived soon after the clothes—blackened chain mail with ebony plates of etched steel and an elegantly sculpted helm that emphasized his piecing eyes. A bejeweled broadsword and dagger, both heirlooms from his father, accompanied the armor.

Two days later, a cavalry regiment from the Iron Guard galloped up. The general who led it dismounted and knelt in the dust before kissing Froan's hand. Afterward, as a demonstration of its prowess, the Iron Guard handily slaughtered everyone who had accompanied their new lord except the priest. Lord Bahl found the display impressive, stimulating, and especially symbolic, for it seemed to mark the end of his old life and the beginning of his new one.

The Iron Guard escorted their lord for another day before they entered Bahland. Its border was marked by a pair of basalt steles that resembled gigantic stone fingers flanking the road. When Froan peered at the wintry landscape ahead, he thought that it possessed a starkness that was due to more than just the season. Nothing seemed to have been done to please the eye. The piled stones that marked the boundaries were haphazardly assembled. Refuse lay in open sight. The fields were filled with brown stubble and rot, and the untilled places were rank with thorny weeds.

The mounted column proceeded down the road with the cavalrymen riding four abreast. The regiment was unequally divided, with a smaller contingent preceding their lord and a greater one trailing him. Froan rode in the gap between, accompanied by Stregg and the general, whose name was Drak.

When a village appeared in the distance, General Drak pulled his horse alongside Froan's. "My lord, your subjects will be gathered to show their devotion and obeisance. They will present gifts. You, in turn, will give them justice."

"Justice? What form of justice?"

"Felons shall be brought forth to feel your blade upon their necks. It's a time-honored custom."

As the column drew nearer to the village, Froan could see its main street was lined with folk. They stood closely packed and silent, and it seemed that everyone had turned out regardless of age or health. The drab settlement about them appeared as stark as the surrounding landscape. Gray stone was the principal building material, and the structures built from it lacked ornamentation or grace. Soot coated the stones and the unpainted wooden doors and shutters, giving them a somber look. Garbage had been removed from the streets by pushing it to the sides where the crowds trampled it underfoot. The overall impression was of squalor, poverty, and neglect.

Closer up, most of the village's inhabitants matched their dismal abodes. Even the ragged children appeared grim. Everyone was dressed in brown, gray, or black. The only color in evidence was the circle painted on everyone's forehead; it was freshly brushed in blood. Even before Froan reached the village, its people began to cheer, and the cheering spread like windblown fire through a dry field. By the time he was riding down the street, a roar reverberated through it.

Froan gazed at the screaming mob, surprised by their enthusiasm. Everyone appeared caught up in frenzied acclamation. Glancing about, Froan sensed why. *They believe their submission will keep them safe.* Since no one could hide from his penetrating gaze, Froan saw that the most terrified shouted his praises the loudest.

The column halted when Froan reached the center of the village, which was an unpaved square of modest dimensions. There, the crowd was most tightly packed. A group of men, somewhat better dressed than most, stood at the forefront of the crowd. Several black-robed priests flanked them. When Froan reined in his horse, the priests bowed and the men knelt in the slushy mud.

"Oh, Great and Dread Lord," called out the foremost kneeling man, "we are most honored by your visit. Your humble and loyal subjects pray to present you gifts in thanks for the grace you've shown us."

"You may rise and do this," said Froan.

The men rose and advanced, bowing after each step. The man who had spoken held something bundled in black cloth. He pulled the cloth away to reveal a goblet wrought from solid gold. He handed it to Froan with many bows. Froan examined it. The work was crudely executed, but the goblet was heavy. "All have paid to have this made, my lord."

"It pleases me," said Froan.

The man looked greatly relieved. "And we have sent seventeen sons for your Iron Guard, your lordship. And seven cows, and thirteen sheep, and fifty fowls for your feast. And we have pledged half again this harvest's tithe."

"All this is good," replied Froan.

The man bowed and made a gesture. Then the crowd behind him parted and a young man and an even younger woman were brought forth. Their lips had been stitched shut and their arms were tightly bound behind their backs. Both were shoeless and wore thin tunics that provided scant protection against the frigid weather. "This pair offended your laws, my lord. Will you render justice?"

Stregg had coached Froan on what to say. "Aye. I will give them death. Bring out the block, so all may see the fate of those who transgress against my laws."

As Froan dismounted, a wooden block was brought forward, and the young man was forced to kneel and place his head upon it. Froan drew his broadsword and strode up to the kneeling man, who was shivering from either the cold or fear or both. Froan had never used such a heavy blade before, and he felt awkward as he gripped the huge sword with both hands to raise it high above his head.

The execution proved a clumsy business. Froan's first blow missed the neck entirely, striking the man just below the shoulders. The wound was grievous, but not immediately fatal. Neither was the second one, but at least it struck the unfortunate man's neck. A third blow finished him, but didn't sever his head; an additional stroke was required for that.

After the bloody corpse was dragged away, they brought forth the young woman. She was trembling violently, and Froan made the error of glancing into her eyes. Immediately, he sensed her despair and understood that neither she nor the young man had done anything to deserve their fates. The law was only a pretext to deliver them as sacrifices to a ruthless lord and his bloody god.

At that instant, Froan was himself and not Lord Bahl. He was about to show the woman mercy until he glanced about. The rabid faces gazing back at him betrayed the general sentiment: all the folk with blood-painted foreheads were eager to see him kill. Froan readily saw that they regarded the execution as an entertaining spectacle, one of the few diversions from a drab and hard life.

Forced to kneel, the woman's face was hidden from him, but her entire body shook. Froan pitied her, but he felt that he must meet expectations. The only mercy he could afford to show was to slay her quickly. He swung his broadsword and succeeded. When the crowd roared its approval, Froan's merciful impulse seemed foolhardy. *A lord must be stern*, he thought, *for his subjects require an iron hand*. The headless body was dragged away. The dark thing within Froan exulted, and strengthened by the two deaths, it suppressed the vestiges of regret. When Froan mounted his horse, he was Lord Bahl again. He smiled coldly as he rode to the next village.

*   *   *

On Froan's journey to the Iron Palace, the visit to the first village proved the pattern for all subsequent stops. The settlements varied from tiny hamlets to good-sized towns, but everywhere he went all the inhabitants turned out. The value of the gifts also varied, as did the number of unfortunates brought forth for "justice." Practice made Froan more adept with the broadsword. After his first executions, he grew more hardened, and he was tempted to show mercy only once again. That was in a village that brought out an entire family for beheading—mother, father, and their five children. In the end, they perished like all the others.

The stops en route to the Iron Palace slowed Froan's advance, but it gave him a feel for the domain that he was to rule. His subjects seemed fittingly subservient, but otherwise hardened and brutal. Judging from the Iron Guard, they made excellent soldiers. They were also adept at displaying loyalty. When Froan passed before the cheering throngs, it was impossible not to feel exalted and powerful. The regiment took a route that passed through most of Bahland, and Froan deduced that someone had taken pains to ensure that the march was a triumphal one. He suspected that person was the Most Holy Gorm.

Thirteen days after Froan crossed the border, he caught his first glimpse of the Iron Palace. Nothing in his travels prepared him for the sight. At first, he couldn't believe that the structure was man-made; it simply looked too big. It stood above a town in splendid isolation on a bluff with the sky as its only backdrop. Before Froan could get a closer view, he had to pass through the town. His greeting there was the most lavish and enthusiastic one on his entire march. Black banners hung from all the buildings, the crowd was immense, the gifts were extravagant, and thirteen people were brought forth to die. Froan endured the pomp and show impatiently, solely concerned with reaching the palace quickly.

When the ceremonies were over at last, Froan rode to his new home. The closer he got to it, the more its size impressed him. If it hadn't been so symmetrical, he might have believed it was a hite formed from black, oiled iron. Its basic form was that of a huge square enclosed by walls that slanted inward as they rose to the height of more than ten men. There were flat-topped, square-sided towers at each corner. A fifth tower rose from near the middle of the rear wall. It was different from the others in that it was much higher, lacked windows, and its top tapered inward to form a pyramid with its tip sliced off. The flat portion appeared to be a small deck. The other towers had crenellations on their tops, as did the outer walls. This feature gave them a spiky look, since each crenellation was capped with a steep-sided pyramid.

Froan could see the upper stories of a huge building rising from within the walls. The only other feature in view was the gatehouse that projected from the front of the palace. It was also gigantically proportioned, rising nearly as high as the walls behind it. An iron gate filled its immense, pointed archway. As the column rode toward it, ten horsemen abreast, the gate slowly rose into the arch, revealing a black, gaping hole.

Gazing upon the Iron Palace, Froan was amazed that such an edifice belonged to a single man. He was even more amazed to be that man. The mere idea of it thrilled and awed him. It seemed a grandiose fantasy, a dream from which he might awake and find himself in the fens again. *How can such a thing be happening to me?* he wondered. It seemed both wonderful and unsettling at once.

The column, still riding ten abreast, passed through the gate into a spacious and frigid courtyard. A massive rectangular building projected into the courtyard, taking up much of its space. The building's upper story was pierced by high, thin windows capped with pointed arches, and it was crowned by a steeply pitched slate roof. Froan assumed the structure was the actual palace. Like the towers and the exterior of the stronghold's walls, it was covered with iron plates. All the other structures flanking the courtyard were built with the same stone that paved it—black basalt. The effect was gloomy but impressive.

Men dressed in black poured out of the palace and rushed over to him. Froan assumed they were servants, and their timid behavior confirmed his conclusion. As one got on all fours to become a human stepping stool, the others bowed low. "O most powerful master," said one, "to fulfill your every wish is our sole desire. We are yours to command."

Then a second spoke. "The Most Holy Gorm awaits you."

It seemed to Froan that the second man contradicted the first, but he replied to him by commanding to be taken to the Most Holy One.

The interior of the palace was as overwhelming as its exterior. Froan passed through a succession of large, shadowy chambers, moving so rapidly that his most vivid impression—other than their darkness—was their smell. The chilly air had a faint but pervasive odor. At first, Froan couldn't place it. Then he recalled the stale scent of the desiccated corpse he had found atop Twin Hite. If folk had built tombs in the Grey Fens, Froan imagined they would have smelled like the somber rooms—ancient, with a whiff of death.

Entering the great hall felt like standing outdoors again, for the vast room exceeded all Froan's conceptions of what a room could be. It seemed far too large for human needs. The black columns appeared like trees to him, especially where they curved at their tops to form the pointed arches of the ceiling. The greenish glass in the high windows dimmed the light and tinted it to an underwater hue. Most striking of all was the hall's emptiness, the way it swallowed sound and made him feel minute.

At the far end of the room was a raised platform, and on

it were two chairs. One was ornate and empty. The other was simple and a man sat in it. When he rose from his seat, the servants retreated, leaving Froan and the man alone. Froan strode toward him. At first, the other man was just a tiny figure dwarfed by the immense proportions of the vacant hall. But eventually, Froan could see him better. He had a full black beard and wore the ebony robes of a priest. However, the simple iron pendant of the Devourer was suspended from an elaborate gold chain. The man bowed, and called to Froan. "Lord Bahl, your chair has long stood empty. Come sit in it while we talk."

Froan advanced closer. When he was near enough to clearly view the man's deeply tanned face, he had two contradictory impressions: The man looked youthful, seemingly Froan's elder by just a dozen winters. At the same time, his gray eyes appeared ancient. The man bowed. "Your lordship, I am the Most Holy Gorm, highest in the order that serves your cause. Long have I awaited this meeting."

Froan gazed into Gorm's eyes and discovered that he was unable to penetrate beneath their surface. He discerned only what any keen observer might see: that Gorm was unafraid of him and that he exuded an air of triumph.

FIFTY

FROAN CLIMBED the short flight of stairs leading to the platform. He was still in his armor, which was stained with the blood of the thirteen he had executed. Gorm grinned at the sight of him. "Every bit a lord," he said. "It is as if you had grown up within these walls." He paused to appraise him. "You possess your father's gaze but your mother's coloring."

"You knew her?" asked Froan.

"Of course. I was there when she betrayed your father. Where did she hide you all this time?"

"The Grey Fens."

"That dismal bog?" said Gorm. "Your arrival is proof of your greatness. A lesser man would have never escaped."

"You said she betrayed my father. Did she slay him?"

"She cut out his heart," said the Most Holy One, shaking his head. "Such a traitorous way to repay his devotion."

Froan gazed into Gorm's eyes again, but they remained impervious to his scrutiny. "Why?"

"I believe that she thought she could work magic with it. She had another lover—"

"I know," said Froan. "Honus. She claimed he was my father and said he was a goatherd. That was also a lie. My father's spirit revealed that Honus was a Sarf."

Gorm's eyes widened, as if he were surprised. "You were visited by your father's ghost?"

"Yes. He hinted at my heritage, but only that."

"Then what happened? Did your mother release you?"

"No," said Froan. "We fought."

"I'm hardly surprised."

"And I killed her."

Gorm raised an eyebrow. "Are you sure?"

"Yes. I cut her throat."

"The memory seems to pain you."

"Somewhat. It was an accident. She was grabbing for my dagger and fell onto my blade."

"Well, don't blame yourself. There's such a thing as fate, and your mother's treachery sealed hers. Before you mourn her, think upon this: your father's death was no accident."

"Still," said Froan, "she was the only parent I knew."

"Your father had a premonition of his end and charged me with your care." Gorm bowed his head in a gesture of humility. "A charge I failed. Your mother outwitted me by fleeing before you were born. But by your grace, I'll redeem myself and teach you all you need to know."

"I'd appreciate that," said Froan. "This life is new to me.".

Gorm bowed again. "I thank you for your trust, my lord. I believe you'll master your role quicker than you suppose. After all, you were born to rule."

"That's what my father said."

Gorm smiled. "Never doubt his wisdom."

Froan and Gorm continued talking for quite a while, but their conversation shifted to a mundane discussion of palace life. Froan had the distinct impression that Gorm had learned all he wanted to know at the very onset and that he had been able to discern things left unsaid. Whatever the Most Holy One discovered apparently pleased him, for he seemed to be struggling to hide his satisfaction under a guise of formality. Eventually, the palace chamberlain appeared and Gorm left Froan in the servant's care.

When Froan arrived at his private apartments, he had the eerie sensation that he had been there before. Everything looked vaguely familiar, although he had never seen anything like the elegant rooms in his life. Their walls and high ceilings were paneled in a wood so dark that it was nearly black. The ceilings were elaborately carved, while tapestries depicting battle scenes hung on the walls. One showed soldiers climbing a mound of corpses to surmount a battlement. The figures in the foreground stood knee-deep in blood. It hung in the oversized room where servants stripped off Froan's armor and dressed him in dark red velvet.

In a private dining room, other servants brought out wine and meat. After they piled a table with more than five could eat or drink, Froan sent them away. He grabbed a brimming wine goblet and a haunch of rare meat and then wandered about. He was both exuberant and uneasy.

Everything about his situation felt perfectly right and disturbingly wrong. The latter feeling wasn't as strong as the former, but it was persistent, and he couldn't dismiss it. He felt like someone who would be at perfect ease if it weren't for a grain of sand beneath an eyelid. He had achieved his destiny and become a great lord. He possessed powers beyond the dreams of ordinary men. Nevertheless, it was spoiled by one small thing—the remnants of a conscience that he couldn't banish.

Rage boiled up within him. *This is Mam's fault!* he thought. *She's ruining this for me!* He was certain that his weaknesses arose from her, and the idea infuriated him. *But what can I do? I've already cut her throat.* Ironically, it seemed that his only obstacle to contentment was himself. With mounting fury, he rang for a servant and a man hurried in. "What do you wish, my lord?"

Froan held out the haunch of meat. "Come and look at this!" When the man rushed over, Froan said, "It's overdone. I want it like this." He plunged his dagger into the servant's bowels. "Bloody."

The servant screamed in agony as Froan twisted the blade, feeling a rush of excitement that overwhelmed his ambivalence. After the man fell writhing to the floor and expired, Froan felt both graced by the Devourer and as one with all the lords who had preceded him. That mood persisted throughout the rest of his meal, which he ate in the presence of the servant's corpse. Afterward, he retired to his bedchamber, where a huge window overlooked the bay and the sea beyond. Froan had never seen the ocean before, and he gazed at it for a long while. The setting sun was disappearing into the water, coloring it bloodred. It was a shade that perfectly fit his mood.

Stregg followed the Most Holy Gorm up the winding stairs of the divining tower in a state of anticipation. When he entered the holy chamber, he was surprised by its simplicity. It was a cubic room built of black stone with an iron door engraved with runes. A very young boy, gagged and bound hand and foot, lay shivering on the floor. He regarded Stregg and the Most Holy One with terrified eyes. A single oil lamp illuminated the room. It sat on a massive stone block that served as a table and was the room's sole furnishing. There were a number of items on the table, but Stregg's gaze was immediately drawn to the gleaming silver chain—the emblem of the More Holy One.

"Give me your pendant," said Gorm.

Stregg removed the leather cord that suspended the iron circle that symbolized the Devourer. The rusty pendant was a family heirloom, and precious to him. Gorm took it and smiled. "I remember presenting this same pendant to your great-grandfather when he was younger than you are now." He took a bronze dagger from his robe and cut the cord away. Then walking over to the table, he attached the pendant to the silver chain using an iron clasp. "Kneel."

Stregg knelt, and the Most Holy One slipped the chain over his head. Stregg admired the emblem of his new office. The chain resembled Gorm's except in its material, featuring tiny skulls and interlocking links modeled after bones.

"Rise," said Gorm. "That chain is but a symbol. It confers no power or gifts. Only our master does that, and it does this through the ritual of bone, hair, blood, and flesh." Gorm returned to the table and picked up a yellowed finger bone. "Your predecessor provides the bone. The More Holy Daijen failed our master. Learn from his example." Gorm dropped the bone into a small iron bowl, took up an iron pestle, and ground the bone to powder.

"What happened to him?" asked Stregg.

"He died of old age," replied Gorm, flashing an ironic smile. "It wasn't as gentle a death as you might suppose. Now you must provide the hair, blood, and flesh. By this means, our master will know you." Gorm grabbed a hand-

ful of Stregg's long, greasy hair and cut off a lock with his
dagger. After he added the lock to the bowl, he said, "Now
bare your arm so I might open a vein."

Stregg obeyed. Gorm punctured a vein in the priest's wrist
and held it over the bowl, releasing the arm only when the
bowl was nearly full of blood. "Before you bandage that,"
said Gorm, "I'll take the flesh." Gorm pinched the skin of
Stregg's lower arm just below the elbow and passed his blade
between his fingers and the arm to slice away a piece of skin
the size of a large coin. Stregg clenched his teeth in pain, but
said nothing. "There's cloth to wrap your wounds," said
Gorm as he added the flesh to the bowl.

As Stregg bandaged himself, Gorm continued talking.
"Now, we must contact our master. After you become the
More Holy One, I'll instruct you on how to do this. The
sole thing you need know tonight is that you can do this
only from inside the protection of a circle of blood and the
blood must come from a male."

"A male child?" asked Stregg.

"Any male will do," replied Gorm. "I use children because they're convenient. The important thing is that there
must be no gap in the circle and you cannot leave its confines while our master is present. Break either of these rules
and you'll be fortunate to be only maimed. I knew one man
who was reduced to a living cinder. Now cut that boy's
throat."

Stregg did as he was told. He also painted the circle under Gorm's watchful eye. Afterward, he knelt inside it with
the Most Holy One, who silently performed the necessary
meditations. The Devourer's presence was signaled by a sudden drop in temperature, a dimming of the lamp's flame, and
an oppressive atmosphere of malice. Then the contents of
the bowl, which Gorm had set on the floor outside the circle,
began to boil. The boiling produced thick black smoke that
had a harsh, putrescent stench. It was all Stregg could do to
keep from gagging.

After a while, the bowl stopped smoking. Still, Gorm cautioned Stregg to stay within the circle until the room warmed and the atmosphere of malice dissipated. At last, Gorm stepped from the circle and handed Stregg the bowl. It was still warm, and its contents were reduced to tarry goo. Gorm handed him a spoon. "Eat what's in the bowl and you'll become the More Holy One. Afterward, we'll celebrate with wine. It will help wash the taste away."

Gorm's apartments were at the very top of the palace, adjoining the entrance to the divining tower. The rusty iron door leading to them looked strictly utilitarian. It opened to a short hallway sealed by another equally plain iron door. Consequently, the gold-paneled room behind it seemed all the more dazzling. Huge bas-reliefs depicting historic scenes caught and reflected the light from dozens of candles. Stregg was momentarily stunned by the grandeur of the chamber. When he recovered, he walked over to the nearest relief to examine it more closely. "Does this portray the destruction of Karm's temple?" he asked.

"Yes," replied Gorm. "It's my most recent acquisition. The artist actually participated in the slaughter." He pointed to another relief. "That's the battle of Karvakken Pass." He gestured to a wall covered with flat sheets of gold. "And that's where the Rising will go."

Stregg grinned. "An event that will happen in my lifetime, now that I'm the More Holy One."

"That would be so even if you hadn't become immortal." Gorm clapped his hand, and a girl of perhaps fifteen winters entered the room. She was dressed in a short black tunic so sheer that Stregg could faintly view her nakedness. She was beautiful, but it was her white hair, pink eyes, and pale, almost transparent skin that made her striking. "Bring wine," Gorm commanded.

As the girl hurried to obey, Stregg turned to his host. "She's stunning. What's her name?"

"I don't give them names," said Gorm. "But this one's unusual. I ordered her from Larresh, sight unseen. They had to ship her in a bag, for the sun blisters her."

"So ye think the Rising—" Stregg stopped talking when the girl returned with wine and goblets.

"You can speak freely around her," said Gorm. "I remove the tongues of all my girls."

"A wise precaution," said Stregg, "and a cure for prattling as well."

"Yes," said Gorm. "All they can do is moan."

"So ye think this Lord Bahl may be the final one?"

"I'm sure of it. The boy's shown remarkable abilities for one still incomplete."

"Incomplete?"

"He has yet to drink his mother's blood to realize his true potential. Currently, the Devourer is divided between them."

"But his mother's dead," said Stregg. "Bahl told me so."

Gorm smiled. "I know he believes that, which will make everything much easier. Usually Lord Bahl never sees his mother until the suckling. At the ceremony, she's just some stranger to him. Only afterward do I reveal her identity." Gorm paused, seemingly puzzled. "You'd think it wouldn't bother them, but it always does. And then afterward, the knowledge hardens them. This time, I expect my revelation to have an especially strong effect."

"Don't ye worry about him lashing out?"

"Ha! Lord Bahl is only the Devourer's vessel, and I'm the Most Holy One. This is my palace, in truth. That's why I live in golden rooms while Bahl dwells in wooden ones."

Gorm's slave gave him his wine in a golden goblet and then gave Stregg a silver one. "To the Rising!" said Gorm.

Stregg clinked his goblet against his host's. "To the Rising!" He drank deeply in an effort to cleanse the foul taste from his mouth. "Ye said it will be soon."

"When Lord Bahl's complete, his army will pour into

Averen. All those he doesn't slay, he'll inflame to swell his forces for Vinden's destruction. When the slaughter is sufficient, the Devourer will burst forth from his fleshy prison to stride the world and reign forever. And we'll be his immortal servants, as exalted and feared as the god we serve."

"And when will Bahl be complete?"

"Spring will bring the blood we need."

"The mother's blood?"

"Yes," replied Gorm, his eyes alight. "She'll come on her own accord, bound by the doom that binds the world."

FIFTY·ONE

BY THE time Yim awoke, the glowing sphere that lit the downy chamber had grown dim. The light it shed was no longer the rosy shade of dawn, but the soft blue of twilight. Yim looked about and saw that she was alone; even the rabbits had departed. Her first thought was of Honus. *Thistle said I needn't fear to tup him*, she thought, feeling a warm flush of excitement. For a moment, she wondered if she could trust Thistle's word. *She's no ordinary girl*, Yim reminded herself, recalling how Lila—another faerie-kissed child—had known about her feelings for Honus. *Thistle's no different.* Moreover, Yim desperately wanted to believe her.

Yim felt something in her hand and saw the walnut comb. It reminded her that Thistle had spoken of far grimmer matters. That dampened Yim's mood until she recalled that Thistle had said she should go to Bahland in the spring. "That's moons away," said she aloud, thinking of all the bliss she could fit into that span. With that in mind, Yim was eager to leave the tower. The idea of dressing in the snow was unpleasant, and Yim wanted to get it over quickly. She slithered up the narrow, twisting tunnel as fast as she could manage, steeling herself for the cold that waited. On her second turn, Yim saw greenish light ahead and sped up her pace.

Even before Yim emerged from the burrow, she was puzzled. By the time she exited the hole, she was stunned. There was no snow. Nor were there dead plants. Instead, the interior of the tower was filled with greenery and spring flowers. The oak had shed its brown leaves and was sprouting new ones. Yim looked for her gown and found it blown to the ground. A few shoots had even pushed through the fabric. She could find only one shoe, and some animal had thoroughly gnawed it.

Dressing in the mild air, Yim hoped that the change of seasons was limited to the confines of the tower and the outside world would still be wrapped in winter. When Yim walked to the opening in the tower wall, her wishful thinking was dashed; the countryside was in the flush of spring. She had "napped" through her stretch of potential bliss, and that made her angry. *Why did Thistle trick me?* It seemed cruel until she recalled that Thistle had told her she was safe in the tower. In that light, Yim's nap likened to the time when she had evaded Lord Bahl by hibernating with a bear.

Although disappointed, Yim forgave Thistle. She sighed and said to herself, "I can only hope Honus is still here." Yim was about to cross the log when she noticed a garland in the pathway. It was woven from violets and looked so fresh that Yim glanced about to see if Thistle had just tossed it there. She saw no sign of the girl. As Yim placed the garland on her head, she caught its sweet, spicy fragrance. It stirred earthy feelings that seemed especially appropriate to the season. Yim thought of how fine a spring night would be for love, and her lips curved into a voluptuous smile. She remained smiling as she skipped across the log, climbed down to the courtyard, and hurried to the manor house.

When Yim entered the manor, she could hear the sounds of talk and dining coming from the banquet hall. She peered in its doorway and saw Honus seated at the head table. The meal was an informal one with less than two dozen diners, and Yim had no qualms about interrupting it. Her bare feet made virtually no sound upon the wooden floor, but soon her footsteps were the loudest sound in the hall. Her sudden appearance silenced everyone.

Honus stared at her, transfixed. Yim gazed back at him, ignoring all the other eyes upon her, yet feeling them nonetheless. She was fully aware that she had become the personification of desire. Her eyes, her lips, her every movement bespoke of a woman who knew exactly what she wanted and believed that she deserved it. A heady scent of violets and musk filled the hall, transforming all the diners into flushed-faced statues.

Her eyes ever on Honus, Yim mounted the stairs with sensuous slowness, enjoying the way her hips and breasts moved beneath the fabric of her gown. Her every movement conveyed her feeling that she was both the essence of womanhood and its perfection. Although she hadn't eaten in moons, the smell of food had no affect on her. She was gripped by a different hunger, one that had been denied far longer. Striding up to Honus, Yim softly stroked his face. "Come," she said, her voice low and earthy. "We've waited far too long."

Honus rose from the bench like a man in a dream who is helpless yet willing. No other words were spoken. In the perfection of the moment, the conventions of courtesy seemed meaningless. Yim silently took Honus's hand, and the two departed the hall as those left behind watched dumbstruck. Neither said a word until they reached Honus's room beneath the eaves. It was strewn with so many violets that Yim crushed them with every step, releasing their scent. Yet the unexpected flowers seemed less a marvel than the rapture she felt. "Honus, I've loved you ever since our spirits mingled when I restored your life." It was the first time that Yim had admitted her deed, yet Honus didn't seem surprised. "Our love wasn't Karm's gift," she whispered, "it was yours. And I want—I *need*—to experience it fully." Yim kissed his lips. "Make love to me."

It seemed to Yim that Honus's face softened before her eyes, the way a craggy mountain softens in spring. His fingertips touched her face as gently as a warm breeze. His touch was his answer, and it spoke to her of his tenderness, longing, and adoration. It was also suffused with primal urgency that more than hinted of a memorable night ahead.

Honus's lips softly brushed hers. They lingered there, growing more hungry and passionate as they embraced. When Yim felt that she could no longer stand to have anything between her body and Honus, she pulled off her gown with his help. It felt wonderful to be naked before him, to see his eyes take in her body and feel his hands explore it. She briefly luxuriated in his caresses before she removed his clothes, so she could rediscover his body.

When they were both nude, they retreated to the bed. As the light coming from the dormer window faded, fingers, lips, and tongues did the work of eyes. Yim felt she was a musical instrument strummed by a master. The sweetness of his playing was as delightful as it was new. When he finally entered her, Yim was ready and expectant. She shuddered with delight. Soon joy and pleasure mounted ever higher until it spread like waves surging over her body. She trembled and cried out in ecstasy. Warmth that was more than warmth flowed through her, leaving happy contentment that washed away the taint and pain of her nightmare tryst with Lord Bahl.

"Yim . . . Yim . . . Yim," whispered Honus, his voice as soft and sweet as syrup. He spoke her name like a Seer chanting to the goddess, each word rich with reverence and devotion. She felt truly and totally loved, and it made her want to weep with happiness. She kissed Honus instead.

"That was truly my first time," Yim said. "What happened before never counted."

"Was it worth so long a wait?" asked Honus.

Yim kissed her reply, then giggled. "You know what's the best thing about sleeping for five moons straight? I'm not the least bit sleepy."

"How about hungry?"

Yim moaned. "Oh, why did you say that? I'm suddenly starving."

Honus got out of bed and pulled on his pants. "I'll see if I can get something from the pantry." He opened the door and found a tray on the floor in the hallway. On it was a jug of wine, two goblets, and all manner of delicacies. He brought the tray into the room. "I suspect we have Cara to thank for this. She's always been the romantic."

Yim smiled. "If she had her way, we'd have tupped long ago in the Bridge Inn." Her expression turned serious. "And Lord Bahl would have overrun Averen and the whole world, I suppose."

"You've always put others before your own desires," said Honus.

"Not tonight!" Yim's smile returned and blossomed into a grin. "Let's eat! But before you join me, take off those pants."

They ate nude by candlelight. The food included a small fowl, bread, cheese, and a wide variety of sweets. After Yim took the edge off her hunger, she dipped her fingers into a bowl of honey and smeared some on her nipples. "Well, *somebody* better lick this off," she said. That began a lover's game in which honey was smeared in ever more imaginative places. It concluded with lovemaking on the flower-strewn floor.

Afterward, they ate some more, brushed violets from their moist skin, and retired to bed. There, Yim declared that in homage to Karm she intended to kiss the length of each scar Honus had received in the goddess's service. By then, the candle had burned out, and she was forced to find each one by feel. She managed, although Honus had an extensive collection of old wounds, and she made up a few as she went.

Honus reciprocated, but he didn't have to search for Yim's injuries. He knew them all by heart. First he kissed the small mark on her foot where the dark man had paralyzed her with his venomed sword. Yim was surprised that he knew about it, for she had lied about that encounter. Then he kissed the scar made by an arrow on the night Hommy was slain. It was on Yim's back and he was the one who had stitched it closed. Next he kissed the mark on her chin made by a peasant intent on her death. She had received that one as Honus's Bearer. Last of all, he kissed the long gash in her neck, the other wound she had lied to him about.

Afterward, they tupped one more time in a leisurely way that was more about intimacy and togetherness than passion. That finally spent them, and entangled together, they drifted off to sleep where they entered each other's dreams.

There were ewers of water and a copper tub outside Yim and Honus's door. They discovered them when they rose at midmorning. The water had cooled, but Yim was glad for a chance to bathe. Honus washed her and she washed him. It was pleasantly arousing, and if Yim hadn't felt sore, she might have pulled Honus back into bed. Instead, she suggested that they go to breakfast.

"Cara will be waiting," warned Honus.

"Of course," said Yim. "There'll be no evading her. We're lucky she didn't wake us."

They dressed and went down to the room off the kitchen where the household ate the morning porridge. The room was empty, except for Cara. She was beaming. "Well, Yim, you certainly made an entrance last night! I tingle just recalling it."

"I suppose you want to know what happened," said Honus.

"Zounds, Honus. Do I want to know the sun rises in the morn? Or that the lake is watery? I'm a married woman with an excellent imagination. I'm na curious, I'm happy for you both. And about time, too! So, Yim, what did Violet tell you that I didn't say before?"

"That it'd be safe."

"Safe? I do na understand."

"You know of the thing within me. She assured me that it could do no harm."

"Na harm? Well, *that's* for sure. You look wonderful. Honus, too. Mayhap now you'll think twice about that trip to you know where and choose happiness instead."

"Thistle told me other things," said Yim. "She also said that I should leave in the spring."

Upon that statement, both Honus and Cara stared at Yim. The atmosphere in the room transformed as Yim's eyes welled with tears. Although she was certain that Honus and she would make love again and share moments of tenderness, she felt the previous night would never be duplicated. Her words had unleashed a sense of doom that could never dissipate until she had done what she must do. Better than anyone, Yim understood both the terrible price of inaction as well as the horrors she would face.

Honus grasped Yim's hand and gently squeezed it. "When do you wish to leave?"

Yim sighed. "As soon as we can."

There were no maps of Bahland in the hall. Cara doubted any could be found outside of Bremven, for Lord Bahl's domain was a place few people visited. Nevertheless, she made inquiries and learned of a man who knew something of Bahland because his brother had traveled there. Cara sent for him and he came the following day. The man was a fur trader named Datlan, a lean, middle-aged fellow with a weather-beaten face and a long red beard and matching hair. He met with Honus and Yim in a small room off the entrance hall.

"Clan Mother says you want to go to Bahland," said Datlan. "Take my advice and stay home."

"But your brother made the trip," said Yim.

"Aye, Tommic went there twice to sell black wolf pelts. But he came back only once. They don't take to outsiders, even those with goods they want. Tommic came to harm, I'm certain of it."

"Why?" asked Honus.

"Because black priests run every settlement and enforce Bahl's laws. Your tattooed face is a capital offense. So's bearing a sword or dagger. And traveling without a black robe's leave, well, that dooms you, too. There's lots of laws to break, and every trial ends on the Dark Path."

"So, we'll travel disguised as cursed ones," said Honus.

"That will na work," said Datlan. "Cursed ones are buried alive."

"Then we'll avoid all towns and villages. Is Bahland thickly settled?"

"Tommic said few dwell near the coast, for there are high cliffs and the land's poor."

"Then we'll go that way," said Honus.

"Honus, your face will doom you," said Yim. "I should go alone."

"My runes say otherwise. It's Karm's will."

"Karm decrees nothing, except that everyone is free to choose."

"And I choose to go with you, even if it means my death. I won't abide another separation."

"You're both daft," said Datlan.

"We probably are," said Yim. "But since we're going, do you have any other advice?"

" 'Tis cold in Bahland this time of year. Dress warm, but na well. Folks there favor drab clothes and wear them till they're rags. Trust no one. Avoid the black robes. May I ask what's worth your life to go?"

"I've a son there," said Yim.

"Then you're a brave and loving mother," said Datlan. He shook his head. "But a foolish one."

FIFTY·TWO

AS LORD Bahl, Froan had spent the winter improving his skill with arms, reviewing his ever-growing army, passing out harsh judgments, and indulging himself. Rich foods, fine wines, beautiful women, and all manner of luxuries were his, but as the countryside turned green, his conscience sometimes reappeared. That was partly because his opposite mood, a restless urge for mayhem, was exacerbated by the mild weather. Men and women perished in his sudden and violent rages, from which only Gorm was completely safe.

As His Lordship's mentor, the Most Holy One usually dined with Froan. He was doing so when Froan suddenly felt troubled by one of his recent judgments and asked, "Do you remember the family I condemned to impalement?"

"The one that short-paid their tithe?" asked Gorm.

"Yes," said Froan. "Perhaps I should have spared the children. They would have grown up to be soldiers."

"Mayhap, my lord. But the little ones' deaths served to deter other parents, and they provided souls to god. Your judgment was a wise one."

"How can you be so sure?"

"I speak to god and it answers me."

"Why call the Devourer 'it'?"

"Because it transcends gender."

"Yet Karm's a goddess."

"Which proves my point. She possesses a woman's frailty—a weak deity, worshipped by weaklings. You live in this magnificent palace, while Karm lacks a single temple."

"Are you saying I'm more powerful than Karm?"

"After the suckling, that will be so, for your understanding and power will increase manyfold. So will your self-assurance. I know of your bouts of self-doubt. The ritual will banish those."

"You've never spoken of this ritual before."

"I've been waiting for the priestess to arrive."

"Priestess? I thought the Devourer was served only by men."

"This woman's an exception."

"What does she do? Let me suckle from her breasts?"

Gorm chuckled, "No, you sip her blood. A taste is usually sufficient. Then you'll be complete."

"I don't understand."

"You will, my lord. It'll be quite a revelation."

"Where and when will this take place?"

"Atop the highest tower. As to when—soon, I expect. Very soon."

As usual, Froan sensed that Gorm was holding something back, but he had long ago abandoned attempts to probe him. The Most Holy One was immune to his gaze. Froan wondered if that would change after the suckling. He hoped that it would.

Although Honus prepared for the journey to the Iron Palace with a heavy heart, he strove for a quick departure. He sensed Yim's dread, and knew delay would only prolong it. *Best make the leap without too much reflection*, he thought, fearing that dwelling on the dangers ahead would sap Yim's hope without altering her resolve. Cara helped by providing clothing appropriate for Bahland and rations that needed no cooking.

To speed their journey, they would travel through Averen on horseback with a packhorse to carry their supplies. Then, before they reached Bahland, they would abandon the animals to cross the border inconspicuously on foot. The only drawback to this plan was that a groom would accompany them to take the horses back. That meant they would have less privacy on the pleasant portion of their trip.

The preparations took only three days. Each night, Honus and Yim made love amid the withered violets, and it was bittersweet. Meals in the banquet hall felt the same. The conversation was subdued or had a forced cheerfulness. Cara was mostly quiet. On the fifth morning after Yim's return from Thistle's tower, all was ready. As Honus, Yim, and the groom prepared to mount, Cara rushed out into the courtyard. "I've said so many good-byes already, you must think me daft to say another."

"No, Cara," replied Yim.

"I remember waving from the boat on the night I sailed from Faerie," said Cara. "Then I thought you were going to your love, and it made me feel better. But now . . ."

"Once again, I'm going to my love—my son." Yim smiled and grasped Honus's hand. "And my beloved is going with me."

"You make it sound so fine, but—but . . . I can na say it. I *will* na say it. Oh, Yim! Oh, Honus!"

"This will end well, Cara," said Yim. "I truly believe that."

"Well, your faith's why you're a Bearer, and I'm na."

"I'm no longer a Bearer. I'm a mother. I know you'd do the same for any child of yours."

"Mayhap," said Cara, "I'd like to think so." She embraced Honus. "Take care of her, Honus. And care of yourself." Then she embraced Yim. "May Karm protect you. Now, both of you come back, and do na wait eighteen winters to do it!" Then teary eyed, Cara kissed them both before rushing into the hall.

Honus led the way out the manor gates and through the village. Then he turned down the lane that followed the lakeshore westward. This route would avoid the more traveled roads. When they were nearly past the lake, a voice called from the water. "Mother!" All gazed in its direction and saw a head peering from the lake's choppy surface.

Yim called back. "Thistle?"

"Aye," the girl answered. Then she began swimming toward the shore with powerful strokes. She reached it much sooner than Honus expected, emerging unclothed from the icy water. Striding over to the party, she addressed the groom first. "Hamick, you may return to your family. The Old Ones will see Mama's horses safely home." When the man seemed to hesitate, she added in a more commanding tone, "Now off with you. I must speak with Mother and Karmamatus."

As the groom rode off, Thistle kissed Yim's hand. "Mother, do you have what I gave you?"

"Yes, it's in my hair."

"Remember all I said, for 'twill make sense in time. I've na more to say except the Old Ones will learn how this ends, and I'll tell Mama." Then she turned to Honus. "Karmamatus, you still carry an iron stick. You should heed me."

"I'm a Sarf," replied Honus, "and have need of a sword."

" 'Tis its tool, na hers," replied Thistle. "Think on that."

"I will."

"My love and hope go with you," said Thistle, already striding toward a thicket. "Now I must pick my dress." When she reached the bushes she seemed to vanish.

Honus and Yim rode on, happier to be traveling alone together. When they took one last glance toward Cara's hall, they spied Thistle dressed in greenery and skipping in its direction.

When Yim could ignore her ominous destination, traveling through Averen seemed like her wedding journey. She thought that because she was alone with her love, and because the night after her winter-long nap felt like her wedding night. She quickly grew used to traveling with Honus again, for throughout their times together they had been always on the move. *The longest we were ever in one place*, thought Yim, *was when we spent twelve days with Commodus.* She wondered what it would be like to settle down with Honus; to watch all the seasons from one place; to plant a crop and harvest it; and most of all, to live without fear. It seemed a wonderful dream.

Averen's winters were long and hard, and that gave its springs a special exuberance. The golden green of new leaves was complemented by clouds of wildflowers. Yim and Honus sought out quiet hollows where they made love with desperate abandon, clinging to moments that—like the season—would pass all too soon. They never talked about the future, and seldom about the past. The present was everything, and both wished it would last forever.

Nevertheless, their horses carried them onward, and all too soon Averen's mountains lay to the south. The land flattened and when the wind came from the west, it was chill and damp. "The sea's nearby," said Honus.

"I've never seen it," replied Yim. "What's it like?"

"Judge for yourself. You'll get the chance very soon. It's time to set the horses loose." Honus dismounted and removed his mount's bridle and reins. As Yim did the same, Honus took their packs from the third horse's back and then removed its bridle.

"Are we close to Bahland?" asked Yim.

"I don't know for certain," said Honus, "but I suspect so.

There are markers on the roads, but we don't want to take a road."

Yim patted her horse and nuzzled it. "Thank you," she said to it. Then her horse trotted off and the others followed. As Yim watched them go, she wished that she were going with them. Nevertheless, she shouldered her pack and turned to Honus. "Well, are you going to show me the sea?"

Ever since they had left the mountains, the country seemed all wasteland. The hard ground, which sloped slightly upward to the west, supported mostly course grass, scrub, and a few stunted trees. The wind seemed the reason. It blew incessantly. Yim and Honus needed their cloaks despite the time of year. Honus had chosen their route because its desolation provided safety; a gentler landscape nurtured settlements and spying eyes.

They walked only a short while before the land suddenly fell away and they stood on the edge of a high, black cliff overlooking the ocean. The day was overcast, and the vast expanse of water was the sullen shade of dull pewter. Nonetheless, Yim was enchanted. "How grand!" she exclaimed. "I feel like I did when I visited Faerie: My troubles seem small against something so timeless."

Honus said nothing, but he wrapped his arms around her.

Knowing that the Iron Palace overlooked the sea meant that they could find it by simply following the coastline. That was what they did, moving inland just far enough to avoid the worst of the wind. They traveled warily, avoiding all human contact. Whenever they encountered a dwelling or a settlement, they either made a cautious detour or waited for darkness to move on.

Once they encountered a ragged girl of perhaps eight winters. She was gathering wood when she spied them. Yim glanced at Honus and was alarmed to see that he had

drawn his sword. As she motioned him to sheath it, the gir
dashed off. Yim and Honus ran in the opposite direction
and soon heard the sounds of people searching for them
Fortunately, the encounter had taken place near sunset, and
they were able to slip off in the darkness. Fearful of pursuit
they traveled all night.

Throughout their journey through Bahland, Yim and
Honus made love only once. They did it quickly on a chill
night, wrapped in their damp cloaks. Honus dressed imme
diately afterward, his skin covered with goose bumps. *It'
not just the night's chill*, Yim thought, *it's me.* Ever sinc
they had entered Bahl's domain, her permanent chill ha
deepened. Yim sensed that the Devourer within her ha
grown stronger, despite its quiescence otherwise. The chang
was worrisome, and it caused Yim to increase her struggle
against her inner foe. She was certain that Honus notice
when she turned inward and grew quiet and grim faced
Yim didn't know if he guessed the nature of those episodes
but she suspected he did. Nevertheless, Honus never com
mented on them, just as he never mentioned her unnatura
chill.

After nine days of nerve-racking travel, they spied a tin
spot of black in the distance. Upon her first glimpse of i
Yim felt a malign presence that left no doubt that she wa
viewing the Iron Palace. All the horrific memories of he
first encounter with Lord Bahl—memories she had strive
so hard to suppress—welled up. For a moment, she wa
paralyzed by fear. *But this time, Lord Bahl's my son. Sh*
hoped it would make a difference.

Yim felt Honus gently shaking her. "We shouldn't ap
proach any closer by daylight," he said. "Let's find a plac
to wait for night."

Yim simply nodded and followed Honus to a scruff
clump of low, woody bushes. They crawled among the
and lay down both to avoid being seen and to get some r

lief from the wind. Yim was cold despite her cloak and Honus's arms around her. She endured her discomfort in stoic silence, for she wanted to seem brave and confident despite feeling frightened and miserable.

FIFTY·THREE

DUE TO the time of year, the sun set late. Thus Honus spent a long time hiding in the scrub with Yim. She had fallen silent, and Honus felt certain that he knew the reason; she was steeling herself for what she had to do. Honus knew there was nothing he could say to aid her. With all his heart, he wanted to dissuade her from going onward. To him, Yim's quest was as unfathomable as it was dangerous. *Save Lord Bahl? What could possibly do that?* Honus didn't have a clue, and he worried that Yim didn't either. *Yet that won't stop her.*

Honus would not try to stop her, either. He loved Yim in her entirety, and this quest was part of who she was. He suspected that it might even be her essence. Moreover, he felt that he was still Yim's Sarf, whether she saw herself as his Bearer or not. Accordingly, he believed his role was to help her in any way she deemed fit. He would die for her if necessary; it was something he had trained to do.

At dusk, Yim and Honus ate as they waited for darkness. Cara had provided them with cheese, sausages, and traveler's hardbread. "Remember our journey through Luvein?" asked Yim. "How I dreamed of sausages and cheese!"

"Cara gave us tasty fare," replied Honus, "far better

than I'm used to." He smiled, glad that Yim was talking again.

"You're the expert on fortifications. What's our plan for tonight?"

"The moon should rise around midnight," replied Honus, "so we'll approach the palace in the dark, and observe it when the moon rises."

"Then what?"

"The seaward cliffs offer many hiding places. I hope to find one close to the palace. I'll need to observe it by daylight, too."

"And what will you be looking for?"

"A weakness to exploit. A way we can get in and find your son. After that, the rest is up to you."

When darkness came at last, they headed toward a destination that neither could see any longer. The Iron Palace became visible again only when the moon rose. It was still distant. Honus gazed at it awhile. "It's like a mountain," he said, "so big, it looks closer than it is."

"Let's keep moving," said Yim. "We won't be seen. It's only a quarter moon."

"Bright enough for keen eyes."

"Why be so cautious when our goal's so risky?" said Yim. "Nothing's safe from now on. Let's go."

Conceding to Yim's logic, Honus headed out again. They continued onward until they were close enough to grasp the Iron Palace's immensity. The stronghold loomed like a gigantic shadow, blotting out much of the sky. No lights were visible; the entire edifice was one black hulk. Honus had never seen anything that approached its scale. The Black Temple in Bremven could be easily fitted six times over within the palace walls and still leave space to spare.

"I guess we're close enough," said Yim in a small voice that reflected awe. "Let's find a place to hide."

They were already close to the steep-sided bay that the

palace overlooked. Honus walked to its edge to gaze about. The entire cliff face was riddled with vertical fissures and a nearby one appeared promising. He went up to it for a closer look. The crack was about a pace across, and extended slightly deeper into the cliff. He thought he saw a ledge at its bottom, though it was hard to tell for certain by peering at black rock in dim moonlight. Honus took off his pack and began to feel the sides of the crevice for holds. The rough rock seemed to have them, but climbing down would require groping blindly with hands and feet.

Honus risked the climb. When he descended nearly twice his height, his feet touched a ledge. It was reasonably flat and just large enough for two. It had been difficult to reach in the dark, but it would be easier by daylight. When he peered over the ledge, all he could see was the white foam of breakers far below. He called up to Yim to toss down his pack and hers. After she did, she whispered loudly, "Now should I throw myself down?"

"I was hoping you'd climb down, but I'll try to catch you if you fall."

"Try? That doesn't sound encouraging."

"Then don't fall."

"Since you put it that way, maybe I won't."

Yim slowly climbed down the crevice, nearly slipping twice. When she reached Honus, she let out a deep sigh of relief. "Well, *this* is cozy!"

"We've slept in worst places," said Honus.

"Better ones, too. But I won't complain. We've made it this far."

They spent the remainder of the night attempting to sleep sitting up. Aided by exhaustion, they managed. When the sun rose, they peeked around the edge of their hiding place and discovered it afforded a good view of the palace's seaward side. The view was equally impressive by daylight. The head of the bay was a high vertical wall of basalt towering over a jumble of massive boulders. Waves made the huge black stones glisten while providing white foam for contrast. Steps had been chiseled into the opposite side of the bay. They led to the wave-washed boulders and provided a sense of scale. A man standing on one of the boulders would appear like an ant on a walnut.

The palace both matched and merged with its grand location. Its black walls seemed an extension of the cliff they crowned, although Honus noted that there was a narrow ledge between the palace's rear wall and the sheer drop to the boulders far below. There was a huge, steep-roofed building that butted against the wall. Judging from its numerous seaward-facing windows and balconies, Honus assumed it was Bahl's residence. A tower was also built into the rear wall. It was the tallest in the palace, yet it didn't seem a watchtower, for it was windowless and its top tapered to a flat deck that lacked crenellations.

Honus's primary interest in the palace was tactical, not architectural. He watched all morning and could discern few signs that it actually functioned as a fortress. Its size, location, and massive walls made it unassailable by any army in the empire or any nearby realm he knew. Honus saw no guards pacing the palace walls or peering from the watchtowers and concluded they were unnecessary. He supposed the palace functioned more as an armory, garrison, and residence than as a stronghold that required an active defense.

Although Honus saw no guards, he did see plenty of activity. An iron-plated building on a seacoast needed constant maintenance, and men were busy brushing blackened oil on its sides. It seemed to be an ongoing project, for Honus noted that rings were set into the top of the walls to aid the oiling. Ropes were threaded through the rings to allow a man standing on the ground to lift another up to oil the walls. The towers had a similar arrangement. Honus watched as more than a dozen men maneuvered about as agilely as spiders dangling from strands of silk.

Late in the afternoon, Honus climbed out of the crevice and crawled through the grass for a closer look at the palace. Nothing contradicted his earlier conclusions. He still could see no sentries. No patrols, either mounted or on foot, scouted for trespassers. No soldiers checked the oilers or supervised them. After the sun set, Honus ventured forth in the dark for an even closer look, intending to circle the entire fortress. He discovered there was only one gate and it was massive. He guessed that the gatehouse would be well guarded, since it was the sole entrance. There seemed no other way into the palace. As far as he and Yim were concerned, Yim's son could have taken up residence on the moon.

Honus finished his inspection of the palace by walking the narrow ledge between its rear wall and the cliff. He hurried, because he wanted to be hidden before moonrise. He also knew that Yim would be worried about him. He was past the midpoint of the wall when he made a discovery: the oilers had left a rope in place. Both ends of a black, oily rope dangled side by side. *I could pull Yim up and climb up after her*, he thought. *Climbing would be tricky, but not impossible.* In order for him to ascend the rope, Yim would need to tie it to the ring so it wouldn't slip.

As soon as Honus made his discovery, he considered not telling Yim about it. He hadn't expected events to move so quickly, and he felt unready. Yet the oilers would undoubtedly find the rope in the morning and remove it. *This might be our only chance for a long time.* Honus decided he couldn't hold back: he would tell Yim about the rope and let her decide what to do.

Yim had begun worrying the moment Honus climbed out of their hiding place to perform his reconnaissance. She knew that he didn't intend to return until well after dark, but knowing his plans didn't ease her anxiety. She envisioned him being discovered and slain, and the thought made her heartsick. She couldn't shake the image from her mind, and as time passed, it seemed ever more probable. *Why did I let him come with me?* She berated herself for her selfishness.

It was long past sunset when she heard a soft voice from above. "Yim."

Yim's heart leapt. "Honus, are you all right?"

"Yes. I found a way into the palace, but we'll have to use it tonight. Do you want to?"

No, thought Yim. "Yes," she said.

"Then climb up with all you need to bring. We'll leave the packs in the crevice."

Yim removed her cloak and positioned the comb in her hair so that her outer locks hid it. Those were her sole preparations. "Ready," she whispered. "Coming up."

Once she stood on the cliff edge, Honus told her about the rope. "After I pull you up the wall, you'll have to tie the rope off so I can climb up after you. Do you know how to tie a double loop?"

"Of course."

Then they were off. It seemed so fast. *I might see Froan before sunrise!* The prospect filled her with both anticipation and dread. They made their way to the palace wall and the dangling rope. There, the air was heavy with the scent of oil despite an ocean breeze. The odor turned Yim's stomach and caused each breath to irritate her throat and lungs.

To fight her queasiness, Yim turned her attention to the rope. At one end, it was tied to form a large loop that passed through holes in the ends of a rectangular piece of wood. The wood formed a seat like that on a child's swing. Like the rope, the seat was black and oily. Yim had watched the oilers and noted that they secured themselves to the ropes on either side of the seat with a leather harness. That safety item was missing. Nonetheless, she sat on the piece of wood and grabbed the ropes. "Pull me up, Honus."

Yim knew from observing the oilers that she would have

to use her feet to keep from being scraped against the wall as she rose. The oilers had made it look as easy as walking. Yim discovered it wasn't. She found herself sliding about on the slippery seat, which tended to pivot forward and backward, and clinging to the ropes so hard that she began to fear her arms might cramp. Several times, she nearly slipped off the seat to go tumbling into the void below.

Yim didn't dare look down, only up. When she finally neared the top of the wall, she saw a major obstacle ahead. The rope passed through a large metal ring at the edge of the wall and the knot that formed the loop would not pass through it. The seat would halt too far below the wall's top edge for her to reach it. Soon after she had that realization, the knot hit the ring and she stopped moving.

The only way you can climb over the wall is by standing on the seat, Yim thought. She wondered if Honus realized that. She would get only one attempt to stand, and if he moved the rope, she'd surely fall. The seat was oily. Her hands were oily. The wall was oily. Nevertheless, she had to try to stand. She pulled her feet up toward the forward edge of the wooden seat. Then, shifting her grip on the ropes as high as she could, Yim pulled her torso upward until she could place her feet on the wood. Once she did that, she moved one hand at a time to ever-higher grips on the rope. Simultaneously, she slowly unbent her knees. Each movement caused her footing on the slippery and teetering seat to shift.

Yim could feel her heart pounding when she touched the ring and grasped it. Then she rose to fully stand. Holding the ring with her left hand for balance, she reached with her right for the inside edge of the wall. She was forced to extend her arm full length before she touched it. Fortunately it was rough stone, not oiled iron. Yim released the ring so she could grip the wall's inner edge with two hands and pull herself over the top. As she pulled, there was a frightening moment when her feet dangled in empty air. Then, for once, the iron's oiliness was helpful, and she slid over the wall's top easily to tumble onto a wide, stone walkway. She looked about to see if anyone had spotted her, but the walkway was deserted.

Yim slumped down and started shaking. Honus must have understood that she had made it, for she could hear the rope sliding through the ring as he lowered the seat. By the time the sound stopped, Yim had calmed her nerves. Honus needed her to secure the rope so he could climb it. As Yim leaned toward the ring that held the rope, she took out the knife she used to slice Cara's sausages. It sliced through rope equally well. As the rope's cut halves fell away, Yim whispered, "Thank you, my love. Keep safe till I return." Then she removed her sandals, the soles of which were smeared with sooty oil, and threw them to the rocks below. She used the hem of her skirt to wipe away what prints the sandals had left, doing it more by feel than sight. Then Yim went to find her son.

FIFTY·FOUR

AS SOON as the two lengths of rope started falling, Honus knew something was wrong. He jumped out of their way as they rapidly formed two piles of loose coils on the ledge. At first, he was gripped by the gut-wrenching fear that Yim had been caught and she would soon come sailing over the wall, either already slain or doomed to splatter on the rocks below. He waited in agony, but no body fell.

However, things did fall. Honus caught a brief glimpse

of two small objects that had been thrown from above. He couldn't tell what they were. He continued to wait for a cry or some other indication of what had happened. While he did, he felt the severed ends of the rope. They had been cut. *By whom?* It occurred to him that Yim might have cut them herself. The reason seemed obvious—to keep him safe. Honus recalled saying that once they had found her son, the rest was up to her. Thinking on that, he regretted his choice of words.

Although Honus had no definite proof that Yim had abandoned him, the other possibilities were far worse. Therefore, he chose to believe the most optimistic scenario for the time being. He found little comfort in it. In fact, he was furious that she would endanger herself for his sake. Simultaneously, he was dreadfully afraid for her. The thought of Yim alone in that evil place tore at him, and it was frustrating to be so helpless.

For a long while, Honus waited in the dark, listening and watching. The tumult in his mind permitted him to do little else. Finally, his self-discipline asserted itself. Concluding that he would discover nothing further, he decided that he should return to the hiding place. The only thing he could do to help Yim at present was to throw the severed rope over the cliff so it wouldn't be discovered. Later, when he was hidden from enemy eyes, he could ponder her actions, her chances, and what to do next.

After Yim cleaned her oily sandal prints away, she crept noiselessly toward the huge building. She assumed that she would be able to enter it from the walkway, and her assumption proved right. There were five large doors facing the sea, and the central one was unlocked and open. Yim gazed up at the building's seaward facade, trying to guess where Froan's bedroom would be. *His father had the highest room in the captured stronghold,* she thought, *and it's likely Froan's living in his father's quarters.* She decided to head for the top floor. It was a logical destination, but still only a guess. Froan could be anywhere.

Yim paused before entering the doorway, and reviewed what she would say if she found her son. She counted on the shock of her sudden appearance to get his attention. She imagined that he'd listen to her for curiosity's sake if nothing else. *I'll begin by talking about "his shadow,"* she thought, *his shadow and mine. Then I'll show how he can control it. After that, I'll go by instinct.* Despite pondering her plan for moons, it hadn't really changed since she had left the Grey Fens.

Yim peered in the open doorway. The room beyond it was unlit. Being constructed of black stone, its features were difficult to discern. She stared long and hard before she thought that she saw an archway at its far side and stairs going to the upper floors. Feeling her way with bare feet, she advancing into the room.

She was midway across it when she heard doors slam and was plunged into absolute darkness. There were the sounds of soft-soled footsteps, and then Yim felt hands on her body. There were too many hands to count, and though they were groping in the dark, their owners seemed to know what they were doing. Almost instantly, Yim's arms were seized. A hand touched her face and then her nose before sliding over her mouth to cover it just as she was about to shout. Hands discovered her legs and traveled down them to grip her ankles.

A voice spoke. "Do you have her?"

Many voices answered, "Aye."

Yim heard the inner door being opened. A voice called, "Bring light!" Soon the stairway reflected torchlight. A moment later, Yim saw the torchbearers descend the stairs. They wore the robes of the Devourer's priests. When they stepped into the room, Yim could see her captors. The seven men restraining her all looked like soldiers, despite being unarmored and unarmed. However, a priest seemed in charge. "Bind her hands and gag her."

Yim's wrists were crossed behind her back and securely tied with a rope so smooth that it felt like silk. A leather gag quickly replaced the hand covering her mouth. The leather seemed new. It had been oiled with a fragrant spice. Then one of the men searched her clothing and took the knife. "Now the blindfold," said the priest.

Black silk was tied over Yim's eyes, and she was in darkness again. "Good work, men," said the priest's voice. "We'll take her from here." The hands gripping her arms were replaced by different ones. Yim heard retreating footsteps, then the priest spoke again. "My lady, you will need to climb some stairs, quite a few I'm afraid. We'll go slowly so you won't stub a toe."

My lady! thought Yim. *That's what Bahl's men called me before.* They must know who I am! Moreover, Yim realized that they had been expecting her and had prepared a trap. The way she had been so quickly captured in the dark marked precision achieved through long drilling. *That rope was left to lure me here.*

What terrified Yim even more than being captured was the likelihood that her reception was Froan's doing. Instead of stepping up and greeting her, he had her bound like a thief. It certainly boded ill for their talk together, especially the gag.

"Come," said the priest. The hands gripping Yim's arms gently forced her forward. They stopped her a few paces later. She heard one of her captors say, "Ye're afore the steps m'lady." Yim found the first one with her foot. Then she was solicitously forced to climb flight after flight of stairs. Eventually, she halted on a landing where she heard a door open with a creaking, metallic sound. Then she was climbing stairs again, except they were spiral ones and there were no landings. The air was dank and chilly, and it had a foul odor that seemed a mixture of smoke and putrescence.

Yim's legs ached by the time her captors halted her, opened another metal door, and forced her into a chamber. They maneuvered her about until the backs of her knees touched something. "There's a bed behind ye, m'lady. Sit down on it." Yim did. "Now, lie down on yer back." Yim obeyed, and felt her captors grab her ankles. "Don't be alarmed, my lady," said a voice. "Ye'll be treated with the utmost respect." With that, her legs were spread, and her ankles were manacled. The irons felt cushioned inside, but their grip was firm.

Then Yim was made to sit up in the bed so her wrists could be untied. After they were freed, she was told to lie down again and her wrists were put in cushioned manacles also. Yim's restraints forced her into a loosely spread-eagle position. She could move but only within limits, and her hands couldn't touch her face. Finally, to Yim's relief, her blindfold and gag were removed.

Yim looked around. She was in a windowless room with a ceiling, floor, and walls made of dull black stone. She was lying on a feather mattress and shackled to a large bed made of iron. It was elegantly crafted, considering its function. The four posts were cast in the form of richly detailed soldiers, each different but each tugging at a manacle's chain. There was an elaborately carved ebony table holding an oil lamp in the form of a silver skull. A silver tray also sat on the table. It held a golden bowl of honeyed fruit and a golden wine ewer and goblet.

Yim paid less attention to these items than to the men in the room. They were all robed as priests. Initially there were four, but two left after removing her gag and blindfold. Summoning up a voice of outraged authority, Yim said, "What's the meaning of this?"

The elder of the remaining priests smiled, seemingly amused by Yim's tone. "Why, my lady, all this is for your own protection. You must confess that you've been careless with your person. Climbing walls at night! You're fortunate to be uninjured."

"I had to get in some way."

"Our door has always been open to you. All you needed to do was present yourself. We would have welcomed you."

"Like this, I suppose."

"Admit it, you've proved troublesome in the past."

"And what does Lord Bahl have to say of this treatment of his mother?"

The priest smiled. "I'm told he grieves for her untimely death."

Yim gazed into the priest's eyes, and saw that he was partly telling the truth: Froan believed that she was dead, though the priest didn't know if he grieved. "Then he'll be pleased to learn the contrary," Yim said.

The priest shrugged. "Mayhap. Who knows? It's not my place to tell him."

"Whose is it?"

"Why, the Most Holy One. Who else to give such joyous news?" The priest grinned sardonically. "Or not, as he deems best. It's a matter you two can discuss."

"When?"

"In good time, my lady. In good time. Until then, this holy one will tend you." He nodded at the other priest, a young, lanky, thin-faced man, with a hawk nose, pimply face, and a shock of wild blond hair. "He'll give you food and drink, bathe and dress you"—the priest gave a shallow metal pan a distasteful look—"and deal with other necessary functions. My vigil is over. I bid you good riddance, my lady."

The elder priest departed from the room, and Yim focused her attention on the remaining one. "Do you have a name?"

"Ye may call me Holy One."

"What if I don't think you're holy?" asked Yim.

"But I am holy, *m'lady*," said the priest, putting a sarcastic twist on the last word. "Holiness is power, and ye'll find me fulsome powerful. Ye eat and drink at my leave. If ye wish to make water, ye must beg my assistance."

"It seems you forget who I am," said Yim.

"Ye're only a hole to me. One Bahl entered it, and another came out. Don't think ye're something special."

"Your god's within me," said Yim, still trying to gain some leverage. "If you don't believe me, touch my flesh. It's as chill as your lord's."

"My lord's the Most Holy One. Bahl is but his tool. As for yer chill—'twill be departing soon enough, although I doubt ye'll be glad to have it go."

"Do you speak of the suckling?" asked Yim.

The young priest's pale face appeared to grow paler. He refused to answer and seemed to become engrossed in gazing at his fingernails.

"So, I'm not supposed to know about that?"

The priest continued to look away.

"When the Most Holy One visits me—and he most certainly will—I'll say you told me all about it." Yim watched the priest's face grow paler yet. She smiled. "Or not, as I deem best. Now, tell me your name."

"Ye know a word, nothing else."

"The Devourer within my son is incomplete until he drinks my blood in a ritual called the suckling. There's no Rising without the suckling. Until it happens, I'm very precious indeed. So best tell me your name."

"Tymec, m'lady."

"Well, Tymec, serve me some wine. Climbing a wall is thirsty work."

As Tymec went to get Yim's wine, whatever minor satisfaction she felt was quickly swallowed by despair. Her sense of doom was absolute. *I'll never see Froan. Gorm will see to that.* Gorm's trap had worked perfectly, and she was certain that the suckling had been planned with equal thoroughness. *I'll die, and my death will destroy my son, and he'll destroy the world.* Tymec brought the goblet to her lips. Yim drank, barely tasting the wine. Her sole thought was that, of the three things that would inevitably happen, her death would be the least tragic.

FIFTY·FIVE

HONUS WAITED in the crevice for dawn as he mulled over what had happened. He was far too distraught to sleep. To be separated from Yim once again was devastating. Worse, he feared that she was headed for disaster or had already encountered it. As soon as there was light, Honus peered from the crevice at the palace, anxious to discover some indication of Yim's fate.

He noted a change immediately: soldiers manned walls and watchtowers that had previously stood deserted. Watching whole squads of armored men pace behind the crenellations erased any doubt that the Iron Palace was an active fortress. Honus came up with two explanations for the change, and both spelled trouble. The first was that Yim had been caught, and Lord Bahl had set the guards to deter further intruders. The second was that the absent guards had been part of a trap, a ploy to make Yim overconfident. The return of the guards was a sign that the trap had worked.

Either way, Yim was Lord Bahl's prisoner. Nevertheless, Honus liked the second explanation less, not because it was less likely, but because it was more disturbing. It meant that he had failed to be sufficiently wary. In retrospect, the forgotten rope seemed too good to be true, like a door left open to lure in a thief. Too late, Honus concluded that had been the case. Furthermore, a trap meant that Bahl had known that Yim was coming. Probably, he had been informed by sorcery, something that always made Honus uneasy.

Uneasy or not, Honus knew what he must do. Both as Yim's lover and her Sarf, he felt bound to rescue her. "Attempt to rescue her" was more accurate, and Honus realized it. His chances for success were negligible. He was vastly outnumbered and had no clue as to Yim's whereabouts within the huge complex. Nevertheless, he was determined to act because the thought of inaction was unbearable.

Yim's night in the Iron Palace was only a little more restful than Honus's on the rocky ledge. Her bed was luxuriously soft, but horrific dreams lurked and pounced the moment she drifted off to sleep. They startled her awake, and afterward, the memories of them made her loath to shut her eyes again. Yet exhaustion eventually left her with no choice, and she endured the bloody nightmares.

When Yim awoke in the dim, windowless room, she had no idea how long she had slept. She still felt tired, but that could be the result of a troubled sleep and not a short one. Yim was certain that her gruesome dreams were the result of the Devourer's pervasiveness. *Its greater part lurks within Froan, and he's inside the palace—perhaps only a few floors away.* Yim wondered if her presence might somehow affect her son and alert him to her nearness. Upon further reflection, she doubted it. Moreover, even if Froan felt her presence, the Devourer's servants seemed firmly in control.

When Tymec saw that Yim was awake, he fed her and tended her other needs. Afterward, he made Yim maneuver within the confines of her chains so he could position a thick canvas-covered pad beneath her. She discovered its purpose when he undressed and bathed her with cold water that had an unpleasant herbal smell. Tymec tried to hide his interest in her body, but his manner of washing betrayed his lust. Yim chose to ignore him and stared at the ceiling throughout. To her great relief, Tymec didn't wash her hair and discover the comb.

When Yim was washed and dried, the pad was pulled

away and she was dressed in new clothes. Her outfit consisted solely of a long tunic fashioned out of a rectangle of fine black cloth. It had a neck hole in its center, and when it was pulled over her and tied closed with a silken cord, it was a fairly modest garment. After Tymec finished dressing Yim, he pulled a chain suspended from a hole in the ceiling. That seemed to confirm Yim's assumption that she was being prepared for something. *The suckling!* Yim forced herself to appear calm, but her heart started pounding rapidly.

Yim waited a long while before the door to her room opened. The Most Holy Gorm entered, looking not a day older than the last time she had seen him. Tymec immediately rose to his feet and bowed. "Wait outside" was all Gorm said. He waited until the door was closed before approaching Yim with a grin. "One of the advantages of long life is that it teaches patience. I always knew this moment would come."

"That's a lie," said Yim. "You had no idea when we last spoke."

"You mistake my meaning," replied Gorm. "The intervening period was different than I expected. The other mothers lived in luxury, not a bog. But this ending was foreordained."

"You mean the suckling?"

For an instant, Gorm looked surprised. "How did you learn about that?"

"General Var told me before he lost his head. So when does the party start?"

"You might as well ask the general. You'll find me no more talkative."

"I ask because I'm resigned to my fate. My only wish is to see my son before I die and speak with him one last time."

"So now you're asking, not demanding?"

"It's but a small request. What difference could it make?"

"Let's stop this game. You know my answer. No."

"Why?"

"I'd not permit it, if only to cause you grief. But I've other reasons, too."

"What are they?"

"The only thing I'll tell you is that you'll soon die. Perhaps Var revealed the manner of your death. If so, know it's unavoidable." Gorm paused a moment. "On second thought, I'll tell you something more: whatever you did to your son in the bog didn't take. He was quite bloodthirsty by the time we found him. He'd already recruited a band of cutthroats, slaughtered an entire town, and was marching east, slaying everyone in his path. As they say, blood will always show. He was thrilled to learn he was Lord Bahl.

"Moreover, he's proved adept in other ways. Inflaming minds comes easily to him. He gained the knack without instruction. This bodes well for the Rising. Before next spring, Bremven will be awash in blood, and Karm will only be a curse upon the lips of the dying."

"How grandiose are your delusions and how arrogant," said Yim. "The goddess has thwarted you before, and she'll do so again."

"What do you expect from your defiance? My respect? My annoyance?"

"I expect nothing from you. I'm merely stating the truth."

"You sound pathetic with your false bravado. But I didn't come to bandy words. Now listen to me: I've brought two men to make a cast of your face. If you cooperate, your remaining time will be easy. If you don't, I'll subdue you with potions, and after the cast is made, I'll have you tortured with venomed needles."

"I'll behave," said Yim.

"See that you do."

Gorm opened the door and ushered in two men who weren't dressed as priests. The younger of the pair had a good-sized wooden box that was slung from his shoulder by a leather strap. As he set it on the floor, Gorm addressed the older man. "Ring the bell if she causes you the slightest trouble."

"I shall, Most Holy One."

"I want it made of gold. The More Holy One will provide all you need. This mask will become a keepsake, so its interior should be a perfect likeness. But the exterior features mustn't resemble hers. Make the eyes closed and the expression peaceful. A half smile would be a fitting touch."

"We shall, Most Holy One. Will it require straps? And should we make allowance for a gag?"

"Neither will be necessary, for she'll be rendered unable to speak or move."

Gorm cast Yim a wry smile. "So now you've learned you'll be under the power of a potion. But also know this: Although you'll be completely helpless, you'll be fully aware and feel everything."

With those words, Gorm left the chamber. Yim glimpsed Tymec beyond the door. He seemed about to return when Gorm pulled him aside and began talking in a low voice. Before Yim could make out anything he said, Gorm shut the door. Yim turned her attention to the two strangers. One was mixing water and white powder in a bowl. The other approached her bearing a small jar. "My lady, we'll be taking an impression of your face by covering it with plaster. 'Tis like mud that hardens quickly. While it does, you mustn't move. You'll breathe through straws in your nostrils. This grease will prevent the plaster from sticking to your eyebrows, lashes, or skin."

Soon, Yim's grease-coated face was encrusted by a thick layer of plaster, which grew warmer the longer it was in place. The men tapped the covering occasionally to monitor its hardening. As she waited for it to be removed, she heard one man say, "Get the gold right away; this must be done in two days."

"Two days for such a work!"

"Aye, and the Most Holy One expects perfection."

"By the circle, we'll get not a wink of sleep."

"That's for sure. We have only till two bells afore sundown of the second day, not a moment more."

As Yim listened, she felt certain that she had just learned when she would die.

Honus's first step in rescuing Yim was to sleep. If his reckless endeavor had any chance of success, it would require flawless execution, and he knew a rested body and mind would be essential. Having a goal allowed him to focus on achieving it. Thus, to save Yim, he willed himself to forget her awhile and doze.

After Honus woke in the afternoon, he decided to take his first gamble. The only way into the Iron Palace seemed through its gate, so he needed to observe the traffic passing through it. Simply exiting the crevice in daylight was risky, and from then on, the risks would escalate. To improve his odds, Honus made some preparations. First, he took a piece of hardbread and crushed it into powder with a stone. Then he meticulously picked out specks of fat from a sausage until he collected a sizable lump. He mixed the fat with the powered hardbread to make a paste, adding pinches of dirt and a few drops of his blood until it approximated the color of flesh. Then he smeared it on his face to hide his tattoos. Honus had no way of telling if the paste covered his dark-blue markings or whether he had applied it well. The best he could hope was that he wouldn't be recognized as a Sarf; being a stranger in Bahland was perilous enough.

Next, Honus adjusted the straps on his scabbard and his sword belt so he could wear his sword on his back. That way, his cloak would hide it better, although he'd have to shed it to reach the hilt. Honus was well aware that drawing his blade outside the palace would be a last resort and the first act in a final stand.

Having made those preparations, Honus ate the mangled sausage, grabbed a water skin, and made a quick exit from his hiding place. He headed away from the palace, taking advantage of what cover could be had, and traced a circuitous route toward the palace gate. He was unable to approach it closely, for the grounds surrounding the palace were kept clear of any growth that might hide an enemy. Nevertheless, he was able to observe the comings and goings on the road from a clump of weeds.

Honus noted numerous motley batches of young men who were marched by soldiers toward the palace. He assumed they were fresh conscripts. Other human traffic was more sporadic, but it moved in both directions. Honus spotted squads of foot soldiers, cavalry troops, many black-robed priests, and all sorts of common folk. He also saw a great deal of wagon traffic. The influx of recruits indicated that the huge palace was a garrison. That meant it was probably as populous as a city and possessed all a city's needs for food, fuel, and fodder.

Most of the wagons on the road were returning from the palace empty. That seemed to mark a pattern of morning deliveries. Honus recalled his and Yim's trip to Bremven with Hamin the wool trader. Hamin had parked his wagon in a camp that catered to wagoners who were forced to wait for the city gate to open. It made Honus think that there might be a similar place nearby.

Honus saw no point in looking for the wagoners' campground until late at night. The waning moon wouldn't rise until early in the morning, providing ample time for his search. When dusk came, Honus moved his sword back to its customary position, and wiped the paste from his face. A blue face would be harder to see at night, as would the way a sword on the hip changed the drape of a cloak.

It was long after sunset when Honus followed the road toward the town. He found the wagon camp easily. All that remained of its campfires were a few dull embers, and there was no sound of anyone stirring. Honus skirted the camp's perimeter until he saw a wagon to his liking. It was piled high with hay. He crept toward the wagon, only to discover that its driver was asleep on his load. Honus continued looking, but after reviewing his other options, he returned to his original choice. He crept over to the hay wagon, climbed up its low wooden side, and rolled over its top rail, all the while hoping the wagoner wasn't a light sleeper. The weight of his body partly wedged him between the wagon's side and the pile of loose hay. In the quiet night, the rustling of the hay seemed loud to his ears.

Honus froze, listening for sounds from the man above. The wagoner stirred a bit, then settled down. Honus was by no means hidden, but he took his time worming into the hay, moving only sporadically and in short bursts. Eventually, he was out of sight. Then, as slowly as he had done the burrowing, Honus pushed his hand through the hay to grasp his sword hilt.

When that was done, Honus meditated so he would be calm enough to sleep. In the morning, the wagon's movements would serve to wake him. When the hay was unloaded, he would rise from it, sword in hand. What would happen next would depend on what he encountered. Honus assumed that he would emerge in a stable, but he had no idea where in the palace it would be or whom he would face. If he survived his arrival, his only plan was to try to enter the main building, head for the upper floors, and see what developed. He hadn't a clue as to what to expect, but it seemed likely that once he drew his sword he'd never sheath it again.

FIFTY·SIX

YIM WOKE with a start, just as she had done ever since she had become a prisoner. This time, something more alarming than a nightmare occupied her thoughts. *Do I have one or two days left to live?* Yim had lost her sense of time because she had no way to mark its passing. The windowless room never changed. Her meals followed no schedule, for Tymec fed her only when she asked. Furthermore, she slept erratically, and the young priest never left the room. After his conversation with Gorm, he avoided eye contact and seldom answered her questions. Nevertheless, Yim attempted to speak with him. "How long have I been here?"

Tymec silently gazed elsewhere.

Yim recalled how she had once forced Commodus to tell the truth and had even been able to probe Gorm's thoughts briefly. She thought she could easily do the same with Tymec. *But I'll have to look him in the eyes.* Yim thought of a ploy that might work. When she spoke again, her voice was soft and shy. "I know I'm doomed. I was wondering . . . well . . . hoping that . . . Oh, Tymec, will you tup me?"

That got his attention. Tymec glanced at Yim, and in that instant, she pounced. The priest's eyes widened when he realized that he couldn't look away.

"When's the suckling?"

"I don't know."

Yim knew he was telling the truth. "When did those men come?"

"Yesterday morn."

Yim assumed that meant she would die tomorrow evening. In her desperation, she decided to test the full extent of her power. Instead of simply extracting information from Tymec, she would try to force him to do her bidding. Yim summoned all her will and directed it at the priest held captive by her gaze. "Unchain me."

"I can't. I don't have the key."

In full control of Tymec's mind, Yim no longer doubted anything he said. "Then go get it."

"I can't. I'm locked in the room with you."

Certain that Tymec would have attempted to get the key if he had been able, Yim tried to think of what else he might do to help her. *I could have him ring the bell. That would get the door opened, but it might also summon Gorm.* She rejected the idea. Then she thought of her comb with its neigin seeds. *They would make me immune to Gorm's potion.* Yim envisioned herself popping up just before the ritual began and pulling off her golden mask to expose Gorm's duplicity to Froan.

"Come here," said Yim. Tymec obeyed. "Feel my hair in the back. You'll find a small comb. Take it out." Yim lifted her head, and Tymec did as he was told. When he had the comb in his hand, Yim spoke again. "Pull off those little seeds and put them in my mouth." Tymec pried the seeds off with his nails and pushed them—one by one—past Yim's lips. There were three in all. Yim cracked them between her teeth and her mouth filled with a bitter taste. *It's done*, she thought.

Tymec still leaned over the bed, totally in her power. Yim pondered if there was anything else she should force him to do, but she couldn't think of anything. Then she remembered the comb. "Put it back in my hair." After Tymec did that, she said, "Forget this happened and especially forget that I asked you to tup me."

Tymec sprang back like a small animal released from a

snare. As he retreated to a corner of the room, his gaze looked vacant. Yim hoped the effect was only temporary. The bitter taste in her mouth grew more intense. "Could I have a sip of wine?" she asked.

Tymec walked over to the table and filled the golden goblet. When he brought it over to her, Yim tried to see if the empty look had departed from his eyes. She couldn't tell, because he kept his face turned away.

The wagon ride to the Iron Palace was fraught with delays, but from his hiding place Honus didn't know their causes. After the better part of the morning, the sound made by the wagon's wheels altered as they began to roll over smooth stone paving. That seemed to indicate they had passed through the palace gate. Soon the wagon halted, and Honus heard a voice call out. "Where to?"

"Holy ones' stable, middle bay. Give this to the tithe master."

"That's only two tallies!"

"New lord, new tithes. Complain to him."

"I've a mind to."

"Ha!"

The wagon began moving again. Then it halted. Honus heard the driver climb down, muttering. Next, he heard the squeal of rusty hinges. Soon afterward, the wagon moved forward a short distance and halted once more. This time, it remained still. Honus heard the driver climb down again. Honus prepared to spring from his hiding place, but before he did, he waited and listened. After a while, it seemed to him that someone other than the driver would unload the hay.

Instead of bursting from his hiding place, Honus emerged as quietly as possible. He quickly glanced around to get his bearings. As he had expected, he was in a stable. It was large, but smaller than one of a cavalry regiment. There were also people working at tending horses and cleaning stalls. *Soon one will come to unload this hay*, thought Honus. He silently dropped to the floor and scurried from the wagon to crouch behind a small pile of hay. It didn't offer much concealment, but because it was close to the open door, it provided a view of the palace courtyard.

The courtyard was spacious, despite the fact that a huge iron-covered building occupied much of it. Honus assumed the structure was Lord Bahl's residence and the likely site of Yim's imprisonment. That made it his objective. He estimated that the building was at least a hundred paces from his position. The open space between the stable and Bahl's iron residence was paved with black stone. It was also alive with activity: Soldiers drilled. Common folk moved about, some purposely and some looking lost. Wagoners made deliveries. Flocks of sheep and a herd of cattle were driven by peasants. A man and a woman were being impaled on stakes as a crowd watched. Oil-smeared men pushed handcarts filled with buckets and ropes. Many men and women in black livery hurried to and fro. The abundant priests moved at a statelier pace.

Honus pondered how he could get his tattooed face past so many eyes without provoking an alarm. While he was thinking, he heard someone coming. Honus retreated into an empty stall. As he heard the sound of hay being forked and thrown, he peered from the stall. There was a door close by. It was open, revealing a room where tack was stored. Along with saddles, bridles, and such, Honus saw something of use. He darted into the room.

What had caught his eye were some foul-weather riding cloaks. The voluminous garments were made of heavy wool and designed not only to cover the rider but also the rear of the horse. They were black and hooded. Honus took one down and cut a long strip of material to wrap about his face. That done, he donned another cloak and grabbed a saddle and bridle. Peering out of the doorway, he spied a horse nearby. There was a man at the far end of the stables mucking out stalls. Nevertheless, Honus strode to the horse, saddled and bridled it, and then led it from its stall. The man never looked up.

Honus's tactic for reaching his goal depended on audacity, not stealth. Knowing that he would cut a bizarre figure swathed in winter gear on a spring day, he planned to gallop across the courtyard before anyone could react. He counted on folk not going out of their way to investigate, but merely shaking their heads in puzzlement and going about their business.

Honus quickly mounted the horse and urged it to a gallop, directing it toward a door in the ironclad building where he had seen many servants enter and exit. His rapid passage across the courtyard created the confusion that he had hoped it would. Honus reined in his horse just before the door, quickly dismounted, shed his bulky cloak, and dashed in the doorway with his face still wrapped. Finding himself in a huge, bustling kitchen, he gazed about for an exit that would take him farther into the building and spied a likely set of double doors. Honus strode toward them confidently and purposefully. Either due to his bluff or his threatening appearance, no one challenged him until he had almost reached the doors. Then a burly man stepped in his way. "Ye there!" he shouted. "What do ye—"

Honus answered with his blade before the question was completed. His interrogator toppled to the floor, and Honus stepped around his corpse without slowing. As he passed through the double doors, he heard a woman scream. *It's begun*, Honus thought, keeping his blade unsheathed. He dashed into an empty dining hall to remove his sandals so he could move more quietly. That done, he trotted off, looking for a stairway.

Honus soon ran into a woman bearing a basket of soiled towels. She dropped it when Honus pointed his sword at her. "Do you wish to live?"

The woman nodded, too frightened to speak.

"Then show me the way to the upper floors, for I'm in need of a priest. Now move quickly!"

The woman gave a soft whimper, then hurried off with Honus right behind her. They passed through a maze of rooms, sometimes encountering other servants, who seemed strangely incurious about Honus. When they arrived at a broad stairway, the woman managed to say, "There, sire."

Honus pointed his blade at her throat. "If you speak of this, I think you'll have more to fear from your master than from me. Now run off and live a long life."

As the woman hurried away, Honus jogged up the stairs with a quick but regular pace, his bare feet making almost no sound. With each new flight, the stairway became broader and grander. The basalt treads became black marble ones. The iron balustrades grew more elaborate. When Honus rounded the fifth landing, he saw a priest at the top of the stairs. Honus charged at once and skewered the man before he could react. Then Honus grabbed the dead priest, dragged him to a corner, and stripped off his robes. Honus quickly shed his own garments and donned those of his victim.

Discarding the wrapping about his face, Honus continued to climb to the upper floors, still lacking a plan of what he would do when he arrived there. Plagued with uncertainty, it seemed to Honus that only the goddess could aid him. Then Thistle's parting words returned to trouble him. *She said a sword's the Devourer's tool, not Karm's.*

The sound of voices and footsteps on the stairs above interrupted Honus's thoughts. Their source was not yet in view, so Honus darted halfway up the next flight of stairs and halted. Then he turned his back to the oncoming sounds, knowing that he would seem a priest from the rear. The ruse worked. The men continued to descend the stairs. When they were close, Honus whirled and surprised two black-robed men. He decapitated both. Their heads bounced down the stairs with their bodies tumbling after.

Honus sprinted up the stairs, aware that each new slaying increased the chances of an alarm. Before that happened, he wanted to accomplish something. *What?* he asked himself. *Nothing I've done will help Yim.* Honus realized that, unless a miracle happened, nothing would help her. No miracle had saved his first Bearer; Bahl's hordes had torn him to pieces. *And now Yim's in Bahl's hands.* It seemed to Honus that all he could do was to fall upon the enemy and reflect the wrath needled on his face. *Is it Karm's wrath or mine?* Honus saw a priest, and the question fell from his consciousness as he rushed to kill the man.

One more flight of stairs brought Honus to a broad landing. The walls on either side were carved with scenes from the battle of Karvakken Pass. Honus recognized the stronghold depicted in them. Straight ahead was a large, pointed archway that afforded a view of a vast hall built of black stone and bathed in dim greenish light. At its far end was a raised platform. Two figures were seated there. The distance made them look tiny. Standing beneath them were many men robed in black. Honus wondered what was going on and who were the men on the platform. Their position made them seem important. One of them might be Yim's son, the new Lord Bahl. Suddenly, Honus believed in the possibility of miracles. If he could reach the boy, perhaps one might happen.

From lower in the stairwell, Honus heard footsteps, clamoring voices, and the unmistakable clink of armor. The alarm had been raised. Honus charged into the vast hall, hoping that the alarm had been raised too late. As he sped across the floor, the size of the hall let him advance unnoticed for quite a distance. But eventually the incongruity of a priest with a Sarf's face was noticed. So was Honus's raised sword. Then the assembled priests turned as one and drew daggers from their black robes. Many of the blades were stained with poison.

The daggers didn't deter Honus. He charged those who grasped them, using his longer blade to reap a black harvest. When the foremost priests fell before him, their fellows appeared to lose their nerve. As a rule, they weren't the kind that killed openly, and Honus's skill and ferocity caused them to retreat, despite their numbers. The raised platform blocked one avenue of escape. It had stairs, but the priests seemed loath to climb them. Instead, they tried to run around Honus and flee toward the archway. Honus, in turn, acted like a herd dog to cut them off and cut them down.

Upon hearing the sounds of soldiers entering the hall, Honus redoubled his efforts. He had just stabbed a priest through the neck when he saw another priest striding toward him. The man wore an elaborate silver chain, and although he appeared unarmed, his manner was confident and menacing. Honus withdrew his sword from the other priest's neck, severing an artery, and then swung at the advancing priest.

The last thing Honus saw was a flash of brilliant blue light as his blade touched the man's flesh. Simultaneously, he felt an excruciating jolt in his sword arm. It seared all consciousness from his mind, and he didn't have time to recall that he had been overcome by an iron spell once before. Honus stood briefly as the blindingly bright light in his head faded to black. Then he fell senseless to the stone floor.

Froan had watched the onslaught with more fascination than apprehension. Each death gave him an invigorating surge and provided the Devourer with a freshly harvested soul. He was unconcerned that priests died to provide them. In fact, it seemed ironically appropriate. After the intruder had fallen, the priests rediscovered their courage and advanced on the prone body with their blades raised. "No one touch him!" Froan commanded. The priests drew back.

Froan turned to Gorm. "Why does that man have a blue face?"

"Those are tattoos, my lord, permanent designs needled into his flesh. They mark him as a Sarf. Such men are the enemy's servants, and quite rare nowadays."

"I wonder if he's Honus," said Froan. "Both Mam and my father's spirit spoke of him, but in quite different ways. Mam said he was my father and a gentle goatherd. But my real father said he was a Sarf and a deadly man."

"Well, this fellow's certainly that," said Gorm. "And I think I can find out his identity."

"Then do," said Froan. "But whether he's Honus or not, let's sacrifice him at the suckling. He seems a far more worthy foe than that chieftain in my dungeon."

"An excellent idea, my lord," replied Gorm. He regarded the guardsmen who had just arrived. "The More Holy Stregg has accomplished your work for you. Your lord wishes the man imprisoned. Restrain him well before the spell wears off."

Froan finished counting the slain priests and addressed the guardsmen. "Did he slay others besides these?"

The ranking guardsman bowed. "Five that we know of, my lord. A cook and four priests."

"Twenty-three in all," said Froan. "Quite impressive." He turned to Gorm. "I look forward to cutting his throat tomorrow."

"As well you might," replied Gorm. "It will make a fitting end to a memorable evening."

FIFTY·SEVEN

YIM FELT the Devourer within her stir. It was responding to violent death with surges of malign excitement. She had experienced the sensation frequently during her imprisonment in the Iron Palace. It seemed that people died all the time within its walls, and the nearness of their deaths made the sensations stronger. The latest surges stood out in both the rapidness of their occurrence and their number. Having nothing else to do, Yim counted them. There were twenty-three in all. It made her wonder what new atrocity was taking place, though she was certain that she'd never find out.

Enchained in the dim room, Yim had to endure both anxiety and boredom. She had done everything she could to prepare for her upcoming ordeal. All there was left to do was wait for the first test. That would take place after she drank Gorm's potion. The seeds she had eaten would render it harmless, so she would have to mimic its effects. Yim worried that appearing conscious but paralyzed wouldn't be easy to pull off. Until then, there was nothing to distract her from her fears. Food and drink were definitely out. The wine she had sipped was not sitting well, and she concluded it would be wise to avoid ingesting anything further. Sleep promised escape, but she was too anxious to doze.

Later, when Gorm entered the room, Yim was almost glad for the diversion. He had a faint smile on his face, and he gazed directly into her eyes as if challenging her to probe him. Yim returned his gaze calmly, knowing that he had veiled his thoughts, just as she had veiled hers.

"Honus is dead," said Gorm.

The statement wrenched Yim, and for just an instant, her shock broke through her calm facade. Summoning all her self-control, she quickly recovered. "Who's Honus?"

Yim realized that she hadn't been quick enough, for Gorm was grinning triumphantly. "He's just a corpse," replied Gorm. "I would have brought you his head, but your son stuck it on a pole. He said you told him Honus was his father and a timid man as well. How droll! Honus slew twenty-three trying to cut his way to you."

"You're lying."

"In your heart, you know I'm not. He was the Sarf who plagued us for moons and then saved you. How we cursed his dogged persistence! Did you truly think he wouldn't try to save you again?"

Of course he'd try, Yim thought. *Cutting the rope was pointless.* Yim saw with the clarity of hindsight how their love had doomed him. *He didn't stand a chance, and still he came for me!* Yim burst out sobbing, even though it made Gorm grin more broadly. She had nothing to gain by hiding the truth. The only way Gorm could have learned Honus's identity was by capturing him, since neither he nor Froan had ever met him. *Gorm didn't know his name and Froan didn't know he was a Sarf.* Certain that her silence no longer protected Honus, Yim gave him her tears, so that he might have one person who wept rather than gloated over his death.

Gorm waited until Yim's sobbing trailed off before asking, "After we captured you the first time, did Honus slay all your guards single-handedly?"

Yim saw no reason to deny it. "He did." She sighed. "He was relentless."

"Then he was a worthy foe," said Gorm, seeming to

mean it. As he turned to leave, he glanced at Tymec for the first time and came to an abrupt stop. "Come here!" he barked at the young priest. "Look me in the eye!" Tymec obeyed. "What did she do to you?"

Tymec's voice had a heavy quality to it, as if he had just awakened from a deep sleep or his wits were addled. "Nothing, Most Holy One."

"You gazed into her eyes, even though I warned you not to!"

"Nay, Most Holy One. I don't recall looking her way. Not once."

"No. Of course you don't, you stupid ass!" Gorm drew his dagger and stabbed the young man in the heart. Tymec gave a long, rattling gasp and collapsed to the floor. Then Gorm turned to stare at Yim with cold fury. "Perhaps you'd like to take me on rather than a gullible boy."

Yim felt the Most Holy One try to invade her mind. He had tried once before, and she had beaten off his assault. She struggled to do so again. The contest between them was intense and ferocious, despite being silent and motionless. As before, it ended in a draw.

Yim expected Gorm to leave, but instead, he climbed onto the bed and sat on her chest. Placing his shins on her shoulders, Gorm shifted his weight to them. His position inflicted pain, but it permitted Yim to breathe. Then Gorm squeezed her head with his knees, immobilizing it. Yim prepared for a second round in their contest, but Gorm spoke to her instead. "I don't know what Tymec could have told you. Certainly nothing of consequence, for I chose him for his ignorance."

"I don't know what you're talking about."

"Oh, I believe you do," replied Gorm. "And I suspect you did more than just ask him questions. He seemed thoroughly befuddled."

"Nonsense."

"Perhaps," replied Gorm. "But I think you revealed your hand. Lucky for me. Less so for you."

Yim saw the dagger point only the instant before it entered her eye. With a burst of pain, the eye's vision blurred and darkened. Liquid spilled on her cheek. Helpless, all Yim could do was close her remaining eye. Gorm used one hand to pull its lid open. The last thing Yim ever saw was Gorm's other hand holding the blade. Pain and darkness followed. The only defiance she could offer was not to scream or sob. Then she heard Gorm's voice. "Although your gaze no longer poses a threat, since you abused your last attendant, you won't get another."

Yim remained silent. Gorm wiped the liquid from her face, then left the chamber. Alone with Tymec's corpse, Yim trembled violently. Her pain was easier to endure than her sense of violation. Worst was the fact that the deed was irrevocable. Although Yim still hoped that she could survive the upcoming ritual, Gorm's cruelty had ensured her life would be forever diminished. *I'll never see Froan again*, she thought, *but that doesn't mean I can't save him*. That one idea was her only barrier against total despair, and Yim clung to it in the darkness.

Awareness returned to Honus, one realization at a time. He was cold. He was lying on a floor. It was stone. Two men stood nearby. He was bound. He was doomed.

Then more details surfaced. The men were priests and both were tall and massively built. One was blond and bearded, the other dark haired and clean shaven. Honus saw that he was no longer dressed as a priest, but wearing his old clothes again. Apparently someone had found them next to the body of the first priest he had slain. He was bound hand and foot in an elaborate manner that appeared decorative as well as effective. Coils of black rope neatly encircled his legs in crossing loops from his ankle to just below the knee. His wrists and arms were secured behind his back, so he couldn't see how they were bound, except that two bands of rope—each five coils wide—passed across his chest. The upper band was also wrapped about his upper arms. Honus was unable to speak due to a leather gag in his mouth.

The blond priest noted Honus's eyes were open. "Well, our 'honored foe' is awake at last."

"Just in time," said the dark-haired one.

"I thought Sarfs were supposed to be tough. This one was out an entire day."

" 'Twas the power of the spell, not the weakness of the man. He slew more than a score of our brethren, and fell only because the More Holy One is graced with might."

"Aye, he's mighty now, but I remember when—"

"Best swallow those words afore they summon trouble."

The blond priest wisely changed the subject. "So what was that writing on the Sarf's back?"

"Some say it foretells his fate," replied his companion. "Mayhap it does, but to me, it's gibberish."

The blond priest laughed. "You mean he strolled through life with 'Lord Bahl will cut my throat' needled on his hide? That must have cheered him up."

Wrapped in her personal darkness, Yim awaited the ordeal ahead as stoically as possible. Her suffering made her recall a vision of the goddess on a long-ago morning outside Bremven. Then, Karm had appeared to her with a mournful face and covered in blood. *She said some of it was mine.* Yim felt that she fully understood the depths of the goddess's sorrow for the first time, as well as her cryptic guidance to do "what's necessary." Yim sensed that she would soon be put to her final trial in a lifetime of trials. Moreover, she was certain what was necessary. *I must save my son.*

Yim heard the door open and footsteps on the stone floor. Then someone lifted her into a sitting position. She heard Gorm's voice. "You can drink willingly or we can force it down your throat. Which will it be?"

Yim replied in a resigned tone. "I'll cooperate." When she felt the rim of a goblet touch her lips, she opened them to drink its contents. The liquid was laced with honey to hide its bitter undertone. Whoever was holding the goblet, tilted it so she had to gulp. Yim swallowed as fast as she could, but even so, some potion flowed down her chin and neck. After the goblet was drained, she lay down. Someone wiped the spilled liquid away and scrubbed the dried crust from beneath her eyes.

Yim heard Gorm's voice. "Give it a while to take effect, then test her with the needle. Bring her up when she's ready." Then Yim heard someone leave. She assumed it was Gorm.

The priests took turns carrying Honus over their shoulders up the long flight of spiral stairs. Honus considered resisting, but he couldn't see the advantage in it. Struggling would change nothing, just as his futile assault had changed nothing. Besides, his weight was causing the priests enough trouble, making them sweat and pant as they climbed upward. Eventually, they pushed open a trapdoor and emerged onto a square deck of oiled iron. It was only six paces across. Honus realized that he was atop the highest tower in the palace. The platform lacked railings and possessed only two features. A rectangular block of basalt occupied its center. The stone was waist high and proportioned so a person might lie upon it. The other feature was an iron pole near the edge of the platform. Honus didn't recall observing it from the ground and suspected it had been erected only recently.

Four priests stood waiting on the deck, and they helped the other two take hold of Honus and move him toward the pole. Using extra men for the task proved wise on their part, for when they brought Honus close to the platform's edge, he struggled to jump off and take several of his captors with him. Subdued by their numbers, Honus was tightly bound to the pole so that he faced the stone block. Afterward, all the priests departed.

Honus could still move his head, so he glanced around. The sun was low in the sky, brightening the ocean and the bay with flecks of gold. The beauty of his lofty view contrasted with the direness of his circumstances. Upon the block of stone was a knife made out of obsidian. The glassy, black rock was sometimes used for knives because it could be flaked into an extremely sharp, albeit brittle, edge. The leaf-shaped stone blade was large, with one end wrapped in boiled leather to form a handle. Honus suspected that it would be used to cut his throat in some sorcerous ritual.

Yim lay perfectly still, expecting to feel a needle any moment. The waiting seemed to take forever. Then she felt a hand grab her foot and was grateful for the warning. Soon afterward, a needle entered the tenderest part of her sole. She focused all her will on not reacting in any way, fully aware that her fate depended on it. The needle must have been coated with venom, for it inflicted far more pain than usual. Nevertheless, Yim remained passive. Even after the needle was withdrawn, her foot continued to hurt.

"She seems ready," said a voice.

One by one, the shackles on her ankles and wrists were removed. Each time, Yim let the limb fall limply. She was stripped of her clothes and bathed in cold, pungent water. On this occasion, her hair was washed, and the comb was found and discarded. After Yim was dried, she was dressed in what felt like a sleeveless tunic that extended just past her knees. A girdle was tied about her waist, and cloth—perhaps a scarf—was wrapped around her neck so that her scar was covered. Throughout all this, she was handled like a rag-stuffed doll, and she tried to behave like one.

When those things were done, she was thrown over

someone's shoulder and carried from the room. Soon, whoever was carrying her changed his gait, giving Yim the impression that he was climbing stairs. She heard the sound of
squealing hinges and metal striking metal. After she was
carried up a few more steps, she felt wind and smelled the
sea. Yim also heard the muffled sound of someone moaning. He or she sounded highly distressed. Next, she was
laid upon something hard and cool. It felt like stone. As
someone arranged the folds of her garment, she felt metal
cover her face. *That must be my mask.* Its interior con-
formed to her features. Yim could breathe through her nostrils but not her mouth. She knew that above her lips rested
a golden pair and they were half smiling.

From the feel of the salt breeze and the slight warmth of
sunlight on her skin, Yim sensed that her bare feet pointed
toward the ocean. The only place she could be was atop the
windowless tower. *They're preparing for the suckling,* Yim
thought. The fact that they had placed her on the stone un-
masked seemed evidence that Froan was not yet present.
Therefore, she remained perfectly motionless. *Unmasking
too soon will ruin everything. I'll only have one chance to
surprise Gorm.* Yim knew that she must wait for a clear
sign that Froan had arrived. *I won't do anything until I
hear his voice.*

After being bound to the iron pole, Honus had been left
alone until the sun neared the horizon. Then the trapdoor
opened again and a priest emerged bearing a limp woman
in a white sleeveless tunic. Honus's apprehension heightened as soon as he saw her long, walnut-colored hair, but it
became agony when he saw her face. He tried to scream
"Yim!" but his gag transformed her name into an incoherent moan. The priest placed her on the stone block and
covered her face with a golden mask. It resembled a smiling
hooked-nosed woman with a pointed chin and seemed to
mock Yim's beauty. However, Honus was more concerned

by other things. Foremost, was Yim's limpness, which made him worry that she was either dead or under a spell. Her eyes also worried him. They were shut, but they didn't look right. The mask covered them before he could get a good view, but he thought they appeared sunken.

Honus was somewhat relieved when he saw that Yim was breathing. Then it occurred to him that his relief was selfish. If Yim was dead, she'd be immune to further harm. Then Honus feared that he'd been brought there to witness some atrocity done to Yim before he died. As if to confirm his fears, more priests arrived bearing bowls of blood that steamed slightly in the cool ocean breeze. With wide brushes, they painted a bloody circle upon the platform, encompassing everything but its four corners. The oil on the iron deck hampered their work, and they were forced the reapply the blood many times before the circle was perfect.

The priests worked silently, communicating with hand gestures, so that the only human sounds were Honus's attempts to call Yim's name. Eventually, he also fell silent. When they finished painting the circle of blood, the priests departed. Soon afterward, a new priest emerged from the trapdoor. Honus recognized the silver chain that suspended the priest's pendant; it marked him as the one who had employed the iron spell. This priest carefully inspected the bloody circle before descending through the trapdoor and returning with two other men. One was a dark-haired and bearded priest, who had a young face and whose iron pendant hung from a chain of gold.

It was the third person who riveted Honus's attention. He was a young man whose sleeveless tunic was identical to Yim's except that it was black. His walnut hair and his features so closely resembled Yim's that there was no question he was her son. Nevertheless, the similarities underscored differences. While Yim's face was tender, Froan's face was harsh. It lacked the degree of malevolence found in the bearded priest's expression, but the potential was there. Moreover, the piercing eyes were definitely Lord Bahl's. Yim's irises were dark brown, but Froan's irises were so light as to seem a faint brownish haze encircling two black holes.

Froan or Lord Bahl—Honus couldn't decide which name best applied—caught Honus's gaze and smiled at him in a disturbing way. Then the bearded priest touched the younger man's shoulder, and he looked away. Everyone seemed to know what to do next, and they did it silently. Yim's son moved to where his mother's head lay upon the stone. The bearded priest picked up the obsidian knife and moved beside him. The other priest stepped back a pace. Then the priest with the knife turned to look at the sun. Honus followed his gaze. The sun was so red its light seemed to turn the sea to blood. It was sinking rapidly. When it touched the water, Honus caught movement from the corner of his eye as the priest plunged the stone knife downward.

FIFTY-EIGHT

WITH KEENLY attuned ears, Yim waited for a sign that Froan had arrived. After the moaning had stopped, all she heard was wind and soft footsteps. People were moving about on the ironclad deck and climbing up and down the stairs, but she had little idea what they were doing. *Probably preparing for the ritual*, thought Yim. *They're silent because they're only servants*. A new odor mingled with those of the ocean and the pungent herbs that scented her skin: it was the smell of blood. That suggested the ritual was about to begin, but nothing happened, just more comings and goings. Yim continued to listen for her son's voice.

Then Yim felt a blade enter the side of her neck and blood spurt out. An instant later, she felt cold lips upon the wound. *Froan's lips!* Nevertheless, as traumatic and shocking as both sensations were, another one dominated: Yim felt the malevolent thing inside her swell with triumph as its two parts united. It had become whole again as blood passed from her to Froan. The Devourer remained within her, but it was retreating rapidly toward Froan. Yet for the moment, it united and bound them like an umbilical cord. Yim instinctively knew that Froan was unable to draw his lips away. That would be possible only after the Devourer was entirely within him.

Then Yim recalled the Old Ones' counsel to hold fast to the shadow, and she finally understood its meaning. *The Devourer is now one and can occupy only one body—Froan's or mine.* With all her will and all her mother's love, Yim resolved that the body would not be her son's. Strengthened by her struggles to subdue her shadow, Yim seized it. It was less a physical act than one like a movement upon the Dark Path, where thought was equivalent to action. Regardless, the struggle was intense.

Yim felt that she was grasping something frigid and slimy, a being that likened to an immense and powerful slug. It was so foul that she had to fight the impulse to let go. She held tight, but her opponent continued to slip into her son. It seemed that all her life had led to this single contest and she was losing it. In her despair, Yim thought, *How can I overcome the power of malice?* Then words echoed in head: *Love is your strength.* Yim couldn't tell if the statement came from Karm or was her own. All she knew was that it was true.

Yim thought of those she loved: Froan and Honus, Cara

and Cronin. Hommy and Hamin. Gurdy. Hendric. Rappali. Even Gatt. Each name suggested another, and when she ran out of names she thought of the nameless ones who had suffered: The faithful slaughtered in Karm's temple. The victims of war and feuding. Those enslaved. All souls yearning for compassion. *Lila and Thistle called me Mother*, she thought. *So did the Old Ones.* At last, Yim felt the name fit, for at that moment she was everyone's mother, struggling for everyone's sake. She loved all who had ever lived, and from that love came strength.

The Devourer's power lay in fear and hate. Love was alien to it, and so was love's might. That gave Yim the advantage of surprise. The thing she grasped writhed, unable to break free. Then Yim strained to pull it toward her. Soon she realized that she was drawing the evil from her son. Yim could feel it growing within her—a vile thing, cold and baleful—but she didn't relent. Once Yim understood that she was winning, she redoubled her efforts. Suddenly, the lips upon her neck turned warm and fell away. Yim contained the entirety of her foe. She knew precisely what to do. *What's necessary.* She rose and bounded toward the sun and the sea.

Honus knew that the priest's knife stroke had severed an artery when he saw a stream of blood spurt from Yim's neck. All too familiar with the sadism of Bahl's minions, he was surprised that the priest would inflict such a relatively quick death. That opinion changed to horror when he witnessed Yim's son kneel down to suck the wound. His revulsion grew when he saw that the lad was not merely tasting her blood but gulping it down like an infant suckling from a breast. Honus was about to turn his face away in disgust when something caught his eye.

Yim's every muscle tensed. At first, Honus thought it was from pain, but that didn't seem quite right. Yim raised her hands over her chest, her splayed fingers seeming to grasp the empty air above it. Then the air didn't seem entirely empty. There was something nebulous there. It looked like dark haze.

Despite its vaporous appearance, the thing Yim grasped terrified Honus. The air turned so chill it nearly stopped his breath. Moreover, an aura of malevolence sapped his strength. He wasn't alone in his reaction. Both of the priests stood white-faced and immobile, their mouths slack with fear. Only Froan appeared unaffected as his lips remained on his mother's neck. As Honus continued to watch, the haze grew darker until it resembled a shadow given physical form. It was as repulsive as a gigantic leech.

Froan fell back. As he stared up at his mother, she sat upright and the mask fell away. Then Honus saw that Yim had been blinded. Although she was sightless, she moved with purpose and vigor. Still clutching the dark thing close, Yim slid from the stone block, and with three powerful bounds, dashed off the platform and sailed into the sky. For an instant, she seemed suspended in air—a swirl of white and black. Then she silently plummeted from view.

Everyone upon the deck was perfectly still. Honus had no choice. Froan stared at the patch of sky that had held his mother. He appeared changed, and despite Honus's earlier impressions, his feelings went out to the boy. The two priests looked stunned, apparently unable to grasp what had taken place.

The priest who wore the gold chain moved first, or rather his skin moved. It developed a wet sheen and began to ripple as if tiny creatures were moving beneath its surface. The priest's face turned grayish and swelled a bit before those creatures began emerging from his pores. To Honus, they looked like maggots, except they were gray and grew with unnatural speed. As they commenced consuming the man's flesh, he still didn't seem to understand what was happening. He raised his hands to his face to touch it, but gray worms also covered his fingers. As he watched, his nails fell off like withered leaves. Honus could glimpse patches of yellow bone beneath the crawling gray.

When the priest saw his ruined hands, he screamed in terror, but the horrendous noise was soon muffled by the gray, living vomit that boiled from his mouth. Then it seemed to Honus that all the agents of decay feasted on the man without ending his suffering. He lost his skin, yet his lidless eyes still moved, filled with panic and agony. They continued doing so even when they peered from sockets in a yellowish skull. The mouth opened and closed long after its lips, cheeks, and tongue were gone. It stopped only when the jawbone tumbled to the iron deck.

Still, the man remained standing for far longer than Honus believed possible, a living skeleton swathed in black. At last, the gruesome remnant of the priest collapsed, yet still it moved feebly. The remaining priest watched in appalled silence as the man was reduced to bone that crumbled into dust that the sea wind blew away.

The whole process seemed quick, but when it was over, Honus realized that it was dusk. Both the priest and Froan appeared as stunned as Honus felt, but the priest recovered first. He grinned and lifted up the golden chain from the dusty pile of crumpled clothes. Then he held it up to admire in the dying light. A single gray maggot fell from the links onto his wrist. He tried to flick it off, but it disappeared beneath his skin. Dropping the gold chain, the priest clawed at his wrist with his nails. Although he bloodied himself, it was of no use. His hand turned grayish and began to swell. When maggots broke through his skin, the man shrieked. He glanced about in panic, then leapt from the deck. His screams stopped only when he struck the rocks below.

That left Froan and Honus atop the tower. Throughout the priests' grisly deaths, Froan's attention remained focused on the empty sky, and his expression was a combination of revelation and despair. Then he rose as one waking from a nightmare. He picked up the stone blade and walked toward Honus. For an instant, Honus thought the boy would cut his throat. Then he saw Froan's eyes. They had become as dark as Yim's, and tears streamed from them. Without a word, Froan carefully sliced through Honus's bindings. It took a while, and when Honus was finally free, Froan held out the knife. "Kill me. I deserve it."

Honus took the knife. Froan shut his flowing eyes. Then it finally occurred to Honus that the boy's grief might match his own. Honus's feelings of shock and loss were so great that he could scarcely think, but he realized that he must. He had to, for Yim's sake. She had sacrificed her life for Froan. Honus felt his duty was to ensure her sacrifice hadn't been pointless. He tried to use his training to subdue his grief, but only his love for Yim allowed him to succeed.

Froan was still waiting for the fatal blow, so Honus raised the knife. Then, with all his strength, Honus threw it down on the iron deck. As the blade shattered, he grabbed Froan in case the boy tried to leap to his death. Hugging him close, Honus said, "Your mother traded her life for yours. She wanted you to live."

Froan began to sob, and each sob racked his entire body. All the while, Honus held him in a gentle but firm grip. It was a long time before Froan was able to speak. "I didn't know she was Mam. I thought she was dead." Froan seemed on the verge of sobbing again. "Why should I live? I've led such an evil life!"

"Your mother never believed you were evil, only that evil possessed you," said Honus. "Now you're free of the De-vourer, and the world is also. Today, your mother fulfilled her life's purpose."

"Her life's purpose? Mam was only a goatherd."

"She was far more than that. Karm named her the Cho-sen. Your mother was destined to bear you, and she believed that she was destined to save you, too."

Froan looked confused. "The Chosen?" he said. "She never told me that."

"How could she? You were possessed by the Devourer. But know this: Your mother was holy."

"And I thought . . . I thought she was nobody."

"Because she wore no golden chain about her neck?"

Tears welled in Froan's eyes. "Because she was just my mam."

"For a while, I thought she was just a slave, someone to carry my pack."

"What changed your mind?"

"One night in Karm's ruined temple, she revealed herself to me. Not all of herself, but enough that I saw her holiness and became her Sarf. Then my role was to serve her and follow her guidance. I believe that's still my role. Allow me to serve her by helping you."

"Mam spoke of you," said Froan. "She said you were my father."

The revelation came as a surprise, and it was a long moment before Honus replied. "I should take that as an omen."

"Then tell me what to do."

"For a start, get far from here."

"But I can't leave Mam lying on the rocks."

"No, we can't," said Honus. "But we should go to her now. Chaos will soon rule this place."

"I know a way," said Froan.

Before leaving the tower's platform, Honus retrieved the golden mask, but he left the gold chain untouched. After they exited the tower through an iron door and descended two flights of stairs, Froan led Honus to a luxurious suite of rooms paneled in dark wood. In one of them, Froan pulled aside a particularly gruesome tapestry. Behind it was a paneled wall that looked no different from the others. Yet when Froan pushed against the wood, the paneling proved to be a door. Beyond it were torches, along with the means to light them, and spiral stairs leading downward.

Froan lit a torch, handed it to Honus, and lit one for himself. "I've never used these stairs, but they're supposed to lead to the bottom of the cliff."

"Do you want to get anything before we leave?" asked Honus.

"Everything here belongs to Lord Bahl," said Froan. "I'll take nothing but this robe on my back." He pulled the door closed.

The climb down the second set of spiral stairs was far longer than the climb from the tower. Honus surmised they had passed below the palace's lowest floor when the stairs and walls were no longer built of stone blocks but were carved from solid rock. The effort required to create such a stairway seemed evidence of Lord Bahl's power. Honus reflected that Yim had succeeded in overcoming that power while army after army had failed. That thought caused his grief to return with renewed force, and he had to struggle against it. *There'll be ample time to mourn later*, he told himself. *Get Froan to safety first.*

The stairway was narrow and steep. It also seemed endless, but eventually they reached an iron door. "When this door closes," said Froan, "we won't be able to open it from the outside."

"Then say farewell to the Iron Palace."

They pushed the heavy door open and discovered its exterior was covered with stone. Beyond the opening was a jumble of huge boulders. No moon shone, so the black rocks outside the circle of torchlight blended into a mass of shadow. Froan and Honus advanced into the shadow to search for Yim's remains. Behind them, the door slammed shut and merged with the cliff.

The damp air was filled with the sounds and smells of the restless sea, which left pools in the low places between boulders. In one such pool, he found what was left of the

More Holy Stregg. His shattered corpse was crawling with crabs. Honus hoped that Yim had fared better. He and Froan wandered about for a long time before Froan's torch illuminated something white atop the highest boulder. He called to Honus, and they went to investigate together.

They discovered Yim's tunic. It was perfectly dry and the girdle was still tied about its waist. That was all they found. There was no body, nor even a bloodstain. The garment lay there as if Yim had stripped it off and cast it down before vanishing into thin air. Honus stared at it, shaking his head in puzzlement. "Let's keep looking," said Froan.

Seeking clues of Yim's final moments, Honus attempted to trance. However, for the first time since he was a small boy, he was unable to visit the Dark Path. He tried for a long while before concluding that Karm had withdrawn her gift. Afterward, Honus resumed searching for Yim, even though he was convinced that they would find nothing. He had no explanation for his conviction, so he didn't mention it to Froan. They searched long into the night, but the tunic proved the only trace of Yim. At last, as gently as possible, Honus suggested that they leave. "I fear what the dawn will bring," he said. Then he told a lie. "And I'm certain the sea has claimed your mother's body."

The two climbed the steps carved into the bayside cliff and crossed the narrow ledge behind the palace's rear wall. When Honus reached the crevice containing the hidden packs, he climbed down to retrieve them. He also brought up Yim's cloak and gave it to Froan. They headed south just as the sky was beginning to lighten in the east. Both Froan and Honus were tired, but they knew that Bahland was on the brink of anarchy and not all evil had departed from the world. They trudged onward until noon. Then they rested as a column of black smoke began to rise from the direction of the Iron Palace.

FIFTY·NINE

HONUS AND Froan ate their first meal together in awkward silence. Instead of talking, they watched smoke from the distant palace smudge the sky. Honus was unsure what to say, and he sensed Froan felt the same way. Although Honus had become Theodus's Sarf at only sixteen, he couldn't help but see Froan as a boy. Moreover, their differences went far beyond age. Every aspect of their lives differed: Froan had grown up with Yim in the Grey Fens. Honus had reached manhood in Karm's temple without ever seeing his parents. Aside from those few facts, Honus knew nothing of Froan's life, except that he had been Lord Bahl. He assumed Froan was equally ignorant about him.

Yim is all we have in common, thought Honus. Nevertheless, that seemed a significant bond. Yim had loved Froan, and to honor her, Honus felt that he should try to befriend her son. Wondering how to bridge the gap between the boy and himself, he thought of Yim and was inspired. "Did you ever eat a wood grub?"

Froan shifted his eyes to Honus, clearly surprised by the question. "They were Mam's favorite treat." Froan smiled sadly at the memory. "She'd get so excited when she found some. Then we'd have a little feast."

"You liked them, too?"

"Of course. They're like mushrooms, only creamy."

"That's what your mother told me. But, to speak truth, I couldn't bear the sight of them. Your mother laughed at me and said 'I thought Sarfs were brave.' She was only my slave then, but already I suspected she had power."

"I never thought of Mam as powerful."

"By the time she terrorized me with those grubs, she had also cured a madwoman, overcome a sorcerer, and received a vision of the massacre at Karvakken Pass."

"There were pictures of that battle all over the Iron Palace," said Froan. "Did she say anything about it?"

"It horrified her," said Honus, recalling the aftermath of Yim's vision and how shaken and vulnerable she had seemed. "She said she had been waist-deep in blood."

Froan shook his head. "I always thought that tapestry exaggerated the blood." He shuddered. "That palace was a pit of horrors. To think I called it home!"

"It wasn't your home. It was the Devourer's lair."

"And Gorm's."

"Who's he?"

"The priest with the gold chain. He said he witnessed that battle, and I believe he told the truth. But he lied about other things. That ritual, for example. He had to know that Mam was beneath that mask, and yet he . . ." Froan's face reddened. "He deserved what happen to him!"

"And now he'll stand before Karm for judgment. If you're right, then it's a judgment he long evaded."

"Even when I was Lord Bahl, I was afraid of him." Froan shook his head. "I suspect it was he who killed my father, not Mam."

"Your mother certainly didn't."

"Then my father's spirit lied to me, or at least, he twisted the truth. That's why I ran away. He said I was destined to be a great lord, though he didn't say which one." Froan sighed. "I'm a fool, and a wicked one, too."

"You're only those things if you refuse to change," said Honus. "Do you feel up to some more walking?"

"Let's go. If I couldn't walk from here, I'd crawl."

As the two trekked through the back ways of Bahland, they continued reminiscing about Yim, each filling in gaps that the other didn't know. The more they conversed, the more accustomed they grew to each other. When dusk arrived, they camped without a fire, though a chill wind blew from the west. Froan knew his former subjects well enough to agree with Honus on the wisdom of avoiding them. Since Honus had lost his cloak in the Iron Palace, they shared Yim's.

Cara woke with a start. Havren was peacefully snoring beside her, but there seemed to be a ghost at the foot of their bed. Then she realized that it was only Thistle. Her pale skin seemed white in the dim bedroom, and it was still wet from her long swim from the faerie dell. She wore a garland of white roses in her wet hair and nothing else. Cara was about to scold her for going about unclothed, when she wondered how her daughter had entered the manor house, which had been locked for the night.

"Mama," said Thistle in a soft voice infused with wonder. "Mother has saved the world!"

"Do you mean Yim?"

"Aye."

"When is she coming back?"

"Never."

Cara's eyes filled with tears. "She's dead."

"Do na be sad, Mama. Only Mother's body died."

"And Honus?"

"Karmamatus lives. But his heart's wounded, and he must journey far to heal it. Do na look to see him in the living world."

"So I'm never to learn what becomes of him?"

"You will in time, Mama. One day we'll journey to Bremven and hear the tale from your namesake. She'll be the one who'll know it best."

Cara was confused, but turned to awake her husband and

tell him what news made sense to her. When she glanced back toward Thistle, she was gone.

It took Honus and Froan seven days to reach Bahland's borders and three more to reach a sizable village. Over that space of time, they'd grown easy in their companionship. When the village came into sight, Honus shed his pack, took out the golden mask, and handed it to Froan. "With this, you'll have the means to start your new life."

Froan regarded him with a surprised and slightly hurt expression. "What do you mean?"

"I've brought you to safety to honor your mother. You owe me nothing for that, so I won't burden you further. This gold can buy you a fine holding where you can raise goats or crops as you deem fit. Or you can purchase the means to follow a trade, though I hope not one involving arms."

"I thought we'd be a pair," said Froan. "Like you and Theodus were."

"Theodus was a holy man. I'm only a Sarf. No . . . I'm not even that."

"I lost Mam. Am I to lose you, too?"

Honus looked at Froan and saw tears welling in his eyes. "I'm old and useless. What good is a Sarf who's renounced the sword?"

"When did you do that?"

"The counsel of a child has been much on my mind. She said weapons aren't Karm's tools. After what I've seen, I've decided to heed her wisdom," replied Honus. "Since my only skill is killing, I won't be much use."

"You'd serve as a good example," said Froan, "especially to one who was once Lord Bahl. Please, Honus, there's no reason for us to part ways."

"But what do you want to do?"

"I've no idea," said Froan. "What do *you* want to do?"

"I've wandered all my life," said Honus. "It might be good to settle down."

"That sounds fine to me. But where?"

"Somewhere off the beaten track." Honus thought a moment. "Luvein."

"The province ruined by the first Lord Bahl?"

"The same. It may sound like a strange choice, but if the world has changed—and I believe it has—then Luvein will have changed the most."

A portion of the mask was sufficient to purchase a horse and cart and to fill it with tools, seed stock, and other supplies. Since it was late to start planting, Honus and Froan hurried their trip to Luvein. Along the way, Froan procured some goats. In light of his recent experiences, the routine of milking no longer seemed unpleasant and it reminded him of his mother. Moreover, he missed her cheese. They entered the former province from the west, and when they reached the abandoned imperial highway, they took it north.

That portion of their journey followed the route Honus had traveled with Yim, and it was there that Honus found the changes most pronounced. Luvein no longer seemed cursed. Freed of its pall of malevolence, the land responded with renewed fecundity. Flowers crowded out the withered nettles and prickly weeds. The trees shed their shrouds of thorny vines. The meadows were filled with birdsong and the woods ran thick with game. The echoes of war and devastation had dwindled to peaceful silence.

When Honus reached the ruined bridge where he and Yim had camped, he took Froan to see the dark man's castle. There, he told how Yim had rescued him from the sorcerer and then lied to hide her deed. He found the castle's interior overgrown where once it had been barren. The keep's roof had fallen in and some good-sized trees grew in the space. The courtyard was also reverting to forest.

They returned to the road and traveled a short way farther until they spied a lush field where two boys and three girls were working. The oldest boy seemed nearly Froan's age. Honus halted the cart and watched them awhile before calling out, "Have any of you heard of a woman named Tabsha?"

"Aye," replied the eldest boy. "She be our mam."

"Mam!" shouted one of the girls. "Thar be a blue-faced man askin' 'bout ya."

Froan whispered to Honus, "Who's Tabsha?"

"Your mother and I helped plant her field when she was widowed and starving," said Honus. He declined to say that Tabsha had pitied Yim for being a slave.

A woman emerged from the stone hut at the field's edge to stare in amazement. Despite all the time that had passed, Honus recognized her immediately. Tabsha had fleshed out, and though there were gray streaks in her hair, she actually seemed younger than when Honus had seen her last. "'Onus? Be tha' ya?"

Honus bowed from the seat of the cart. "Yes, Mother. It's good to see you well."

Tabsha turned to her children. "'Onus be tha man who saved mah life. Go fetch yar da an' tell 'im." She turned to Honus and Froan. "Will ya stay an' sup with us?"

"We'd be honored," replied Honus.

"Ya 'ad a slave with ya las' time," said Tabsha.

"Yes," said Honus. "Yim."

"Wha' 'appened ta 'er?"

"I freed her."

"Ah'm glad."

"And this is her son, Froan."

Honus and Froan had climbed down from the cart by the time Gowen, Tabsha's husband, arrived in the tow of his youngest daughter. He was a robust man with a thick beard, thinning hair, and an effusive manner. By the time he reached Honus he had already bowed to him half a dozen times and was grinning broadly. "By Karm, 'tis 'Onus 'imself," he said, bowing twice more. "Now Ah ken finally thank ya fer savin' mah sweet Tabsha."

At dinner that evening, Honus made inquiries about vacant lands and learned of a nearby ruin with an intact cellar that might be suitable for cheese making. He and Froan visited it the following day. The roofless structure topped a hillside and consisted of four stone walls pierced by arches that once had held windows. The walls enclosed dead leaves, scrubs, and a few slender trees. At first sight, the structure appeared more suitable for a goat pen than a residence, but its cellars were large and cool. Honus thought they had stored wine long ago.

They moved in the following day and set to work. Following Gowen's advice, they quickly cleared a plot by girdling trees, rather than cutting them, and put in a crop of roots and beans. They built a small hut using a corner of the ruin for two of the walls. The rest of the building became a goat pen.

The garden flourished, the goats thrived, and before long, the hut felt like a home. At times, Honus reflected that he was living the same simple life as Gan and his mam, who had provided shelter to Yim and him on their second night together. They had lived in a ruin also, and Yim's visit had changed their lives. Since Honus was unable to trance, when thoughts of Yim made his heart heavy, he turned to the living world for solace. He found it in simple things: milking goats, seeing his crops grow, working with his hands, and viewing the changes of the world from one spot.

Where Honus found refuge, Froan found redemption. Freed at last from the evil that had oppressed him throughout his life, he seemed to blossom before Honus's eyes. His disposition became kind and cheerful. He was patient and never lost his temper. He became interested in everything and tackled all tasks with energy. He enjoyed helping others.

He mastered cheese making, although he claimed his mother's cheeses were far superior. In many ways, Froan reminded Honus of Yim, and not just in appearance. It took Honus a long time to figure out why, and when he did, his conclusion startled him. Froan seemed holy. It wasn't a word that Honus took lightly, and one he never thought he'd associate with Lord Bahl. Nevertheless, upon further reflection, it seemed likely that Yim's child would be serene and good. Honus kept that judgment to himself, for he knew Froan would smile and refuse to believe it.

SIXTY

RAPPALI STOOD on the northern slope of Tararc Hite, peering at the fen's twisted waterways. Frost had caused the reeds to die back, and from her vantage point, nearly everything was tan or blue. Blue dominated. Tangled strands of azure joined the Turgen's broad cobalt band, which in turn, touched the bright autumn sky. It was a lovely sight, but that wasn't why she had climbed so high. Rappali was there to view something else, and she strained her eyes to find it.

At last, she saw what she was looking for—a speck moving among the blue. It was making its way toward the hite and her. As she watched it grow ever larger, her heart pounded faster. Finally, when she felt it would burst from joy, she ran down the path to the shore. For a while, the reeds obscured her view. Then she saw the boat turn into the channel. It wasn't a reed boat, but a wooden one. The tall young man who stood upon its deck wore strange clothes, and instead of poling his craft to propel it, he sculled it with a single oar. Rappali scarcely noticed those things, for the young man was her son whom she had thought she had lost forever.

"Telk! Telk! Telk!" she cried out between sobs of joy. "Yim said ya'd come home taday."

"How could she do that?"

"She spoke ta me in a dream."

"Did she say I went off with Froan, and he's Lord Bahl?"

"Aye, but Froan's Bahl no more. Yim saved him."

"Then good for her. Oh, Mam, 'twas like some terrible dream. What things I saw! What things I did!"

The boat touched the shore, and Telk bounded into his mother's arms.

The following spring brought more traffic on Luvein's roads. Some of the travelers were tradesmen, and one of them was an itinerant carpenter. Honus and Froan had spent most of the winter clearing trees, and they paid the man with a piece of the gold mask to help them turn the logs into a wooden floor and a proper roof for their hut. Before the carpenter departed, they contracted with him to bring a crew in the fall for more extensive improvements.

By the next spring, the ruined house enclosed a smaller one that even possessed two glazed windows. One afternoon, Honus discovered a white-haired stranger peering at the dwelling. The man's expression was one of wonderment that increased dramatically when he spied Honus. Then he bowed very low. "Oh, Karmamatus, this is a most extraordinary day!"

"You shouldn't address me that way," replied Honus. "Call me Honus, for I'm only a farmer and goatherd."

"Oh ho! Just wait!" replied the man, appearing not to have heard Honus. "I must get my daughter. She didn't believe me. Scoffed at the very idea of it. But now . . . Oh, just wait!" Then he hurried off.

Honus watched the man and saw that he was heading

for a heavily loaded wagon at the base of the hill. A young woman sat on the bench at its front, reading a scroll. Soon the man had taken her hand to drag her up the hillside. He appeared to be talking the entire way, and soon Honus could make out what he was saying. ". . . a house within a house. Those were her exact words. And the Sarf! In Luvein! Even you must confess it passes your strictest test."

When the woman saw Honus, she bowed gracefully. She was lithe and fair-featured, with long russet hair and dark eyes, and seemed far too young to be the man's daughter. In fact, she appeared no older than Froan. "Greetings, Karmamatus," she said.

"As I explained to your father," replied Honus, "that greeting doesn't apply."

"But your face marks you as a Sarf."

"I've renounced the sword."

"A blade's not necessary to serve the goddess," replied the woman. "Indeed, I believe it's ill suited for the task."

Her father bowed. "Pardon my daughter's impudence," he said. "She's outspoken concerning the goddess."

"I wasn't offended," replied Honus. "I've reached the same conclusion. But why are you here?"

"I'm Vaccus, and this is my only child, Memlea. I've come all the way from Argenor, and though I am a sound sleeper by nature, last autumn, just after the first pressing, I—"

"Eventually, Father will tell you Karm sent us. He claims to have had a vision." Memlea gazed about. "And now I believe him."

"Pardon my daughter's bluntness," said Vaccus. "However, what she says is true. The goddess sent me here, although she by no means provided a clear set of directions. All I had were pictures in my head. The first I recognized was an inn by a long and ancient bridge. An excellent establishment. Its Vinden red was quite good, though lacking somewhat in body. Nevertheless, its balance and—"

"After his vision," said Memlea, "he sold our winery, bought grape root cuttings, and headed here to start a vineyard."

"On this very hill," said Vaccus. "The goddess was insistent. There seemed little choice but to follow her wisdom, though I need not tell you that Memlea was less than supportive. 'Karm doesn't care about wine.' That's what she said. Ha! Have you ever heard such nonsense? Everything— I mean *everything*—is just as in my vision. So where's the lad? The one named Frost."

"Do you mean Froan?" asked Honus.

"Frost, Froan—they mean the same thing."

"He's in the cellar, making cheese."

Vaccus beamed at his daughter. "You see? It already has a cellar! Of course, the goddess understands the grape. That's why we're in Luvein. It was legendary for its vintages. Yes, yes, that was long ago, but soil remains soil. Memlea? Memlea, are you listening?"

One glance at Memlea, and it was obvious that she wasn't. Her face had taken on a rosy hue, and she was staring at the ruined house with her lips parted in a cryptic expression that could have been shock, recognition, or even wonder. Honus followed her gaze, and saw Froan. He had emerged from the ruin, but appeared to have halted in midstride. His face was a mirror of Memlea's. Honus had heard of persons who knew his or her love immediately, but only in tales. His own experience was far different, and he regarded such accounts as mere inventions of the bards. However, at that moment, he was less certain. It made him speculate that Vaccus may have misunderstood his vision, for it seemed to him that Karm's interests lay elsewhere than in wine.

"Honus, I'm certain that we can reach some accommodation," said Vaccus. "After all, soil that's best for grapes is not so good for other crops. I've some of the finest rootstock to be found, a lifetime of experience, and a daughter who—despite an interest in things spiritual—is a hard worker. A winery requires the labor of many hands, but the rewards can be great. Besides, all this is Karm's will. A man with your background must surely see her hand in our arrival."

For once, Honus thought he did. "Froan," he called. "Come meet Vaccus and his daughter, Memlea. Vaccus has a proposition and an interesting tale as well."

Yim had believed in choice, not fate. Though Honus deferred to her wisdom, he still thought Froan and Memlea were fated to choose each other. That was not to say they fell in love immediately. There was friendship from the start, for they were much alike in their good natures. Moreover, they worked well together. The deeper feelings came more slowly.

One day, the pair disappeared. When they returned, Froan's eyes were red from weeping, while Memlea regarded him with sympathy and understanding. Then Honus knew that Froan had revealed everything about his past. After that unburdening, their love grew more apparent and more light-hearted, too. They talked incessantly, laughed often, and found reasons to work side by side. It seemed to Honus they were two vines growing together until they were so intertwined they appeared as one. The joy they found together made Honus wistfully recall his times with Yim. But this couple had no doom overhanging them.

Possessing the energy of youth, Froan and Memlea did most of the hard work of clearing and planting a vineyard. Vaccus helped, dispensing a lifetime of experience. When he spoke of vintages that he would never taste, it was apparent that they were doing more than planting grapes.

Honus settled into the more routine chores of milking and gardening. Their slower pace suited him, for his many winters of trancing had exacted a toll on his body, and it seemed to him that life was moving overly fast. It often tired him out. To no one's surprise, Froan and Memlea wed after the harvest. The simple Karmish ceremony of gifts and vows took place on the hilltop overlooking the new vines. Afterward, there was a feast for all the neighbors, but no wedding trip. There was far too much to do. Although there wouldn't be enough grapes to press for several more harvests, Vaccus was already preparing for their first vintage. It seemed to Honus that making wine was an overly complicated business. Nonetheless, it seemed to fascinate Froan.

Autumn's painted leaves had mostly fallen when Karm's summer arrived, a stretch of warm days that were most likely the season's last. Froan and Vaccus had gone to Tabsha and Gowen's place to help erect a fowl house. Honus, thinking it would be a good day to hunt, asked Memlea if she would do the milkings. When she agreed, he took his sling and headed for the woods. He moved more slowly than his normal pace, for his chest had been paining him of late. Nevertheless, it was a fine day to be out. Honus breathed in deeply, savoring the rich scent of newly fallen leaves and wild apples.

As Honus moved among the trees with the silent tread of a Sarf, his thoughts were less on the current hunt than on former ones. He recalled the first time Yim had roasted hares and how she had suggested using his sword as a spit. He remembered the game they had shared with Tabsha when she was starving. He thought of the pheasants Yim and he had eaten on the day of Gatt's funeral. *The day she revealed what it meant to be the Chosen.* Reliving his disappointment, Honus wondered if Yim foresaw where that role would lead her. *I doubt she knew until she leapt from the tower.* Honus found that he was weeping.

As the day drew toward its end, Honus was still in the woods and still empty-handed. He didn't mind; it hadn't seemed a good day for killing any creature. Before heading home for dinner, he decided to go to the brook and wash. It flowed not far from the base of their hill, where the landscape was still mostly wild. Honus headed for a sandy section of the stream bank. There, Froan and he had partly blocked the brook with stones so that the water formed a pool. Though he reached the spot near sundown, the sand was still warm. Honus lay down upon it, for its warmth soothed his back.

Then it was evening. Honus woke from his unplanned nap beneath a full moon. Before he returned home, he squatted by the brook's edge to throw water on his face. As his hands reached toward the pool, he saw movement from the corner of his eye. Honus turned and looked upstream. In the moonlight, the brook resembled a path of silver, and a woman was striding down its center. She wore a simple, sleeveless robe that ended just below the knee. It was white, and her bare feet trod upon the water's surface without getting wet. He had seen the woman's face thousands of times in Karm's temple, where it had been rendered in mosaic. Then she spoke. "Honus."

"Goddess?"

Karm smiled. "You may call me Yim, for I was her and still am."

"How can that be?"

"The true question is not 'how' but 'why.'"

"Then why?"

"Because when I made the world, I gave all its creatures the freedom to choose their paths. A creation ruled by fate would be as static as a scripted play. Yet that same freedom constrains my actions. In the living world, only the living can oppose evil. Hence, the need for the Chosen."

"So Yim was an ordinary woman?"

"Yes. Yim possessed all the qualities of the living—uncertainty, mortality, and the freedom to choose well or poorly. But she never knew that she was also me."

"I still don't understand."

"Do you doubt I can be in two places at once?"

"No. The Seers taught that you can."

"And they're right," said Karm. "So why doubt I can be two things at once—divine and mortal."

Karm squatted down before Honus, her feet still resting on the pool's shimmering surface. "Look at me. Who do you see before you?"

"Yim."

Yim smiled. "And I see my beloved." She leaned forward and softly kissed Honus. He expected her lips to be cold, but they were warm. Then she dipped her hands into the brook and brought up water to wash his face. The water was warm also. "This is not the face of wrath," she said. As the water fell back into the brook, Honus saw that it was stained. Gazing down, he viewed his reflection. There were no marks upon his face, neither those made by a tattoo needle nor those etched by time.

Yim rose, and Honus rose with her. They embraced with the intensity of longing and suffering transmuted into joy. Honus felt Yim's warmth against his skin and realized that he was unclothed. Then he saw that he was also standing on the brook. The water felt soft and slightly spongy beneath his soles. He glanced at the stream bank and saw a worn-out man slumped upon the sand. *That was me*, he thought.

With that realization, the world around him changed. It resembled a faerie dell in its lushness, except everything had the perfection of innocence. Beauty was everywhere. There were plants, animals, and people, and all were bathed in opalescent light. "Where am I?" he asked.

"This is how the Dark Path appears to spirits after they forget their lives."

"But I remember mine," said Honus, "every bit of it."

"When I restored your life, our spirits merged," said Yim. "I experienced love in a new way." She kissed him passionately on the mouth. "I shall never forget that."

Then Honus realized that Yim's robe had been only an illusion, and he reached out to caress her body. As he savored the softness of her skin and saw how she delighted in his touch, Honus had another realization. Like the robe, Yim's body was only an illusion. There was no barrier between them, and when he entered her, it would be totally and forever.

It was dark by the time the fowl house was erected. Vaccus lingered to sup with Gowen, Tabsha, and their children, but Froan headed home. Memlea greeted him at the door. Tears trailed freely down her cheeks, but her face was also radiant. "Dearest," she said, "Karm appeared to me."

Froan felt trepidation over what Memlea might say, for her expression mingled grief with joy. His wife went over and kissed him before she spoke. "Honus is embraced by the goddess."

Froan let out a great sob, and Memlea held him. "It is a joyous thing for him. We'll find him by the brook, and his still face will be marked by rapture."

"Yet, I'll miss him," said Froan.

"I, too. He was a good man and gentle at heart." Memlea squeezed Froan tighter. "And Karm said that I'll bear our first child on this day next fall. A daughter whom we're to name Cara."

Then Froan and Memlea walked hand in hand into the warm Karm's summer eve to go where Honus had at last found peace.

From the *Scroll of Karm*

Morvus the Ill-fated perished upon Bahland's fall. Then Geraldus the Wise, who tore down the Black Temple, was emperor for twenty-three winters. Brucus the Younger succeeded him, and in the fifteenth autumn of his reign, Cara of Luvein entered Bremven. There she spoke to all those who would listen, and many proclaimed that she was the one whom Frodoric the Farsighted had sung about, he the bard inspired by the goddess.

Yet Cara said in humility, "I am but a winemaker's daughter and not mighty in the eyes of men." Although she spoke those words, her deeds proved otherwise, and when she took to living within Karm's temple, its curse at long last departed. Then many came to hear her wisdom, and she spoke with authority.

Thus was the temple restored, but not all its customs. Sarfs no longer learned the ways of death, nor were their faces marked. No children were sundered from their parents to follow the goddess's path. When some asked why these traditions were abandoned, Cara replied unto them, "Of late, the goddess walked among us, a woman tasting life's sweetness and bitterness. After that, how could she be unmoved?"

Acknowledgments

FOR ME, this trilogy was an eight-year journey. Many people aided me along the way, and I'm deeply grateful for their help. My agent, Richard Curtis, was with me from the onset with advice and encouragement. My editor, Betsy Mitchell, proved an insightful guide. Gerald Burnsteel, Bruce Younger, Carol Hubbell, Justin Hubbell, and Nathaniel Hubbell provided the fresh perspective of careful readers. Finally, I wish to thank all my readers whose enthusiasm spurred me on.